The Man In Black
An Historical Novel Of The Days Of Queen Anne

By

G. P. R. James

Double9
BOOKS

The Man in Black
An Historical Novel of the Days of Queen Anne
by G. P. R. James

ISBN: 978-93-63059-98-6

Published by

DOUBLE 9 BOOKS

2/13-B, Ansari Road
Daryaganj, New Delhi – 110002
info@double9books.com
www.double9books.com
Tel. 011-40042856

ABOUT THE AUTHOR

George Payne Rainsford James, a London-born novelist and historian, was born on August 9, 1799, and died on June 9, 1860. He served as the British Consul for a long time in a number of locations across the continent and in the United States. During the final years of William IV's reign, he was the honorary British Historiographer Royal. In 1799, George Payne Rainsford James was born in London's Hanover Square on St. George Street. His father was a doctor who had been in the navy and had fought alongside Benedict Arnold in the Battle of Groton Heights in America during the Revolutionary War. James went to the Putney school run by Reverend William Carmalt. He became passionate in learning new languages, such as Arabic, Persian, Greek, and Latin. When he was younger, he also studied medicine, but his preferences took him in a different way. His father, who had served in the navy himself, opposed his desire to enlist, which ultimately led to him being able to enlist in the army. James was injured in a minor battle after the Battle of Waterloo and remained in the army for a brief period of time during the Hundred Days as a lieutenant.

CONTENTS

CHAPTER I

Let me take you into an old-fashioned country house, built by architects of the early reign of James the First. It had all the peculiarities--I might almost say the oddities--of that particular epoch in the building art. Chimneys innumerable had it. Heaven only knows what rooms they ventilated; but their name must have been legion. The windows were not fewer in number, and much more irregular: for the chimneys were gathered together in some sort of symmetrical arrangement, while the windows were scattered all over the various faces of the building, with no apparent arrangement at all. Heaven knows, also, what rooms they lighted, or were intended to light, for they very little served the purpose, being narrow, and obstructed by the stone mullions of the Elizabethan age. Each, too, had its label of stone superincumbent, and projecting from the brick-work, which might leave the period of construction somewhat doubtful--but the gables decided the fact.

They, too, were manifold; for although the house had been built all at once, it seemed, nevertheless, to have been erected in detached masses, and joined together as best the builder could; so that there were no less than six gables, turning north, south, east, and west, with four right angles, and flat walls between them. These gables were surmounted--topped, as it were, by a triangular wall, somewhat higher than the acute roof, and this wall was constructed with a row of steps, coped with freestone, on either side of the ascent, as if the architect had fancied that some man or statue would, one day or another, have to climb up to the top of the pyramid, and take his place upon the crowning stone.

It was a gloomy old edifice: the bricks had become discolored; the livery of age, yellow and gray lichen, was upon it; daws hovered round the chimney tops; rooks passed cawing over it, on the way to their conventicle hard by; no swallow built under the eaves; and the trees, as if repelled by its stern, cold aspect, retreated from it on three sides, leaving it alone on its own flat ground, like a moody man amidst a gay society. On the fourth side, indeed, an avenue--that is to say, two rows of old elms--crept cautiously up to it in a winding and sinuous course, as if afraid of approaching too rapidly; and at the distance of some five or six hundred yards, clumps of old trees, beeches, and ever-green oaks, and things of sombre foliage, dotted the park, only enlivened by here and there a herd of deer.

Now and then, a milk-maid, a country woman going to church or market, a peasant, or at game-keeper, might be seen traversing the dry brown expanse of grass, and but rarely deviating from a beaten path, which led from one stile over the path wall to another. It was all sombre and monotonous: the very spirit of dulness seemed to hang over it; and the clouds themselves--the rapid sportive clouds, free denizens of the sky, and playmates of the wind and sunbeam--appeared to grow dull and tardy, as they passed across the wide space open to the view, and to proceed with awe and gravity, like timid youth in the presence of stern old age.

Enough of the outside of the house. Let me take you into the interior, reader, and into one particular room--not the largest and the finest; but one of the highest. It was a little oblong chamber, with one window, which was ornamented--the only ornament the chamber had--with a decent curtain of red and white checked linen. On the side next the door, and between it and the western wall, was a small bed. A walnut-tree table and two or three chairs were near the window. In one corner stood a washing-stand, not very tidily arranged, in another chest of drawers; and opposite the fire-place, hung from nails driven into the wall, two or three shelves of the same material as the table, each supporting a row of books, which, by the dark black covers, brown edges, and thumbed corners, seemed to have a right to boast of some antiquity and much use.

At the table, as you perceive, there is seated a boy of some fifteen years of age, with pen and ink and paper, and an open book. If you look over his shoulder, you will perceive that the words are Latin. Yet he reads it with ease and facility, and seeks no aid from the dictionary. It is the "Cato Major" of Cicero. Heaven! what a book for a child like that to read! Boyhood studying old age!

But let us turn from the book, and examine the lad himself more closely. See that pale face, with a manlike unnatural gravity upon it. Look at that high broad brow, towering as a monument above the eyes. Remark those eyes themselves, with their deep eager thought; and then the gleam in them--something more than earnestness, and less than wildness--a thirsty sort of expression, as if they drank in that they rested on, and yet were unsated.

The brow rests upon the pale fair hand, as if requiring something to support the heavy weight of thoughts with which the brain is burdened. He marks nothing but the lines of that old book. His whole soul is in the as well as the form he carried in his arms, spoke as plainly as words could have done that some accident had happened; and she called to him, at some distance, to ask what was the matter.

"Matter, child! matter!" cried the clergyman, "I believe I have half killed this poor boy."

"Killed him!" exclaimed the girl, with a look of doubt as well as surprise.

"Ay, Mistress Rachael," replied the old man, "killed him by unkindly and rashly telling him of his brother's death, without preparation."

"You intended it for kind, I am sure," murmured the girl in a sweet low tone, coming down the steps, and gazing on his pale face, while the clergyman carried the lad up the steps.

"There, Miss Marshal, do not stay staring," said Dr. Paulding; "but pray call some of the lackeys, and bid them bring water or hartshorn, or something. Your lady-mother must have some essences to bring folks out of swoons. There is nothing but swooning at Court, I am told--except gaming, and drinking, and profanity."

The girl was already on her way, but she looked back, saying, "My father and mother are both out; but I will soon find help."

When the lad opened his eyes, there was something very near, which seemed to him exceedingly beautiful--rich, warm coloring, like that of a sunny landscape; a pair of liquid, tender eyes, deeply fringed and full of sympathy; and the while some sunny curls of bright brown hair played about his cheek, moved by the hay-field breath of the sweet lips that bent close over him.

"Where am I?" he said. "What is the matter? What has happened? Ah! now I recollect. My brother--my poor brother! Was it a dream?"

"Hush, hush!" said a musical voice. "Talk to him, sir. Talk to him, and make him still."

"It is but too true, my dear Philip," said the old clergyman; "your brother is lost to us. But recollect yourself, my son. It is weak to give way in this manner. I announced your misfortune somewhat suddenly, it is true, trusting that your philosophy was stronger than it is--your Christian fortitude. Remember, all these dispensations are from the hand of the most merciful God. He who gives the sunshine, shall he not bring the clouds?

Doubt not that all is merciful; and suffer not the manifestations of His will to find you unprepared or unsubmissive."

"I have been very weak," said the young man, "but it was so sudden! Heaven! how full of health and strength he looked when he went away! He was the picture of life--almost of immortality. I was but as a reed beside him--a weak, feeble reed, beside a sapling oak."

"'One shall be taken, and the other left,'" said the sweet voice of the young girl; and the eyes both of the youth and the old clergyman turned suddenly upon her.

Philip Hastings raised himself upon his arm, and seemed to meditate for a moment or two. His thoughts were confused and indistinct. He knew not well where he was. The impression of what had happened was vague and indefinite. As eyes which have been seared by the lightning, his mind, which had lost the too vivid impression, now perceived everything in mist and confusion.

"I have been very weak," he said, "too weak. It is strange. I thought myself firmer. What is the use of thought and example, if the mind remains thus feeble? But I am better now I will never yield thus again;" and flinging himself off the sofa on which they had laid him, he stood for a moment on his feet, gazing round upon the old clergyman and that beautiful young girl, and two or three servants who had been called to minister to him.

We all know--at least, all who have dealt with the fiery things of life--all who have felt and suffered, and struggled and conquered, and yielded and grieved, and triumphed in the end--we all know how short-lived are the first conquests of mind over body, and how much strength and experience it requires to make the victory complete. To render the soul the despot, the tyranny must be habitual.

Philip Hastings rose, as I have said, and gazed around him. He struggled against the shock which his mere animal nature had received, shattered as it had been by long and intense study, and neglect of all that contributes to corporeal power. But everything grew hazy to his eyes again. He felt his limbs weak and powerless; even his mind feeble, and his thoughts confused. Before he knew what was coming, he sunk fainting on the sofa again, and when he woke from the dull sort of trance into which he had fallen, there were other faces around him; he was stretched quietly in bed in a strange room, a physician and a beautiful lady of mature years were standing by his bedside, and he felt the oppressive lassitude of fever in every nerve and in every limb.

But we must turn to good Doctor Paulding. He went back to his rectory discontented with himself, leaving the lad in the care of Lady Annabelle Marshal and her family. The ordinary--as the man who carried the letters, was frequently called in those days--was to depart in an hour, and he knew that Sir John Hastings expected his only remaining eon in London to attend the body of his brother down to the family burying place. It was impossible that the lad could go, and the old clergyman had to sit down and write an account of what had occurred.

There was nothing upon earth, or beyond the earth, which would have induced him to tell a lie. True, his mind might be subject to such self-deceptions as the mind of all other men. He might be induced to find excuses to his own conscience for anything he did that was wrong--for any mistake or error in judgment; for, willfully, he never did what was wrong; and it was only by the results that he knew it. But yet he was eagerly, painfully upon his guard against himself. He knew the weakness of human nature--he had dealt with it often, and observed it shrewdly, and applied the lesson with bitter severity to his own heart, detecting its shrinking from candor, its hankering after self-defense, its misty prejudices, its turnings and windings to escape conviction; and he dealt with it as hardly as he would have done with a spoiled child.

Calmly and deliberately he sat down to write to Sir John Hastings a full account of what had occurred, taking more blame to himself than was really his due. I have his feet, gazing round upon the old clergyman called it a full account, though it occupied but one page of paper, for the good doctor was anything but profuse of words; and there are some men who can say much in small space. He blamed himself greatly, anticipating reproach; but the thing which he feared the most to communicate was the fact that the lad was left ill at the house of Colonel Marshal, and at the house of a man so very much disliked by Sir John Hastings.

There are some men--men of strong mind and great abilities--who go through life learning some of its lessons, and totally neglecting others--pre-occupied by one branch of the great study, and seeing nothing in the course of scholarship but that. Dr. Paulding had no conception of the change which the loss of their eldest son had wrought in the heart of Sir John and Lady Hastings. The second--the neglected one--had now become not only the eldest, but the only one. His illness, painfully as it affected them, was a blessing to them. It withdrew their thoughts from their late bereavement. It occupied their mind with a new anxiety. It withdrew it from grief and from disappointment. They thought little or nothing of whose house he was at, or whose care he was under; but leaving the body of their dead child to be brought down by slow and solemn procession to the country, they hurried on before, to watch over the one that was left.

Sir John Hastings utterly forgot his ancient feelings toward Colonel Marshal. He was at the house every day, and almost all day long, and Lady Hastings was there day and night.

Wonderful how--when barriers are broken down--we see the objects brought into proximity under a totally different point of view from that in which we beheld them at a distance. There might be some stiffness in the first meeting of Colonel Marshal and Sir John Hastings, but it wore off with exceeding rapidity. The Colonel's kindness and attention to the sick youth were marked. Lady Annabelle devoted herself to him as to one of her own children. Rachael Marshal made herself a mere nurse. Hard hearts could only withstand such things. Philip was now an only child, and the parents were filled with gratitude and affection.

CHAPTER III

The stone which covered the vault of the Hastings family had been raised, and light and air let into the cold, damp interior. A ray of sunshine, streaming through the church window, found its way across the mouldy velvet of the old coffins as they stood ranged along in solemn order, containing the dust of many ancestors of the present possessors of the manor. There, too, apart from the rest were the coffins of those who had died childless; the small narrow resting-place of childhood, where the guileless infant, the father's and mother's joy and hope, slept its last sleep, leaving tearful eyes and sorrowing hearts behind, with naught to comfort but the blessed thought that by calling such from earth, God peoples heaven with angels; the coffins, too, of those cut off in the early spring of manhood, whom the fell mower had struck down in the flower before the fruit was ripe. Oh, how his scythe levels the blossoming fields of hope! There, too, lay the stern old soldier, whose life had been given up to his country's service, and who would not spare one thought or moment to soften domestic joys; and many another who had lived, perhaps and loved, and passed away without receiving love's reward.

Amongst these, close at the end of the line, stood two tressels, ready for a fresh occupant of the tomb, and the church bell tolled heavily above, while the old sexton looked forth from the door of the church toward the gates of the park, and the heavy clouded sky seemed to menace rain.

"Happy the bride the sun shines upon: happy the corpse the heaven rains upon!" said the old man to himself. But the rain did not come down; and presently, from the spot where he stood, which overlooked the park-wall, he saw come on in slow and solemn procession along the great road to the gates, the funeral train of him who had been lately heir to all the fine property around. The body had been brought from London after the career of youth had been cut short in a moment of giddy pleasure, and father and mother, as was then customary, with a long line of friends, relations, and dependents, now conveyed the remains of him once so dearly loved, to the cold grave.

Only one of all the numerous connections of the family was wanting on this occasion, and that was the brother of the dead; but he lay slowly recovering from the shock he had received, and every one had been told that it was impossible for him to attend. All the rest of the family had hastened to the hall in answer to the summons they had received, for though Sir John Hastings was not much loved, he was much respected and somewhat feared--at least, the deference which was paid to him, no one well knew why, savored somewhat of dread.

It is a strange propensity in many old persons to hang about the grave to which they are rapidly tending, when it is opened for another, and to comment--sometimes even with a bitter pleasantry--upon an event which must soon overtake themselves. As soon as it was known that the funeral procession had set out from the hall door, a number of aged people, principally women, but comprising one or two shriveled men, tottered forth from the cottages, which lay scattered about the church, and made their way into the churchyard, there to hold conference upon the dead and upon the living.

"Ay, ay!" said one old woman, "he has been taken at an early time; but he was a fine lad, and better than most of those hard people."

"Ay, Peggy would praise the devil himself if he were dead," said an old man, leaning on a stick, "though she has never a good word for the living. The boy is taken away from mischief, that is the truth of it. If he had lived to come down here again, he would have broken the heart of my niece's daughter Jane, or made a public shame of her. What business had a gentleman's son like that to be always hanging about a poor cottage girl, following her into the corn-fields, and luring her out in the evenings?"

"Faith! she might have been proud enough of his notice," said an old crone; "and I dare say she was, too, in spite of all your conceit, Matthew. She is not so dainty as you pretend to be; and we may see something come of it yet."

"At all events," said another, "he was better than this white-faced, spiritless boy that is left, who is likely enough to be taken earlier than his brother, for he looks as if breath would blow him away."

"He will live to do something yet, that will make people talk of him;" said a woman older than any of the rest, but taller and straighter; "there is a spirit in him, be it angel or devil, that is not for death so soon."

"Ay! they're making a pomp of it, I warrant," said another old woman, fixing her eyes on the high road under the park wall, upon which the procession now entered. "Marry, there are escutcheons enough, and coats of arms! One would think he was a lord's son, with all this to do! But there is a curse upon the race anyhow; this man was the last of eleven brothers, and I have heard say, his father died a bad death. Now his eldest son must die by drowning--saved the hangman something, perchance--we shall see what comes of the one that is left. 'Tis a curse upon them ever since Worcester fight, when the old man, who is dead and gone, advised to send the poor fellows who were taken, to work as slaves in the colonies."

As she spoke, the funeral procession advanced up the road, and approached that curious sort of gate with a penthouse over it, erected probably to shelter the clergyman of the church while receiving the corpse at the gate of the burial-ground, which was then universally to be found at the entrance to all cemeteries. She broke off abruptly, as if there was something still on her mind which she had not spoken, and ranging themselves on each side of the church-yard path, the old men and women formed a lane down which good Dr. Paulding speedily moved with book in hand. The people assembled, whose numbers had been increased by the arrival of some thirty or forty young and middle-aged, said not a word as the clergymen marched on, but when the body had passed up between them, and the bereaved father followed as chief-mourner, with a fixed, stern, but tearless eye, betokening more intense affliction perhaps, in a man of his character, than if his cheeks had been covered with drops of womanly sorrow, several voices were heard saying aloud. "God bless and comfort you, Sir John."

Strange, marvelously strange it was, that these words should come from tongues, and from those alone, which had been so busily engaged in carping censure and unfeeling sneers but the moment before. It was the old men and women alone who had just been commenting bitterly upon the fate, history, and character of the family, who now uttered the unfelt expressions of sympathy in a beggar-like, whining tone. It was those who really felt compassion who said nothing.

The coffin had been carried into the church, and the solemn rites, the beautiful service of the Church of England, had proceeded some way, when another person was added to the congregation who had not at first been there. All eyes but those of the father of the dead and the lady who sat weeping by his side, turned upon the new-comer, as with a face as pale as death, and a faltering step, he took his place on one of the benches somewhat remote from the rest. There was an expression of feeble lassitude in the young man's countenance, but of strong resolution, which overcame the weakness of the frame. He looked as if each moment he would have fainted, but yet he sat out the whole service of the Church, mingled with the crowd when the body was lowered into the vault, and saw the handful of earth hurled out upon the velvet coffin, as if in mockery of the empty pride of all the pomp and circumstance which attended the burial of the rich and high.

No tear came into his eyes--no sob escaped from his bosom; a slight quivering of the lip alone betrayed that there was strong agitation within. When all was over, and the father still gazing down into the vault, the young lad crept quietly back into a pew, covered his face with his hand, and wept.

The last rite was over. Ashes to ashes, dust to dust were committed. Sir John Hastings drew his wife's arm through his own, and walked with a heavy, steadfast, and unwavering step down the aisle. Everybody drew back respectfully as he passed; for generally, even in the hardest hearts, true sorrow finds reverence. He had descended the steps from the church into the burying ground, and had passed half way along the path toward his carriage, when suddenly the tall upright old woman whom I have mentioned thrust herself into his way, and addressed him with a cold look and somewhat menacing tone--

"Now, Sir John Hastings," she said, "will you do me justice about that bit of land? By your son's grave I ask it. The hand of heaven has smitten you. It may, perhaps, have touched your heart. You know the land is mine. It was taken from my husband by the usurper because he fought for the king to whom he had pledged his faith. It was given to your father because he broke his faith to his king and brought evil days upon his country. Will you give me back the land, I say? Out man! It is but a garden of herbs, but it is mine, and in God's sight I claim it."

"Away out of my path," replied Sir John Hastings angrily. "Is this a time to talk of such things? Get you gone, I say, and choose some better hour. Do you suppose I can listen to you now?"

"You have never listened, and you never will," replied the old woman, and suffering him to pass without further opposition, she remained upon the path behind him muttering to herself what seemed curses bitter and deep, but the words of which were audible only to herself.

The little crowd gathered round her, and listened eagerly to catch the sense of what she said, but the moment after the old sexton laid his hand upon her shoulder and pushed her from the path, saying, "Get along with you, get along with you, Popish Beldam. What business have you here scandalizing the congregation, and brawling at the church door? You should be put in the stocks!"

"I pity you, old worm," replied the old woman, "you will be soon among those you feed upon," and with a hanging head and dejected air she quitted the church-yard.

In the meanwhile Dr. Paulding had remained gazing down into the vault, while the stout young men who had come to assist the sexton withdrew the broad hempen bands by which the coffin had been lowered, from beneath it, arranged it properly upon the tressels in its orderly place among the dead, and then mounted by a ladder into the body of the church, again preparing to replace the stone over the mouth of the vault. He then turned to the church door and looked out, and then quietly approached a pew in the side aisle.

"Philip, this is very wrong," he said; "your father never wished or intended you should be here."

"He did not forbid me," replied the young man. "Why should I only be absent from my brother's funeral?"

"Because you are sick. Because, by coming, you may have risked your life," replied the old clergyman.

"What is life to a duty?" replied the lad. "Have you not taught me, sir, that there is no earthly thing--no interest of this life, no pleasure, no happiness, no hope, that ought not to be sacrificed at once to that which the heart says is right?"

"True--true," replied the old clergyman, almost impatiently; "but in following precept so severely, boy, you should use some discrimination. You have a duty to a living father, which is of more weight than a mere imaginary one to a dead brother. You could do no good to the latter; as the Psalmist wisely said, 'You must go to him, but he can never come back to you.' To your father, on the contrary, you have high duties to perform; to console and cheer him in his present affliction; to comfort and support his declining years. When a real duty presents itself, Philip, to yourself, to your fellow men, to your country, or to your God--I say again, as I have often said, do it in spite of every possible affection. Let it cut through everything, break through every tie, thrust aside every consideration. There, indeed, I would fain see you act the old Roman, whom you are so fond of studying, and be a Cato or a Brutus, if you will. But you must make very sure that you do not make your fancy create unreal duties, and make them of greater importance in your eyes than the true ones. But now I must get you back as speedily as possible, for your mother, ere long, will be up to see you, and your father, and they must not find you absent on this errand."

The lad made no reply, but readily walked back toward the court with Dr. Paulding, though his steps were slow and feeble. He took the old man's arm, too, and leaned heavily upon it; for, to say the truth, he felt already the consequences of the foolish act he had committed; and the first excitement past, lassitude and fever took possession once more of every limb, and his feet would hardly bear him to the gates.

The beautiful girl who had been the first to receive him at that house, met the eyes both of the young man and the old one, the moment they entered the gardens. She looked wild and anxious, and was wandering about with her head uncovered; but as soon as she beheld the youth, she ran toward him, exclaiming, "Oh, Philip, Philip, this is very wrong and cruel of you. I have been looking for you everywhere. You should not have done this. How could you let him, Dr. Paulding?"

"I did not let him, my dear child," replied the old man, "he came of his own will, and would not be let. But take him in with you; send him to bed as speedily as may be; give him a large glass of the fever-water he was taking, and say as little as possible of this rash act to any one."

The girl made the sick boy lean upon her rounded arm, led him away into the house, and tended him like a sister. She kept the secret of his rashness, too, from every one; and there were feelings sprang up in his bosom toward her during the next few hours which were never to be obliterated. She was so beautiful, so tender, so gentle, so full of all womanly graces, that he fancied, with his strong imagination, that no one perfection of body or mind could be wanting; and he continued to think so for many a long year after.

CHAPTER IV

Enough of boyhood and its faults and follies. I sought but to show the reader, as in a glass, the back of a pageant that has past. Oh, how I sometimes laugh at the fools--the critics--God save the mark! who see no more in the slight sketch I choose to give, than a mere daub of paint across the canvas, when that one touch gives effect to the whole picture. Let them stand back, and view it as a whole; and if they can find aught in it to make them say "Well done," let them look at the frame. That is enough for them; their wits are only fitted to deal with "leather, and prunella."

I have given you, reader--kind and judicious reader--a sketch of the boy, that you may be enabled to judge rightly of the man. Now, take the lad as I have moulded him--bake him well in the fiery furnace of strong passion, remembering still that the form is of hard iron--quench and harden him in the cold waters of opposition, and disappointment, and anxiety--and bring him forth tempered, but too highly tempered for the world he has to live in-- not pliable--not elastic; no watch-spring, but like a graver's tool, which must cut into everything opposed to it, or break under the pressure.

Let us start upon our new course some fifteen years after the period at which our tale began, and view Philip Hastings as that which he had now become.

Dr. Paulding had passed from this working day world to another and a better--where we hope the virtues of the heart may be weighed against vices of the head--a mode of dealing rare here below. Sir John Hastings and his wife had gone whither their eldest son had gone before them; and Philip Hastings was no longer the boy. Manhood had set its seal upon his brow only too early; but what a change had come with manhood!--a change not in the substance, but in its mode.

Oh, Time! thy province is not only to destroy! Thou worker-out of human destinies--thou new-fashioner of all things earthly--thou blender of races--thou changer of institutions--thou discoverer--thou concealer--thou builder up--thou dark destroyer; thy waters as they flow have sometimes a petrifying, sometimes a solvent power, hardening the soft, melting the strong, accumulating the sand, undermining the rock! What had been thine effect upon Philip Hastings?

All the thoughts had grown manly as well as the body. The slight youth had been developed into the hardy and powerful man; somewhat inactive-- at least so it seemed to common eyes--more thoughtful than brilliant, steady in resolution, though calm in expression, giving way no more to bursts of boyish feeling, somewhat stern, men said somewhat hard, but yet extremely just, and resolute for justice. The poetry of life--I should have said the poetry of young life--the brilliancy of fancy and hope, seemed somewhat dimmed in him--mark, I say seemed, for that which seems too often is not; and he might, perhaps, have learnt to rule and conceal feelings which he could not altogether conquer or resist.

Still there were many traces of his old self visible: the same love of study, the same choice of books and subjects of thought, the same subdued yet strong enthusiasms. The very fact of mingling with the world, which had taught him to repress those enthusiasms, seemed to have concentrated and rendered them more intense.

The course of his studies; the habits of his mind; his fondness for the school of the stoics, it might have been supposed, would rather have disgusted him with the society in which he now habitually mingled, and made him look upon mankind--for it was a very corrupt age--with contempt, if not with horror.

Such, however, was not the case. He had less of the cynic in him than his father--indeed he had nothing of the cynic in him at all. He loved mankind in his own peculiar way. He was a philanthropist of a certain sort; and would willingly have put a considerable portion of his fellow-creatures to death, in order to serve, and elevate, and improve the rest.

His was a remarkable character--not altogether fitted for the times in which he lived; but one which in its wild and rugged strength, commanded much respect and admiration even then. Weak things clung to it, as ivy to an oak or a strong wall: and its power over them was increased by a certain sort of tenderness--a protecting pity, which mingled strangely with his harder and ruder qualities. He seemed to be sorry for everything that was weak, and to seek to console and comfort it, under the curse of feebleness. It seldom offended him--he rather loved it, it rarely came in his way; and his feeling toward it might approach contempt but never rose to anger.

He was capable too of intense and strong affections, though he could not extend them to many objects. All that was vigorous and powerful in him concentrated itself in separate points here and there; and general things were viewed with much indifference.

See him as he walks up and down there before the old house, which I have elsewhere described. He has grown tall and powerful in frame: and yet his gait is somewhat slovenly and negligent, although his step is firm and strong. He is not much more than thirty-one years of age; but he looks forty at the least; and his hair is even thickly sprinkled with gray. His face is pale, with some strong marked lines and indentations in it; yet, on the whole, it is handsome, and the slight habitual frown, thoughtful rather than stern, together with the massive jaw, and the slight drawing down of the corners of the mouth, give it an expression of resolute firmness, that is only contradicted by the frequent variation of the eye, which is sometimes full of deep thought, sometimes of tenderness; and sometimes is flashing with a wild and almost unearthly fire.

But there is a lady hanging on his arm which supports her somewhat feeble steps. She seems recovering from illness; the rose in her cheek is faint and delicate; and an air of languor is in her whole face and form. Yet she is very beautiful, and seems fully ten years younger than her husband, although, in truth, she is of the same age--or perhaps a little older. It is Rachael Marshal, now become Lady Hastings.

Their union did not take place without opposition; all Sir John Hastings' prejudices against the Marshal family revived as soon as his son's attachment to the daughter of the house became apparent. Like most fathers, he saw too late; and then sought to prevent that which had become inevitable. He sent his son to travel in foreign lands; he even laid out a scheme for marrying him to another, younger, and as he thought fairer. He contrived that the young man should fall into the society of the lady he had selected, and he fancied that would be quite sufficient; for he saw in her character, young as she was, traits, much more harmonious, as he fancied, with those of his son, than could be found in the softer, gentler, weaker Rachael Marshal. There was energy, perseverance, resolution, keen and quick perceptions-- perhaps a little too much keenness. More, he did not stay to inquire; but, as is usual in matters of the heart, Philip Hastings loved best the converse of himself. The progress of the scheme was interrupted by the illness of Sir John Hastings, which recalled his son from Rome. Philip returned, found his father dead, and married Rachael Marshal.

They had had several children; but only one remained; that gay, light, gossamer girl, like a gleam darting along the path from sunny rays piercing through wind-borne clouds. On she ran with a step of light and careless air, yet every now and then she paused suddenly, gazed earnestly at a flower, plucked it, pored into its very heart with her deep eyes, and, after seeming to labor under thought for a moment, sprang forward again as light as ever.

The eyes of the father followed her with a look of grave, thoughtful, intense affection. The mother's eyes looked up to him, and then glanced onward to the child.

She was between nine and ten years old--not very handsome, for it is not a handsome age. Yet there were indications of future beauty--fine and sparkling eyes, rich, waving, silky hair, long eyelashes, a fine complexion, a light and graceful figure, though deformed by the stiff fashions of the day.

There was a sparkle too in her look--that bright outpouring of the heart upon the face which is one of the most powerful charms of youth and innocence. Ah! how soon gone by! How soon checked by the thousand loads which this heavy laboring world casts upon the buoyancy of youthful spirits--the chilling conventionality--the knowledge, and the fear of wrong-- the first taste of sorrow--the anxieties, cares, fears--even the hopes of mature life, are all weights to bear down the pinions of young, lark-like joy. After twenty, does the heart ever rise up from her green sod and fling at Heaven's gate as in childhood? Never--eh, never! The dust of earth is upon the wing of the sky songster, and will never let her mount to her ancient pitch.

That child was a strange combination of her father and her mother. She was destined to be their only one; and it seemed as if nature had taken a pleasure in blending the characters of both in one. Not that they were intimately mingled, but that they seemed like the twins of Laconia, to rise and set by turns.

In her morning walk: in her hours of sportive play; when no subject of deep thought, no matter that affected the heart or the imagination was presented to her, she was light and gay as a butterfly; the child--the happy child was in every look, and word, and movement. But call her for a moment from this bright land of pleasantness--present something to her mind or to her fancy which rouses sympathies, or sets the energetic thoughts at work, and she was grave, meditative, studious, deep beyond her years.

She was a subject of much contemplation, some anxiety, some wonder to her father. The brightness of her perceptions, her eagerness in the pursuit of knowledge, her vigorous resolution even as a child, when convinced that she was right, showed him his own mind reflected in hers. Even her tenderness, her strong affections, he could comprehend; for the same were in his own heart, and though he believed them to be weaknesses, he could well understand their existence in a child and in a woman.

But that which he did not understand--that which made him marvel--was her lightness, her gayety, her wild vivacity--I might almost say, her trifling, when not moved by deep feeling or chained down by thought.

This was beyond him. Yet strange! the same characteristics did not surprise nor shook him in her mother--never had surprised or shocked him; indeed he had rather loved her for those qualities, so unlike his own. Perhaps it was that he thought it strange, his child should, in any mood, be so unlike himself; or perhaps it was the contrast between the two sides of the same character that moved his wonder when he saw it in his child, he might forget that her mother was her parent as well as himself; and that she had an inheritance from each.

In his thoughtful, considering, theoretical way, he determined studiously to seek a remedy for what he considered the defect in his child--to cultivate with all the zeal and perseverance of paternal affection, supported by his own force of character, those qualities which were most like his own--those, in short, which were the least womanly. But nature would not be baffled. You may divert her to a certain degree; but you cannot turn her aside from her course altogether.

He found that he could not--by any means which his heart would let him employ--conquer what he called, the frivolity of the child. Frivolity! Heaven save us! There were times when she showed no frivolity, but on the contrary, a depth and intensity far, far beyond her years. Indeed, the ordinary current of her mind was calm and thoughtful. It was but when a breeze rippled it that it sparkled on the surface. Her father, too, saw that this was so; that the wild gayety was but occasional. But still it surprised and pained him--perhaps the more because it was occasional. It seemed to hie eyes an anomaly in her nature. He would have had her altogether like himself. He could not conceive any one possessing so much of his own character, having room in heart and brain for aught else. It was a subject of constant wonder to him; of speculation, of anxious thought.

He often asked himself if this was the only anomaly in his child--if there were not other traits, yet undiscovered, as discrepant as this light volatility with her general character: and he puzzled himself sorely.

Still he pursued her education upon his own principles; taught her many things which women rarely learned in those days; imbued her mind with thoughts and feelings of his own; and often thought, when a season of peculiar gravity fell upon her, that he made progress in rendering her character all that he could wish it. This impression never lasted long, however; for sooner or later the bird-like spirit within her found the cage door open, and fluttered forth upon some gay excursion, leaving all his dreams vanished and his wishes disappointed.

Nevertheless he loved her with all the strong affection of which his nature was capable; and still he persevered in the course which he thought for her benefit. At times, indeed, he would make efforts to unravel the mystery of her double nature, not perceiving that the only cause of mystery was in himself: that what seemed strange in his daughter depended more upon his own want of power to comprehend her variety than upon anything extraordinary in her. He would endeavor to go along with her in her sportive moods--to let his mind run free beside hers in its gay ramble to find some motive for them which he could understand; to reduce them to a system; to discover the rule by which the problem was to be solved. But he made nothing of it, and wearied conjecture in vain.

Lady Hastings sometimes interposed a little; for in unimportant things she had great influence with her husband. He let her have her own way wherever he thought it not worth while to oppose her; and that was very often. She perfectly comprehended the side of her daughter's character which was all darkness to the father; and strange to say, with greater penetration than his own, she comprehended the other side likewise. She recognized easily the traits in her child which she knew and admired in her husband, but wished them heartily away in her daughter's case, thinking such strength of mind, joined with whatever grace and sweetness, somewhat unfeminine.

Though she was full of prejudices, and where her quickness of perception failed her, altogether unteachable by reason, yet she was naturally too virtuous and good to attempt even to thwart the objects of the father's efforts in the education of his child. I have said that she interfered at times, but it was only to remonstrate against too close study, to obtain frequent and healthful relaxation, and to add all those womanly accomplishments on which she set great value. In this she was not opposed. Music, singing, dancing, and a knowledge of modern languages, were added to other branches of education, and Lady Hastings was so far satisfied.

CHAPTER V

The Italian singing-master was a peculiar man, and well worthy of a few words in description. He was tall and thin, but well built; and his face had probably once been very handsome, in that Italian style, which, by the exaggeration of age, grows so soon into ugliness. The nose was now large and conspicuous, the eyes bright, black, and twinkling, the mouth good in shape, but with an animal expression about it, the ear very voluminous.

He was somewhat more than fifty years of age, and his hair was speckled with gray; but age was not apparent in wrinkles and furrows, and in gait he was firm and upright.

At first Sir Philip Hastings did not like him at all. He did not like to have him there. It was against the grain he admitted him into the house. He did it, partly because he thought it right to yield in some degree to the wishes of his wife; partly from a grudging deference to the customs of society.

But the Signor was a shrewd and world-taught man, accustomed to overcome prejudices, and to make his way against disadvantages; and he soon established himself well in the opinion of both father and mother. It was done by a peculiar process, which is well worth the consideration of all those who seek _les moyens de parvenir_.

In his general and ordinary intercourse with his fellow-men, he had a happy middle tone,--a grave reticent manner, which never compromised him to anything. A shrewd smile, without an elucidatory remark, served to harmonize him with the gay and vivacious; a serious tranquillity, unaccompanied by any public professions, was enough to make the sober and the decent rank him amongst themselves. Perhaps that class of men--whether pure at heart or not--have always overestimated decency of exterior.

All this was in public however. In private, in a _tête-à-tête_, Signor Guardini was a very different man. Nay more, in each and every _tête-à-tête_ he was a different man from what he appeared in the other. Yet, with a marvelous art, he contrived to make both sides of his apparent character harmonize with his public and open appearance. Or rather perhaps I should say that his public demeanor was a middle tint which served to harmonize the opposite extremes of coloring displayed by his character. Nothing could exemplify this more strongly than the different impressions he produced on Sir Philip and Lady Hastings. The lady was soon won to his side. She was predisposed to favor him; and a few light gay sallies, a great deal of conventional talk about the fashionable life of London, and a cheerful bantering tone of persiflage, completely charmed her. Sir Philip was more difficult to win. Nevertheless, in a few short sentences, hardly longer than those which Sterne's mendicant whispered in the ear of the passengers, he succeeded in disarming many prejudices. With him, the Signor was a stoic; he had some tincture of letters, though a singer, and had read sufficient of the history of his own land, to have caught all the salient points of the glorious past.

Perhaps he might even feel a certain interest in the antecedents of his decrepit land--not to influence his conduct, or to plant ambitious or nourish pure and high hopes for its regeneration--but to waken a sort of touchwood enthusiasm, which glowed brightly when fanned by the stronger powers of others. Yet before Sir Philip had had time to communicate to him one spark of his own ardor, he had as I have said made great progress in his esteem. In five minutes' conversation he had established for himself the character of one of a higher and nobler character whose lot had fallen in evil days.

"In other years," thought the English gentleman, "this might have been a great man--the defender unto death of his country's rights--the advocate of all that is ennobling, stern, and grand."

What was the secret of all this? Simply that he, a man almost without character, had keen and well-nigh intuitive perceptions of the characters of others; and that without difficulty his pliable nature and easy principles would accommodate themselves to all.

He made great progress then in the regard of Sir Philip, although their conversations seldom lasted above five minutes. He made greater progress still with the mother. But with the daughter he made none--worse than none.

What was the cause, it may be asked. What did he do or say--how did he demean himself so as to produce in her bosom a feeling of horror and disgust toward him that nothing could remove?

I cannot tell. He was a man of strong passions and no principles: that his after--perhaps his previous--life would evince. There is a touchstone for pure gold in the heart of an innocent and high-minded woman that detects all baser metals: they are discovered in a moment: they cannot stand the test.

Now, whether his heart-cankering corruption, his want of faith, honesty, and truth, made themselves felt, and were pointed out by the index of that fine barometer, without any overt act at all--or whether he gave actual cause of offense, I do not know--none has ever known.

Suddenly, however, the gay, the apparently somewhat wayward girl, now between fifteen and sixteen, assumed a new character in her father's and mother's eyes. With a strange frank abruptness she told them she would take no more singing lessons of the Italian; but she added no explanation.

Lady Hastings was angry, and expostulated warmly; but the girl was firm and resolute. She heard her mother's argument, and answered in soft and humble tones that she would not,--could not learn to sing any longer--that she was very sorry to grieve or to offend her mother; but she had learned long enough, and would learn no more.

More angry than before, with the air of indignant pride in which weakness so often takes refuge, the mother quitted the room; and the father then, in a calmer spirit, inquired the cause of her resolution.

She blushed like the early morning sky; but there was a sort of bewildered look upon her face as she replied, "I know no cause--I can give no reason, my dear father; but the man is hateful to me. I will never see him again."

Her father sought for farther explanation, but he could obtain none. Guardini had not said anything nor done anything, she admitted, to give her offense; but yet she firmly refused to be his pupil any longer.

There are instincts in fine and delicate minds, which, by signs and indications intangible to coarser natures discover in others thoughts and feelings, wishes and designs, discordant--repugnant to themselves. They are instincts, I say, not amenable to reason, escaping analysis, incapable of explanation--the warning voice of God in the heart, bidding them beware of evil.

Sir Philip Hastings was not a man to allow aught for such impulses--to conceive or understand them in the least. He had been accustomed to delude himself with reasons, some just, others very much the reverse, but he had never done a deed or entertained a thought for which he could not give some reason of convincing power to his own mind.

He did not understand his daughter's conduct at all; but he would not press her any farther. She was in some degree a mysterious being to him. Indeed, as I have before shown, she had always been a mystery; for he had no key to her character in his own. It was written in the unknown language.

Yet, did he love or cherish her the less? Oh no! Perhaps a deeper interest gathered round his heart for her, the chief object of his affections. More strongly than ever he determined to cultivate and form her mind on his own model, in consequence of what he called a strange caprice, although he could not but sometimes hope and fancy that her resolute rejection of any farther lessons from Signor Guardini arose from her distaste to what he himself considered one of the frivolous pursuits of fashion.

Yet she showed no distaste for singing: for somehow every day she would practice eagerly, till her sweet voice, under a delicate taste, acquired a flexibility and power which charmed and captivated her father, notwithstanding his would-be cynicism. He was naturally fond of music; his nature was a vehement one, though curbed by such strong restraints; and all vehement natures are much moved by music. He would sit calmly, with his eyes fixed upon a book, but listening all the time to that sweet voice, with feelings working in him--emotions, thrilling, deep, intense, which he would have felt ashamed to expose to any human eye.

All this however made her conduct toward Guardini the more mysterious; and her father often gazed upon her beautiful face with a look of doubting inquiry, as one may look on the surface of a bright lake, and ask, What is below?

That face was now indeed becoming very beautiful. Every feature had been refined and softened by time. There was soul in the eyes, and a gleam of heaven upon the smile, besides the mere beauties of line and coloring. The form too had nearly reached perfection. It was full of symmetry and grace, and budding charms; and while the mother marked all these attractions, and thought how powerful they would prove in the world, the father felt their influence in a different manner: with a sort of abstract admiration of her loveliness, which went, no farther than a proud acknowledgment to his own heart that she was beautiful indeed. To him her beauty was as a gem, a picture, a beautiful possession, which he had no thought of ever parting with--something on which his eyes would rest well pleased until they closed forever. How blessed he might have been in the possession of such a child could he have comprehended her--could he have divested his mind of the idea that there was something strange and inharmonious in her character! Could he have made his heart a woman's heart for but one hour, all mystery would have been dispelled; but it was impossible, and it remained.

No tangible effect did it produce at the time; but preconceptions of another's character are very dangerous things. Everything is seen through their medium, everything is colored and often distorted. That which produced no fruit at the time, had very important results at an after period.

But I must turn now to other scenes and more stirring events, having I trust made the reader well enough acquainted with father, mother, and daughter, at least sufficiently for all the purposes of this tale. It is upon the characters of two of them that all the interest if there be any depends. Let them be marked then and remembered, if the reader would derive pleasure from what follows.

CHAPTER VI

Reader, can you go back for twenty years? You do it every day. You say, "Twenty years ago I was a boy--twenty years ago I was a youth--twenty years ago I played at peg-top and at marbles--twenty years ago I wooed--was loved--I sinned--I suffered!"

What is there in twenty years that should keep us from going back over them? You go on so fast, so smoothly, so easily on the forward course--why not in retrogression? But let me tell you: it makes a very great difference whether Hope or Memory drives the coach.

But let us see what we can do. Twenty years before the period at which the last chapter broke off, Philip Hastings, now a father of a girl of fifteen, was a lad standing by the side of his brother's grave. Twenty years ago Sir John Hastings was the living lord of these fine lands and broad estates. Twenty years ago he passed, from the mouth of the vault in which he had laid the clay of the first-born, into the open splendor of the day, and felt sorrow's desolation in the sunshine. Twenty years age, he had been confronted on the church-yard path by a tall old woman, and challenged with words high and stern, to do her right in regard to a paltry rood or two of land. Twenty years ago he had given her a harsh, cold answer, and treated her menaces with impatient scorn.

Do you remember her, reader? Well, if you do, that brings us to the point I sought to reach in the dull flat expanse of the far past; and we can stand and look around us for awhile.

That old woman was not one easily to forget or lightly to yield her resentments. There was something perdurable in them as well as in her gaunt, sinewy frame. As she stood there menacing him, she wanted but three years of seventy. She had battled too with many a storm--wind and weather, suffering and persecution, sorrow and privation, had beat upon her hard--very hard. They had but served to stiffen and wither and harden, however.

Her corporeal frame, shattered as it seemed, was destined to outlive many of the young and fair spirit-tabernacles around it--to pass over, by long years, the ordinary allotted space of human life; and it seemed as if even misfortune had with her but a preserving power. It is not wonderful, however, that, while it worked thus upon her body, it should likewise have stiffened and withered and hardened her heart.

I am not sure that conscience itself went untouched in this searing process. It is not clear at all that even her claim upon Sir John Hastings was not an unjust one; but just or unjust his repulse sunk deep and festered.

Let us trace her from the church-yard after she met him. She took her path away from the perk and the hamlet, between two cottages, the ragged boys at the doors of which called her "Old Witch," and spoke about a broomstick.

She heeded them little: there were deeper offences rankling at her heart.

She walked on, across a corn-field and a meadow, and then she came upon some woodlands, through which a little sandy path wound its way, round stumps of old trees long cut down, amidst young bushes and saplings just springing up, and catching the sunshine here and there through the bright-tinted foliage overhead. Up the hill it went, over the slope on which the copse was scattered, and then burst forth again on the opposite side of wood and rise, where the ground fell gently the other way, looking down upon the richly-dressed grounds of Colonel Marshall, at the distance of some three miles.

Not more than a hundred yards distant was a poor man's cottage, with an old gray thatch which wanted some repairing, and was plentifully covered with herbs, sending the threads of their roots into the straw. A. little badly-cultivated garden, fenced off from the hill-side by a loose stone wall, surrounded the horse, and a gate without hinges gave entrance to this inclosed space.

The old woman went in and approached the cottage door. When near it she stopped and listened, lifting one of the flapping ears of her cotton cap to aid the dull sense of hearing. There were no voices within; but there was a low sobbing sound issued forth as if some one were in bitter distress.

"I should not wonder if she were alone," said the old woman; "the ruffian father is always out; the drudging mother goes about this time to the town. They will neither stay at home, I wot, to grieve for him they let too often into that door, nor to comfort her he has left desolate. But it matters little whether they be in or out. It were better to talk to her first. I will give her better than comfort--revenge, if I judge right. They must play their part afterwards."

Thus communing with herself, she laid her hand upon the latch and opened the door. In an attitude of unspeakable grief sat immediately before her a young and exceedingly beautiful girl, of hardly seventeen years of age.

The wheel stood still by her side; the spindle had fallen from her hands; her head was bowed down as with sorrow she could not bear up against; and her eyes were dropping tears like rain.

The moment she heard the door open she started, and looked up with fear upon her face, and strove to dash the tears from her eyes; but the old women bespoke her softly, saying, "Good even, my dear; is your mother in the place?"

"No," replied the girl; "she has gone to sell the lint, and father is out too. It is very lonely, and I get sad here."

"I do not wonder at it, poor child," said the old woman; "you have had a heavy loss, my dear, and may well cry. You can't help what is past, you know; but we can do a good deal for what is to come, if we but take care and make up our minds in time."

Many and strange were the changes of expression which came upon the poor girl's face as she heard these few simple words. At first her cheek glowed hot, as with the burning blush of shame; then she turned pale and trembled, gazing inquiringly in her visitor's face, as if she would have asked, "Am I detected?" and then she cast down her eyes again, still pale as ashes, and the tears rolled forth once more and fell upon her lap.

The old woman sat down beside her, and talked to her tenderly; but, alas! very cunningly too. She assumed far greater knowledge than she possessed. She persuaded the poor girl that there was nothing to conceal from her; and what neither father nor mother knew, was told that day to one comparatively a stranger. Still the old woman spoke tenderly--ay, very tenderly; excused her fault--made light of her fears--gave her hope--gave her strength. But all the time she concealed her full purpose. That was to be revealed by degrees. Whatever had been the girl's errors, she was too innocent to be made a party to a scheme of fraud and wrong and vengeance at once. All that the woman communicated was blessed comfort to a bruised and bleeding heart; and the poor girl leaned her head upon her old companion's shoulder, and, amidst bitter tears and sobs and sighs, poured out every secret of her heart.

But what is that she says, which makes the old woman start with a look of triumph?

"Letters!" she exclaimed; "two letters: let me see them, child--let me see them! Perhaps they may be more valuable than you think."

The girl took them from her bosom, where she kept them as all that she possessed of one gone that day into the tomb.

The old woman read them with slow eyes, but eager attention; and then gave them back, saying, "That one you had better destroy as soon as possible--it tells too much. But this first one keep, as you value your own welfare--as you value your child's fortune, station, and happiness. You can do much with this. Why, here are words that may make your father a proud man. Hark! I hear footsteps coming. Put them up--we must go to work cautiously, and break the matter to your parents by degrees."

It was the mother of the girl who entered; and she seemed faint and tired. Well had the old woman called her a drudge, for such she was--a poor patient household drudge, laboring for a hard, heartless, idle, and cunning husband, and but too tenderly fond of the poor girl whose beauty had been a snare to her.

She seemed somewhat surprised to see the old woman there; for they were of different creeds, and those creeds made wide separation in the days I speak of. Perhaps she was surprised and grieved to see the traces of tears and agitation on her daughter's face; but of that she took no notice; for there were doubts and fears at her heart which she dreaded to confirm. The girl was more cheerful, however, than she had been for the last week--not gay, not even calm; but yet there was a look of some relief.

Often even after her mother's entrance, the tears would gather thick in her eyes when she thought of the dead; but it was evident that hope had risen up: that the future was not all darkness and terror. This was a comfort to her; and she spoke and looked cheerfully. She had sold all the thread of her and her daughter's spinning, and she had sold it well. Part she hid in a corner to keep a pittance for bread from her husband's eyes; part she reserved to give up to him for the purchase of drink: but while she made all these little arrangements, she looked somewhat anxiously at the old woman, from time to time, as if she fain would have asked, "What brought you here?"

The crone was cautious, however, and knew well with whom she had to deal. She talked in solemn and oracular tones, as if she had possessed all the secrets of fate, but she told nothing, and when she went away she said in a low voice but authoritative manner, "Be kind to your girl--be very kind; for she will bring good luck and fortune to you all." The next day she laid wait for the husband, found and forced him to stop and hear her. At first he was impatient, rude, and brutal; swore, cursed, and called her many and evil names. But soon he listened eagerly enough: looks of intelligence and eager design passed between the two, and ere they parted they perfectly understood each other.

The man was then, on more than one day, seen going down to the hall. At first he was refused admission to Sir John Hastings; for his character was known. The next day, however, he brought a letter, written under his dictation by his daughter, who had been taught at a charitable school of old foundation hard by; and this time he was admitted. His conversation with the Lord of the Manor was long; but no one knew its import. He came again and again, and was still admitted.

A change came over the cottage and its denizens. The fences were put in order, the walls were repaired, the thatch renewed, another room or two was added; plenty reigned within; mother and daughter appeared in somewhat finer apparel; and money was not wanting.

At the end of some months there was the cry of a young child in the house. The neighbors were scandalized, and gossips spoke censoriously even in the father's ears; but he stopped them fiercely, with proud and mysterious words; boasted aloud of what they had thought his daughter's shame; and claimed a higher place for her than was willingly yielded to her companions. Strange rumors got afloat, but ere a twelvemonth had passed, the father had drank himself to death. His widow and her daughter and her grandson moved to a better house, and lived at ease on money none knew the source of, while the cottage, now neat and in good repair, became the dwelling of the old woman, who had been driven with scorn from Sir John's presence. Was she satisfied--had she sated herself? Not yet.

CHAPTER VII

There was a lady, a very beautiful lady indeed, came to a lonely house, which seemed to have been tenanted for several years by none but servants, about three years after the death of Sir John Hastings. That house stood some miles to the north of the seat of that gentleman, which now had passed to his son; and it was a fine-looking place, with a massive sort of solemn brick-and-mortar grandeur about it, which impressed the mind with a sense of the wealth and long-standing of its owners.

The plural has slipped from my pen, and perhaps it is right; for the house looked as if it had had many owners, and all of them had been rich.

Now, there was but one owner,--the lady who descended from that lumbering, heavy coach, with the two great leathern wings on each side of the door. She was dressed in widow's weeds, and she had every right to wear them. Though two-and-twenty only, she stood there orphan, heiress, and widow. She had known many changes of condition, but not of fate, and they did not seem to have affected her much. Of high-born and proud parentage, she had been an only child for many years before her parents' death. She had been spoiled, to use a common, but not always appropriate phrase; for there are some people who cannot be spoiled, either because the ethereal essence within them is incorruptible, or because there is no ethereal essence to spoil at all. However, she had been spoiled very successfully by fate, fortune, and kind friends. She had never been contradicted in her life; she had never been disappointed--but once. She had travelled, seen strange countries--which was rare in those days with women--had enjoyed many things. She had married a handsome, foolish man, whom she chose--few knew rightly why. She had lost both her parents not long after; got tired of her husband, and lost him too, just when the loss could leave little behind but a decent regret, which she cultivated as a slight stimulant to keep her mind from stagnating. And now, without husband, child, or parents, she returned to the house of her childhood, which she had not seen for five long years.

Is that all her history? No, not exactly all. There is one little incident which may as well be referred to here. Her parents had entered into an arrangement for her marriage with a very different man from him whom she afterwards chose,--Sir Philip Hastings; and foolishly they had told her of what had been done, before the young man's own assent had been given. She did not see much of him--certainly not enough to fall in love with him. She even thought him a strange, moody youth; but yet there was something in his moodiness and eccentricity which excited her fancy. The reader knows that he chose for himself; and the lady also married immediately after.

Thus had passed for her a part of life's pageant; and now she came to her own native dwelling, to let the rest march by as it might. At first, as she slowly descended from the carriage, her large, dark, brilliant eyes were fixed upon the ground. She had looked long at the house as she was driving towards it, and it seemed to have cast her into a thoughtful mood. It is hardly possible to enter a house where we have spent many early years, without finding memory suddenly seize upon the heart and possess it totally. What a grave it is! What a long line of buried ancestors may not _the present_ always contemplate there.

Nor are there many received into the tomb worth so much respect as one dead hour. All else shall live again: lost hours have no resurrection.

There were old servants waiting around, to welcome her, new ones attending upon her orders; but for a moment or two she noticed no one, till at length the old housekeeper, who knew her from a babe, spoke out, saying, "Ah, madam I do not wonder to see you a little sad on first coming to the old place again, after all that has happened."

"Ah, indeed, Arnold," replied the lady, "many sad things have happened since we parted. But how are you, Goody? You look blooming:" and walking into the house, she heard the reply in the hall.

From the hall, the old housekeeper led her lady through the house, and mightily did she chatter and gossip by the way. The lady listened nearly in silence; for Mrs. Arnold was generous in conversation, and spared her companion all expense of words. At length, however, something she said seemed to rouse her mistress, and she exclaimed with a somewhat bitter laugh, "And so the good people declared I was going to be married to Sir Philip Hastings?"

"_Mr_. Hastings he was then, madam," answered the housekeeper "to be sure they did. All the country around talked of it, and the tenants listened at church to hear the banns proclaimed."

The lady turned very red, and the old woman went on to say, "Old Sir John seemed quite sure of it; but he reckoned without his host, I fancy."

"He did indeed," said the lady with an uncheerful smile, and there the subject dropped for the time. Not long after, however, the lady herself brought the conversation back to nearly the same point, asked after Sir Philip's health and manner of living, and how he was liked in the neighborhood, adding, "He seemed a strange being at the time I saw him, which was only once or twice--not likely to make a very pleasant husband, I thought."

"Oh dear, yes, madam, he does," answered Mrs. Arnold, "many a worse, I can assure you. He is very fond of his lady indeed, and gives up more to her than one would think. He is a little stern, they say, but very just and upright; and no libertine fellow, like his brother who was drowned-- which I am sure was a providence, for if he was so bad when he was young, what would he have been when he was old?"

"Better, perhaps," replied her mistress, with a quiet smile; "but was he so very wicked? I never heard any evil of him."

"Oh dear me, madam! do not you know?" exclaimed the old woman; and then came the whole story of the cotter's daughter on the hill, and how she and her father and old Mother Danby--whom people believed to be a witch--had persuaded or threatened Sir John Hastings into making rich people of them.

"Persuaded or threatened Sir John Hastings!" said the lady in a tone of doubt. "I knew him better than either of his sons; and never did I see a man so little likely to yield to persuasion or to bow to menace;" and she fell into a deep fit of musing, which lasted long, while the old housekeeper rambled on from subject to subject, unlistened to, but very well content.

Let us dwell a little on the lady, and on her character. There is always something to interest, something to instruct, in the character of a woman. It is like many a problem in Euclid, which seems at first sight as plain and simple as the broad sunshine; but when we come to study it, we find intricacies beneath which puzzle us mightily to resolve. It is a fine, curious, delicate, complicated piece of anatomy, a woman's heart. I have dissected many, and I know the fact. Take and lay that fibre apart--take care, for heaven's sake! that you do not tear the one next to it; and be sure you do not dissever the fragments which bind those most opposite parts together! See, here lies a muscle of keen sensibility; and there--what is that? A cartilage, hard as a nether millstone. Look at those light, irritable nerves, quivering at the slightest touch; and then see those tendons, firm, fixed, and powerful as the resolution of a martyr. Oh, that wonderful piece of organization who can describe it accurately?

I must not pretend to do so; but I will give a slight sketch of the being before me.

There she stands, somewhat above the usual height, but beautifully formed, with every line rounded and flowing gracefully into the others. There is calmness and dignity in the whole air, and in every movement; but yet there is something very firm, very resolute, very considerate, in the fall of that small foot upon the carpet. She cannot intend her foot to stay there for ever; and yet, when she sets it down, one would be inclined to think she did. Her face is very beautiful--every feature finely cut--the eyes almost dazzling in their dark brightness. How chaste, how lovely the fine lines of that mouth. Yet do you see what a habit she has of keeping the pearly teeth close shut--one pure row pressed hard against the other. The slight sarcastic quiver of the upper lip does not escape you; and the expanded nostril and flash of the eye, contradicted by the fixed motionless mouth.

Such is her outward appearance, such is she too within--though the complexion there is somewhat darker. Much that, had it been cultivated and improved, would have blossomed into womanly virtue; a capability of love, strong, fiery, vehement, changeless--not much tenderness--not much pity,--no remorse--are there. Pride, of a peculiar character, but strong, ungovernable, unforgiving, and a power of hate and thirst of vengeance, which only pride can give, are there likewise. Super-add a shrewdness--a policy--a cunning--nay, something greater--something approaching the sublime--a divination, where passion is to be gratified, that seldom leads astray from the object.

Yes, such is the interior of that fair temple, and yet, how calm, sweet, and promising it stands.

I have omitted much perhaps; for the human heart is like the caldron of the witches in Macbeth, and one might go on throwing in ingredients till the audience became tired of the song. However, what I have said will be enough for the reader's information; and if we come upon any unexplained phenomena, I must endeavor to elucidate them hereafter.

Let us suppose the lady's interview with her housekeeper at an end--all her domestic arrangements made--the house restored to its air of habitation-

-visits received and paid. Amongst the earliest visitors were Sir Philip and Lady Hastings. He came frankly, and in one of his most happy moods, perfectly ignorant that she had ever been made aware of there having been a marriage proposed between himself and her and she received him and his fair wife with every appearance of cordiality. But as soon as these visits and all the ceremonies were over, the lady began to drive much about the country, and to collect every tale and rumor she could meet with of all the neighboring families. Her closest attention, however, centred upon those affecting the Hastings' race; and she found the whole strange story of the cottage girl confirmed, with many another particular added. She smiled when she heard this--smiled blandly--it seemed to give her pleasure. She would fain have called upon the girl and her mother too. She longed to do so, and to draw forth with skill, of which she possessed no small share, the key secret of the whole. But her station, her reputation, prevented her from taking a step which she knew might be noised abroad and create strange comments.

She resolved upon another move, however, which she thought would do as well. There would be no objection to her visiting her poorer neighbors, to comfort, to relieve; and she went to the huts of many. At length one early morning, on a clear autumn day, the carriage was left below on the high road, and the lady climbed the hill alone towards the cottage, where the girl and her parents formerly lived. She found the old woman, who was now its occupant, busily cooking her morning meal; and sitting down, she entered into conversation with her. At first she could obtain but little information; the old woman was in a sullen mood, and would not speak of any thing she did not like. Money was of no avail to unlock her eloquence.

She had never asked or taken charity, the old woman said, and now she did not need it.

The lady pondered for a few minutes, considering the character of her ancient hostess, trying it by her experience and intuition; and thus she boldly asked her for the whole history of young John Hastings and the cottage girl.

"Tell me all," she said, "for I wish to know it--I have an interest in it."

"Ay?" said the old woman, gazing at her, "then you are the pretty lady Sir Philip was to have married, but would not have her?"

"The same," replied the visitor, and for an instant a bright red spot arose upon her cheek--a pang like a knife passed through her heart.

That was the price she paid for the gratification of her curiosity. But it probably was gratified, for she stayed nearly an hour and a half in the cottage--so long, indeed, that her servants, who were with the carriage, became alarmed, and one of the footmen walked up the hill. He met his lady coming down.

"Poor thing," she said, as if speaking of the old woman she had just left, "her senses wander a little; but she is poor, and has been much persecuted. I must do what I can for her. Whenever she comes to the house, see she is admitted."

The old woman did come often, and always had a conference with the lady of the mansion; but here let us leave them for the present. They may appear upon the stage again.

CHAPTER VIII

"MY DEAR SIR PHILIP:

"I have not seen you or dear Lady Hastings for many months; nor your sweet Emily either, except at a distance, when one day she passed my carriage on horseback, sweeping along the hill-side like a gleam of light. My life is a sad, solitary one here; and I wish my friends would take more compassion upon me and let me see human faces oftener--especial faces that I love.

"But I know that you are very inexorable in these respects, and, sufficient to yourself, cannot readily conceive how a lone woman can pine for the society of other more loving friends than books or nature. I must, therefore, attack the only accessible point I know about you, meaning your compassion, which you never refuse to those who really require it. Now I do require it greatly; for I am at this present engaged in business of a very painful and intricate nature, which I cannot clearly understand, and in which I have no one to advise me but a country attorney, whose integrity as well as ability I much doubt. To whom can I apply so well as to you, when I need the counsel and assistance of a friend, equally kind, disinterested, and clear-headed? I venture to do so, then, in full confidence, and ask you to ride over as soon as you can, to give me your advice, or rather to decide for me, in a matter where a considerable amount of property is at stake, and where decision is required immediately. I trust when you do come you will stay all night, as the business is, I fear, of so complicated a nature, that it may occupy more than one day of your valuable time in the affairs of

Your faithful and obliged servant, CAROLINE HAZLETON."

"Is Mrs. Hazleton's messenger waiting?" asked Sir Philip Hastings, after having read the letter and mused for a moment.

The servant answered in the affirmative; and his master rejoined, "Tell him I will not write an answer, as I have some business to attend to; but I beg he will tell his mistress that I will be with her in three hours."

Lady Hastings uttered a low-toned exclamation of surprise. She did not venture to ask any question--indeed she rarely questioned her husband on any subject; but when anything excited her wonder, or, as was more frequently the case, her curiosity, she was accustomed to seek for satisfaction in a somewhat indirect way, by raising her beautiful eyebrows with a doubtful sort of smile, or, as in the present instance, by exclaiming, "Good gracious! Dear me!" or giving voice to some other little vocative, with a note of interrogation strongly marked after it.

In this case there was more than one feeling at the bottom of her exclamation. She was surprised; she was curious; and she was, moreover, in the least degree in the world, jealous. She had her share of weaknesses, as I have said; and one of them was of a kind less uncommon than may be supposed. Of her husband's conduct she had no fear--not the slightest suspicion. Indeed, to have entertained any would have been impossible-- but she could not bear to see him liked, admired, esteemed, by any woman- -mark, me, I say by _any woman_; for no one could feel more triumphant joy than she did when she saw him duly appreciated by men. She was a great monopolizer: she did not wish one thought of his to be won away from her by another woman; and a sort of irritable feeling came upon her even when she saw him seated by any young and pretty girl, and paying her the common attentions of society. She was too well bred to display such sensations except by those slight indications, or by a certain petulance of manner, which he was not close observer enough of other people's conduct to remark.

Not to dwell too long on such things, Sir Philip Hastings, though perfectly unconscious of what was going on in her heart, rarely kept her long in suspense, when he saw any signs of curiosity. He perhaps might think it a point of Roman virtue to spoil his wife, although she had very little of the Portia in her character. On the present occasion, he quietly handed over to her the letter of Mrs. Hazleton; and then summoned a servant and gave orders for various preparations.

"Had not I and Emily better go with you?" asked Lady Hastings, pointing out to him the passage in the letter which spoke of the long absence of all the family.

"Not when I am going on business," replied her husband gravely, and quitted the room.

An hour after, Philip Hastings was on horseback with a servant carrying a valise behind him, and riding slowly through the park. The day was far advanced, and the distance was likely to occupy about an hour and a half in travelling; but the gentleman had fallen into a reverie, and rode very slowly. They passed the park gates; they took their way down the lane by the church and near the parsonage. Here Sir Philip pulled in his horse suddenly, and ordered the man to ride on and announce that he would be at Mrs. Hazleton's soon after. He then fastened his horse to a large hook, put up for the express purpose on most country houses of that day in England, and walked up to the door. It was ajar, and without ceremony he walked in, as he was often accustomed to do, and entered the little study of the rector.

The clergyman himself was not there; but there were two persons in the room, one a young and somewhat dashing-looking man, one or two and twenty years of age, exceedingly handsome both in face and figure; the other personage past the middle age, thin, pale, eager and keen-looking, in whom Sir Philip instantly recognized a well known, but not very well reputed attorney, of a country town about twenty miles distant. They had one of the large parish books before them, and were both bending over it with great appearance of earnestness.

The step of Sir Philip Hastings roused them, and turning round, the attorney bowed law, saying, "I give you good day, Sir Philip. I hope I have the honor of seeing you well."

"Quite so," was the brief reply, and it was followed by an inquiry for the pastor, who it seemed had gone into another room for some papers which were required.

In the mean time the younger of the two previous occupants of the room had been gazing at Sir Philip Hastings with a rude, familiar stare, which the object of it did not remark; and in another moment the clergyman himself appeared, carrying a bundle of old letters in his hand.

He was a heavy, somewhat timid man, the reverse of his predecessor in all things, but a very good sort of person upon the whole. On seeing the baronet there, however, something seemed strangely to affect him--a sort of confused surprise, which, after various stammering efforts, burst forth as soon as the usual salutation was over, in the words, "Pray, Sir Philip, did you come by appointment?"

Sir Philip Hastings, as the reader already knows, was a somewhat unobservant man of what was passing around him in the world. He had his own deep, stern trains of thought, which he pursued with a passionate earnestness almost amounting to monomania. The actions, words, and even looks of those few in whom he took an interest, he could sometimes watch and comment on in his own mind with intense study. True, he watched without understanding, and commented wrongly; for he had too little experience of the motives of others from outward observation, and found too little sympathy with the general motives of the world, in his own heart, to judge even those he loved rightly. But the conduct, the looks, the words of ordinary men, he hardly took the trouble of remarking; and the good parson's surprise and hesitation, passed like breath upon a mirror, seen perhaps, but retaining no hold upon his mind for a moment. Neither did the abrupt question surprise him; nor the quick, angry look which it called up on the face of the attorney attract his notice; but he replied quietly to Mr. Dixwell, "I do not remember having made any appointment with you."

The matter was all well so far; and would have continued well; but the attorney, a meddling fellow, had nearly spoiled all, by calling the attention of Philip Hastings more strongly to the strangeness of the clergyman's question.

"Perhaps," said the man of law, interrupting the baronet in the midst, "Perhaps Mr. Dixwell thought, Sir Philip, that you came here to speak with me on the business of the Honorable Mrs. Hazleton. She told me she would consult you, and I can explain the whole matter to you."

But the clergyman instantly declared that he meant nothing of the kind; and at the same moment Sir Philip Hastings said, "I beg you will not, sir. Mrs. Hazleton will explain what she thinks proper to me, herself. I desire no previous information, as I am now on my way to her. Why my good friend here should suppose I came by appointment, I cannot tell. However, I did not; and it does not matter. I only wish, Mr. Dixwell, to say, that I hear the old woman Danley is ill and dying. She is a papist, and the foolish people about fancy she is a witch. Little help or comfort will she obtain from them, even if they do not injure or insult her. As I shall be absent all night, and perhaps all to-morrow, I will call at her cottage as I ride over to Mrs. Hazleton's and inquire into her wants. I will put down on paper, and leave there, what I wish my people to do for her; but there is one thing which I must request you to do, namely, to take every means, by exhortation and remonstrance, to prevent the ignorant peasantry from troubling this poor creature's death-bed. Her sad errors in matters of faith should only at such a moment make us feel the greater compassion for her."

Mr. Dixwell thought differently, for though a good man, he was a fanatic. He did not indeed venture to think of disobeying the injunction of the great man of the parish--the man who now held both the Hastings and the Marshal property; but he would fain have detained Sir Philip to explain and make clear to him the position--as clear as a demonstration in Euclid to his own mind--that all Roman Catholics ought to be, at the very least, banished from the country for ever.

But Sir Philip Hastings was not inclined to listen, and although the good man began the argument in a solemn tone, his visitor, falling into a fit of thought, walked slowly out of the room, along the passage, through the door, and mounted his horse, without effectually hearing one word, though they were many which Mr. Dixwell showered upon him as he followed.

At his return to his little study, the parson found the young man and the lawyer, no longer looking at the book, but conversing together very eagerly, with excited countenances and quick gestures. The moment he entered, however, they stopped, the young man ending with an oath, for which the clergyman reproved him on the spot.

"That is very well, Mr. Dixwell," said the attorney, "and my young friend here will be much the better for some good admonition; and for sitting under your ministry, as I trust he will, some day soon; but we must go I fear directly. However, there is one thing I want to say; for you had nearly spoiled every thing to-day. No person playing at cards--"

"I never touch them," said the parson, with a holy horror in his face.

"Well, others do," said the attorney, "and those who do never show their hand to their opponent. Now, law is like a game of cards--"

"In which the lawyer is sure to get the odd trick," observed the young man.

"And we must not have Sir Philip Hastings know one step that we are taking," continued the lawyer. "If you have conscience, as I am sure you have, and honor, as I know you have, you will not suffer any thing that we have asked you, or said to you, to transpire; for then, of course, Sir Philip would take every means to prevent our obtaining information."

"I do not think it," said the parson.

"And justice and equity would be frustrated," proceeded the attorney, "which you are bound by your profession to promote. We want nothing but justice, Mr. Dixwell: justice, I say; and no one can tell what card Sir Philip may play."

"I will trump it with the knave," said the young man to himself; and having again cautioned the clergyman to be secret, not without some obscure menaces of danger to himself, if he failed, the two gentlemen left him, and hurried down, as fast as they could go, to a small alehouse in the village, where they had left their horses. In a few minutes, a well known poacher, whose very frequent habitation was the jail or the cage, was seen to issue forth from the door of the ale-house, then to lead a very showy looking horse from the stable, and then to mount him and take his way over the hill. The poacher had never possessed a more dignified quadruped than a dog or a donkey in his life; so that it was evident the horse could not be his. That he was not engaged in the congenial but dangerous occupation of stealing it, was clear from the fact of the owner of the beast gazing quietly at him out of the window while he mounted; and then turning round to the attorney, who sat at a table hard by, and saying, "he is off, I think."

"Well, let him go," replied the lawyer, "but I do not half like it, Master John. Every thing in law should be cool and quiet. No violence--no bustle."

"But this is not a matter of law," replied the younger man, "it is a matter of safety, you fool. What might come of it, if he were to have a long canting talk with the old wretch upon her death-bed?"

"Very little," replied the attorney, in a calm well-assured tone, "I know her well. She is as hard as a flint stone. She always was, and time has not softened her. Besides, he has no one with him to take depositions, and if what you say is true, she'll not live till morning."

"But I tell you, she is getting frightened, as she comes near death!" exclaimed the young man. "She has got all sorts of fancies into her head; about hell, and purgatory, and the devil knows what; and she spoke to my mother yesterday about repentance, and atonement, and a pack of stuff more, and wanted extreme unction, and to confess to a priest. It would be a fine salve, I fancy, that could patch up the wounds in her conscience; but if this Philip Hastings were to come to her with his grave face and solemn tone, and frighten her still more, he would get any thing out of her he pleased."

"I don't think it," answered the lawyer deliberately; "hate, Master John, is the longest lived passion I know. It lasts into the grave, as I have often seen in making good men's wills when they were dying--sanctified, good men, I say. Why I have seen a man who has spent half his fortune in charity, and built alms-houses, leave a thoughtless son, or a runaway daughter, or a plain-spoken nephew, to struggle with poverty all his life, refusing to forgive him, and comforting himself with a text or a pretence. No, no; hate is the only possession that goes out of the world with a man: and this old witch, Danby, hates the whole race of Hastings with a goodly strength that will not decay as her body does. Besides, Sir Philip is well-nigh as puritanical as his father--a sort of cross-breed between an English fanatic and an old Roman cynic. She abominates the very sound of his voice, and nothing would reconcile her to him but his taking the mass and abjuring the errors of Calvin. Ha! ha! ha! However, as you have sent the fellow, it cannot be helped. Only remember I had nothing to do with it if violence follows. That man is not to be trusted, and I like to keep on the safe side of the law."

"Ay, doubtless, doubtless," answered the youth, somewhat thoughtfully; "it is your shield; and better stand behind than before it. However, I don't doubt Tom Cutter in the least. Besides, I only told him to interrupt them in their talk, and take care they had no private gossip; to stick there till he was gone, and all that."

"Sir Philip is not a man to bear such interruption," said the attorney, gravely; "he is as quiet looking as the deep sea on a summer's day; but there can come storms, I tell you, John, and then woe to those who have trusted the quiet look."

"Then, if he gets in a passion, and mischief comes of it," replied the young man, with a laugh, "the fault is his, you know, Shanks."

"True," answered the attorney, meditating, "and perhaps, by a little clever twisting and timing, we might make something of it if he did, were there any other person concerned but this Tom Cutter, and we had a good serviceable witness or two. But this man is such a rogue that his word is worth nothing; and to thrash him--though the business of the beadle--would be no discredit to the magistrate. Besides, he is sure to give the provocation, and one word of Sir Philip's would be worth a thousand oaths of Tom Cutter's, in any court in the kingdom."

"As to thrashing him, that few can do," replied the youth; "but only remember, Shanks, that I gave no orders for violence."

"I was not present," replied the attorney, with a grin; "you had better, by a great deal, trust entirely to me, in these things, Master John. If you do, I will bring you safely through, depend upon it; but if you do not, nobody can tell what may come. Here comes Folwell, the sexton. Now hold your tongue, and let me manage him, sir. You are not acquainted with these matters."

The Man In Black | 55

CHAPTER IX

Did you ever examine an ant-hill, dear reader? What a wonderful little cosmos it is--what an epitome of a great city--of the human race! See how the little fellows run bustling along upon their several businesses--see how some get out of each other's way, how others jostle, and others walk over their fellows' heads! But especially mark that black gentleman, pulling hard to drag along a fat beetle's leg and thigh, three times as large as his own body. He cannot get it on, do what he will; and yet he tugs away, thinking it a very fine haunch indeed. He does not perceive, what is nevertheless the fact, that there are two others of his own race pulling at the other end, and thus frustrating all his efforts.

And thus it is with you, and me, and every one in the wide world. We work blindly, unknowing the favoring or counteracting causes that are constantly going on around us, to facilitate or impede our endeavors. The wish to look into futurity is vain, irrational, almost impious; but what a service would it be to any man if he could but get a sight into Fate's great workshop, and see only that part in which the events are on the anvil that affect our own proceedings. Still, even if we did, we might not understand the machinery after all, and only burn or pinch our fingers in trying to put pieces together which fate did not intend to fit.

In the mean time--that is to say while the attorney and his companion were talking together at the alehouse--Sir Philip Hastings rode quietly up the hill to the cottage I have before described, and therefore shall not describe again, merely noticing that it now presented an appearance of neatness and repair which it had not before possessed. He tied his horse to the palings, walked slowly up the little path, gazing right and left at the cabbages and carrots on either side, and then without ceremony went in.

The cottage had two tenants at this time, the invalid old woman, and another, well-nigh as old but less decrepit, who had been engaged to attend upon her in her sickness. How she got the money to pay her no one knew, for her middle life and the first stage of old age had been marked by poverty and distress; but somehow money seems to have a natural affinity for old age. It grows upon old people, I think, like corns; and certainly she never wanted money now.

There she was, lying in her bed, a miserable object indeed to see. She was like a woman made of fungus--not of that smooth, putty-like, fleshy fungus which grows in dank places, but of the rough, rugged, brown, carunculated sort which rises upon old stumps of trees and dry-rot gate-posts. Teeth had departed nearly a quarter of a century before, and the aquiline features had become more hooked and beaky for their loss; but the eyes had now lost their keen fire, and were dull and filmy.

The attorney was quite right. Hate was the last thing to go out in the ashes where the spark of life itself lingered, but faintly. At first she could not see who it was entered the cottage; for the sight now reached but a short distance from her own face. But the sound of his voice, as he inquired of the other old woman how she was going on, at once showed her who it was, and hate at least roused "the dull cold ear of death."

For a moment or two she lay muttering sounds which seemed to have no meaning; but at length she said, distinctly enough, "Is that Philip Hastings?"

"Yes, my poor woman," said the baronet; "is there any thing I can do for you?"

"Come nearer, come nearer," she replied, "I cannot see you plainly."

"I am close to you, nevertheless," he answered. "I am touching the bed on which you lie."

"Let me feel you," continued she--"give me your hand."

He did as she asked him; and holding by his hand, she made a great struggle to raise herself in bed; but she could not, and lay exhausted for a minute before she spoke again.

At length, however, she raised her voice louder and shriller than before--"May a curse rest upon this hand and upon that head!" she exclaimed; "may the hand work its own evil, and the head its own destruction! May the child of your love poison your peace, and make you a scoff, and a by-word, and a shame! May the wife of your bosom perish by----"

But Sir Philip Hastings withdrew his hand suddenly, and an unwonted flush came upon his cheek.

"For shame!" he said, in a low stern tone, "for shame!"

The next moment, however, he recovered himself perfectly; and turning to the nurse he added, "Poor wretch! my presence only seems to excite evil feelings which should long have passed away, and are not fit counsellors for the hour of death. If there be any thing which can tend to her bodily comfort that the hall can supply, send up for it. The servants have orders. Would that any thing could be done for her spiritual comfort; for this state is terrible to witness."

"She often asks for a priest, your worship," said the nurse. "Perhaps if she could see one she might think better before she died."

"Alas, I doubt it," replied the visitor; "but at all events we cannot afford her that relief. No such person can be found here."

"I don't know, Sir Philip," said the old woman, with a good deal of hesitation; "they do say that at Carrington, there is--there is what they call a seminary."

"You do not mean a papist college!" exclaimed the baronet, with unfeigned surprise and consternation.

"Oh, dear, no sir," replied the nurse, "only a gentleman--a seminary--a seminary priest, I think they call it; a papist certainly; but they say he is a very good gentleman, all but that."

Sir Philip mused for a minute or two, and then turned to the door, saying, "Methinks it is hard that a dying woman cannot have the consolations of the rites of her own faith--mummery though they be. As a magistrate, my good woman, I can give no authority in this business. You must do as you think fit. I myself know of no priest in this neighborhood, or I should be bound to cause his apprehension. I shall take no notice of your word, however, and as to the rest, you must, as I have said, act as you think fit. I did not make the laws, and I may think them cruel. Did I make them, I would not attempt to shackle the conscience of any one. Farewell," and passing through the door, he remounted his horse and rode away.

It was in the early autumn time of the year, and the scene was peculiarly lovely. I have given a slight description of it before, but I must pause and dwell upon it once more, even as Sir Philip Hastings paused and dwelt upon its loveliness at that moment, although he had seen and watched it a thousand times before. He was not very impressible by fine scenery. Like the sages of Laputa, his eyes were more frequently turned inwards than outwards; but there was something in that landscape which struck a chord in his heart, that is sure to vibrate easily in the heart of every one of his countrymen.

It was peculiarly English--I might say singularly English; for I have never seen any thing of exactly the same character anywhere else but in Old England--except indeed in New England, where I know not whether it be from the country having assimilated itself to the people, or from the people having chosen the country from the resemblance to their own paternal dwelling place, many a scene strikes the eye which brings back to the wandering Englishman all the old, dear feelings of his native land, and for a moment he may well forget that the broad Atlantic rolls between him and and the home of his youth.

But let me return to my picture. Sir Philip Hastings sat upon his horse's back, very nearly at the summit of the long range of hills which bisected the county in which he dwelt. I have described, in mentioning his park, the sandy character of the soil on the opposite slope of the rise; but here higher up, and little trodden by pulverizing feet, the sandstone rock itself occasionally broke out in rugged maps, diversifying the softer characteristics of the scene. Wide, and far away, on either hand, the eye could wander along the range, catching first upon some bold mass of hill, or craggy piece of ground, assuming almost the character of a cliff, seen in hard and sharp distinctness, with its plume of trees and coronet of yellow gorse, and then, proceeding onward to wave after wave, the sight rested upon the various projecting points, each softer and softer as they receded, like the memories of early days, till the last lines of the wide sweep left the mind doubtful whether they were forms of earth or clouds, or merely fancy.

Such was the scene on either hand, but straightforward it was very different, but still quite English. Were you ever, reader, borne to the top of a very high wave in a small boat, and did you ever, looking down the watery mountain, mark how the steep descent, into the depth below, was checkered by smaller waves, and these waves again by ripples? Such was the character of the view beneath the feet of the spectator. There was a gradual, easy descent from the highest point of the whole county down to a river-nurtured valley, not unbroken, but with lesser and lesser waves of earth, varying the aspect of the scene. These waves again were marked out, first by scattered and somewhat stunted trees, then by large oaks and chestnuts, not undiversified by the white and gleaming bark of the graceful birch. A massive group of birches here and there was seen; a scattered cottage, too, with its pale bluish wreath of smoke curling up over the tree-tops. Then, on the lower slope of all, came hedgerows of elms, with bright green rolls of verdant turf between; the spires of churches; the roofs and white walls of many sorts of man's dwelling-places, and gleams of a bright river, with two or three arches of a bridge. Beyond that again appeared a rich wide valley--I might almost have called it a plain, all in gay confusion, with fields, and houses, and villages, and trees, and streams, and towns, mixed altogether in exquisite disorder, and tinted with all the variety of colors and shades that belong to autumn and to sunset.

Down the descent, the eye of Sir Philip Hastings could trace several roads and paths, every step of which he knew, like daily habits. There was one, a bridle-way from a town about sixteen miles distant, which, climbing the hills almost at its outset, swept along the whole range, about midway between the summit and the valley. Another, by which he had come, and along which he intended to proceed, traversed the crest of the hills ere it reached the cottage, and then descended with a wavy line into the valley, crossing the bridle-path I have mentioned. A wider path--indeed it might be called a road, though it was not a turnpike--came over the hills from the left, and with all those easy graceful turns which Englishmen so much love in their highways, and Frenchmen so greatly abhor, descended likewise into the valley, to the small market-town, glimpses of which might be caught over the tops of the trees. As the baronet sat there on horseback, and looked around, more than one living object met his eye. To say nothing of some sheep wandering along the uninclosed part of the hill, now stopping to nibble the short grass, now trotting forward for a sweeter bite,--not to notice the oxen in the pastures below, there was a large cart slowly winding its way along an open part of the road, about half a mile distant, and upon the bridle-path which I have mentioned, the figure of a single horseman was seen, riding quietly and easily along, with a sauntering sort of air, which gave the beholder at once the notion that he was what Sterne would have called a "picturesque traveller," and was enjoying the prospect as he went.

On the road that came over the hill from the left, was another rider of very different demeanor, going along at a rattling pace, and apparently somewhat careless of his horse's knees.

The glance which Sir Philip Hastings gave to either of them was but slight and hasty. His eyes were fixed upon the scene before him, feeling, rather than understanding, its beauties, while he commented In his mind, after his own peculiar fashion. I need not trace the procession of thought through his brain. It ended, however, with the half uttered words,

"Strange, that such a land should have produced so many scoundrels, tyrants, and knaves!"

He then slowly urged his horse forward, down the side of the hill, soon reached some tall trees, where the inclosures and hedgerows commenced, and was approaching the point at which the road he was travelling, crossed the bridle-path, when he heard some loud, and as it seemed to him, angry words, passing between two persons he could not see.

"I will soon teach you that;" cried a loud, coarse tongue, adding an exceedingly blasphemous oath, which I will spare the reader.

"My good friend," replied another milder voice, "I neither desire to be taught any thing, just now, nor would you be the teacher I should chose, if I did, though perchance, in case of need, I might give you a lesson, which would be of some service to you."

Sir Philip rode on, and the next words he heard were spoken by the first voice, to the following effect; "Curse me, if I would not try that, only my man might get off in the mean time; and I have other business in hand than yours. Otherwise I would give you such a licking in two minutes, you would be puzzled to find a white spot on your skin for the neat month."

"Two minutes would not detain you long," replied the calmer voice, "and, as I have never had such a beating, I should like to see, first, whether you could give it, and secondly, what it would be like."

"Upon my soul, you are cool!" exclaimed the first speaker with another oath.

"Perfectly," replied the second; and, at the same moment, Sir Philip Hastings emerged from among the trees, at the point where the two roads crossed, and where the two speakers were face to face before his eyes.

The one, who was in truth the sauntering traveller whom he has seen wending along the bridle-path, was a tall, good-looking young man, of three or four and twenty years of age. In the other, the Baronet had no difficulty in recognizing at once, Tom Cutter, the notorious poacher and bruiser, whom he had more than once had the satisfaction of committing to jail. To see him mounted on a very fine powerful horse, was a matter of no slight surprise to Sir Philip; but, naturally concluding that he had stolen it, and was making off with his prize for sale to the neighboring town, he rode forward and put himself right in the way, determined to stop him.

"Ay, ay! Here is my man!" cried Tom Cutter, as soon as he saw him. "I will settle with him first, and then for you, my friend."

"No, no, to an old proverb, first come must be first served," replied the traveller, pushing his horse forward a few steps.

"Keep the peace, in the King's name!" exclaimed Sir Philip Hastings. "I, as a magistrate, charge you, sir, to assist me in apprehending this man!-- Thomas Cutter, get off that horse!"

The only reply was a coarse and violent expletive, and a blow with a thick heavy stick, aimed right at Sir Philip's head. The magistrate put up his arm, which received the blow, and was nearly fractured by it; but at the same moment, the younger traveller spurred forward his horse upon the ruffian, and with one sweep of his arm struck him to the ground.

Tom Cutter was upon, his feet again in a moment. He was accustomed to hard blows, and like the immortal hero of Butler, could almost tell the quality of the stick he was beat withal. He was not long in discovering, therefore, that the fist which struck him was of no ordinary weight, and was directed with skill as well as with vigor; but he was accustomed to make it his boast, that he had never taken a licking "from any man," which vanity caused him at once to risk such another blow, in the hope of having his revenge.

Rushing upon the young stranger then, stick in hand, he prepared to knock him from his horse; for the other appeared to have no defensive arms, but a slight hazel twig, pulled from a hedge.

"He will jump off the other side of his horse," thought Tom Cutter; "and then, if he do, I'll contrive to knock the nag over upon him. I know that trick, well enough."

But the stranger disappointed him. Instead of opposing the horse between him and his assailant, he sprung with one bound out of the saddle, on the side next to the ruffian himself, caught the uplifted stick with one hand, and seized the collar of the bruiser's coat with the other.

Tom Cutter began to suspect he had made a mistake; but, knowing that at such close quarters the stick would avail him little, and that strength of thews and sinews would avail him much, he dropped the cudgel, and grappled with the stranger in return.

It was all the work of a moment. Sir Philip Hastings had no time to interfere. There was a momentary struggle, developing the fine proportions and great strength and skill of the wrestlers; and then, Tom Cutter lay on his back upon the ground. The next instant, the victor put his foot upon his chest, and kept the ruffian forcibly down, notwithstanding all his exclamations of "Curse me, that isn't fair! When you give a man a fall, let him get up again!"

"If he is a fair fighter, I do," replied the other; "but when he plays pirate, I don't--" Then turning to Sir Philip Hastings, who had by this time dismounted, he said, "What is to be done with this fellow, sir? It seems he came here for the express purpose of assaulting you, for he began his impertinence, with asking if you had passed, giving a very accurate description of your person, and swearing you should find every dog would have his day."

"His offence towards myself," replied the Baronet, "I will pass over, for it seems to me, he has been punished enough in his own way; but I suspect he has stolen this horse. He is a man of notoriously bad character, who can never have obtained such an animal by honest means."

"No, I didn't steal him, I vow and swear," cried the ruffian, in a piteous tone; for bullies are almost always cravens; "he was lent to me by Johny Groves--some call him another name; but that don't signify.--He lent him to me, to come up here, to stop your gab with the old woman, Mother Danty; and mayhap to give you a good basting into the bargain. But I didn't steal the horse no how; and there he is, running away over the hill-side, and I shall never catch him; for this cursed fellow has well nigh broken my back."

"Served you quite right, my friend," replied the stranger, still keeping him tightly down with his foot. "How came you to use a cudgel to a man who had none? Take my advice, another time, and know your man before you meddle with him."

In the mean time Sir Philip Hastings had fallen into a profound reverie, only repeating to himself the words "John Groves." Now the train of thought which was awakened in his mind, though not quite new, was unpleasant to him; for the time when he first became familiar with that name was immediately subsequent to the opening of his father's will, in which had been found a clause ordering the payment of a considerable sum of money to some very respectable trustees, for the purpose of purchasing an annuity in favor of one John Groves, then a minor.

There had been something about the clause altogether which the son and heir of Sir John Hastings could not understand, and did not like. However, the will enjoined him generally to make no inquiry whatsoever into the motives of any of the bequests, and with his usual stern rigidity in what he conceived right, he had not only asked no questions, but had stopped bluntly one of the trustees, who was about to enter into some explanations. The money was paid according to directions received, and he had never heard the name of John Groves from that moment till it issued from the lips of the ruffian upon the present occasion.

"What the man says may be true," said Sir Philip Hastings, at length; "there is a person of the name he mentions. I know not how I can have offended him. It may be as well to let him rise and catch his horse if he can; but remember, Master Cutter, my eye is upon you; two competent witnesses have seen you in possession of that horse, and if you attempt to sell him, you will hang for it."

"I know better than to do that," said the bruiser, rising stiffly from the ground as the stranger withdrew his foot; "but I can tell you, Sir Philip, others have their eyes upon you, so you had better look to yourself. You hold your head mightily top high, just now: but it may chance to come down."

Sir Philip Hastings did not condescend to reply, even by a look; but turning to the stranger, as if the man's words had never reached his ear, he said, "I think we had better ride on, sir. You seem to be going my way. Night is falling fast, and in this part of the country two is sometimes a safer number to travel with than one."

The other bowed his head gravely, and remounting their horses they proceeded on the way before them, while Tom Cutter, after giving up some five minutes to the condemnation of the eyes, limbs, blood, and soul of himself and several other persons, proceeded to catch the horse which he had been riding as fast as he could. But the task proved a difficult one.

CHAPTER X

The two horsemen rode on their way. Neither spoke for several minutes. Sir Philip Hastings pondering sternly on all that had passed, and his younger companion gazing upon the scene around flooded with the delicious rays of sunset, as if nothing had passed at all.

Sir Philip, as I have shown the reader, had a habit of brooding over any thing which excited much interest in his breast--nay more, of extracting from it, by a curious sort of alchemy, essence very different from its apparent nature, sometimes bright, fine, and beneficial, and others dark and maleficent. The whole of the transaction just past disturbed him much; it puzzled him; it set his imagination running upon a thousand tracks, and most of them wrong ones; and thought was not willing to be called from her vagaries to deal with any other subject than that which preoccupied her.

The young stranger, on the other hand, seemed one of those characters which take all things much more lightly. In the moment of action, he had shown skill, resolution, and energy enough, but as he sat there on his horse's back, looking round at every point of any interest to an admirer of nature with an easy, calm and unconcerned air, no one who saw him could have conceived that he had been engaged the moment before in so fierce though short a struggle. There was none of the heat of the combatant or the triumph of the victor in his air or countenance, and his placid and equable expression of face contrasted strongly with the cloud which sat upon the brow of his companion.

"I beg your pardon, sir, for my gloomy silence," said Sir Philip Hastings, at length, conscious that his demeanor was not very courteous, "but this affair troubles me. Besides certain relations which it bears to matters of private concernment, I am not satisfied as to how I should deal with the ruffian we have suffered to depart so easily. His assault upon myself I do not choose to treat harshly; but the man is a terror to the country round, committing many an act to which the law awards a very insufficient punishment, but with cunning sufficient to keep within that line, the passage beyond which would enable society to purge itself of such a stain upon it; how to deal with him, I say, embarrasses me greatly. I have committed him two or three times to prison already; and I am inclined to regret that I did not, on this occasion, when he was in the very act of breaking the law, send my sword through him, and I should have been well justified in doing so."

"Nay, sir, methinks that would have been too much," replied his companion; "he has had a fall, which, if I judge rightly, will be a sufficient punishment for his assault upon you. According to the very _lex talionis_, he has had what he deserves. If he has nearly broke your arm, I think I have nearly broken his back."

"It is not his punishment for any offence to myself, sir, I seek," replied the baronet; "it is a duty to society to free it from the load of such a man whenever he himself affords the opportunity of doing so. Herein the law would have justified me, but even had it not been so, I can conceive many cases where it may be necessary for the benefit of our country and society to go beyond what the law will justify, and to make the law for the necessity."

"Brutus, and a few of his friends, did so," replied the young stranger with a smile, "and we admire them very much for so doing, but I am afraid we should hang them, nevertheless, if they were in a position to try the thing over again. The illustration of the gibbet and the statue might have more applications than one, for I sincerely believe, if we could revive historical characters, we should almost in all cases erect a gallows for those to whom we now raise a monument."

Sir Philip Hastings turned and looked at him attentively, and saw his face was gay and smiling. "You take all these things very lightly sir," he said.

"With a safe lightness," replied the stranger.

"Nay, with something more," rejoined his companion; "in your short struggle with that ruffian, you sprang upon him, and overthrew him like a lion, with a fierce activity which I can hardly imagine really calmed down so soon."

"O yes it is, my dear sir," replied the stranger, "I am somewhat of a stoic in all things. It is not necessary that rapidity of thought and action, in a moment of emergency, should go one line beyond the occasion, or sink one line deeper than the mere reason. The man who suffers his heart to be fluttered, or his passions to be roused, by any just action he is called upon to do, is not a philosopher. Understand me, however; I do not at all pretend to be quite perfect in my philosophy; but, at all events, I trust I schooled myself well enough not to suffer a wrestling match with a contemptible animal like that, to make my pulse beat a stroke quicker after the momentary effort is over."

Sir Philip Hastings was charmed with the reply; for though it was a view of philosophy which he could not and did not follow, however much he might agree to it, yet the course of reasoning and the sources of argument were so much akin to those he usually sought, that he fancied he had at length found a man quite after his own heart. He chose to express no farther opinion upon the subject, however, till he had seen more of his young companion; but that more he determined to see. In the mean time he easily changed the conversation, saying, "You seemed to be a very skilful and practised wrestler, sir."

"I was brought up in Cornwall," replied the other, "though not a Cornish man, and having no affinity even with the Terse and the Tees--an Anglo Saxon, I am proud to believe, for I look upon that race as the greatest which the world has yet produced."

"What, superior to the Roman?" asked Sir Philip.

"Ay, even so," answered the stranger, "with as much energy, as much resolution, less mobility, more perseverance, with many a quality which the Roman did not possess. The Romans have left us many a fine lesson which we are capable of practising as well as they, while we can add much of which they had no notion."

"I should like much to discuss the subject with you more at large," said Sir Philip Hastings, in reply; "but I know not whether we have time sufficient to render it worth while to begin."

"I really hardly know, either," answered the young stranger; "for, in the first place, I am unacquainted with the country, and in the next place, I know not how far you are going. My course tends towards a small town called Hartwell--or, as I suspect it ought to be Hartswell, probably from some fountain a which hart and hind used to come and drink."

"I am going a little beyond it," replied Sir Philip Hastings, "so that our journey will be for the next ten miles together;" and with this good space of time before him, the baronet endeavored to bring his young companion back to the subject which had been started, a very favorite one with him at all times.

But the stranger seemed to have his hobbies as well as Sir Philip, and having dashed into etymology in regard to Hartwell, he pursued it with an avidity which excluded all other topics.

"I believe," he said, not in the least noticing Sir Philip's dissertation on Roman virtues--"my own belief is, that there is not a proper name in England, except a few intruded upon us by the Normans, which might not easily be traced to accidental circumstances in the history of the family or the place. Thus, in the case of Aylesbury, or Eaglestown, from which it is derived, depend upon it the place has been noted as a resort for eagles in old times, coming thither probably for the ducks peculiar to that place. Bristol, in Anglo Saxon, meaning the place of a bridge, is very easily traceable; and Costa, or Costaford, meaning in Anglo Saxon the tempter's ford, evidently derives its name from monk or maiden having met the enemy of man or womankind at that place, and having had cause to rue the encounter. All the Hams, all the Tons, and all the Sons, lead us at once to the origin of the name, to say nothing of all the points of the compass, all the colors of the rainbow, and every trade that the ingenuity of man has contrived to invent."

In vain Sir Philip Hastings for the next half hour endeavored to bring him back to what he considered more important questions. He had evidently had enough of the Romans for the time being, and indulged himself in a thousand fanciful speculations upon every other subject but that, till Sir Philip, who at one time had rated his intellect very highly, began to think him little better than a fool. Suddenly, however, as if from a sense of courtesy rather than inclination, the young man let his older companion have his way in the choice of subject, and in his replies showed such depth of thought, such a thorough acquaintance with history, and such precise and definite views, that once more the baronet changed his opinion, and said to himself, "This is a fine and noble intellect indeed, nearly spoiled by the infection of a corrupt and frivolous world, but which might be reclaimed, if fortune would throw him in the way of those whose principles have been fixed and tried."

He pondered upon the matter for some short time. It was now completely dark, and the town to which the stranger was going distant not a quarter of a mile. The little stars were looking out in the heavens, peering at man's actions like bright-eyed spies at night; but the moon had not risen, and the only light upon the path was reflected from the flashing, dancing stream that ran along beside the road, seeming to gather up all the strong rays from the air, and give them back again with interest.

"You are coming very near Hartwell," said Sir Philip, at length; "but it is somewhat difficult to find from this road, and being, but little out of my way, I will accompany you thither, and follow the high road onwards."

The stranger was about to express his thanks, but the Baronet stopped him, saying, "Not in the least, my young friend. I am pleased with your conversation, and should be glad to cultivate your acquaintance if opportunity should serve. I am called Sir Philip Hastings, and shall be glad to see you at any time, if you are passing near my house."

"I shall certainly wait upon you, Sir Philip, if I stay any time in this county," replied the other. "That, however, is uncertain, for I come here merely on a matter of business, which may be settled in a few hours--indeed it ought to be so, for it seems to me very simple. However, it may detain me much longer, and then I shall not fail to take advantage of your kind permission."

He spoke gravely, and little more was said till they entered the small town of Hartwell, about half through which a large gibbet-like bar was seen projecting from the front of a house, suspending a large board, upon which was painted a star. The light shining from the windows of an opposite house fell upon the symbol, and the stranger, drawing in his rein, said, "Here is my inn, and I will now wish you good night, with many thanks, Sir Philip."

"Methinks it is I should thank you," replied the Baronet, "both for a pleasant journey, and for the punishment you inflicted on the ruffian Cutter."

"As for the first," said the stranger, "that has been more than repaid, if indeed it deserved thanks at all; and as for the other, that was a pleasure in itself. There is a great satisfaction to me in breaking down the self-confidence of one of these burly bruisers."

As he spoke, he dismounted, again wishing Sir Philip good night, and the latter rode on upon his way. His meditations, as he went, were altogether upon the subject of the young stranger; for, as I have shown, Sir Philip rarely suffered two ideas to get any strong grasp of his mind at the same time. He revolved, and weighed, and dissected every thing the young man had said, and the conclusion that he came to was even more favorable than at first. He seemed a man after his own heart, with just sufficient differences of opinion and diversities of character to make the Baronet feel a hankering for some opportunity of moulding and modelling him to his own standard of perfection. Who he could be, he could not by any means divine. That he was a gentleman in manners and character, there could be no doubt. That he was not rich, Sir Philip argued from the fact of his not having chosen the best inn in the little town, and he might also conclude that he was of no very distinguished family, as he had not thought fit to mention his own name in return for the Baronet's frank invitation.

Busy with these thoughts Sir Philip rode on but slowly, and took nearly half an hour to reach the gates of Mrs. Hazleton's park, though they stood only two miles' distance from the town. He arrived before them at length, however, and rang the bell. The lodge-keeper opened them but slowly, and putting his horse to a quicker pace, Sir Philip trotted up the avenue towards the house. He had not reached it, however, when he heard the sound of horses feet behind him, and, as he was dismounting at the door, his companion of the way rode quickly up and sprang to the ground, saying, with a laugh--

"I find, Sir Philip, that we are both to enjoy the same quarters to-night, for, on my arrival at Hartwell, I did not expect to visit this house till to-morrow morning. Mrs. Hazleton, however, has very kindly had my baggage brought up from the inn, and therefore I have no choice but to intrude upon her to-night."

As he spoke the doors of the house were thrown open, servants came forth to take the horses, and the two gentlemen were ushered at once into Mrs. Hazleton's receiving-room.

CHAPTER XI

Mrs. Hazleton was looking as beautiful as she had been at twenty--perhaps more so; for the few last years before the process of decay commences, sometimes adds rather than detracts from woman's loveliness. She was dressed with great skill and taste too; nay, even with peculiar care. The hair, which had not yet even one silver thread in its wavy mass, was so arranged as to hide, in some degree, that height and width of forehead which gave almost too intellectual an expression to her countenance--which, upon some occasions, rendered the expression (for the features were all feminine) more that of a man than that of a woman. Her dress was very simple in appearance though costly in material; but it had been chosen and fitted by the nicest art, of colors which best harmonized with her complexion, and in forms rather to indicate beauties than to display them.

Thus attired, with grace and dignity in every motion, she advanced to meet Sir Philip Hastings, frankly holding out her hand to him, and beaming on him one of her most lustrous smiles. It was all thrown away upon him indeed; but that did not matter. It had its effect in another quarter. She then turned to the younger gentleman with a greater degree of reserve in manner, but yet, as she spoke to him and welcomed him to her house, the color deepened on her cheek with a blush that would not have been lost to Sir Philip if he had been at all in the custom of making use of them. They had evidently met before, but not often and her words, "Good evening, Mr. Marlow, I am glad to see you at my house at length," were said in the tone if one who was really glad, but did not wish to show it too plainly.

"You have come with my friend, Sir Philip Hastings," she added; "I did not know you were acquainted."

"Nor were we, my dear madam, till this evening," replied the Baronet, speaking for himself and his companion of the road, "till we met by accident on the hill-side on our way hither. We had a somewhat unpleasant encounter with a notorious personage of the name of Tom Cutter, which brought us first into acquaintance; though, till you uttered it, my young friend's name was unknown to me."

"Tom Cutter! is that the man who poaches all my game?" said the lady, in a musing tone.

Nor was she musing of Tom Cutter, or the lost game, or of the sins and iniquities of poaching; neither one or the other. The exclamation and inquiry taken together were only one of those little half-unconscious stratagems of human nature, by which we often seek to amuse the other parties in conversation--and sometimes amuse our own outward man too--while the little spirit within is busily occupied with some question which we do not wish our interlocutors to have any thing to do with. She was asking herself, in fact, what had been the conversation with which Sir Philip Hastings and Mr. Marlow had beguiled the way--whether they had talked of her--whether they had talked of her affairs--and how she could best get some information on the subject without seeming to seek it.

She soon had an opportunity of considering the matter more at leisure, for Sir Philip Hastings, with some remark as to "dusty dresses not being fit for ladies' drawing-rooms," retired for a time to the chamber prepared for him. The fair lady of the house detained Mr. Marlow indeed for a few minutes, talking with him in a pleasant and gentle tone, and making her bright eyes do their best in the way of captivating. She expressed regret that she had not seen him more frequently, and expressed a hope, in very graceful terms, that even the painful question, which those troublesome men of law had started between them, might be a means of ripening their acquaintance into friendship.

The young gentleman replied with all gallantry, but with due discretion, and then retired to his room to change his dress. He certainly was a very good-looking young man; finely formed, and with a pleasing though not regularly handsome countenance; and perhaps he left Mrs. Hazleton other matters to meditate of than the topics of his conversation with Sir Philip Hastings. Certain it is, that when the baronet returned very shortly after, he found his beautiful hostess in a profound reverie, from which his sudden entrance made her start with a bewildered look not common to her.

"I am very glad to talk to you for a few moments alone, my dear friend," said Mrs. Hazleton, after a moment's pause. "This Mr. Marlow is the gentleman who claims the very property on which you now stand;" and she proceeded to give her hearer, partly by spontaneous explanations, partly by answers to his questions, her own view of the case between herself and Mr. Marlow; laboring hard and skilfully to prepossess the mind of Sir

Philip Hastings with a conviction of her rights as opposed to that of her young guest.

"Do you mean to say, my dear madam," asked Sir Philip, "that he claims the whole of this large property? That would be a heavy blow indeed."

"Oh, dear, no," replied the lady; "the great bulk of the property is mine beyond all doubt, but the land on which this house stands, and rather more than a thousand acres round it, was bought by my poor father before I was born, I believe, as affording the most eligible site for a mansion. He never liked the old house near your place, and built this for himself. Mr. Marlow's lawyers now declare that his grand-uncle, who sold the land to my father, had no power to sell it; that the property was strictly entailed."

"That will be easily ascertained," said Sir Philip Hastings; "and I am afraid, my dear madam, if that should prove the case, you will have no remedy but to give up the property."

"But is not that very hard?" asked Mrs. Hazleton, "the Marlows certainly had the money."

"That will make no difference," replied Sir Philip, musing; "this young man's grand-uncle may have wronged your father; but he is not responsible for the act, and I am very much afraid, moreover, that his claim may not be limited to the property itself. Back rents, I suspect, might be claimed."

"Ay, that is what my lawyer, Mr. Shanks, says," replied Mrs. Hazleton, with a bewildered look; "he tells me that if Mr. Marlow is successful in the suit, I shall have to pay the whole of the rents of the land. But Shanks added that he was quite certain of beating him if we could retain for our counsel Sargeant Tutham and Mr. Doubledo."

"Shanks is a rogue," said Sir Philip Hastings, in a calm, equable tone; "and the two lawyers you have named bear the reputation of being learned and unscrupulous men. The first point, my dear madam, is to ascertain whether this young gentleman's claim is just, and then to deal with him equitably, which, in the sense I affix to the term, may be somewhat different from legal."

"I really do not know what to do," cried Mrs. Hazleton, with a slight laugh, as if at her own perplexity. "I Was never in such a situation in my life;" and then she added, very rapidly and in a jocular tone, as if she were afraid of pausing upon or giving force to any one word, "if my poor father had been alive, he would have settled it all after his own way soon enough.

He was a great match-maker you know, Sir Philip, and he would have proposed, in spite of all obstacles, a marriage between the two parties, to settle the affair by matrimony instead of by law," and she laughed again as if the very idea was ridiculous.

Unlearned Sir Philip thought so too, and most improperly replied, "The difference of age would of course put that out of the question;" nor when he had committed the indiscretion, did he perceive the red spot which came upon Mrs. Hazleton's fair brow, and indicated sufficiently enough the effect his words had produced. There was an ominous silent pause, however, for a minute, and then the Baronet was the person to resume the discourse in his usual calm, argumentative tone. "I do not think," he said, "from Mr. Marlow's demeanor or conversation, that he is likely to be very exacting in this matter. His claim, however, must be looked to in the first place, before we admit any thing on your part. If the property was really entailed, he has undoubtedly a right to it, both in honesty and in law; but methinks there he might limit his claim if his sense of real equity be strong; but the entail must be made perfectly clear before you can admit so much as that."

"Well, well, sir," said Mrs. Hazleton, hastily, for she heard a step on the outer stairs, "I will leave it entirely to you, Sir Philip, I am sure you will take good care of my interests."

Sir Philip did not altogether like the word interests, and bowing his head somewhat stiffly, he added, "and of your honor, my dear madam."

Mrs. Hazleton liked his words as little as he did hers, and she colored highly. She made no reply, indeed, but his words that night were never forgotten.

The next moment Mr. Marlow entered the room with a quiet, easy air, evidently quite unconscious of having been the subject of conversation. During the evening he paid every sort of polite attention to his fair hostess, and undoubtedly showed signs and symptoms of thinking her a very beautiful and charming woman. Whatever was her game, take my word for it, reader, she played it skilfully, and the very fact of her retiring early, at the very moment when she had made the most favorable impression, leaving Sir Philip Hastings to entertain Mr. Marlow at supper, was not without its calculation.

As soon as the lady was gone, Sir Philip turned to the topic of Mrs. Hazleton's business with his young companion, and managed the matter more skilfully than might have been expected. He simply told him that Mrs.

Hazleton had mentioned a claim made upon her estate by his lawyers, and had thought it better to leave the investigation of the affair to her friend, rather than to professional persons.

A frank good-humored smile came upon Mr. Marlow's face at once. "I am not a rich man, Sir Philip," he said, "and make no professions of generosity, but, at the same time, as my grand-uncle undoubtedly had this money from Mrs. Hazleton's father, I should most likely never have troubled her on the subject, but that this very estate is the original seat of our family, on which we can trace our ancestors back through many centuries. The property was undoubtedly entailed, my father and my uncle were still living when it was sold, and performed no disentailing act whatever. This is perfectly susceptible of proof, and though my claim may put Mrs. Hazleton to some inconvenience, I am anxious to avoid putting her to any pain. Now I have come down with a proposal which I confidently trust you will think reasonable. Indeed, I expected to find her lawyer here rather than an independent friend, and I was assured that my proposal would be accepted immediately, by persons who judged of my rights more sanely perhaps than I could."

"May I hear what the proposal is?" asked Sir Philip.

"Assuredly," replied Mr. Marlow, "it is this: that in the first place Mrs. Hazleton should appoint some gentleman of honor, either at the bar or not, as she may think fit, to investigate my claim, with myself or some other gentleman on my part, with right to call in a third as umpire between them. I then propose that if my claim should be distinctly proved, Mrs. Hazleton should surrender to me the lands in question, I repaying her the sum which my grand-uncle received, and--"

"Stay," said Sir Philip Hastings, "are you aware that the law would not oblige you to do that?"

"Perfectly," replied Mr. Marlow, "and indeed I am not very sure that equity would require it either, for I do not know that my father ever received any benefit from the money paid to his uncle. He may have received a part however, without my knowing it, for I would rather err on the right side than on the wrong. I then propose that the rents of the estate, as shown by the leases, and fair interest upon the value of the ground surrounding this house, should be computed during the time that it has been out of our possession, while on the other hand the legal interest of the money paid for the property should be calculated for the same period, the smaller sum deducted from the larger, and the balance paid by me to Mrs. Hazleton or by Mrs. Hazleton to me, so as to replace every thing in the same state as if this unfortunate sale had never taken place."

Sir Philip Hastings mused without reply for more than one minute. That is a long time to muse, and many may be the thoughts and feelings which pass through the breast of man during that space. They were many in the present instance, and it would not be very easy to separate or define them. Sir Philip thought of all the law would have granted to the young claimant under the circumstances of the case: the whole property, all the back rents, every improvement that had been made, the splendid mansion in which they were then standing, without the payment on his part of a penny: he compared these legal rights with what he now proposed, and he saw that he had indeed gone a great way on the generous side of equity. There was something very fine and noble in this conduct, something that harmonized well with his own heart and feelings. There was no exaggeration, no romance about it: he spoke in the tone of a man of business doing a right thing well considered, and the Baronet was satisfied in every respect but one. Mrs. Hazleton's words I must not say had created a suspicion, but had suggested the idea that other feelings might be acting between her and his young companion, notwithstanding the difference of age which he had so bluntly pointed out, and he resolved to inquire farther.

In the mean time, however, Mr. Marlow somewhat misinterpreted his silence, and he added, after waiting longer than was pleasant, "Of course you understand, Sir Philip, that if two or three honest men decide that my case is unfounded--although I know that cannot be the case--I agree to drop it at once and renounce it for ever. My solicitors and counsel in London judged the offer a fair one at least."

"And so do I," said Sir Philip Hastings, emphatically; "however, I must speak with Mrs. Hazleton upon the subject, and express my opinion to her. Pray, have you the papers regarding your claim with you?"

"I have attested copies," replied Mr. Marlow, "and I can bring them to you in a moment. They are so unusually clear, and seem to put the matter so completely beyond all doubt, that I brought them down to satisfy Mrs. Hazleton and her solicitor, without farther trouble, that my demand at least had some foundation in justice."

The papers were immediately brought, and sitting down deliberately, Sir Philip Hastings went through them with his young friend, carefully weighing every word. They left not even a doubt on his mind; they seemed not to leave a chance even for the chicanery of the law, they were clear, precise, and definite. And the generosity of the young man's offer stood out even more conspicuously than before.

"For my part, I am completely satisfied," said Sir Philip Hastings, when he had done the examination, "and I have no doubt that Mrs. Hazleton will be so likewise. She is an excellent and amiable person, as well as a very beautiful woman. Have you known her long? have you seen her often?"

"Only once, and that about a year ago," replied Mr. Marlow; "she is indeed very beautiful as you say--for a woman of her period of life remarkably so; she puts me very much in mind of my mother, whom I in the confidence of youthful affection used to call 'my everlasting.' I recollect doing so only three days before the hand of death wrote upon her brow the vanity of all such earthly thoughts."

Sir Philip Hastings was satisfied. There was nothing like passion there. Unobservant as he was in most things, he was more clear-sighted in regard to matters of love, than any other affection of the human mind. He had himself loved deeply and intensely, and he had not forgotten it.

It was necessary, before any thing could be concluded, to wait for Mrs. Hazleton's rising on the following morning; and, bidding Mr. Marlow good night with a warm grasp of the hand, Sir Philip Hastings retired to his room and passed nearly an hour in thought, pondering the character of his new acquaintance, recalling every trait he had remarked, and every word he had heard. It was a very satisfactory contemplation. He never remembered to have met with one who seemed so entirely a being after his own heart. There might be little flaws, little weaknesses perhaps, but the confirming power of time and experience would, he thought, strengthen all that was good, and counsel and example remedy all that was weak or light.

"At all events," thought the Baronet, "his conduct on this occasion shows a noble and equitable spirit. We shall see how Mrs. Hazleton meets it to-morrow."

When that morrow came, he had to see the reverse of the picture, but it must be reserved for another chapter.

CHAPTER XII

Mrs. Hazleton was up in the morning early. She was at all times an early riser, for she well knew what a special conservator of beauty is the morning dew, but on this occasion certain feelings of impatience made her a little earlier than usual. Besides, she knew that Sir Philip Hastings was always a matutinal man, and would certainly be in the library before she was down. Nor was she disappointed. There she found the Baronet reaching up his hand to take down Livy, after having just replaced Tacitus.

"It is a most extraordinary thing, my dear madam," said Sir Philip, after the salutation of the morning, "and puzzles me more than I can explain."

Mrs. Hazleton fancied that her friend had discovered some very knotty point in the case with Mr. Marlow, and she rejoiced, for her object was not, to emulate but to entangle. Sir Philip, however, went on to put her out of all patience by saying, "How the Romans, so sublimely virtuous at one period of their history, could fall into so debased and corrupt a state as we find described even by Sallust, and depicted in more frightful colors still by the latter historians of the empire."

Mrs. Hazleton, as I have said, was out of all patience, and ladies in that state sometimes have recourse to homely illustration. "Their virtue got addled, I suppose," she replied, "by too long keeping. Virtue is an egg that won't bear sitting upon--but now do tell me, Sir Philip, had you any conversation with Mr. Marlow last night upon this troublesome affair of mine?"

"I had, my dear madam," replied Sir Philip, with a very faint smile, for Sir Philip could not well bear any jesting on the Romans. "I did not only converse with Mr. Marlow on the subject, but I examined carefully the papers he brought down with him, and perceived at once that you have not the shadow of a title to the property in question."

Mrs. Hazleton's brow grew dark, and she replied in a somewhat sullen tone, "You decided against me very rapidly, Sir Philip. I hope you did not let Mr. Marlow see your strong prepossession--opinion I mean to say--in his favor."

"Entirely," replied Sir Philip Hastings.

Mrs. Hazleton was silent, and gazed down upon the carpet as if she were counting the threads of which it was composed, and finding the calculation by no means satisfactory.

Sir Philip let her gaze on for some time, for he was not very easily moved to compassion in cases where he saw dishonesty of purpose as well as suffering. At length, however, he said, "My judgment is not binding upon you in the least; I tell you simply, my dear madam, what is my conclusion, and the law will tell you the same."

"We shall see," muttered Mrs. Hazleton between her teeth; but then putting on a softer air she asked, "Tell me, Sir Philip, would you, if you were in my situation, tamely give up a property which was honestly bought and paid for, without making one struggle to retain it?"

"The moment I was convinced I had no legal right to it," replied Sir Philip. "However, the law is still open to you, if you think it better to resist; but before you take your determination, you had better hear what Mr. Marlow proposes, and you will pardon me for expressing to you what I did not express to him: an opinion that his proposal is founded upon the noblest view of equity."

"Indeed," said Mrs. Hazleton, with her eyes brightening, "pray let me hear this proposal."

Sir Philip explained it to her most distinctly, expecting that she would be both surprised and pleased, and never doubted that she would accept it instantly. Whether she was surprised or not, did not appear, but pleased she certainly was not to any great extent, for she did not wish the matter to be so soon concluded. She began to make objections immediately. "The enormous expense of building this house has not been taken into consideration at all, and it will be very necessary to have the original papers examined before any thing is decided. There are two sides to every question, my dear Sir Philip, and we cannot tell that other papers may not be found, disentailing this estate before the sale took place."

"This is impossible," answered Sir Philip Hastings, "if the papers exhibited to me are genuine, for this young gentleman, on whom, as his father's eldest son, the estate devolved by the entail, was not born when the sale took place. By his act only could it be disentailed, and as he was not born, he could perform no such act."

He pressed her hard in his cold way, and it galled her sorely.

"Perhaps they are not genuine," she said at length.

"They are all attested," replied Sir Philip, "and he himself proposes that the originals should be examined as the basis of the whole transaction."

"That is absolutely necessary," said Mrs. Hazleton, well satisfied to put off decision even for a time. But Sir Philip would not leave her even that advantage.

"I think," he said; "you must at once decide whether you accept his proposal, on condition that the examination of the papers proves the justice of his claim to the satisfaction of those you may appoint to examine it. If there are any doubts and difficulties to be raised afterwards, he might as well proceed by law at once."

"Then let him go to law," exclaimed Mrs. Hazleton with a flashing eye. "If he do, I will defend every step to the utmost of my power."

"Incur enormous expense, give yourself infinite pain and mortification, and ruin a fine estate by a spirit of unnecessary and unjust resistance," added Sir Philip, in a calm and somewhat contemptuous tone.

"Really, Sir Philip, you press me too hard," exclaimed Mrs. Hazleton in a tone of angry mortification, and, sitting down to the table, she actually wept.

"I only press you for your own good," answered the Baronet, not at all moved, "you are perhaps not aware that if this gentleman's claim is, just, and you resist it, the whole costs will fall upon you. All that could be expected of him was to submit his claim to arbitration, but he now does more; he proposes, if arbitration pronounce it just, to make sacrifices of his legal rights to the amount of many thousand pounds. He is not bound to refund one penny paid for this estate, he is entitled to back rents for a considerable number of years, and yet he offers to repay the money, and far from demanding the back rents, to make compensation for any loss of interest that may have been sustained by this investment. There are few men in England, let me tell you, who would have made such a proposal, and if you refuse it you will never have such another."

"Do not you think, Sir Philip," asked Mrs. Hazleton sharply, "that he never would have made such a proposal if he had not known there was something wrong about his title?"

Now there was something in this question which doubly provoked Sir Philip Hastings. He never could endure a habit which some ladies have of recurring continually to points previously disposed of, and covering the reiteration by merely putting objections in a new form. Now the question as to the validity of Mr. Marlow's title, he looked upon as entirely disposed of by the proposal of investigation and arbitration. But there was something more than this; the very question which the lady put showed an incapacity for conceiving any generous motive, which thoroughly disgusted him, and, turning with a quiet step to the window, he looked down upon the lawn which spread far away between two ranges of tall fine wood, glowing in the yellow sunshine of a dewy autumnal morning. It was the most favorable thing he could have done for Mrs. Hazleton. Even the finest and the strongest and the stoutest minds are more frequently affected unconsciously by external things than any one is aware of. The sweet influences or the irritating effects of fine or bad weather, of beautiful or tame scenery, of small cares and petty disappointments, of pleasant associations or unpleasant memories, nay of a thousand accidental circumstances, and even fancies themselves, will affect considerations totally distinct and apart, as the blue or yellow panes of a stained glass window cast a melancholy hue or a yellow splendor upon the statue and carvings of the cold gray stone.

As Sir Philip gazed forth upon the fair scene before his eyes, and thought what a lovely spot it was, how calm, how peaceful, how refreshing in its influence, he said to himself, "No wonder she is unwilling to part with it."

Then again, there was a hare gambolling upon the lawn, at a distance of about a hundred yards from the house, now scampering along and beating up the dew from the morning grass, now crouched nearly flat so as hardly to be seen among the tall green blades, then hopping quietly along with an awkward, shuffling gait, or sitting up on its hind legs, with raised ears, listening to some distant sound; but still as it resumed its gambols, again going round and round, tracing upon the green sward a labyrinth of meandering lines. Sir Philip watched it for several moments with a faint smile, and then said to himself, "It is the beast's nature--why not a woman's?"

Turning himself round he saw Mrs. Hazleton, sitting at the table with her head leaning in a melancholy attitude upon her hand, and he replied to her last words, though he had before fully made up his mind to give them no answer whatever.

"The question in regard to title, my dear madam," he said, "is one which is to be decided by others. Employ a competent person, and he will insure, by full investigation, that your rights are maintained entire. Your acceptance of Mr. Marlow's proposals contingent on the full recognition of his claim, will be far from prejudicing your case, should any flaw in your title be discovered. On the contrary, should the decision of a point Of law be required, it will put you well with the court. By frankly doing so, you also meet him in the same spirit in which I am sure he comes to you; and as I am certain he has a very high sense of equity, I think he will be well inclined to enter into any arrangement which may be for your convenience. From what he has said himself, I do not believe he can afford to keep such an establishment as is necessary for this house, and if you cling to it, as you may well do, doubtless it may remain your habitation as long as you please at a very moderate rent. Every other particular I think may be settled in the same manner, if you will but show a spirit of conciliation, and--"

"I am sure I have done that," said Mrs. Hazleton, interrupting him. "However, Sir Philip, I will leave it all to you. You must act for me in this business. If you think it right, I will accept the proposal conditionally as you mention, and the title can be examined fully whenever we can fix upon the time and the person. All this is very hard upon me, I do think; but I suppose I must submit with a good grace."

"It is certainly the best plan," replied Sir Philip; and while Mrs. Hazleton retired to efface the traces of tears from her eyelids, the Baronet walked into the drawing-room, where he was soon after joined by Mr. Marlow. He merely told him, however, that he had conversed with the lady of the house, and that she would give him her answer in person. Now, whatever were Mrs. Hazleton's wishes or intentions, she certainly was not well satisfied with the precise and rapid manner in which Sir Philip brought matters of business to an end. His last words, however, had afforded her a glimmering prospect of somewhat lengthy and frequent communication between herself and Mr. Marlow, and one thing is certain, that she did not at all desire the transaction between them to be concluded too briefly. At the same time, it was not her object to appear otherwise than in the most favorable light to his eyes; and consequently, when she entered the drawing-room she held out her hand to him with a gracious though somewhat melancholy smile, saying, "I have had a long conversation with Sir Philip this morning, Mr. Marlow, concerning the very painful business which brought you here. I agree at once to your proposal in regard to the arbitration and the rest;" and she then went on to speak of the whole business as if she had made not the slightest resistance whatever, but had been struck at once by the liberality of his proposals, and by the sense of equity which they displayed. Sir Philip took little notice of all this; for he had fallen into one of his fits of musing, and Mr. Marlow had quitted the room to bring some of the papers for the purpose of showing them to Mrs. Hazleton, before the Baronet awoke out of his reverie. The younger gentleman returned a moment after, and he and Sir Philip and Mrs. Hazleton were busily looking at a long list of certificates of births, deaths and marriages, when the door opened, and Mr. Shanks, the attorney, entered the room, booted, spurred, and dusty as if from a long ride. He was a man to whom Sir Philip had a great objection; but he said nothing, and the attorney with a tripping step advanced towards Mrs. Hazleton.

The lady looked confused and annoyed, and in a hasty manner put back the papers into Mr. Marlow's hand. But Mr. Shanks was one of the keen and observing men of the world. He saw every thing about him as if he had been one of those insects which have I do not know how many thousand pair of lenses in each eye. He had no scruples or hesitation either; he was all sight and all remark, and a lady of any kind was not at all the person to inspire him with reverence.

He was, in short, all law, and loved nothing, respected nothing, but law.

"Dear me, Mrs. Hazleton," he exclaimed, "I did not expect to find you so engaged. These seem to be law papers--very dangerous, indeed, madam, for unprofessional persons to meddle with such things. Permit me to look at them;" and he held out his hand towards Mr. Marlow, as if expecting to receive the papers without a word of remonstrance. But Mr. Marlow held them back, saying, in a very calm, civil tone, "Excuse me, sir! We are conversing over the matter in a friendly manner; and I shall show them to a lawyer only at Mrs. Hazleton's request."

"Very improper--that is, I mean to say very unprofessional!" exclaimed Mr. Shanks, "and let me say very hazardous too," rejoined the lawyer abruptly; but Mrs. Hazleton herself interposed, saying in a marked tone and with an air of dignity which did not always characterize her demeanor towards her "right hand man," as she was accustomed sometimes to designate Mr. Shanks, "We do not desire any interference at this moment, my good sir. I appointed you at twelve o'clock. It is not yet nine."

"O I can see, I can see," replied Mr. Shanks, while Sir Philip Hastings advanced a step or two, "his worship here never was a friend of mine, and has no objection to take a job or two out of my hands at any time."

"We have nothing to do with jobs, sir," said Sir Philip Hastings, in his usual dry tone, "but at all events we do not wish you to make a job where there is none."

"I must take the liberty, however, of warning that lady, sir," said Mr. Shanks, with the pertinacity of a parrot, which he so greatly resembled, "as her legal adviser, sir, that if----"

"That if she sends for an attorney, she wants him at the time she appoints," interposed Sir Philip; "that was what you were about to say, I suppose."

"Not at all, sir, not at all," exclaimed the lawyer; for very shrewd and very oily lawyers will occasionally forget their caution and their coolness when they see the prospect of a loss of fees before them. "I was going to say no such thing. I was going to warn her not to meddle with matters of business of which she can understand nothing, by the advice of those who know less, and who may have jobs of their own to settle while they are meddling with hers."

"And I warn you to quit this room, sir," said Sir Philip Hastings, a bright spot coming into his usually pale cheek; "the lady has already expressed her opinion upon your intrusion, and depend upon it, I will enforce mine."

"I shall do no such thing, sir, till I have fully----"

He said no more, for before he could conclude the sentence, the hand of Sir Philip Hastings was upon his collar with the grasp of a giant, and although he was a tall and somewhat powerful man, the Baronet dragged him to the door in despite of his half-choking struggles, as a nurse would haul along a baby, pulled him across the stone hall, and opening the outer door with his left hand, shot him down the steps without any ceremony; leaving him with his hands and knees upon the terrace.

This done, the Baronet returned into the house again, closing the door behind him. He then paused in the hall for an instant, reproaching himself for certain over-quick beatings of the heart, tranquillized his whole look and demeanor, and then returning to the drawing-room, resumed the conversation with Mrs. Hazleton, as if nothing had ever occurred to interrupt it.

CHAPTER XIII

Mrs. Hazleton was or affected to be a good deal flustered by the event which had just taken place, but after a number of certain graceful attitudes, assumed without the slightest appearance of affectation, she recovered her calmness, and proceeded with the business in hand. That business was soon terminated, so far as the full and entire acceptance of Mr. Marlow's proposal went, and immediately after the conclusion of breakfast, Sir Philip Hastings ordered his horses to depart. Mrs. Hazleton fain would have detained him, for she foresaw that his going might be a signal for Mr. Marlow's going also, and it was not a part of her policy to assume the matronly character so distinctly as to invite him to remain in her house alone. Sir Philip however was inexorable, and returned to his own dwelling, renewing his invitation to his new acquaintance.

Mrs. Hazleton bade him adieu, with the greatest appearance of cordiality; but I am very much afraid, if one had possessed the power of looking into her heart, one would have a picture very different from that presented by her face. Sir Philip Hastings had said and done things since he had entered her dwelling the night before, which Mrs. Hazleton was not a woman to forget or forgive. He had thwarted her schemes, he had mortified her vanity, he had wounded her pride; and she was one of those women who bide their time, but have a strong tenacity of resentments.

When he was gone, however, she played a new game with Mr. Marlow. She insisted upon his remaining for the day, but with a fine sense of external proprieties, she informed him that she expected a charming elderly lady of her acquaintance to pass a few days with her, to whom she should particularly like to introduce him.

This was false, be it remarked; but she immediately took measures to make it true. Now, there is in every neighborhood more than one of that class called good creatures. For this office, an abundant store of real or assumed soft stupidity is required; but it is a somewhat difficult part to play, for with this stupidity there must also be a considerable portion of fine tact, to guard the performer against any of those blunders into which good-natured people are continually plunging. Drill and discipline are also necessary, in order to be always on the look out for hints, to appreciate them properly, to comprehend that friends may say one thing and mean another, and to ask no questions of any kind. There were no less than three of these good creatures in this Mrs. Hazleton's immediate neighborhood; and during a few moments' retreat to her own little writing-room, she laid her finger upon her fair temple, and thought them well over. Mrs. Winifred Edgeby was the first who suggested herself to the mind of the fair lady. She had many of the requisites. She dressed well, talked well, and had an air of style and fashion about her; was perfectly innocuous, and skilful in divining the purposes and wishes of a friend or patron; but there was an occasional touch of subacrid humor about her which Mrs. Hazleton did not half like. It gave an impression of seeing too clearly, of perceiving much more than she pretended to perceive.

The second was Mrs. Warmington, a widow, not very rich, and not indeed very refined; gay, talkative, somewhat boisterous, yet full of a sound discretion in never committing herself or a friend. She had also much experience, for she had been twice married, and twice a widow, and thus had had her misfortunes. The third was a Miss Goodenough, the most silent, quiet, stilly person in the world, moving about the house with the step of a cat, and a face of infinite good nature to the whole human race. She was to all appearance the pink of gentleness and weak good nature; but her silence was invaluable.

After some consideration Mrs. Hazleton decided upon the widow, and instantly dispatched a note with her own carriage, begging Mrs. Warmington to come over immediately and spend a few days with her, as a young gentleman had arrived upon a visit, and it would be indecorous to entertain him alone.

Mrs. Warmington understood it all in an instant. She said to her. If, "Ho, ho! a young gentleman come to stay--wanted a duenna! Matrimony in the wind! Heigho! she must be six and thirty--six and thirty from two and fifty leave sixteen points against me, and long odds. Well, well,--I have had my share;" and Mrs. Warmington laughed aloud. However, she would neither keep Mrs. Hazleton's carriage waiting, nor Mrs. Hazleton herself in suspense, for there were various little comforts and conveniences in the good will of that lady which Mrs. Warmington was eager to cultivate. She had, too, a shrewd suspicion that the enmity of Mrs. Hazleton might become a thing to be seriously dreaded; and therefore, whichever side of the question she looked at, she saw reasons for seeking the beautiful widow's good graces. Her maid was called, her clothes packed up, and she entered the carriage and drove away, while in the mean time Mrs. Hazleton had been expatiating to Mr. Marlow upon all the high qualities and points of excellence in her friend Mrs. Warmington. She was too skilful, moreover, to bring her good taste and judgment into question with her young friend, by raising expectations which might be disappointed. She therefore threw in insinuations of a few faults and failings in dear Madam Warmington's manner and demeanor. But then she said she was such a good creature at heart, that although the very fastidious affected to censure, she herself forgot all little blemishes in the inherent excellence of the person.

Moreover, upon the plea of looking at the ground which was the subject of Mr. Marlow's claim, she led him out for a long, pleasant ramble through the park. She took him amongst old hawthorn trees, through groves of chestnuts by the banks of the stream, and along paths where the warm sunshine played through the brown and yellow leaves above, gilding their companions which had fallen earlier than themselves to the sward below. It was a very lover-like walk indeed--one where nature speaks to the heart, wakening sweet influences, and charming the spirit up from hard and cold indifference. Mrs. Hazleton felt sure that Mr. Marlow would not forget that walk, and she took care to impress it as deeply as possible upon his memory. Nor did she want any of the means to do so. Her mind was highly cultivated for the age in which she lived, her taste fine, her information extensive. She could discourse of foreign lands, of objects and scenes of deep interest, great beauty, and rich associations,--of courts and cities far away, of music, painting, flowers in other lands, of climates rich in sunshine and of genial warmth; and through the whole she had the art to throw a sort of magic glow from her own mind which brightened all she spoke of.

She was very charming that day, indeed, and Mr. Marlow felt the spell, but he did not fall in love.

Now what was the object of using all these powers upon him? Was Mrs. Hazleton a person very susceptible, or very covetous of the tender passion? Since her return to England she had refused some half-dozen very eligible offers from handsome, agreeable, estimable men, and the world in general had set her down for a person as cold as a stone. It might be so, but there are some stones, which, when you heat them, acquire intense fervor, and retain it longer than any other substance. Every body in the world has his peculiarities, his whims, caprices, crochets if you will. Mrs. Hazleton had gazed over the handsome, the glittering and the gay, with the most perfect indifference. She had listened to professions of love with a tranquil, easy balance power, which weighed to a grain the advantages of matrimony and widowhood, without suffering the dust of passion to give even a shake to the scale. Before the preceding night she had only seen Mr. Marlow once, but the moment she set eyes upon him--the moment she heard his voice, she had said to herself, "If ever I marry again, that is the man." There is no explaining these sympathetic attractions, impulses, or whatever they may be called; but I think, from some observation of human nature, it will be found that in those persons where they are the least frequent, they are the most powerful and persevering when they do exist.

Not long after their first meeting, some intimation occurred of a claim on the part of Mr. Marlow to a portion of the lady's property--that portion that she loved best. The very idea of parting with it at all, of being forced to give it up, was most painful and distressing to her. Yet that made no difference whatever in her feelings towards Mr. Marlow. Communications of various kinds took place between lawyers, and the opposite counsel were as firm as a rock. Mrs. Hazleton thought it very hard, very unjust, very wrong; but that changed not in the least her feelings towards Mr. Marlow. Nay more, with that delicate art of combination in which ladies are formed to excel, she conceived and manipulated with great dexterity a scheme for bringing herself and Mr. Marlow into frequent personal communication, and for causing somebody to suggest to him a marriage with her own beautiful self, as the best mode of settling the disputed claim.

O those fine and delicate threads of intrigue, how frail they are, and how much depends upon every one of them, be it in the warp or the woof of a scheme! We have seen that in this case, one of them gave way under the rough handling of Sir Philip Hastings, and the whole fabric was in imminent danger of running down and becoming nothing but a raveled skein. Mrs. Hazleton was resolved that it should not be so, and now she was busily engaged in the attempt to knot together the broken thread, and to lay all the others straight and in right order again. This was the secret of the whole matter.

She exerted all her charms, and could Waller but have seen her we should have had such an account of the artillery of her eyes, the insidious attack of her smile, and the whole host of powerful adversaries brought to bear against the object of her assault in her gracefully moving form and heaving bosom, that Saccharissa would have melted away like a wet lump of sugar in the comparison.

Then again when she had produced an effect, and saw clear and distinctly that he thought her lovely, and very charming too, she seemed to fall into a pleasant sort of languid melancholy, which was even more charming still. The brook was bubbling and murmuring at their feet, dashing clear and bright over its stony bed, and changing the brown rock, the water weed, or the leaf beneath, into gems by the magic of its own brightness. The boughs were waving over head, covered with many-colored foliage, and the sun, glancing through, not only enriched the tints above, but checkered the mossy path along which they wandered like a chess-board of brown and gold. Some of the late autumn birds uttered their short sweet songs from the copse hard by, and the musical wind came sighing up from the valley, as if nature had furnished Eolus with a harp. It was in short quite a scene, and a moment for a widow to make love to a young man. They were silent for some little time, and then Mrs. Hazleton said, with her soft, sweet, round voice, "Is not all this very charming, Mr. Marlow?"

Her tone was quite a sad one, but not with that sort of pleasant sadness which often mingles with our happiest moments, giving them even a higher zest, like the flattened notes when a fine piece of music passes gently from the major into the minor key, but really sad, profoundly sad.

"Very charming, indeed," replied her young companion, looking round to her face with some surprise.

"And what am I to do without it, when you turn me out of my house!" said the lady, answering his glance with a melancholy smile.

"Turn you out of your house!" exclaimed Mr. Marlow; "I hope you do not suppose, my dear madam, that I could dream of such a thing. Oh, no! I would not for the world deprive such a scene of its brightest ornament. Some arrangement can be easily effected, even if my claim should prove satisfactory to those you appoint to investigate it, by which the neighborhood will not be deprived of the happiness of your presence."

Mrs. Hazleton felt that she had made a great step, and as she well knew that there was no chance of his proposing then and there, she resolved not to risk losing ground by any farther advance, even while she secured some present benefits from that which was gained. "Well, well," she said, "Mr. Marlow, I am quite sure you are very kind and very generous, and we can talk of that matter hereafter. Only there is one thing you must promise me, which is, that in regard to any arrangements respecting the house you will not leave them to be settled by cold lawyers or colder friends, who cannot enter into my feelings in regard to this place, or your own liberal and kindly feelings either. Let us settle it some day between ourselves," she added, with a light laugh, "in a tête-à-tête like this. I do not suppose you are afraid of being overreached by me in a bargain. But now let us turn our steps back towards the house, for I expect Mrs. Warmington early, and I must not be absent when she arrives."

Mrs. Warmington was there already; for the tête-à-tête had lasted longer than Mrs. Hazleton knew. However, Mrs. Hazleton's first task was to inform her fair friend and counsellor of the cause of Mr. Marlow's being there; her next to tell her that all had been settled as to the claim, by that tiresome man Sir Philip Hastings, without what she considered due deliberation, and that the only thing which remained to be arranged was in regard to the house, respecting which Mrs. Hazleton communicated a certain portion of her own inclinations, and of Mr. Marlow's kind view of the matter.

Now, strange to say, this was the turning point of fate for Mrs. Hazleton, Mr. Marlow, and most of the persons mentioned in this history. It was then that Mrs. Warmington suggested a scheme which she thought would suit her friend well.

"Why do you not offer him in exchange--for the time at all events--your fine old house on the side of Hartwell--Hartwell Place? It is only seven miles off. It is ready furnished to his hand, and must be worth a great deal more than the bare walls of this. Besides it would be pleasant to have him in the neighborhood."

Pause, Mrs. Hazleton! pause and meditate over all the consequences; for be assured much depends upon these few simple words.

Mrs. Hazleton did pause--Mrs. Hazleton did meditate. She ran over in her head the list of all the families in the neighborhood. In none of them could she see a probable rival. There were plenty of married women, old maids, young girls; but she saw nobody to fear, and with a proud consciousness of her own beauty and worth; she took her resolution. That very evening she proposed to Mr. Marlow what her friend had suggested. It was accepted.

Mrs. Hazleton had made one miscalculation, and her fate and Mr. Marlow's were decided.

CHAPTER XIV

Occasionally in the life of man, as in the life of the world--History--or in the course of a stream towards the sea, come quiet lapses, sunny and calm, reflecting nothing but the still motionless objects around, or the blue sky and moving clouds above. Often too we find that this tranquil expanse of silent water follows quickly after some more rapid movement, comes close upon some spot where a dashing rapid has diversified the scene, or a cataract, in roar and confusion and sparkling terror, has broken the course of the stream.

Such a still pause, silent of action--if I may use the term--followed the events which I have related in the last chapter, extending over a period of nearly six months. Nothing happened worthy of any minute detail. Peace and tranquillity dwelt in the various households which I have noticed in the course of this story, enlivened in that of Sir Philip Hastings by the gay spirit of Emily Hastings, although somewhat shadowed by the sterner character of her father; and in the household of Mrs. Hazleton brightened by the light of hope, and the fair prospect of success in all her schemes which for a certain time continued to open before her.

Mr. Marlow only spent two days at her house, and then went away to London, but whatever effect her beauty might have produced upon him, his society, brief as it was, served but to confirm her feelings towards him, and before he left her, she had made up her mind fully and entirely, with her characteristic vigor and strength of resolution, that her marriage with Mr. Marlow was an event which must and should be. There was under this conviction, but not the less strong, not the less energetic, not the less vehement, for being concealed even from herself--a resolution that no sacrifice, no fear, no hesitation at any course, should stand in the way of her purpose. She did not anticipate many difficulties certainly; for Mr. Marlow clearly admired her; but the resolution was, that if difficulties should arise, she would overcome them at all cost. Hers was one of those characters of which the world makes its tragedies, having within itself passions too strong and deep to be frequently excited--as the more profound waters which rise into mountains when once in motion require a hurricane to still them--together with that energetic will, that fixed unbending determination, which like the outburst of a torrent from the hills, sweeps away all before it. But let it be ever remembered that her energies were exerted upon herself as well as upon others, not in checking passion, not in limiting desire, but in guarding scrupulously every external appearance, guiding every thought and act with careful art towards its destined object. Mrs. Hazleton suffered Mr. Marlow to be in London more than a month before she followed to conclude the mere matters of business between them. It cost her a great struggle with herself, but in that struggle she was successful, and when at length she went, she had several interviews with him. Circumstances--that great enemy of schemes, was against her. Sometimes lawyers were present at their interviews, sometimes impertinent friends; but Mrs. Hazleton did not much care: she trusted to the time he was speedily about to pass in the country, for the full effect, and in the mean time took care that nothing but the golden side of the shield should be presented to her knight.

The continent was at that time open to Englishmen for a short period, and Mr. Marlow expressed his determination of going to the Court of Versailles for a month or six weeks before he came down to take possession of Hartwell place, everything now having been settled between them in regard to business.

Mrs. Hazleton did not like his determination, yet she did not much fear the result; for Mr. Marlow was preeminently English, and never likely to wed a French woman. Still she resolved that he should see her under another aspect before he went. She was a great favorite of the Court of those days; her station, her wealth, her beauty, and her grace rendered her a brightness and an ornament wherever she came. She was invited to one of the more private though not less splendid assemblies at the Palace, and she contrived that Mr. Marlow should be invited also, though neither by nature or habit a courtier. She obtained the invitation for him skilfully, saying to the Royal Personage of whom she asked it, that as he won a lawsuit against her, she wished to show him that she bore no malice. He went, and found her the brightest in the brilliant scene; the great and the proud, the handsome and the gay, all bending down and worshipping, all striving. for a smile, and obtaining it but scantily. She smiled upon him, however, not sufficiently to attract remark from others, but quite sufficiently to mark a strong distinction for his own eyes, if he had chosen to use them. He went away to France, and Mrs. Hazleton, returned to the country; the winter passed with her in arranging his house for him; and, in so doing, she often had to write to him. His replies were always prompt, kind, and grateful; and at length came the spring, and the pleasant tidings that he was on his way back to his beloved England.

Alas for human expectation! Alas for the gay day-dream of youth--maturity--middle age--old age--for they have all their day-dreams! Every passion which besets man from the cradle to the grave has its own visionary expectations. Each creature, each animal, from the tiger to the beetle, has its besetting insect, which preys upon it, gnaws it, irritates it, and so have all the ages of the soul and of the heart. Alas for human speculation of all kinds! Alas for every hope and aspiration! for those that are pure and high, but, growing out of earth, bear within themselves the bitter seeds of disappointment; and those that are dark or low produce the germ of the most poisonous hybrid, where disappointment is united with remorse.

Happy is the man that expecteth nothing, for verily he shall not be disappointed! It is a quaint old saying; and could philosophy ever stem the course of God's will, it would be one which, well followed, might secure to man some greater portion of mortal peace than he possesses. But to aspire was the ordinance of God; and, viewed rightly, the withering of the flowers upon each footstep we have taken upwards, is no discouragement; for if we shape our path aright, there is a wreath of bright blossoms crowning each craggy peak before us, as we ascend to snatch the garland of immortal glory, placed just beyond the last awful leap of death.

Mrs. Hazleton's aspirations, however, were all earthly. She thought of little beyond this life. She had never been taught so to think. There are some who are led astray from the path of noble daring, to others as difficult and more intricate, by some loud shout of passion on the right or on the left--and seek in vain to return; some who, misled by an apparent similarity in the course of two paths, although the finger post says, "Thus shalt thou go!" think that the way so plainly beaten, and so seemingly easy, must surely lead them to the same point. Others again never learn to read the right path from the wrong (and she was one), while others shut their eyes to all direction, fix their gaze upon the summit, and strain up, now amidst flowers and now amidst thorns, till they are cast back from the face of some steep precipice, to perish in the descent or at the foot.

Mrs. Hazleton's aspirations were all earthly; and that was the secret of her only want in beauty. That divine form, that resplendent face, beamed with every earthly grace, sparkled forth mind and intellect in every glance, but they were wanting in soul, in spirit, and in heart. Life was there, but the life of life, the intense flame of immortal, over-earthly intelligence, was wanting. She might be the grandest animal that ever was seen, the most bright and capable intellect that ever dealt with mortal things; but the fine golden chain which leads on the electric fire from intellectual eminence to spiritual preeminence, from mind to soul, from earth to heaven, was wanting, or had been broken. Her loveliness none could doubt, her charm of manner none could deny, her intellectual superiority all admitted, her womanly softness added a grace beyond them all; but there was one grace wanting--the grace of a high, holy soul, which, in those who have it, be they fair, be they ugly, pours forth as an emanation from every look and every action, and surrounds them with a cloud of radiance, faintly imaged by the artist's glory round a saint.

Alas for human aspirations! Alas for the expectations of this fair frail creature! How eagerly she thought of Mr. Marlow's return how she had anticipated their meeting again! How she had calculated upon all that would be said and done during the next few weeks! The first news she received was that he had arrived, and with a few servants had taken possession of his new dwelling. She remained all day in her own house; she ordered no carriage; she took no walk: she tried to read; she played upon various instruments of music; she thought each instant he would come, at least for a few minutes, to thank her for all the care she had bestowed to make his habitation comfortable. The sun gilded the west; the melancholy moon rose up in solemn splendor; the hours passed by, and he came not.

The next morning, she heard that he had ridden over to the house of Sir Philip Hastings, and indignation warred with love in her bosom. She thought he must certainly come that day, and she resolved angrily to upbraid him for his want of courtesy. Luckily, however, for her, he did not come that day; and a sort of melancholy took possession of her. Luckily, I say; for when passion takes hold of a scheme it is generally sure to shake it to pieces, and that melancholy loosens the grasp of passion for a time. The next day he did come, and with an air so easy and unconscious of offence as almost to provoke her into vehemence again. He knew not what she felt--he had no idea of how he had been looked for. He was as ignorant that she had ever thought of him as a husband, as she was that he had ever compared her in his mind to his own mother.

He talked quietly, indifferently, of his having been over to the house of Sir Philip Hastings, adding merely--not as an excuse, but as a simple fact-- that he had been unable to call there as he had promised before leaving the country. He dilated upon the kind reception he had met with from Lady Hastings, for Sir Philip was absent upon business; and he went on to dwell rather largely upon the exceeding beauty and great grace of Emily Hastings.

Oh how Mrs. Hazleton hated her! It requires but a few drops of poison to envenom a whole well.

He did worse: he proceeded to descant upon her character--upon the blended brightness and deep thought--upon the high-souled emotions and childlike sparkle of her disposition--upon the simplicity and complexity, upon the many-sided splendor of her character, which, like the cut diamond, reflected each ray of light in a thousand varied and dazzling hues. Oh how Mrs. Hazleton hated her--hated, because for the first time she began to fear. He had spoken to her in praise of another woman--with loud encomiums too, with a brightened eye, and a look which told her more than his words. These were signs not to be mistaken. They did not show in the least that he loved Emily Hastings, and that she knew right well; but they showed that he did not love her; and there was the poison in the cup.

So painful, so terrible was the sensation, that, with all her mastery over herself, she could not conceal the agony under which she writhed. She became silent, grave, fell into fits of thought, which clouded the broad brow, and made the fine-cut lip quiver. Mr. Marlow was surprised and grieved. He asked himself what could be the matter. Something had evidently made her sorrowful, and he could not trace the sorrow to its source; for she carefully avoided uttering one word in depreciation of Emily Hastings. In this she showed no woman's spirit. She could have stabbed her, had the girl been there in her presence; but she would not scratch her. Petty spite was too low for her, too small for the character of her mind. Hers was a heart capable of revenge, and would be satisfied with nothing less.

Mr. Marlow soothed her, spoke to her kindly, tenderly, tried to lead her mind away, to amuse, to entertain her. Oh, it was all gall and bitterness to her. He might have cursed, abused, insulted her, without, perhaps, diminishing her love--certainly without inflicting half the anguish that was caused by his gentle words. It is impossible to tell all the varied emotions that went on in her heart--at least for me. Shakspeare could have done it, but none less than Shakspeare. For a moment she knew not whether she loved or hated him; but she soon felt and knew it was love; and the hate, like lightning striking a rock, and glancing from the solid stone to rend a sapling, all turned away from him, to fall upon the head of poor unconscious Emily Hastings.

Though she could not recover from the blow she had received, yet she soon regained command over herself, conversed, smiled, banished absorbing thoughts, answered calmly, pertinently, even spoke in her own bright, brilliant way, with a few more figures and ornaments of speech than usual; for figures are things rather of the head than of the heart, and it was from the head that she was now speaking.

At length Mr. Marlow took his leave, and for the first time in life she was glad he was gone.

Mrs. Hazleton gave way to no burst of passion: she shed not a tear; she uttered no exclamation. That which was within her heart, was too intense for any such ordinary expression. She seated herself at a table, leaned her head upon her hand, and fixed her eyes upon one bright spot in the marquetry. There she sat for more than an entire hour, without a motion, and in the meantime what were the thoughts that passed through her brain? We have shown the feelings of her heart enough.

She formed plans; she determined her course; she looked around for means. Various persons suggested themselves to her mind as instruments. The three women, I have mentioned in a preceding chapter--the good sort of friends. But it was an agent she wanted, not a confidant. No, no, Mrs. Hazleton knew better than to have a confidant. She was her own best council-keeper, and she knew it. Nevertheless, these good ladies might serve to act in subordinate parts, and she assigned to each of them their position in her scheme with wonderful accuracy and skill. As she did so, however, she remembered that it was by the advice of Mrs. Warmington that she had brought Mr. Marlow to Hartwell Place; and in her heart's secret chamber she gave her fair friend a goodly benediction. She resolved to use her nevertheless--to use her as far as she could be serviceable; and she forgot not that she herself had been art and part in the scheme that had failed. She was not one to shelter herself from blame by casting the whole storm of disappointment upon another, She took her own full share. "If she was a fool so to advise," said Mrs. Hazleton, "'twas a greater fool to follow her advice."

She then turned to seek for the agent. No name presented itself but that of Shanks, the attorney; and she smiled bitterly when she thought of him. She recollected that Sir Philip Hastings had thrown him head-foremost down the steps of the terrace, and that was very satisfactory to her; for, although Mr. Shanks was a man who sometimes bore injuries very meekly, he never forgot them.

Nevertheless, she had somewhat a difficult part to play, for most agents have a desire of becoming confidants also, and that Mrs. Hazleton determined her attorney should not be. The task was to insinuate her purposes rather than to speak them--to act, without betraying the motive of action--to make another act, without committing herself by giving directions.

Nevertheless, Mrs. Hazleton arranged it all to her own satisfaction; and as she did so, amongst the apparently extinct ashes of former schemes, one small spark of hope began to glow, giving promise for the time to come. What did she propose? At first, nothing more than to drive Sir Philip Hastings and his family from the country, mingling the gratification of personal hatred with efforts for the accomplishment of her own purposes. It was a bold attempt, but Mrs. Hazleton had her plan, and she sat down and wrote for Mr. Shanks, the attorney.

CHAPTER XV

Decorum came in with the house of Hanover. I know not whether men and women in England were more virtuous before--I think not--but they certainly were more frank in both their virtues and their vices. There were fewer of those vices of conventionality thrown around the human heart--fewer I mean to say of those cold restraints, those gilded chains of society, which, like the ornaments that ladies wear upon their necks and arms, seem like fetters; but, I fear me, restrain but little human action, curb not passion, and are to the strong will but as the green rushes round the limbs of the Hebrew giant. Decorum came into England with the house of Hanover; but I am speaking of a period before that, when ladies were less fearful of the tongue of scandal, when scandal itself was fearful of assailing virtue, when honesty of purpose and purity of heart could walk free in the broad day, and men did not venture to suppose evil acts perpetrated whenever, by a possibility, they could be committed.

Emily Hastings walked quietly along by the side of Mr. Marlow, through her father's park. There was no one with him, no keen matron's ear to listen to and weigh their words, no brother to pretend to accompany them, and either feel himself weary with the task or lighten it by seeking his own amusement apart. They were alone together, and they talked without restraint. Ye gods, how they did talk! The dear girl was in one of her brightest, gayest moods. There was nothing that did not move her fancy or become a servant to it. The clouds as they shot across the sky, the blue fixed hills in the distance, the red and yellow and green coloring of the young budding oaks, the dancing of the stream, the song of the bird, the whisper of the wind, the misty spring light which spread over the morning distance, all had illustrations for her thoughts. It seemed that day as if she could not speak without a figure--as if she revelled in the flowers of imagination, like a child tossing about the new mown grass in a hay-field. And he, with joyous sport, took pleasure in furnishing her at every moment with new material for the bounding joy of fancy.

They had not known each other long; but there was something in the young man's manner--nay, let me go farther--in his character, which invited confidence, which besought the hearts around to throw off all strange disguise, and promised that he would take no base advantage of their openness. That something was perhaps his earnestness: one felt that he was true in all he said or did or looked: that his words were but his spoken feelings: his countenance a paper on which the heart at once recorded its sensations. But let me not be mistaken. Do not let it be supposed that when I say he was earnest, I mean that he was even grave. Oh no! Earnestness can exist as well in the merriest as in the soberest heart. One can be as earnest, as truthful, even as eager in joy or sport, as in sorrow or sternness. But he was earnest in all things, and it was this earnestness which probably found a way for him to so many dissimilar hearts.

Emily knew not at all what it was doing with hers; but she felt that he was one before whom she had no need to hide a thought: that if she were gay, she might be gay in safety: that if she were inclined to muse, she might muse on in peace.

Onward they walked, talking of every thing on earth but love. It was in the thoughts of neither. Emily knew nothing about it: the tranquil expanse of life had never for her been even rippled by the wing of passion. Marlow might know more; but for the time he was lost in the enjoyment of the moment. The little enemy might be carrying on the war against the fortress of each unconscious bosom; but if so, it was by the silent sap and mine, more potent far than the fierce assault or thundering cannonade--at least in this sort of warfare.

They were wending their way towards a gate, at the very extreme limit of the park, which opened upon a path leading by a much shorter way to Mr. Marlow's own dwelling than the road he usually pursued. He had that morning come to spend but an hour at the house of Sir Philip Hastings, and he had an engagement at his own house at noon. He had spent two hours instead of one with Emily and her mother, and therefore short paths were preferable to long ones for his purpose. Emily had offered to show him the way to the gate, and her company was sure to shorten the road, though it might lengthen the time it took to travel.

Now in describing the park of Sir Philip Hastings, I have said that there was a wide open space around the mansion; but I have also said, that at some distance the trees gathered thick and sombre. Those nearest the house gathered together in clumps, confusing the eye in a wilderness of hawthorns, and bushes, and evergreen oaks, while beyond appeared a dense mass of wood; and, through the scattered tufts of trees and thick woodland at the extreme of the park ran several paths traced by deer, and park-keepers, and country folk. Thus for various reasons some guidance was needful to Marlow on his way, and for more reasons still he was well pleased that the guide should be Emily Hastings. In the course of their walk, amongst many other subjects they spoke of Mrs. Hazleton, and Marlow expatiated warmly on her beauty, and grace, and kindness of heart. How different was the effect of all this upon Emily Hastings from that which his words in her praise had produced upon her of whom he spoke! Emily's heart was free. Emily had no schemes, no plans, no purposes. She knew not that there was one feeling in her bosom with which praise of Mrs. Hazleton could ever jar. She loved her well. Such eyes as hers are not practised in seeing into darkness. She had divined the Italian singer--perhaps by instinct, perhaps by some distinct trait, which occasionally will betray the most wily. But Mrs. Hazleton was a fellow-woman--a woman of great brightness and many fine qualities. Neither had she any superficial defects to indicate a baser metal or a harder within. If she was not all gold, she was doubly gilt.

Emily praised her too, warmed with the theme; and eagerly exclaimed, "She always seems to me like one of those dames of fairy tales, upon whom some enchanter has bestowed a charm that no one can resist. It is not her beauty; for I feel the same when I hear her voice and shut my eyes. It is not her conversation; for I feel the same when I look at her and she is silent. It seems to breathe from her presence like the odor of a flower. It is the same when she is grave as when she is gay."

"Aye, and when she is melancholy," replied Marlow. "I never felt it more powerfully than a few days ago when I spent an hour with her, and she was not only grave but sad."

"Melancholy!" exclaimed Emily. "I never saw her so. Grave I have seen her--thoughtful, silent--but never sad; and I do not know that she has not seemed more charming to me in those grave, stiller moods, than in more cheerful ones. Do you know that in looking at the beautiful statues which I have seen in London, I have often thought they might lose half their charm if they would move and speak? Thus, too, with Mrs. Hazleton; she seems to me even more lovely, more full of grace, in perfect stillness than at any other time. My father," she added, after a moment's pause, "is the only one who in her presence seems spell-proof."

Her words threw Marlow into a momentary fit of thought. "Why," he asked himself, "was Sir Philip Hastings spell-proof when all others were charmed?"

Men have a habit of depending much upon men's judgment, whether justly or unjustly I will not stop to inquire. They rely less upon woman's judgment in such matters; and yet women are amongst the keenest discerners--when they are unbiassed by passion. But are they often so? Perhaps it is from a conviction that men judge less frequently from impulse, decide more generally from cause, that this presumption of their accuracy exists. Woman--perhaps from seclusion, perhaps from nature--is more a creature of instincts than man, They are given her for defence where reason would act too slowly; and where they do act strongly, they are almost invariably right. Man goes through the slower process, and naturally relies more firmly on the result; for reason demonstrates where instinct leads blindfold. Marlow judged Sir Philip Hastings by himself, and fancied that he must have some cause for being spell-proof against the fascinations of Mrs. Hazleton. This roused the first doubt in his mind as to her being all that she seemed. He repelled the doubt as injurious, but it returned from time to time in after days, and at length gave him a clue to an intricate labyrinth.

The walk came to an end, too soon he thought. Emily pointed out the gate as soon as it appeared in sight, shook hands with him and returned homeward. He thought more of her after they had parted, than when she was with him. There are times when the most thoughtful do not think-- when they enjoy. But now, every word, every look of her who had just left him, came back to memory. Not that he would admit to himself that there was the least touch of love in his feelings. Oh no! He had known her too short a time for such a serious passion as love to have any thing to do with his sensations. He only thought of her--mused--pondered--recalled all she had said and done, because she was so unlike any thing he had seen or heard of before--a something new--a something to be studied.

She was but a girl--a mere child, he said; and yet there was something more than childish grace in that light, but rounded form, where beauty was more than budding, but not quite blossomed, like a moss-rose in its loveliest state of loveliness. And her mind too; there was nothing childish in her thoughts except their playfulness. The morning dew-drops had not yet exhaled; but the day-star of the mind was well up in the sky.

She was one of those, on whom it is dangerous for a man afraid of love to meditate too long. She was one the effect of whose looks and words is not evanescent. That of mere beauty passes away. How many a face do we see and think it the loveliest in the world; yet shut the eyes an hour after, and try to recall the features--to paint them to the mind's eye. You cannot. But there are others that link themselves with every feeling of the heart, that twine themselves with constantly recurring thoughts, that never can be effaced--never forgotten--on which age or time, disease or death, may do its work without effecting one change in the reality embalmed in memory. Destroy the die, break the mould, you may; but the medal and the cast remain. Had Marlow lived a hundred years--had he never seen Emily Hastings again, not one line of her bright face, not one speaking look, would have passed from his memory. He could have painted a portrait of her had he been an artist. Did you ever gaze long at the sun, trying your eyes against the eagle's? If so, you have had the bright orb floating before your eyes the whole day after. And so it was with Marlow: throughout the long hours that followed, he had Emily Hastings ever before him. But yet he did not love her. Oh dear no, not in the least. Love he thought was very different from mere admiration. It was a plant of slower growth. He was no believer in love at first sight. He was an infidel as to Romeo and Juliet, and he had firmly resolved if ever he did fall in love, it should be done cautiously.

Poor man! he little knew how deep he was in already.

In the meanwhile, Emily walked onward. She was heart-whole at least. She had never dreamed of love. It had not been one of her studies. Her father had never presented the idea to her. Her mother had often talked of marriage, and marriages good and bad; but always put them in the light of alliances--compacts--negotiated treaties. Although Lady Hastings knew what love is as well as any one, and had felt it as deeply, yet she did not wish her daughter to be as romantic as she had been, and therefore the subject was avoided. Emily thought a good deal of Mr. Marlow, it is true. She thought him handsome, graceful, winning--one of the pleasantest companions she had ever known. She liked him better than any one she had ever seen; and his words rang in her ears long after they were spoken. But even imagination, wicked spinner of golden threads as she is, never drew one link between his fate and hers. The time had not yet come, if it was to come.

She walked on, however, through the wood; and just when she was emerging from the thicker part into the clumps and scattered trees, she saw a stranger before her, leaning against the stump of an old hawthorn, and seeming to suffer pain. He was young, handsome, well-dressed, and there was a gun lying at his feet. But as Emily drew nearer, she saw blood slowly trickling from his arm, and falling on the gray sand of the path.

She was not one to suffer shyness to curb humanity; and she exclaimed at once, with a look of alarm, "I am afraid you are hurt, sir. Had you not better come up to the house?"

The young man looked at her, fainted, and answered in a low tone, "The gun has gone off, caught by a branch, and has shattered my arm. I thought I could reach the cottage by the park gates, but I feel faint."

"Stay, stay a moment," cried Emily, "I will run to the hall and bring assistance--people to assist you upon a carriage."

"No, no!" answered the stranger quickly, "I cannot go there--I will not go there! The cottage is nearer," he continued more calmly. "I think with a little help I could reach it, if I could staunch the blood.

"Let me try," exclaimed Emily; and with ready zeal, she tied her handkerchief round his arm, not without a shaking hand indeed, but with firmness and some skill.

"Now lean upon me," she said, when she had done; "the cottage is indeed nearer, but you would have better tendance if you could reach the hall."

"No, no, the cottage," replied the stranger, "I shall do well there."

The cottage was perhaps two hundred yards nearer to the spot on which they stood than the hall; but there was an eagerness about the young man's refusal to go to the latter, which Emily remarked. Suspicion indeed was alive to her mind; but those were days when laws concerning game, which have very year been becoming less and less strict, were hardly less severe than in the time of William Rufus. Every day, in the country life which she led, she heard some tale of poaching or its punishment. The stranger had a gun with him; she had found him in her father's park; he was unwilling even in suffering and need of help to go up to the hall for succor; and she could not but fancy that for some frolic, perhaps some jest, or some wild whim, he had been trespassing upon the manor in pursuit of game. That he was an ordinary poacher she could not suppose; his dress, his appearance forbade such a supposition.

But there was something more.

In the young man's face--more in its expression than its features perhaps--more in certain marking lines and sudden glances than in the general whole--there was something familiar to her--something that seemed akin to her. He was handsomer than her father; of a more perfect though less lofty character of beauty; and yet there was a strange likeness, not constant, but flashing occasionally upon her brow, in what, when, she could hardly determine.

It roused another sort of sympathy from any she had felt before; and once more she asked him to go up to the hall.

"If you have been taking your sport," she said, "where perhaps you ought not, I am sure my father will look over it without a word, when he sees how you are hurt. Although people sometimes think he is stern and severe, that is all a mistake. He is kind and gentle, I assure you, when he does not feel that duty requires him to be rigid."

The stranger gave a quick start, and replied in a tone which would have been haughty and fierce, had not weakness subdued it, "I have been shooting only where I have a right to shoot. But I will not go up to the hall, till--but I dare say I can get down to the cottage without help, Mistress Emily. I have been accustomed to do without help in the world;" and he withdrew his arm from that which supported him. The next moment, however, he tottered, and seemed ready to fall, and Emily again hurried to help him. There were no more words spoken. She thought his manner somewhat uncivil; she would not leave him, and the necessity for her kindness was soon apparent. Ere they were within a hundred yards of the cottage, he sunk slowly down. His face grew pale and death-like, and his eyes closed faintly as he lay upon the turf. Emily ran on like lightning to the cottage, and called out the old man who lived there. The old man called his son from the little garden, and with his and other help, carried the fainting man in.

"Ay, master John, master John," exclaimed the old cottager, as he laid him in his own bed; "one of your wild pranks, I warrant!"

His wife, his son, and he himself tended the young man with care; and a young boy was sent off for a surgeon.

Emily did not know what to do; but compassion kept her in the cottage till the stranger recovered his consciousness, and then after inquiring how he felt, she was about to withdraw, intending to send down further aid from the hall. But the stranger beckoned her faintly to come nearer, and said in tones of real gratitude, "Thank you a thousand times, Mistress Emily; I never thought to need such kindness at your hands. But now do me another, and say not a word to any one at the mansion of what has happened. It will be better for me, for you, for your father, that you should not speak of this business."

"Do not! do not! Mistress Emily!" cried the old man, who was standing near. "It will only make mischief and bring about evil."

He spoke evidently under strong apprehension, and Emily was much surprised, both to find that one quite a stranger to her knew her at once, and to find the old cottager, a long dependant upon her family, second so eagerly his strange injunction.

"I will say nothing unless questions are asked me," she replied; "then of course I must tell the truth."

"Better not," replied the young man gloomily.

"I cannot speak falsely," replied the beautiful girl "I cannot deal doubly with my parents or any one," and she was turning away.

But the stranger besought her to stop one moment, and said, "I have not strength to explain all now; but I shall see you again, and then I will tell you why I have spoken as you think strangely. I shall see you again. In common charity you will come to ask if I am alive or dead. If you knew how near we are to each other, I am sure you would promise!"

"I can make no such promise," replied Emily; but the old cottager seemed eager to end the interview; and speaking for her, he exclaimed, "Oh, she will come, I am sure, Mistress Emily will come;" and hurried her away, seeing her back to the little gate in the park wall.

CHAPTER XVI

Mrs. Hazleton found Mr. Shanks, the attorney, the most difficult person to deal with whom she had ever met in her life. She had remarked that he was keen, active, intelligent, unscrupulous, confident in his own powers, bold as a lion in the wars of quill, parchment, and red tape; without fear, without hesitation, without remorse. There was nothing that he scrupled to do, nothing that he ever repented having done. She had fancied that the only difficulty which she could have to encounter was that of concealing from him, at least in a degree, the ultimate objects and designs which she herself had in view.

So shrewd people often deceive themselves as to the character of other shrewd people. The difficulty was quite different. It was a peculiar sort of stolidity on the part of Mr. Shanks, for which she was utterly unprepared.

Now the attorney was ready to do any thing on earth which his fair patroness wished. He would have perilled his name on the roll in her service; and was only eager to understand what were her desires, even without giving her the trouble of explaining them. Moreover, there was no point of law or equity, no manner of roguery or chicanery, no object of avarice, covetousness, or ambition, which he could not have comprehended at once. They were things within his own ken and scope, to which the intellect and resources of his mind were always open. But to other passions, to deeper, more remote motives and emotions, Mr. Shanks was as stolid as a doorpost. It required to hew a way as it were to his perceptions, to tunnel his mind for the passage of a new conception.

The only passion which afforded the slightest cranny of an opening was revenge; and after having tried a dozen other ways of making him comprehend what she wished without committing herself, Mrs. Hazleton got him to understand that she thought Sir Philip Hastings had injured--at all events, that he had offended--her, and that she sought vengeance. From that moment all was easy. Mr. Shanks could understand the feeling, though not its extent. He would himself have given ten pounds out of his own pocket--the largest sum he had ever given in life for any thing but an advantage--to be revenged upon the same man for the insult he had received; and he could perceive that Mrs. Hazleton would go much further, without, indeed, being able to conceive, or even dream of, the extent to which she was prepared to go.

However, when he had once got the clue, he was prepared to run along the road with all celerity; and now she found him every thing she had expected. He was a man copious in resources, prolific of schemes. His imagination had exercised itself through life, in devising crooked paths; but in this instance the road was straight-forward before him. He would rather it had been tortuous, it is true; but for the sake of his dear lady he was ready to follow even a plain path, and he explained to her that Sir Philip Hastings stood in a somewhat dangerous position.

He was proceeding to enter into the details, but Mrs. Hazleton interrupted him, and, to his surprise, not only told him, but showed him, that she knew all the particulars.

"The only question is, Mr. Shanks," she said, "can you prove the marriage of his elder brother to this woman before the birth of the child?"

"We think we can, madam," replied the attorney, "we think we can. There is a very strong letter, and there has been evidently--"

He paused and hesitated, and Mrs. Hazleton demanded, "There has been what, Mr. Shanks?"

"There has been evidently a leaf torn out of the register," replied the lawyer.

There was something in his manner which made the lady gaze keenly in his face; but she would ask no questions on that subject, and she merely said, "Then why has not the case gone on, as it was put in your hands six months ago?"

"Why, you see, my dear madam," replied Shanks, "law is at best uncertain. One wants two or three great lawyers to make a case. Money was short; John and his mother had spent all last year's annuity. Barristers won't plead without fees, and besides--"

He paused again, but an impatient gesture from the lady urged him on. "Besides," he said, "I had devised a little scheme, which, of course, I shall abandon now, for marrying him to Mistress Emily Hastings. He is a very handsome young fellow, and--"

"I have seen him," said Mrs. Hazleton, thoughtfully, "but why should you abandon this scheme, Mr. Shanks? It seems to me by no means a bad one."

The poor lawyer was now all at sea again, and fancied himself as wide of the lady's aim as ever.

Mrs. Hazleton suffered him to remain in this dull suspense for some time. Wrapped up in her own thoughts, and busy with her own calculations, she suffered several minutes to elapse without adding a word to that which had so much surprised the attorney. Then, however, she said, in a meditative tone, "There is only one way by which it can be accomplished. If you allow it to be conducted in a formal manner, you will fail utterly. Sir Philip will never consent. She will never even yield."

"But if Sir Philip is made to see that it will save him a tremendous lawsuit, and perhaps his whole estate," suggested Mr. Shanks.

"He will resist the more firmly," answered the lady; "if it saved his life, he would reject it with scorn--no! But there is a way. If you can persuade her--if you can show her that her father's safety, his position in life, depends upon her conduct, perhaps you may bring her by degrees to consent to a private marriage. She is young, inexperienced, enthusiastic, romantic. She loves her father devotedly, and would make any sacrifice for him."

"No great sacrifice, I should think, madam," replied Mr. Shanks, "to marry a handsome young man who has a just claim to a large fortune."

"That is as people may judge," replied the lady; "but at all events this claim gives us a hold upon her which we must not fail to use, and that directly. I will contrive means of bringing them together. I will make opportunity for the lad, but you must instruct him how to use it properly. All I can do is to co-operate without appearing."

"But, my dear madam, I really do not fully understand," said Mr. Shanks. "I had a fancy--a sort of imagination like, that you wished--that you desired--"

He hesitated; but Mrs. Hazleton would not help him by a single word, and at last he added, "I had a fancy that you wished this suit to go on against Sir Philip Hastings, and now--but that does not matter--only do you really wish to bring it all to an end, to settle it by a marriage between John and Mistress Emily?"

"That will be the pleasantest, the easiest way of settling it, sir," replied Mrs. Hazleton, coolly; "and I do not at all desire to injure, but rather to serve Sir Philip and his family."

That was false, for though to marry Emily Hastings to any one but Mr. Marlow was what the lady did very sincerely desire; yet there was a long account to be settled with Sir Philip Hastings which could not well be discharged without a certain amount of injury to him and his. The lady was well aware, too, that she had told a lie, and moreover that it was one which Mr. Shanks was not at all likely to believe. Perhaps even she did not quite wish him to believe it, and at all events she knew that her actions must soon give it contradiction. But men make strange distinctions between speech and action, not to be accounted for without long investigation and disquisition. There are cases where people shrink from defining in words their purposes, or giving voice to their feelings, even when they are prepared by acts to stamp them for eternity. There are cases where men do acts which they dare not cover by a lie.

Mrs. Hazleton sought for no less than the ruin of Sir Philip Hastings; she had determined it in her own heart, and yet she would not own it to her agent--perhaps she would not own it to herself. There is a dark secret chamber in the breast of every one, at the door of which the eyes of the spirit are blindfolded, that it may not see the things to which it is consenting. Conscience records them silently, and sooner or later her book is to be opened; it may be in this world: it may be in the next: but for the time that book is in the keeping of passion, who rarely suffers the pages to be seen till purpose has been ratified by act, and remorse stands ready to pronounce the doom.

There was a pause after Mrs. Hazleton had spoken, for the attorney was busy also with thoughts he wished to utter, yet dared not speak. The first prospect of a lawsuit--the only sort of the picturesque in which he could find pleasure--a long, intricate, expensive lawsuit, was fading before his eyes as if a mist were coming over the scene. Where were his consultations, his letters, his briefs, his pleas, its rejoinders, his demurrers, his appeals? Where were the fees, the bright golden fees? True, in the hopelessness of his young client's fortunes, he had urged the marriage with a proviso, that if it took place by his skilful management, a handsome bonus was to be his share of the spoil. But then Mrs. Hazleton's first communication had raised brighter hopes, had put him more in his own element, had opened to him a scene of achievements as glorious to his notions as those of the listed field to knights of old; and now all was vanishing away. Yet he did not venture to tell her how much he was disappointed, still less to show her why and how.

It was the lady who spoke first; and she did so in as calm, deliberate, passionless a tone as if she had been devising the fashion of a new Mantua.

"It may be as well, Mr. Shanks," she said, "in order to produce the effect we wish upon dear Emily's mind"--dear Emily!--"to commence the suit against Sir Philip--I mean to take those first steps which may create some alarm. I cannot of course judge what they ought to be, but you must know; and if not, you must seek advice from counsel learned in the law. You understand what I mean, doubtless."

"Oh, certainly, madam, certainly," replied Mr. Shanks, with a profound sigh of relief. "First steps commit us to nothing: but they must be devised cautiously, and I am very much afraid that--that--"

"Afraid of what, sir?" asked Mrs. Hazleton, in a tone somewhat stern.

"Only that the expense will be greater than my young client can afford," answered the lawyer, seeing that he must come to the point.

"Let not that stand in the way," said Mrs. Hazleton at once; "I will supply the means. What will be the expense?"

"Would you object to say five hundred pounds?" asked the lawyer, cautiously.

"A thousand," replied the lady, with a slight inclination of the head; and then, weary of circumlocution, she added in a bolder tone than she had yet used, "only remember, sir, that what is done must be done effectually; no mistakes, no errors, no flaws! See that you use all your eyes--see that you bend every nerve to the task. I will have no procrastination for the sake of fresh fees--nothing omitted one day to be remembered the next-- no blunders to be corrected after long delays and longer correspondence. I know you lawyers and your ways right well; and if I find that for the sake of swelling a bill to the bursting, you attempt to procrastinate, the cause will be taken at once from your hands and placed in those who will do their work more speedily. You can practise those tricks upon those who are more or less in your power; but you shall not play them upon me."

"I declare, my dear madam, I can assure you," said Mr. Shanks; but Mrs. Hazleton cut him short. "There, there," she said, waving her fair hand, "do not declare--do not assure me of any thing. Let your actions speak, Mr. Shanks. I am too much accustomed to declarations and assurances to set much value upon them. Now tell me, but in as few words and with as few cant terms as possible, what are the chances of success in this suit? How does the young man's case really stand?"

Mr. Shanks would gladly have been excused such explanations. He never liked to speak clearly upon such delicate questions, but he would not venture to refuse any demand of Mrs. Hazleton's, and therefore he began with a circumlocution in regard to the uncertainty of law, and to the impossibility of giving any exact assurances of success.

The lady would not be driven from her point, however. "That is not what I sought to know," she said. "I am as well aware of the law's uncertainty--of its iniquity, as you. But I ask you what grounds you have to go upon? Were they ever really married? Is this son legitimate?"

"The lady says they were married," replied Mr. Shanks cautiously, "and I have good hope we can prove the legitimacy. There is a letter in which the late Mr. John Hastings calls her 'my dear little wife;' and then there is clearly a leaf torn out of the marriage register about that very time."

Mr. Shanks spoke the last words slowly and with some hesitation; but after a pause he went on more boldly and rapidly. "Then we have a deposition of the old woman Danby that they were married. This is clear and precise," he continued with a grin: "she wanted to put in something about 'in the eyes of God,' but I left that out as beside the question; and she did the swearing very well. She might have broken down under cross-examination, it is true; and therefore it was well to put off the trial till she was gone. We can prove, moreover, that the late Sir John always paid an annuity to both mother and child, in order to make them keep secret--nay more, that he bribed the old woman Danby. This is our strong point; but it is beyond doubt--I can prove it, madam--I can prove it. All I fear is the mother; she is weak--very weak; I wish to heaven she were out of the way till the trial is over."

"Send her out of the way," cried Mrs. Hazleton, decidedly; "send her to France;" and then she added, with a bitter smile, "she may still figure amongst the beauties of Versailles.

"But she will not go," replied Mr. Shanks. "Madam, she will not go. I hinted at such a step--mentioned Cornwall or Ireland--any where she could be concealed."

"Cornwall or Ireland!" exclaimed Mrs. Hazleton, "of course she would not go. Why did not you propose Africa or the plantations? She shall go, Mr. Shanks. Leave her to me. She shall go. And now, set to work at once--immediately, I say--this very day. Send the youth to-morrow, and let him bring me word that some step is taken. I will instruct him how to act, while you deal with the law."

Mr. Shanks promised to obey, and retired overawed by all he had seen and heard. There had, it is true, been no vehement demonstration of passion; no fierce blaze; no violent flash; but there had been indications enough to show the man of law all that was raging within. It had been for him like gazing at a fine building on fire at that period of the conflagration where dense smoke and heavy darkness brood over the fearful scene, while dull, suddenly-smothered flashes break across the gloom, and tell how terrible will be the flame when it does burst freely forth.

He had never known Mrs. Hazleton before--he had never comprehended her fully. But now he knew her--now, though perhaps the depths were still unfathomable to his eyes, he felt that there was a strong commanding will within that beautiful form which would bear no trifling. He had often treated her with easy lightness--with no want of apparent respect indeed--but with the persuasions and arguments such as men of business often address to women as beings inferior to themselves either in intellect or experience. Now Mr. Shanks wondered how he had escaped so long and so well, and he resolved that for the future his conduct should be very different.

Mrs. Hazleton, when he left her, sat down to rest--yes, to rest; for she was very weary. There had been the fatiguing strife of strong passions in the heart--hopes--expectations--schemes--contrivances; and, above all, there had been a wrestling with herself to deal calmly and softly where she felt fiercely. It had exhausted her; and for some minutes she sat listlessly, with her eyes half shut, like one utterly tired out. Ere a quarter of an hour had passed, wheels rolled up to the door; a carriage-step was let down, and there was a footfall in the hall.

"Dear Mrs. Warmington, delighted to see you!" said Mrs. Hazleton, with a smile sweet and gentle as the dawn of a summer morning.

CHAPTER XVII

Circumstance will always have its finger in the pie with the best-laid schemes; but it does not always happen that thereby the pie is spoiled. On the contrary, circumstance is sometimes a very powerful auxiliary, and it happened so in the present instance with the arrangements of Mrs. Hazleton. Before that lady could bring any part of her scheme for introducing Emily to the man whom she intended to drive her into taking as a husband, to bear, the introduction had already taken place, as we have seen, by an accident.

It was likely, indeed, to go no further; for Emily thought over what had occurred, before she gave way to her native kindness of heart. She remembered how tenacious all country gentlemen of that day were of their sporting rights, and especially of what she had often heard her father declare, that he looked upon any body who took his game off his property, according to every principle of equity and justice, as no better than a common robber.

"If the only excuse be that it is more exposed to depredation than other property," said Sir Philip, "it only shows that the plunderer of it is a coward as well as a villain, and should be punished the more severely." Such, and many such speeches she had heard from her father at various times, and it became a case of conscience, which puzzled the poor girl much, whether she ought or ought not to have promised not to mention what had occurred in the park. She loved no concealment, and nothing would have induced her to tell a falsehood; but she knew that if she mentioned the facts, especially while the young man whom she had seen crossing the park with a gun lay wounded at the cottage, great evil might have resulted; and though she somewhat reproached herself for rashly giving her word, she would not break it when given.

As to seeing him again, however--as to visiting him at the cottage, even to inquire after his health, when he had refused all aid from her father's house, that was an act she never dreamed of. His last words, indeed, had puzzled her; and there was something in his face, too, which set her fancy wandering. It was not exactly what she liked; but yet there was a resemblance, she thought, to some one she knew and was attached to. It could not be to her father, she said to herself, and yet her father's face recurred to her mind more frequently than any other when she thought of that of the young man she had seen; and from that fact a sort of prepossession in the youth's favor took possession of her, making her long to know who he really was.

For some days Emily did not go near the cottage, but at length she ventured on the road which passed it--not without a hope, indeed, that she might meet one of the old people who tenanted it, and have an opportunity of inquiring after his health--but certainly not, as some good-natured reader may suppose, with any expectation of seeing him herself. As she approached, however, she perceived him sitting on a bench at the cottage-door, and, by a natural impulse, she turned at once into another path, which led back by a way nearly as short to the hall. The young man instantly rose, and followed her, addressing her by name, in a voice still weak, in truth, but too loud for her not to hear, or to affect not to hear.

She paused, rather provoked than otherwise, and slightly inclined her head, while the young man approached, with every appearance of respect, and thanked her for the assistance she had rendered him.

He had had his lesson in the mean time, and he played his part not amiss. All coarse swagger, all vulgar assumption was gone from his manner; and referring himself to some words he had spoken when last they had met, he said: "Pardon me, Miss Hastings, for what I said some days ago, which might seem both strange and mysterious, and for pressing to see you again; but at that time I was faint with loss of blood, and knew not how this might end. I wished to tell you something I thought you ought to hear; but now I am better; and I will find a more fitting opportunity ere long."

"It will be better to say any thing you think fit to my father," replied Emily. "I am not accustomed to deal with any matters of importance; and any thing of so much moment as you seem to think this is, would, of course, be told by me to him."

"I think not," replied the other, with a mysterious smile; "but of that you will judge when you have heard all I have to say. Your father is the last person to whom I would mention it myself, because I believe, notwithstanding all his ability, he is the last person who would judge sanely of it, as he would of most other matters; but, of course, you will speak of it or not, as you think proper. At present," he added, "I am too weak to attempt the detail, even if I could venture to detain you here. I only wished to return you my best thanks, and assure you of my gratitude;" and bowing low, he left her to pursue her way homeward.

Emily went on musing. No woman's breast is without curiosity--nor any man's, either--and she asked herself what could be the meaning of the stranger's words, at least a dozen times. What could he have to tell her, and why was there so much mystery? She did not like mystery, however; and though she felt interested in the young man--felt pity, in fact--yet it was by no means the interest that leads to, nor the pity which is akin to love. On the contrary, she liked him less than the first time she saw him. There was a certain degree of cunning in his mysterious smile, a look of self-confidence, almost of triumph in his face, which, in spite of his respectful demeanor, did not please her.

Emily's father was absent from home at this time; but he returned two or three days after this last interview, and remarked that his daughter was unusually grave. To her, and to all that affected her in any way, his eyes were always open, though he often failed to comprehend that which he observed. Lady Hastings, too, had noticed Emily's unusual gravity, and as she had no clue to that which made her thoughtful, she concluded that the solitude of the country had a depressing influence upon her spirits, as it frequently had upon her own and she determined to speak to her husband upon the matter. To him she represented that the place was very dull; that they had but few visitors; that even Mr. Marlow had not called for a week; and that Emily really required some variety of scene and amusement.

She reasoned well according to her notions, and though Sir Philip could not quite comprehend them, though he abhorred great cities, and loved the country, she had made some impression at least by reiteration, when suddenly a letter arrived from Mrs. Hazleton, petitioning that Emily might be permitted to spend a few days with her.

"I am quite alone," she said, "and not very well (she never was better in her life), and I propose next week to make some excursions to all the beautiful and interesting spots in the neighborhood. But you know, dear Lady Hastings, there is but small pleasure in such expeditions when they must be solitary; but with such a mind as that of your dear Emily for my companion, every object will possess a double interest."

The reader has perceived that the letter was addressed to Lady Hastings; but it was written for the eye of Sir Philip, and to him it was shown. Lady

Hastings observed, as she put the note into her husband's hand, that it would be much better to go to London. The change from their own house to Mrs. Hazleton's was not enough to do Emily any good; and that, as to these expeditions to neighboring places, she had always found them the dullest things imaginable.

Sir Philip thought differently, however. He had been brought to the point of believing that Emily did want change, but not to the conviction that London would afford the best change for her. He inquired of Emily, however, which she would like best, a visit of a week to Mrs. Hazleton's, or a short visit to the metropolis. Much to his satisfaction, Emily decided at once in favor of the former, and Mrs. Hazleton's letter was answered, accepting her invitation.

The day before Emily went, Mr. Marlow spent nearly two hours with her and her father in the sort of musy, wandering conversation which is so delightful to imaginative minds. He paid Emily herself no marked or particular attention; but he never suffered her to doubt that even while talking with her father, he was fully conscious of her presence, and pleased with it. Sometimes his conversation was addressed to her directly, and when it was not, by a word or look he would invite her to join in, and listened to her words as if they were very sweet to his ear.

She loved to listen to him, however, better than to speak herself, and he contrived to please and interest her in all he said, gently moving all sorts of various feelings, sometimes making her smile gayly, sometimes muse thoughtfully, and sometimes rendering her almost sad. If he had been the most practiced love-maker in the world, he could not have done better with a mind like that of Emily Hastings.

He heard of her proposed visit to Mrs. Hazleton with pleasure, and expressed it. "I am very glad to hear you are to be with her," he said, "for I do not think Mrs. Hazleton is well. She has lost her usual spirits, and has been very grave and thoughtful when I have seen her lately."

"Oh, if I can cheer and soothe her," cried Emily eagerly, "how delightful my visit will be to me. Mrs. Hazleton says in her letter that she is unwell; and that decided me to go to her, rather than to London."

"To London!" exclaimed Mr. Marlow, "I had no idea that you proposed such a journey. Oh, Sir Philip, do not take your daughter to London. Friends of mine there are often in the habit of bringing in fresh and beautiful flowers from the country; but I always see that first they become dull and dingy with the smoke and heavy air, and then wither away and perish; and often in gay parties, I have thought that I saw in the young and beautiful around me the same dulling influence, the same withering, both of the body and the heart."

Sir Philip Hastings smiled pleasantly, and assured his young friend that he had no desire or intention of going to the capital except for one month in the winter, and Emily looked up brightly, saying, "For my part, I only wish that even then I could be left behind. When last I was there, I was so tired of the blue velvet lining of the gilt _vis-a-vis_, that I used to try and paint fancy pictures of the country upon it as I drove through the streets with mamma."

At length Emily set out in the heavy family coach, with her maid and Sir Philip for her escort. Progression was slow in those days compared with our own, when a man can get as much event into fifty years as Methuselah did into a thousand. The journey took three hours at the least; but it seemed short to Emily, for at the end of the first hour they were overtaken by Mr. Marlow on horseback, and he rode along with them to the gate of Mrs. Hazleton's house. He was an admirable horseman, for he had not only a good but a graceful seat, and his handsome figure and fine gentlemanly carriage never appeared to greater advantage than when he did his best to be a centaur. The slow progress of the lumbering vehicle might have been of some inconvenience, but his horse was trained to canter to a walk when he pleased, and, leaning to the window of the carriage, and sometimes resting his hand upon it, he contrived to carry on the conversation with those within almost as easily as in a drawing-room.

Just as the carriage was approaching the gate, Marlow said: "I think I shall not go in with you Sir Philip for I have a little business farther on, and I have ridden more slowly than I thought;" but before the sentence was well concluded, the gates of the park were opened by the porter, and Mrs. Hazleton herself appeared within, leaning on the arm of her maid. She had calculated well the period of Emily's arrival, and had gone out to the gate for the purpose of giving her an extremely hospitable welcome. Probably, had she not hated her as warmly and sincerely as she did, she would have stayed at home; our attention is ever doubtful.

But what were Mrs. Hazleton's feelings when she saw Mr. Marlow riding by the side of the carriage? I will not attempt to describe them; but for one instant a strange dark cloud passed over her beautiful face.

It was banished in an instant; but not before Marlow had remarked both the expression itself and the sudden glance of the lady's eyes from him to Emily. For the first time a doubt, a suspicion, a something he did not like to fathom, came over his mind; and he resolved to watch. Neither Emily nor her father perceived that look, and as the next moment the beautiful face was once more as bright as ever, they felt pleased with her kind eagerness to meet them; and alighting from the carriage, walked on with her to the house, while Marlow, dismounted, accompanied them, leading his horse.

"I am glad to see you, Mr. Marlow," said Mrs. Hazleton, in a tone from which she could not do what she would--banish all bitterness. "I suppose I owe the pleasure of your visit to that which you yourself feel in escorting a fair lady."

"I must not, I fear, pretend to such gallantry," replied Marlow. "I overtook the carriage accidentally as I was riding to Mr. Cornelius Brown's; and to say the truth, I did not intend to come in, for I am somewhat late."

"Cold comfort for my vanity," replied the lady, "that you would not have paid me a visit unless you had met me at the gate."

She spoke in a tone rather of sadness than of anger; but Marlow did not choose to perceive any thing serious in her words, and he replied, laughing: "Nay, dear Mrs. Hazleton, you do not read the riddle aright. It shows, when rightly interpreted, that your society is so charming that I cannot resist its influence when once within the spell, even for the sake of the Englishman's god--Business."

"A man always succeeds in drawing some flattery for woman's ear out of the least flattering conduct," answered Mrs. Hazleton.

The conversation then took another turn; and after walking with the rest of the party up to the house, Marlow again mounted and rode away. As soon as the horses had obtained some food and repose, Sir Philip also returned, and Emily was left with a woman who felt at her heart that she could have poniarded her not an hour before.

But Mrs. Hazleton was all gentle sweetness, and calm, thoughtful, dignified ease. She did not suffer her attention to to diverted for one moment from her fair guest: there were no reveries, no absence of mind; and Emily--poor Emily--thought her more charming than ever. Nevertheless, while speaking upon many subjects, and brightly and intelligently upon all, there was an under-current of thought going on unceasingly in Mrs.

Hazleton's mind, different from that upon the surface. She was trying to read Marlow's conduct towards Emily--to judge whether he loved her or not. She asked herself whether his having escorted her to that house was in reality purely accidental, and she wished that she could have seen them together but for a few moments longer, though every moment had been a dagger to her heart. Nay, she did more: she strove by many a dexterous turn of the conversation, to lure out her fair unconscious guest's inmost thoughts--to induce her, not to tell all, for that she knew was hopeless, but to betray all. Emily, however, happily for herself, was unconscious; she knew not that there was any thing to betray. Fortunately, most fortunately, she knew not what was in her own breast; or perhaps I should say, knew not what it meant. Her answers were all simple, natural and true; and plain candor, as often happens, disappointed art.

Mrs. Hazleton retired for the night with the conviction that whatever might be Marlow's feelings towards Emily, Emily was not in love with Marlow; and that was something gained.

"No, no," she said, with a pride in her own discernment, "a woman who knows something of the world can never be long deceived in regard to another woman's heart." She should have added, "except by its simplicity."

"Now," she continued, mentally, "to-morrow for the first great step. If this youth can but demean himself wisely, and will follow the advice I have given him, he has a fair field to act in. He seems prompt and ready enough: he is assuredly handsome, and what between his good looks, kind persuasion by others, and her father's dangerous position, this girl methinks may be easily driven--or led into his arms; and that stumbling-block removed. He will punish her enough hereafter, or I am mistaken."

Punish her for what, Mrs. Hazleton?

CHAPTER XVIII

It was long ere Emily Hastings slept. There was a bright moonlight; but she sat not up by the window, looking out at the moon in love-lorn guise. No, she laid her down in bed, as soon as the toilet of the night was concluded, and having left the window-shutters open, the light of the sweet, calm brightener of the night poured in a long, tranquil ray across the floor. She watched it, with her head resting on her hand for a long time. Her fancy was very busy with it, as by slow degrees it moved its place, now lying like a silver carpet by her bedside, now crossing the floor far away, and painting the opposite wall. Her thoughts then returned to other things, and whether she would or not, Marlow took a share in them. She remembered things that he had said, his looks came back to her mind, she seemed to converse with him again, running over in thought all that had passed in the morning.

She was no castle-builder; there were no schemes, plans, designs, in her mind; no airy structures of future happiness employed fancy as their architect. She was happy in her own heart; and imagination, like a bee, extracted sweetness from the flowers of the present.

Sweet Emily, how beautiful she looked, as she lay there, and made a night-life for herself in the world of her own thoughts!

She could not sleep, she knew not why. Indeed, she did not wish or try to sleep. She never did when sleep did not come naturally; but always remained calmly waiting for the soother, till slumber dropped uncalled and stilly upon her eyelids.

One hour--two hours--the moonbeam had retired far into a corner of the room, the household was all still; there was no sound but the barking of a distant farm-dog, such a long way off; that it reached the ear more like an echo than a sound, and the crowing of a cock, not much more near.

Suddenly, her door opened, and a figure entered, bearing a small night-lamp. Emily started, and gazed. She was pot much given to fear, and she uttered not a sound; for which command over herself she was very thankful, when, in the tall, graceful form before her, she recognized Mrs. Hazleton. She was dressed merely as she had risen from her bed: her rich black hair bound up under her snowy cap, her long night-gown trailing on the ground, and her feet bare. Yet she looked perhaps more beautiful than in jewels and ermine. Her eyes were not fixed and motionless, though there was a certain sort of deadness in them. Neither were her movements stiff and mechanical, as we often see in the representations of somnambulism on the stage. On the contrary, they were free and graceful. She looked neither like Mrs. Siddons nor any other who ever acted what she really was. Those who have seen the state know better. She was walking in her sleep, however: that strange act of a life apart from waking life--that mystery of mysteries, when the soul seems severed from all things on earth but the body which it inhabits--when the mind sleeps, but the spirit wakes--when the animal and the spiritual live together, yet the intellectual lies dead for the time.

Emily comprehended her condition at once, and waited and watched, having heard that it is dangerous to wake suddenly a person in such a state. Mrs. Hazleton walked on past her bed towards a door at the other side of the room, but stopped opposite the toilet-table, took up a ribbon that was lying on it, and held it in her hand for a moment.

"I hate him!" she said aloud; "but strangle him--oh, no! That would not do. It would leave a blue mark. I hate him, and her too! They can't help it-- they must fall into the trap."

Emily rose quietly from her bed, and advancing with a soft step, took Mrs. Hazleton's hand gently. She made no resistance, only gazing at her with a look not utterly devoid of meaning. "A strange world!" she said, "where people must live with those they hate!" and suffered Emily to lead her towards the door. She showed some reluctance to pass it, however, and turned slowly towards the other door. Her beautiful young guide led her thither, and opened it; then went on through the neighboring room, which was vacant, Mrs. Hazleton saying, as they passed the large bed canopied with velvet, "My mother died there--ah, me!" The next door opened into the corridor; but Emily knew not where her hostess slept, till perceiving a light streaming out upon the floor from a room near the end, she guided Mrs. Hazleton's steps thither, rightly judging that it must be the chamber she had just left. There she quietly induced her to go to bed again, taking the lamp from her hand, and bending down her sweet, innocent face, gave her a gentle kiss.

"Asp!" said Mrs. Hazleton, turning away; but Emily remained with her for several minutes, till the eyes closed, the breathing became calm and regular, and natural sleep succeeded to the strange state into which she had fallen.

Then returning to her own room, Emily once more sought her bed; but though the moonlight had now departed, she was farther from sleep than ever.

Mrs. Hazleton's words still rang in her ears. She thought them very strange; but yet she had heard--it was indeed a common superstition in those days--that people talking in their sleep expressed feelings exactly the reverse of those which they really entertained; and her good, bright heart was glad to believe. She would not for the world have thought that the fair form, and gentle, dignified manners of her friend could shroud feelings so fierce and vindictive as those which had breathed forth in the utterance of that one word, "hate." It seemed to her impossible that Mrs. Hazleton could hate any thing, and she resolved to believe so still. But yet the words rang in her ears, as I have said. She had been somewhat agitated and alarmed, too, though less than many might have been, and more than an hour passed before her sweet eyes closed.

On the morning of the following day, Emily was somewhat late at breakfast; and she found Mrs. Hazleton down, and looking bright and beautiful as the morning. It was evident that she had not even the faintest recollection of what had occurred in the night--that it was a portion of her life apart, between which and waking existence there was no communication open. Emily determined to take no notice of her sleep-walking; and she was wise, for I have always found, that to be informed of their strange peculiarity leaves an awful and painful impression on the real somnambulists--a feeling of being unlike the rest of human beings, of having a sort of preternatural existence, over which their human reason can hold no control. They fear themselves--they fear their own acts--perhaps their own words, when the power is gone from that familiar mind, which is more or less the servant, if not the slave, of will, and when the whole mixed being, flesh, and mind, and spirit, is under the sole government of that darkest, least known, most mysterious personage of the three--the soul.

Mrs. Hazleton scolded her jestingly for late rising, and asked if she was always such a lie-abed. Emily replied that she was not, but usually very matutinal in her habits. "But the truth is, dear Mrs. Hazleton," she added, "I did not sleep well last night."

"Indeed," said her fair hostess, with a gay smile; "who were you thinking of to keep your young eyes open?"

"Of you," answered Emily, simply; and Mrs. Hazleton asked no more questions; for, perhaps, she did not wish Emily to think of her too much. Immediately after breakfast the carriage was ordered for a long drive.

"I will give you so large a dose of mountain air," said Mrs. Hazleton, "that it shall insure you a better night's rest than any narcotic could procure, Emily. We will go and visit Ellendon Castle, far in the wilds, some sixteen miles hence."

Emily was well pleased with the prospect, and they set out together, both apparently equally prepared to enjoy every thing they met with. The drive was a long one in point of time, for not only were the carriages more cumbrous and heavy in those days, but the road continued ascending nearly the whole way. Sometimes, indeed, a short run down into a gentle valley released the horses from the continual tug on the collar, but it was very brief, and the ascent commenced almost immediately. Beautiful views over the scenery round presented themselves at every turn; and Emily, who had all the spirit of a painter in her heart, looked forth from the window enchanted.

Mrs. Hazleton marked her enjoyment with great satisfaction; for either by study or intuition she had a deep knowledge of the springs and sources of human emotions, and she knew well that one enthusiasm always disposes to another. Nay, more, she knew that whatever is associated in the mind with pleasant scenes is usually pleasing, and she had plotted the meeting between Emily and him she intended to be her lover with considerable pains to produce that effect. Nature seemed to have been a sharer in her schemes. The day could not have been better chosen. There was the light fresh air, the few floating clouds, the merry dancing gleams upon hill and dale, a light, momentary shower of large, jewel-like drops, the fragment of a broken rainbow painting the distant verge of heaven.

At length the summit of the hills was reached; and Mrs. Hazleton told her sweet companion to look out there, ordering the carriage at the same time to stop. It was indeed a scene well worthy of the gaze. Far spreading out beneath the eye lay a wide basin in the hills, walled in, as it were, by those tall summits, here and there broken by a crag. The ground sloped gently down from the spot at which the carriage paused, so that the whole expanse was open to the eye, and over the short brown herbage, through which a purple gleam from the yet unblossomed heath shone out, the lights and shades seemed sporting in mad glee. All was indeed solitary, uncultivated, and even barren, except where, in the very centre of the wide hollow, appeared a number of trees, not grouped together in a wood, but scattered over a considerable space of ground, as if the remnants of some old deer-park, and over their tall tops rose up the ruined keep of some ancient stronghold of races passed away, with here and there another tower or pinnacle appearing, and long lines of grassy mounds, greener than the rest of the landscape, glancing between the stems of the older trees, or bearing up in picturesque confusion their own growth of wild, fantastic, seedling ashes.

By the name of the spot, Ellendon, which means strong-hill, I believe it is more than probable that the Anglo-Saxons had here some forts before the conquest; but the ruin which now presented itself to the eyes of Emily and Mrs. Hazleton was evidently of a later date and of Norman construction.

Here, probably, some proud baron of the times of Henry, Stephen, or Matilda, had built his nest on high, perchance to overawe the Saxon churls around him, perhaps to set at defiance the royal power itself. Here the merry chase had swept the hills; here revelry and pageantry had checkered a life of fierce strife and haughty oppression. Such scenes, at least such thoughts, presented themselves to the imaginative mind of Emily, like the dreamy gleams that skimmed in gold and purple before her eyes; but the effect of any strong feeling, whether of enjoyment or of grief, was always to make her silent; and she gazed without uttering a word.

Mrs. Hazleton, however, understood some points in her character, and by the long fixed look from beneath the dark sweeping lashes of her eye, by the faint sweet smile that gently curled her young, beautiful lip, and by the sort of gasping sigh after she had gazed breathless for some moments, she knew how intense was that gentle creature's delight in a scene, which to many an eye would have offered no peculiar charm.

She would not suffer it to lose any of its first effect, and after a brief pause ordered the carriage to drive on. Still Emily continued to look onwards out of carriage-window, and as the road turned in the descent, the castle and the ancient trees grouped themselves differently every minute. At length, as they came nearer, she said, turning to Mrs. Hazleton, "There seems to be a man standing at the very highest point of the old keep."

"He must be bold indeed," replied her companion, looking out also. "When you come close to it, dear Emily, you will see that it requires the foot of a goat and the heart of a lion to climb up there over the rough, disjointed, tottering stones. Good Heaven, I hope he will not fall!"

Emily closed her eyes. "It is very foolish," she said.

"Oh, men have pleasure in such feats of daring," answered Mrs. Hazleton, "which we women cannot understand. He is coming down again as steadily as if he were treading a ball-room. I wish that tree were out of the way."

In two or three minutes the carriage passed between two rows of old and somewhat decayed oaks, and stopped between the fine gate of the castle, covered with ivy, and rugged with the work of Time's too artistic hand, and a building which, if it did not detract from the picturesque beauty of the scene, certainly deprived it of all romance. There, just opposite the entrance, stood a small house, built apparently of stones stolen from the ruins, and bearing on a pole projecting from the front a large blue sign-board, on which was rudely painted in yellow, the figure of what we now call a French horn, while underneath appeared a long inscription to the following effect:

"John Buttercross, at the sign of the Bugle Horn, sells wine and aqua vitæ, and good lodgings to man and horse. N. B. Donkeys to be found within."

Emily laughed, and in an instant came down to common earth.

Mrs. Hazleton wished both John Buttercross and his sign in one fire or another; though she could not help owning that such a house in so remote a place might be a great convenience to visitors like herself. She took the matter quietly, however, returning Emily's gay look with one somewhat rueful, and saying, "Ah, dear girl, all very mundane and unromantic, but depend upon it the house has proved a blessing often to poor wanderers in bleak weather over these wild hills; and we ourselves may find it not so unpleasant by and by when Paul has spread our luncheon in the parlor, and we look out of its little casement at the old ruin there."

Thus saying, she alighted from the carriage, gave some orders to her servants, and to an hostler who was walking up and down a remarkably beautiful horse, which seemed to have been ridden hard, and then leaning on Emily's arm, walked up the slope towards the gate.

Barbican and outer walls were gone--fallen long ago into the ditch, and covered with the all-receiving earth and a green coat of turf. You could but tell were they lay, by the undulations of the ground, and the grassy hillock here and there. The great gate still stood firm, however, with its two tall towers, standing like giant wardens to guard the entrance. There were the machicolated parapets, the long loopholes mantled with ivy, the outsloping basement, against which the battering ram might have long played in vain, the family escutcheon with the arms crumbled from it, the portcullis itself showing its iron teeth above the traveller's head. It was the most perfect part of the building; and when the two ladies entered the great court the scene of ruin was more complete. Many a tower had fallen, leaving large gaps in the inner wall; the chapel with only one beautiful window left, and the fragments of two others, showing where the fine line had run, lay mouldering on the right, and at some distance in front appeared the tall majestic keep, the lower rooms of which were in tolerable preservation, though the roof had fallen in to the second story, and the airy summit had lost its symmetry by the destruction of two entire sides. Short green turf covered the whole court, except where some mass of stone, more recently fallen than others, still stood out bare and gray; but a crop of brambles and nettles bristled up near the chapel, and here and there a tree had planted itself on the tottering ruins of the walls.

Mrs. Hazleton walked straight towards the entrance of the keep along a little path sufficiently well worn to show that the castle had frequent visitors, and was within a few steps of the doorway, when a figure issued forth which to say sooth did not at all surprise her to behold. She gave a little start, however, saying in a low tone to Emily, "That must be our climbing friend whose neck we thought in such peril a short time since."

The gentleman--for such estate was indicated by his dress, which was dark and sober, but well made and costly--took a step or two slowly forward, verging a little to the side as if to let two ladies pass whom he did not know; but then suddenly he stopped, gazed for an instant with a well assumed look of surprise and inquiry, and then hurried rapidly towards them, raising hie hat not ungracefully, while Mrs. Hazleton exclaimed, "Ah, how fortunate! Here is a friend who doubtless can tell us all about the ruins."

At the same moment Emily recognized the young man whom she had found accidentally wounded in her father's park.

CHAPTER XIX

"Let me introduce Mr. Ayliffe to you, Emily," said Mrs. Hazleton; "but you seem to know each other already. Is it so?"

"I have seen this gentleman before," replied her young companion, "but did not know his name. I hope you have quite recovered from your wound?"

"Quite, I thank you, Miss Hastings," replied John Ayliffe, in a quiet and respectful tone; but then he added, "the interest you kindly showed on the occasion, I believe did much to cure me."

"Too much, and too soon!" thought Mrs. Hazleton, as she remarked a slight flush pass over Emily's cheek, to which her reply gave interpretation.

"Every one, I suppose, would feel the same interest," answered the beautiful girl, "in suffering such as you seemed to endure when I accidentally met you in the park. Shall we go on into the Castle?"

The last words were addressed to Mrs. Hazleton, who immediately assented, but asked Mr. Ayliffe to act as their guide, and, at the very first opportunity, whispered to him, "not too quick."

He seemed to comprehend in a moment what she meant; and during the rest of the ramble round the ruins behaved himself with a good deal of discretion. His conversation could not be said to be agreeable to Emily; for there was little in it either to amuse or interest. His stores of information were very limited--at least upon subjects which she herself was conversant; and although he endeavored to give it, every now and then, a poetical turn, the attempt was not very successful. On the whole, however, he did tolerably well till after the luncheon at the inn, to which Mrs. Hazleton invited him, when he began to entertain his two fair companions with an account of a rat hunt, which surprised Emily not a little, and drew, almost instantly, from Mrs. Hazleton a monitory gesture.

The young man looked confused, and broke off, suddenly, with an embarrassed laugh, saying, "Oh! I forgot, such exploits are not very fit for ladies' ears; and, to say the truth, I do not much like them myself when there is any thing better to do."

"I should think that something better might always be found," replied Mrs. Hazleton, gravely, taking to her own lips the reproof which she knew was in Emily's heart; "but, I dare say, you were a boy when this happened?"

"Oh, quite a boy," he said, "quite a boy. I have other things to think of now."

But the impression was made, and it was not favorable. With keen acuteness Mrs. Hazleton watched every look, and every turn of the conversation; and seeing that the course of things had begun ill for her purposes, she very soon proposed to order the carriage and return; resolving to take, as it were, a fresh start on the following day. She did not then ask young Ayliffe to dine at her house, as she had, at first, intended; but was well pleased, notwithstanding, to see him mount his horse in order to accompany them on the way back; for she had remarked that his horsemanship was excellent, and well knew that skill in manly exercises is always a strong recommendation in a woman's eyes. Nor was this all: decidedly handsome in person, John Ayliffe had, nevertheless, a certain common--not exactly vulgar--air, when on his feet, which was lost as soon as he was in the saddle. There, with a perfect seat, and upright, dashing carriage, managing a fierce, wild horse with complete mastery, he appeared to the greatest advantage. All his horsemanship was thrown away upon Emily. If she had been asked by any one, she would have admitted, at once, that he was a very handsome man, and a good and graceful rider; but she never asked herself whether he was or not; and, indeed, did not think about it at all.

One thing, however, she did think, and that was not what Mrs. Hazleton desired. She thought him a coarse and vulgar-minded young man; and she wondered how a woman of such refinement as Mrs. Hazleton could be pleased with his society. There was at the end of that day only one impression in his favor, which was produced by an undefinable resemblance to her father, evanescent, but ever returning. There was no one feature like: the coloring was different: the hair, eyes, beard, all dissimilar. He was much handsomer than Sir Philip Hastings ever had been; but ever and anon there came a glance of the eye, or a curl of the lip; a family expression which was familiar and pleasant to her. John Ayliffe accompanied the carriage to the gate of Mrs. Hazleton's park; and there the lady beckoned him up, and in a kind, half jesting tone, bade him keep himself disengaged the next day, as she might want him.

He promised to obey, and rode away; but Mrs. Hazleton never mentioned his name again during the evening, which passed over in quiet conversation, with little reference to the events of the morning.

Before she went to bed, however, Mrs. Hazleton wrote a somewhat long epistle to John Ayliffe, full of very important hints for his conduct the next day, and ending with an injunction to burn the letter as soon as he had read it. This done, she retired to rest; and that night, what with free mountain air and exercise, she and Emily both slept soundly. The next morning, however, she felt, or affected to feel, fatigue; and put off another expedition which had been proposed.

Noon had hardly arrived, when Mr. Ayliffe presented himself, to receive her commands he said, and there he remained, invited to stay to dinner, not much to Emily's satisfaction; but, at length, she remembered that she had letters to write, and, seated at a table in the window, went on covering sheets of paper, with a rapid hand, for more than an hour; while John Ayliffe seated himself by Emily's embroidery frame, and labored to efface the bad impression of the day before, by a very different strain of conversation. He spoke of many things more suited to her tastes and habits than those which he had previously noticed, and spoke not altogether amiss. But yet, there was something forced in it all. It was as if he were reading sentences out of a book, and, in truth, it is probable he was repeating a lesson.

Emily did not know what to do. She would have given the world to be freed from his society; to have gone out and enjoyed her own thoughts amongst woods and flowers; or even to have sat quietly in her own room alone, feeling the summer air, and looking at the glorious sky. To seek that refuge, however, she thought would be rude; and to go out to walk in the park would, she doubted not, induce him to follow. She sat still, therefore, with marvellous patience, answering briefly when an answer was required; but never speaking in reply with any of that free pouring forth of heart and mind which can only take place where sympathy is strong.

She was rewarded for her endurance, for when it had lasted well nigh as long as she could bear it, the drawing-room door opened, and Mr. Marlow appeared. His eyes instantly fixed upon Emily with that young man sitting by her side; and a feeling, strange and painful, came upon him. But the next instant the bright, glad, natural, unchecked look, of satisfaction, with which she rose to greet him, swept every doubt-making jealousy away.

Very different was the look of Mrs. Hazleton. For an instant--a single instant--the same black shadow, which I have mentioned once before, came across her brow, the same lightning flashed from her eye. But both passed away in a moment; and the feelings which produced them were again hidden in her heart. They were bitter enough; for she had read, with the clear eyesight of jealousy, all that Marlow's look of surprise and annoyance--all that Emily's look of joy and relief--betrayed.

They might not yet call themselves lovers--they might not even be conscious that they were so; but that they were and would be, from that moment, Mrs. Hazleton had no doubt. The conviction had come upon her, not exactly gradually, but by fits, as it were--first a doubt, and then a fear, and then a certainty that one, and then that both loved.

If it were so, she knew that her present plans must fail; but yet she pursued them with an eagerness very different than before--a wild, rash, almost frantic eagerness. There was a chance, she thought, of driving Emily into the arms of John Ayliffe, with no love for him, and love for another; and there was a bitter sort of satisfaction in the very idea. Fears for her father she always hoped might operate, where no other inducement could have power, and such means she resolved to bring into play at once, without waiting for the dull, long process of drilling Ayliffe into gentlemanly carriage, or winning for him some way in Emily's regard. To force her to marry him, hating rather than loving him, would be a mighty gratification, and for it Mrs. Hazleton resolved at once to strike; but she knew that hypocrisy was needed more than ever; and therefore it was that the brow was smoothed, the eye calmed in a moment.

To Marlow, during his visit, she was courteous and civil enough, but still so far cold as to give him no encouragement to stay long. She kept watch too upon all that passed, not only between him and Emily, but between him and John Ayliffe; for a quarrel between them, which she thought likely, was not what she desired. But there was no danger of such a result. Marlow treated the young man with a cold and distant politeness--a proud civility, which left him no pretence for offence, and yet silenced and abashed him completely. During the whole visit, till towards its close, the contrast between the two men was so marked and strong, so disadvantageous to him whom Mrs. Hazleton sought to favor, that she would have given much to have had Ayliffe away from such a damaging companion. At length she could endure it no longer, and contrived to send him to seek for some flowers which she pretended to want, and which she knew he would not readily find in her gardens.

Before he returned, Marlow was gone; and Emily, soon after, retired to her own room, leaving the youth and Mrs. Hazleton together.

The three met again at dinner, and, for once, a subject was brought up, by accident, or design--which, I know not--that gave John Ayliffe an opportunity of setting himself in a somewhat better light. Every one has some amenity--some sweeter, gentler spot in the character. He had a great love for flowers--a passion for them; and it brought forth the small, very small portion of the poetry of the heart which had been assigned to him by nature. It was flowers then that Mrs. Hazleton talked of, and he soon joined in discussing their beauties, with a thorough knowledge of, and feeling for his subject. Emily was somewhat surprised, and, with natural kindness, felt glad to find some topic where she could converse with him at ease. The change of her manner encouraged him, and he went on, for once, wisely keeping to a subject on which he was at home, and which seemed so well to please. Mrs. Hazleton helped him greatly with a skill and rapidity which few could have displayed, always guiding the conversation back to the well chosen theme, whenever it was lost for an instant.

At length, when the impression was most favorable, John Ayliffe rose to go--I know not whether he did so at a sign from Mrs. Hazleton; but I think he did. Few men quit a room gracefully--it is a difficult evolution--and he, certainly, did not. But Emily's eyes were in a different direction, and to say the truth, although he had seemed to her more agreeable that evening than he had been before, she thought too little of him at all to remark how he quitted the room, even if her eyes had been upon him.

From time to time, indeed, some of the strange vague words which he had used when she had seen him in the park, had recurred to her mind with an unpleasant impression, and she had puzzled herself with the question of what could be their meaning; but she soon dismissed the subject, resolving to seek some information from Mrs. Hazleton, who seemed to know the young man so well.

On the preceding night, that lady had avoided all mention of him; but that was not the case now. She spoke of him, almost as soon as he was gone, in a tone of some compassion, alluding vaguely and mysteriously to misfortunes and disadvantages under which he had labored, and saying, that it was marvellous to see how much strength of mind, and natural high qualities, could effect against adverse circumstances. This called forth from Emily the inquiry which she had meditated, and although she could not recollect exactly the words John Ayliffe had used, she detailed, with sufficient accuracy, all that had taken place between herself and him; and the strange allusion he had made to Sir Philip Hastings.

Mrs. Hazleton gazed at her for a moment or two after she had done speaking, with a look expressive of anxious concern.

"I trust, my dear Emily," she said, at length, "that you did not repel him at all harshly. I have had much sad experience of the world, and I know that in youth we are too apt to touch hardly and rashly, things that for our own best interests, as well as for good feeling's sake, we ought to deal with tenderly."

"I do not think that I spoke harshly," replied Emily, thoughtfully; "I told him that any thing he had to say must be said to my father; but I do not believe I spoke even that unkindly."

"I am glad to hear it--very glad;" replied Mrs. Hazleton, with much emphasis; and then, after a short pause, she added, "Yet I do not know that your father--excellent, noble-minded, just and generous as he is--was the person best fitted to judge and act in the matter which John Ayliffe might have to speak of."

"Indeed!" exclaimed Emily, becoming more and more surprised, and in some degree alarmed, "this is very strange, dear Mrs. Hazleton. You seem to know more of this matter; pray explain it all to me. I may well hear from you, what would be improper for me to listen to from him."

"He has a kindly heart," said Mrs. Hazleton, thoughtfully, "and more forbearance than I ever knew in one so young; but it cannot last for ever; and when he is of age, which will be in a few days, he must act; and I trust will act kindly and gently--I am sure he will, if nothing occurs to irritate a bold and decided character."

"But act how?" inquired Emily, eagerly; "you forget, dear Mrs. Hazleton, that I am quite in the dark in this matter. I dare say that he is all that you say; but I will own that neither his manners generally, nor his demeanor on that occasion, led me to think very well of him, or to believe that he was of a forbearing or gentle nature."

"He has faults," said Mrs. Hazleton, dryly; "oh yes, he has faults, but they are those of manner, more than heart or character--faults produced by circumstances may be changed by circumstances--which would never have existed, had he had, earlier, one judicious, kind, and experienced friend to counsel and direct him. They are disappearing rapidly, and, if ever he should fall under the influences of a generous and noble spirit, will vanish altogether."

She was preparing the way, skilfully exciting, as she saw, some interest in Emily, and yet producing some alarm.

"But still you do not explain," said the beautiful girl, anxiously; "do not, dear Mrs. Hazleton, keep me longer in suspense."

"I cannot--I ought not, Emily, to explain all to you," replied the lady, "it would be a long and painful story; but this I may tell you, and after that, ask me no more. That young man has your father's fortunes and his fate entirely in his hands. He has forborne long. Heaven grant that his forbearance may still endure."

She ceased, and after one glance at Emily's face, she cast down her eyes, and seemed to fall into thought.

Emily gazed up towards the sky, as if seeking counsel there, and then, bursting into tears, hurriedly quitted the room.

CHAPTER XX

Emily's night was not peaceful. The very idea that her father's fate was in the power of any other man, was, in itself, trouble enough; but in the present case there was more. Why, or wherefore, she knew not; but there was something told her that, in spite of all Mrs. Hazleton's commendations, and the fair portrait she had so elaborately drawn, John Ayliffe was not a man to use power mercifully. She tried eagerly to discover what had created this impression: she thought of every look and every word which she had seen upon the young man's countenance, or heard from his lips; and she fixed at length more upon the menacing scowl which she had marked upon his brow in the cottage, than even upon the menacing language which he had held when her father's name was mentioned.

Sleep visited not her eyes for many an hour, and when at length her eyes closed through fatigue, it was restless and dreamful. She fancied she saw John Ayliffe holding Sir Philip on the ground, trying to strangle him. She strove to scream for help, but her lips seemed paralyzed, and there was no sound. That strange anguish of sleep--the anguish of impotent strong will--of powerless passion--of effort without effect, was upon her, and soon burst the bonds of slumber. It would have been impossible to endure it long. All must have felt that it is greater than any mortal agony; and that if he could endure more than a moment, like a treacherous enemy it would slay us in our sleep.

She awoke unrefreshed, and rose pale and sad. I cannot say that Mrs. Hazleton, when she beheld Emily's changed look, felt any great compunction. If she had no great desire to torture, which I will not pretend to say, she did not at all object to see her victim suffer; but Emily's pale cheek and distressed look afforded indications still more satisfactory; which Mrs. Hazleton remarked with the satisfaction of a philosopher watching a successful experiment. They showed that the preparation she had made for what was coming, was even more effectual than she had expected, and so the abstract pleasure of inflicting pain on one she hated, was increased by the certainty of success.

Emily said little--referred not at all to the subject of her thoughts, but dwelt upon it--pondered in silence. To one who knew her she might have seemed sullen, sulky; but it was merely that one of those fits of deep intense communion with the inner things of the heart--those abstracted rambles through the mazy wilderness of thought, which sometimes fell upon her, was upon her now. At these times it was very difficult to draw her spirit forth into the waking world again--to rouse her to the things about her life. It seemed as if her soul was absent far away, and that the mere animal life of the body remained. Great events might have passed before her eyes, without her knowing aught of them.

On all former occasions but one, these reveries--for so I must call them--had been of a lighter and more pleasant nature. In them it had seemed as if her young spirit had been tempted away from the household paths of thought, far into tangled wilds where it had lost itself--tempted, like other children, by the mere pleasure of the ramble--led on to catch a butterfly, or chase the rainbow. Feeling--passion, had not mingled with the dream at all, and consequently there had been no suffering. I am not sure that on other occasions, when such absent fits fell upon her, Emily Hastings was not more joyous, more full of pure delight, than when, in a gay and sparkling mood, she moved her father's wonder at what he thought light frivolity. But now it was all bitter: the labyrinth was dark as well as intricate, and the thorns tore her as she groped for some path across the wilderness.

Before it had lasted very long--before it had at all reached its conclusion--and as she had sat at the window of the drawing-room, gazing out upon the sky without seeing either white cloud or blue, Sir Philip Hastings himself, on a short journey for some magisterial purpose, entered the room, spoke a few words to Mrs. Hazleton, and then turned to his daughter. Had he been half an hour later, Emily would have cast her arms round his neck and told him all; but as it was, she remained self-involved, even in his presence--answered indeed mechanically--spoke words of affection with an absent air, and let the mind still run on upon the path which it had chosen.

Sir Philip had no time to stay till this fit was past, and Mrs. Hazleton was glad to get rid of him civilly before any other act of the drama began.

But his daughter's mood did not escape Sir Philip's eyes. I have said that for her he was full of observation, though he often read the results wrongly; and now he marked Emily's mood with doubt, and not with pleasure. "What can this mean?" he asked himself, "can any thing have gone wrong?

It is strange, very strange. Perhaps her mother was right after all, and it might have been better to take her to the capital."

Thus thinking, Sir Philip himself fell into a reverie, not at all unlike that in which he had found his daughter. Yet he understood not hers, and pondered upon it as something strange and inextricable.

In the mean time, Emily thought on, till at length Mrs. Hazleton reminded her that they were to go that day to the Waterfall. She rose mechanically, sought her room, dressed, and gazed from the window.

It is wonderful, however, how small a thing will sometimes take the mind, as it were, by the hand, and lead it back out of shadow into sunshine. From the lawn below the window a light bird sprang up into the air, quivered upon its twinkling wings, uttered a note or two, and then soared higher, and each moment as it rose up, up, into the sky, the song, like a spirit heavenward bound, grew stronger and more strong, and flooded the air with melody.

Emily watched it as it rose, listened to it as it sang. Its upward flight seemed to carry her spirit above the dark things on which it brooded; its thrilling voice to waken her to cheerful life again. There is a high holiness in a lark's song; and hard must be the heart, and strong and corrupt, that does not raise the voice and join with it in its praise to God.

When she went down again into the drawing-room, she was quite a different being, and Mrs. Hazleton marvelled what could have happened so to change her. Had she been told that it was a lark's song, she would have laughed the speaker to scorn. She was not one to feel it.

I will not pause upon the journey of the morning, nor describe the beautiful fall of the river that they visited, or tell how it fell rushing over the precipice, or how the rocks dashed it into diamond sparkles, or how rainbows bannered the conflict of the waters, and boughs waved over the struggling stream like plumes. It was a sweet and pleasant sight, and full of meditation; and Mrs. Hazleton, judging perhaps of others by herself, imagined that it would produce in the mind of Emily those softening influences which teach the heart to yield readily to the harder things of life.

There is, perhaps, not a more beautiful, nor a more frequently applicable allegory than that of the famous Amreeta Cup--I know not whether devised by Southey, or borrowed by him from the rich store of instructive fable hidden in oriental tradition. It is long, long, since I read it;

but yet every word is remembered whenever I see the different effect which scenes, circumstances, and events produce upon different characters. It is shown by the poet that the cup of divine wine gave life and immortality, and excellence superhuman, and bliss beyond belief, to the pure heart; but to the lark, earthly, and evil, brought death, destruction, and despair. We may extend the lesson a little, and see in the Amreeta wine, the spirit of God pervading all his works, but producing in those who see and taste an effect, for good or evil, according to the nature of the recipient. The strong, powerful, self-willed, passionate character of Mrs. Hazleton, found, in the calm meditative fall of the cataract, in the ever shifting play of the wild waters, and in the watchful stillness of the air around, a softening, enfeebling influence. The gentle character of Emily turned from the scene with a heart raised rather than depressed, a spirit better prepared to combat with evil and with sorrow, full of love and trust in God, and a confidence strong beyond the strength of this world. There is a voice of prophecy in waterfalls, and mountains, and lakes, and streams, and sunny lands, and clouds, and storms, and bright sunsets, and the face of nature every where, which tells the destiny, not of one, but of many, and at all events, foreshows the unutterable mercy reserved for those who trust. It is a prophecy--and an exhortation too. The words are, "Be holy, and be happy!" The God who speaks is true and glorious. Be true and inherit glory.

Emily had been cheerful as they went. As they returned she was calm and firm. Readily she joined in any conversation. Seldom did she fall into any absent fit of thought, and the effect of that day's drive was any thing but what Mrs. Hazleton expected or wished.

When they returned to the house, a letter was delivered to Emily Hastings, with which, the seal unbroken, she retired to her own room. The hand was unknown to her, but with a sort of prescience something more than natural, she divined at once from whom it came, and saw that the difficult struggle had commenced. An hour or two before, the very thought would have dismayed her. Now the effect was but small.

She had no suspicion of the plans against her; no idea whatever that people might be using her as a tool--that there was any interest contrary to her own, in the conduct or management of others. But yet she turned the key in the door before she commenced the perusal of the letter, which was to the following effect:

"I know not," said the writer, in a happier style than perhaps might have been expected, "how to prevail upon your goodness to pardon all I am going to say, knowing that nothing short of the circumstances in which I am placed, could excuse my approaching you even in thought. I have long known you, though you have known me only for a few short hours. I have watched you often from childhood up to womanhood, and there has been growing upon me from very early years a strong attachment, a deep affection, a powerful--overpowering--ardent love, which nothing can ever extinguish. Need I tell you that the last few days would have increased that love had increase been possible.

"All this, however, I know is no justification of my venturing to raise my thoughts to you--still less of my venturing to express these feelings boldly; but it has been an excuse to myself, and in some degree to others, for abstaining hitherto from that which my best interests, a mother's fame, and my own rights, required. The time has now come when I can no longer remain silent; when I must throw upon you the responsibility of an important choice; when I am forced to tell you how deeply, how devotedly, I love you, in order that you may say whether you will take the only means of saving me from the most painful task I ever undertook, by conferring on me the greatest blessing that woman ever gave to man; or, on the other hand, will drive me to a task repugnant to all my feelings, but just, necessary, inevitable, in case of your refusal. Let me explain, however, that I am your cousin--the son of your father's elder brother by a private marriage with a peasant girl of this county. The whole case is perfectly clear, and I have proof positive of the marriage in my hands. From fear of a lawsuit, and from the pressure of great poverty, my mother was induced to sacrifice her rights after her husband's early death, still to conceal her marriage, to bear even sneers and shame, and to live upon a pittance allowed to her by her husband's father, and secured to her by him after his own death, when she was entitled to honor, and birth, and distinction by the law of the land.

"One of her objects, doubtless, was to secure to herself and her son a moderate competence, as the late Sir John Hastings, my grandfather and yours, had the power of leaving all his estates to any one he pleased, the entail having ended with himself. For this she sacrificed her rights, her name, her fame, and you will find, if you look into your grandfather's will, that he took especial care that no infraction of the contract between him and her father should give cause for the assertion of her rights. Two or three mysterious clauses in that will will show you at once, if you read them, that the whole tale I tell you is correct, and that Sir John Hastings, on the one hand, paid largely, and on the other threatened sternly, in order to conceal the marriage of his eldest son, and transmit the title to the second. But my mother could not bar me of my rights: she could endure unmerited shame for pecuniary advantages, if she pleased; but she could not entail shame upon me; and were it in the power of any one to deprive me of that which Sir John Hastings left me, or to shut me out from the succession to his whole estates, to which--from the fear of disclosing his great secret--he did not put any bar in his will that would have been at once an acknowledgment of my legitimacy, I would still sacrifice all, and stand alone, friendless and portionless in the world, rather than leave my mother's fame and my own birth unvindicated. This is one of the strongest desires, the most overpowering impulses of my heart; and neither you nor any one could expect me to resist it. But there is yet a stronger still--not an impulse, but a passion, and to that every thing must yield. It is love; and whatever may be the difference which you see between yourself and me, however inferior I may feel myself to you in all those qualities which I myself the most admire, still, I feel myself justified in placing the case clearly before you--in telling you how truly, how sincerely, how ardently I love you, and in asking you whether you will deign to favor my suit even now as I stand, to save me the pain and grief of contending with the father of her I love, the anguish of stripping him of the property he so well uses, and of the rank which he adorns; or will leave me to establish my rights, to take my just name and station, and then, when no longer appearing humble and unknown, to plead my cause with no less humility than I do at present.

"That I shall do so then, as now, rest assured--that I would do so if the rank and station to which I have a right were a principality, do not doubt; but I would fain, if it were possible, avoid inflicting any pain upon your father. I know not how he may bear the loss of station and of fortune--I know not what effect the struggles of a court of law, and inevitable defeat may produce. Only acquainted with him by general repute, I cannot tell what may be the effect of mortification and the loss of all he has hitherto enjoyed. He has the reputation of a good, a just, and a wise man, somewhat vehement in feeling, somewhat proud of his position. You must judge him, rather than I; but, I beseech you, consider him in this matter.

"At any time, and at all times, my love will be the same--nothing can change me--nothing can alter or affect the deep love I bear you. When casting from me the cloud which had hung upon my birth, when assuming the rank and taking possession of the property that is my own, I shall still love you as devotedly as ever--still as earnestly seek your hand. But oh!

how I long to avoid all the pangs, the mischances, the anxieties to every one, the ill feeling, the contention, the animosity, which must ever follow such a struggle as that between your father and myself--oh, how I long to owe every thing to you, even the station, even the property, even the fair name that is my own by right Nay, more, far more, to owe you guidance and direction--to owe you support and instruction--to owe you all that may improve, and purify, and elevate me.

"Oh, Emily, dear cousin, let me be your debtor in all things. You who first gave me the thought of rising above fate, and making myself worthy of the high fortunes which I have long known awaited me, perfect your work, redeem me for ever from all that is unworthy, save me from bitter regrets, and your father from disappointment, sorrow, and poverty, and render me all that I long to be.

"Yours, and forever,

"JOHN HASTINGS."

Very well done, Mrs. Hazleton!--but somewhat too well done. There was a difference, a difference so striking, so unaccountable, between the style of this letter, both in thought and composition, and the ordinary style and manners of John Ayliffe, that it could not fail to strike the eyes of Emily. For a moment she felt a little confused--not undecided. There was no hesitation, no doubt, as to her own conduct. For an instant it crossed her mind that this young man had deeper, finer feelings in his nature than appeared upon the surface--that his manner might be more in fault than his nature. But there were things in the letter itself which she did not like--that, without any labored analysis or deep-searching criticism, brought to her mind the conviction that the words, the arguments, the inducements employed were those of art rather than of feeling--that the mingling of threats towards her father, however veiled, with professions of love towards herself, was in itself ungenerous--that the objects and the means were not so high-toned as the professions--that there was something sordid, base, ignoble in the whole proceeding. It required no careful thought to arrive at such a conclusion--no second reading--and her mind was made up at once.

The deep reverie into which she had fallen in the morning had done her good--it had disentangled thought, and left the heart and judgment clear. The fair, natural scene she had passed through since, the intercourse with God's works, had done her still more good--refreshed, and strengthened, and elevated the spirit; and after a very brief pause she drew the table towards her, sat down, and wrote. As she did write, she thought of her father, and she believed from her heart that the words she used were those which he would wish her to employ. They were to the following effect:

"Sir: Your letter, as you may suppose, has occasioned me great pain, and the more so, as I am compelled to say, not only that I cannot return your affection now, but can hold out no hope to you of ever returning it. I am obliged to speak decidedly, as I should consider myself most base if I could for one moment trifle with feelings such as those which you express.

"In regard to your claims upon my father's estates, and to the rank which he believes himself to hold by just right, I can form no judgment; and could have wished that they had never been mentioned to me before they had been made known to him.

"I never in my life knew my father do an unjust or ungenerous thing, and I am quite sure that if convinced another had a just title to all that he possesses on earth, he would strip himself of it as readily as he would of a soiled garment. My father would disdain to hold for an hour the rightful property of another. You have therefore only to lay your reasons before him, and you may be sure that they will have just consideration and yourself full justice. I trust that you will do so soon, as to give the first intelligence of such claims would be too painful a task for

"Your faithful servant,

"EMILY HASTINGS."

She read her letter over twice, and was satisfied with it. Sealing it carefully, she gave it to her own maid for despatch, and then paused for a moment, giving way to some temporary curiosity as to who could have aided in the composition of the letter she had received, for John Ayliffe's alone she could not and would not believe it to be. She cast such thoughts from her very speedily, however, and, strange to say, her heart seemed lightened now that the moment of trial had come and gone, now that a turning-point in her fate seemed to have passed.

Mrs. Hazleton was surprised to see her re-enter the drawing-room with a look of relief. She saw that the matter was decided, but she was too wise to conclude that it was decided according to her wishes.

CHAPTER XXI

Marlow reasoned with his own heart. For the first time in his life it had proved rebellious. It would have its own way. It would give no account of its conduct,--why it had beat so, why it had thrilled so, why it had experienced so many changes of feeling when he saw John Ayliffe sitting beside Emily Hastings, and when Emily Hastings had risen with so joyous a smile to greet him--it would not explain at all. And now he argued the point with it systematically, with a determination to get to the bottom of the matter one way or another. He asked it, as if it had been a separate individual, if it was in love with Emily Hastings. The question was too direct, and the heart said it "rather thought not."

Was it quite sure? he asked again. The heart was silent, and seemed to be considering. Was it jealous? he inquired. "Oh dear no, not in the least."

Then why did it go on in such a strange, capricious, unaccountable way, when a good-looking, vulgar young man was seen sitting beside Emily?

The heart said it "could not tell; that it was its nature to do so."

Marlow was not to be put off. He was determined to know more, and he argued, "If it be your nature to do so, you of course do the same when you see other young men sitting by other young women." The heart was puzzled, and did not reply; and then Marlow begged a definite answer to this question. "If you were to hear to-morrow that Emily Hastings is going to be married to this youth, or to any other man, young or old, what would you do then?"

"Break!" said the heart, and Marlow asked no more questions. Knowing how dangerous it is to enter into such interrogations on horseback, when the pulse is accelerated and the nervous system all in a flutter, he had waited till he got into his own dwelling, and seated himself in his chair, that he might deal with the rebellious spirit in his breast stately, and calmly likewise; but as he came to the end of the conversation, he rose up, resolving to order a fresh horse, and ride instantly away, to confer with Sir Philip Hastings. In so doing he looked round the room. It was not very well or very fully furnished. The last proprietor before Mrs. Hazleton had not been very fond of books, and had never thought of a library. When Marlow brought his own books down he had ordered some cases to be made by a country carpenter, which fitted but did not much ornament the room. They gave it a raw, desolate aspect, and made him, by a natural projection of thought, think ill of the accommodation of the whole house, as soon as he began to entertain the idea of Emily Hastings ever becoming its mistress. Then he went on to ask himself, "What have I to offer for the treasure of her hand? What have I to offer but the hand of a very simple, undistinguished country gentleman-- quite, quite unworthy of her? What have I to offer Sir Philip Hastings as an alliance worthy of even his consideration?--A good, unstained name; but no rank, and a fortune not above mediocrity. Marry! a fitting match for the heiress of the Hastings and Marshall families."

He gazed around him, and his heart fell.

A little boy, with a pair of wings on his shoulders, and the end of a bow peeping up near his neck, stood close behind Marlow, and whispered in his ear, "Never mind all that--only try."

And Marlow resolved he would try; but yet he hesitated how to do so. Should he go himself to Sir Philip? But he feared a rebuff. Should he write? No, that was cowardly. Should he tell his love to Emily first, and strive to win her affections, ere he breathed to her father? No, that would be dishonest, if he had a doubt of her father's consent. At length he made up his mind to go in person to Sir Philip, but the discussion and the consideration had been so long that it was too late to ride over that night, and the journey was put off till the following day. That day, as early as possible, he set out. He called it as early as possible, and it was early for a visit; but the moment one fears a rebuff from any lady one grows marvellously punctilious. When his horse was brought round he began to fancy that he should be too soon for Sir Philip, and he had the horse walked up and down for half an hour.

What would he have given for that half hour, when, on reaching Sir Philip's door, he found that Emily's father had gone out, and was not expected back till late in the day. Angry with himself, and a good deal disappointed, he returned to his home, which, somehow, looked far less cheerful than usual. He could take no pleasure in his books, or in his pictures, and even thought was unpleasant to him, for under the influence of expectation it became but a calculation of chances, for which he had but scanty data. One thing, indeed, he learned from the passing of that evening, which was, that home and home happiness was lost to him henceforth without Emily Hastings.

The following day saw him early in the saddle, and riding away as if some beast of the chase were before him. Indeed, man's love, when it is worth any thing, has always a smack of the hunter in it. He cared not for highlands or bypaths--hedges and ditches offered small impediments. Straight across the country he went, till he approached the end of his journey; but then he suddenly pulled in his rein, and began to ask himself if he was a madman. He was passing over the Marshall property at the time, the inheritance of Emily's mother, and the thought of all that she was heir to cooled his ardor with doubt and apprehension. He would have given one half of all that he possessed that she had been a peasant-girl, that he might have lived with her upon the other.

Then he began to think of all that he should say to Sir Philip Hastings, and how he should say it; and he felt very uneasy in his mind. Then he was angry with himself for his own sensations, and tried philosophy and scolded his own heart. But philosophy and scolding had no effect; and then cantering easily through the park, he stopped at the gate of the house and dismounted.

Sir Philip was in this time; and Marlow was ushered into the little room where he sat in the morning, with the library hard by, that he might have his books at hand. But Sir Philip was not reading now; on the contrary, he was in a fit of thought; and, if one might judge by the contraction of his brow, and the drawing down of the corners of his lips, it was not a very pleasant one.

Marlow fancied that he had come at an inauspicious moment, and the first words of Sir Philip, though kind and friendly, were not at all harmonious with the feeling of love in his young visitor's heart.

"Welcome, my young friend," he said, looking up. "I have been thinking this morning over the laws and habits of different nations, ancient and modern; and would fain satisfy myself if I am right in the conclusion that we, in this land, leave too little free action to individual judgment. No man, we say, must take law in his own hands; yet how often do we break this rule--how often are we compelled to break it. If you, with a gun in your hand, saw a man at fifty or sixty paces about to murder a child or a woman, without any means of stopping the blow except by using your weapon, what would you do?"

"Shoot him on the spot," replied Marlow at once, and then added, "if I were quite certain of his intention."

"Of course--of course," replied Sir Philip. "And yet, my good friend, if you did so, without witnesses---supposing the child too young to testify, or the woman sleeping at whom the blow was aimed--you would be hung for your just, wise, charitable act."

"Perhaps so," said Marlow, abruptly; "but I would do it, nevertheless."

"Right, right," replied Sir Philip, rising and shaking his hand; "right, and like yourself! There are cases when, with a clear consciousness of the rectitude of our purpose, and a strong confidence in the justice of our judgment, we must step over all human laws, be the result to ourselves what it may. Do you remember a man--one Cutter--to whom you taught a severe lesson on the very first day I had the pleasure of knowing you? I should have been undoubtedly justified, morally, and perhaps even legally also, in sending my sword through his body, when he attacked me that day. Had I done so I should have saved a valuable human life, spared the world the spectacle of a great crime, and preserved an excellent husband and father to his wife and children. That very man has murdered the game-keeper of the Earl of Selby; and being called to the spot yesterday, I had to commit him for that crime, upon evidence which left not a doubt of his guilt. I spared him when he assaulted me from a weak and unworthy feeling of compassion, although I knew the man's character, and dimly foresaw his career. I have regretted it since; but never so much as yesterday. This, of course, is no parallel case to that which I just now proposed; but the one led my mind to the other."

"Did the wretched man admit his guilt?" asked Marlow.

"He did not, and could not deny it," answered Sir Philip; "during the examination he maintained a hard, sullen silence; and only said, when I ordered his committal, that I ought not to be so hard upon him for that offence, as it was the best service he could have done me; for that he had silenced a man whose word could strip me of all I possessed."

"What could he mean?" asked Marlow, eagerly.

"Nay, I know not," replied Sir Philip, in an indifferent tone; "crushed vipers often turn to bite. The man he killed was the son of the former sexton here--an honest, good creature too, for whom I obtained his place; his murderer a reckless villain, on whose word there is no dependence. Let us give no thought to it. He has held some such language before; but it never produced a fear that my property would be lost, or even diminished. We do not hold our fee simples on the tenure of a rogue's good pleasure--why do you smile?"

"For what will seem at first sight a strange, unnatural reason for a friend to give, Sir Philip," replied Marlow, determined not to lose the opportunity; "for your own sake and for your country's, I am bound to hope that your property may never be lost or diminished; but every selfish feeling would induce me to wish it were less than it is."

Sir Philip Hastings was no reader of riddles, and he looked puzzled; but Marlow walked frankly round and took him by the hand, saying, "I have not judged it right, Sir Philip, to remain one day after I discovered what are my feelings towards your daughter, without informing you fully of their nature, that you may at once decide upon your future demeanor towards one to whom you have hitherto shown much kindness, and who would on no account abuse it. I was not at all aware of how this passion had grown upon me, till the day before yesterday, when I saw your daughter at Mrs. Hazleton's, and some accidental circumstance revealed to me the state of my own heart."

Sir Philip looked as if surprised; but after a moment's thought, he inquired, "And what says Emily, my young friend?"

"She says nothing, Sir Philip," replied Marlow; "for neither by word nor look, as far as I know, have I betrayed my own feelings towards her. I would not, between us, do so, till I had given you an opportunity of deciding, unfettered by any consideration for her, whether you would permit me to pursue my suit or not."

Sir Philip was in a reasoning mood that day, and he tortured Marlow by asking, "And would you always think it necessary, Marlow, to obtain a parent's consent, before you endeavored to gain the affection of a girl you loved?"

"Not always," replied the young man; "but I should think it always necessary to violate no confidence, Sir Philip. You have been kind to me--trusted me--had no doubt of me; and to say one word to Emily which might thwart your plans or meet your disapproval, would be to show myself unworthy of your esteem or her affection."

Sir Philip mused, and then said, as if speaking to himself, "I had some idea this might turn out so, but not so soon. I fancy, however," he continued, addressing Marlow, "that you must have betrayed your feelings more than you thought, my young friend; for yesterday I found Emily in a strange, thoughtful, abstracted mood, showing that some strong feelings were busy at her heart."

"Some other cause," said Marlow quickly; "I cannot even flatter myself that she was thinking of me. When I saw her the day before, there was a young man sitting with her and Mrs. Hazleton--John Ayliffe, I think, is his name--and I will own I thought his presence seemed to annoy her."

"John Ayliffe at Mrs. Hazleton's!" exclaimed Sir Philip, his brow growing very dark; "John Ayliffe in my daughter's society! Well might the poor child look thoughtful--and yet why should she? She knows nothing of his history. What is he like, Marlow--how does he bear himself?"

"He is certainly handsome, with fine features and a good figure," replied Marlow; "indeed, it struck me that there was some resemblance between him and yourself; but there is a want I cannot well define in his appearance, Sir Philip--in his air--in his carriage, whether still or in motion, which fixes upon him what I am accustomed to call a class-mark, and that not of the best. Depend upon it, however, that it was annoyance at being brought into society which she disliked that affected your daughter as you have mentioned. My love for her she is, and must be, ignorant of; for I stayed there but a few minutes; and before that day, I saw it not myself. And now, Sir Philip, what say you to my suit? May I--as some of your words lead me to hope--may I pursue that suit and strive to win your dear daughter's love?"

"Of course," replied Sir Philip, "of course. A vague fancy has long been floating in my brain, that it might be so some day. She is too young to marry yet; and it will be sad to part with her when the time does come; but you have my consent to seek her affection if she can give it you. She must herself decide."

"Have you considered fully," asked Marlow, "that I have neither fortune nor rank to offer her, that I am by no means--"

Sir Philip waved his hand almost impatiently. "What skills it talking of rank or wealth?" he said. "You are a gentleman by birth, education, manners. You have easy competence. My Emily will desire no more for herself, and I can desire no more for her. You will endeavor, I know, to make her happy, and will succeed, because you love her. As for myself, were I to choose out of all the men I know, you would be the man. Fortune is a good adjunct; but it is no essential. I do not promise her to you. That she must do; but if she says she will give you her hand, it shall be yours."

Marlow thanked him, with joy such as may be conceived; but Sir Philip's thoughts reverted at once to his daughter's situation at Mrs. Hazleton's. "She must stay there no longer, Marlow," he said; "I will send for her home without delay. Then you will have plenty of opportunity for the telling of your own tale to her ear, and seeing how you may speed with her; but, at all events, she must stay no longer in a house where she can meet with John Ayliffe. Mrs. Hazleton makes me marvel--a woman so proud--so refined!"

"It is but justice to say," replied Marlow, thoughtfully, "that I have some vague recollection of Mrs. Hazleton having intimated that they met that young gentleman by chance upon some expedition of pleasure. But had I not better communicate my hopes and wishes to Lady Hastings, my dear sir?"

"That is not needful," replied Emily's father, somewhat sternly; "I promise her to you, if she herself consents. My good wife will not oppose my wishes or my daughter's happiness; for do I suffer opposition upon occasions of importance. I will tell Lady Hastings my determination myself."

Marlow was too wise to say another word, but agreed to come on the following day to dine and sleep at the hall, and took his leave for the time. It was not, indeed, without some satisfaction that he heard Sir Philip order a horse to be saddled and a man to prepare to carry a letter to Mrs. Hazleton; for doubts were rapidly possessing themselves of his mind--not in regard to Emily--but in reference to Mrs. Hazleton herself.

The letter was dispatched immediately after his departure, recalling Emily to her father's house, and announcing that the carriage would be sent for her early on the following morning. That done, Sir Philip repaired to his wife's drawing-room, and informed her that he had given his consent to his young friend Marlow's suit to their daughter. His tone was one that admitted no reply, and Lady Hastings made none; but she entered her protest quite as well, by falling into a violent fit of hysterics.

CHAPTER XXII

In a very gaudily furnished parlor, and in a very gaudy dress, sat a lady of some eight or nine and thirty years of age, with many traces of beauty still to be perceived in a face of no very intellectual expression. Few persons perhaps would have recognized in her the fair and faulty girl whom we have depicted weeping bitterly over the fate of Sir Philip Hastings' elder brother, and over the terrible situation in which he left her. Her features had much changed: the girlish expression--the fresh bloom of youth was gone. The light graceful figure was lost; but the mind had changed as greatly as the person, though, like it, the heart yet retained some traces of the original. When first she appeared before the reader's eyes, though weak and yielding, she was by no means ill disposed. She had committed an error--a great and fatal one; but at heart she was innocent and honest. She was, however, like all weak people, of that plastic clay moulded easily by circumstances into any form; and, in her, circumstances had shaped her gradually into a much worse form than nature had originally given her. To defraud, to cheat, to wrong, had at one time been most abhorrent to her nature. She had taken no active part in her father's dealings with old Sir John Hastings, and had she known all that he had said and sworn, would have shrunk with horror from the deceit. But during her father's short life, she had been often told by himself, and after his death had been often assured by the old woman Denby, that she was rightly and truly the widow of John Hastings, although because it would be difficult to prove, her father had consented to take an annuity for himself and her son, rather than enter into a lawsuit with a powerful man; and she had gradually brought herself to believe that she had been her lover's wife, because in one of his ardent letters he had called her so to stifle the voice of remorse in her bosom. The conviction had grown upon her, till now, after a lapse of more than twenty years, she had forgotten all her former doubts and scruples, believed herself and her son to be injured and deprived of their just rights, and was ready to assert her marriage boldly, though she had at one time felt and acknowledged that there was no marriage at all, and that the words her seducer had used were but intended to soothe her regret and terror. There was a point however beyond which she was not prepared to go. She still shrunk from giving false details, from perjuring herself in regard to particular facts. The marriage, she thought, might be good in the sight of heaven, of herself, and of her lover; but to render it good in the eyes of the law, she had found would require proofs that she could not give--oaths that she dared not take.

Another course, however, had been proposed for her; and now she sat in that small parlor gaudily dressed, as I have said, but dressed evidently for a journey. There were tears indeed in her eyes; and as her son stood by her side she looked up in his face with a beseeching look as if she would fain have said, "Pray do not drive me to this!"

But young John Ayliffe had no remorse, and if he spoke tenderly to her who had spoiled his youth, it was only because his object was to persuade and cajole.

"Indeed, mother," he said, "it is absolutely necessary or I would not ask you to go. You know quite well that I would rather have you here: and it will only be for a short time till the trial is over. Lawyer Shanks told you himself that if you stayed, they would have you into court and cross-examine you to death; and you know quite well you could not keep in one story if they browbeat and puzzled you."

"I would say any where that my marriage was a good one," replied his mother, "but I could not swear all that Shanks would have had me, John-- No, I could not swear that, for Dr. Paulding had nothing to do with it, and if he were to repeat it all over to me a thousand times, I am sure that I should make a blunder, even if I consented to tell such a falsehood. My father and good Mrs. Danby used always to say that the mutual consent made a marriage, and a good one too. Now your father's own letter shows that he consented to it, and God knows I did. But these lawyers will not let well alone, and by trying to mend things make them worse, I think. However, I suppose you have gone too far to go back; and so I must go to a strange out of the way country and hide myself and live quite lonely. Well, I am ready- -I am ready to make any sacrifice for you, my boy--though it is very hard, I must say."

As she spoke, she rose with her eyes running over, and her son kissed her and assured her that her absence should not be long. But just as she was moving towards the door, he put a paper--a somewhat long one--on the table, where a pen was already in the inkstand, saying, "just sign this before you go, dear mother."

"Oh, I cannot sign any thing," cried the lady, wiping her eyes; "how can you be so cruel, John, as to ask me to sign any thing just now when I am parting with you? What is it you want?

"It is only a declaration that you are truly my father's widow," said John Ayliffe; "see here, the declaration, &c., you need not read it, but only just sign here."

She hesitated an instant; but his power over her was complete; and, though, she much doubted the contents, she signed the paper with a trembling hand. Then came a parting full of real tenderness on her part, and assumed affection and regret on his. The post-chaise, which had been standing for an hour at the door, rolled away, and John Ayliffe walked back into the house.

When there, he walked up and down the room for some time, with an impatient thoughtfulness, if I may use the term, in his looks, which had little to do with his mother's departure. He was glad that she was gone-- still gladder that she had signed the paper; and now he seemed waiting for something eagerly expected.

At length there came a sound of a quick trotting horse, and John Ayliffe took the paper from the table hastily, and put it in his pocket But the visitor was not the one he expected. It was but a servant with a letter; and as the young man took it from the hand of the maid who brought it in, and gazed at the address, his cheek flushed a little, and then turned somewhat pale. He muttered to himself, "she has not taken long to consider!"

As soon as the slipshod girl had gone out of the room, he broke the seal and read the brief answer which Emily had returned to his declaration.

It would not be easy for an artist to paint, and it is impossible for a writer to describe, the expression which came upon his face as he perused the words of decided rejection which were written on that sheet; but certainly, had poor Emily heard how he cursed her, how he vowed to have revenge, and to humble her pride, as he called it, she would have rejoiced rather than grieved that such a man had obtained no hold upon her affection, no command of her fate. He was still in the midst of his tempest of passion, when, without John Ayliffe being prepared for his appearance, Mr. Shanks entered the room. His face wore a dark and somewhat anxious expression which even habitual cunning could not banish; but the state in which he found his young client, seemed to take him quite by surprise.

The Man In Black | 151

"Why what is the matter, John?" he cried, "What in the name of fortune has happened here?"

"What has happened!" exclaimed John Ayliffe, "look there," and he handed Mr. Shanks the letter. The attorney took it, and with his keen weazel eyes read it as deliberately as he would have read an ordinary law paper. He then handed it back to his young client, saying, "The respondent does not put in a bad answer."

"Damn the respondent," said John Ayliffe, "but she shall smart for it."

"Well, well, this cannot be helped," rejoined Mr. Shanks; "no need of putting yourself in a passion. You don't care two straws about her, and if you get the property without the girl so much the better. You can then have the pick of all the pretty women in the country."

John Ayliffe mused gloomily; for Mr. Shanks was not altogether right in his conclusion as to the young man's feelings towards Emily. Perhaps when he began the pursuit he cared little about its success, but like other beasts of prey, he had become eager as he ran--desire had arisen in the chase--and, though mortified vanity had the greatest share in his actual feelings, he felt something beyond that.

While he mused, Mr. Shanks was musing also, calculating results and combinations; but at length he said, in a low tone, "Is she gone?--Have you got that accomplished?"

"Gone?--Yes.--Do you mean my mother?--Damn it, yes!--She is gone, to be sure.--Didn't you meet her?"

"No," said Mr. Shanks; "I came the other way. That is lucky, however. But harkee, John--something very unpleasant has happened, and we must take some steps about it directly; for if they work him well, that fellow is likely to peach."

"Who?--what the devil are you talking about?" asked John Ayliffe, with his passion still unsubdued.

"Why, that blackguard whom you would employ--Master Tom Cutter," answered Mr. Shanks. "You know I always set my face against it, John; and now--"

"Peach!" cried John Ayliffe, "Tom Cutter will no more peach than he'll fly in the air. He's not of the peaching sort."

"Perhaps not, where a few months' imprisonment are concerned," answered Mr. Shanks; "but the matter here is his neck, and that makes a mighty difference, let me tell you. Now listen to me, John, and don't interrupt me till I've done; for be sure that we have got into a very unpleasant mess, which we may have some difficulty in getting out of. You sent over Tom Cutter, to see if he could not persuade young Scantling, Lord Selby's gamekeeper, to remember something about the marriage, when he was with his old father the sexton. Now, how he and Tom manage their matters, I don't know; but Tom gave him a lick on the head with a stick, which killed him on the spot. As the devil would have it, all this was seen by two people, a laborer working in a ditch hard by, and Scantling's son, a boy of ten years old. The end of it is, Tom was instantly pursued, and apprehended; your good uncle, Sir John, was called to take the depositions, and without any remand whatever, committed our good friend for trial. Tom's only chance is to prove that it was a case of chance-medley, or to bring it under manslaughter, as a thing done in a passion, and if he thinks that being employed by you will be any defence, or will show that it was a sudden burst of rage, without premeditation, he will tell the whole story as soon as he would eat his dinner."

"I'll go over to him directly, and tell him to hold his tongue," cried John Ayliffe, now fully awakened to the perils of the case.

"Pooh, pooh! don't be a fool," said Mr. Shanks, contemptuously. "Are you going to let the man see that you are afraid of him--that he has got you in his power? Besides, they will not let you in. No, the way must be this. I must go over to him as his legal adviser, and I can dress you up as my clerk. That will please him, to find that we do not abandon him; and we must contrive to turn his defence quite another way, whether he hang for it or not. We must make it out that Scantling swore he had been poaching, when he had done nothing of the kind, and that in the quarrel that followed, he struck the blow accidentally. We can persuade him that this is his best defence, which perhaps it is after all, for nobody can prove that he was poaching, inasmuch as he really was not; whereas, if he were to show that he killed a man while attempting to suborn evidence, he would speedily find himself under a crossbeam."

"Suborn evidence," muttered John Ayliffe to himself; for though ready to do any act that might advance his purpose, he did not like to hear it called by its right name.

However that might be, he agreed to the course proposed by the attorney, and it was determined that, waiting for the fall of night, they should both go over to the prison together, and demand admittance to the felon's cell. The conversation then reverted to Emily's distinct rejection of the young man's suit, and long did the two ponder over it, considering what might be the effect upon the plans they were pursuing.

"It may hurry us desperately," said Mr. Shanks, at length, "unless we can get her to hold her tongue; for depend upon it, as soon as Sir Philip hears what we are doing, he will take his measures accordingly. Don't you think you and Mrs. Hazleton together can manage to frighten her into silence? If I were you, I would get upon my horse's back directly, ride over, and see what can be done. Your fair friend there will give you every help, depend upon it."

John Ayliffe smiled. "I will see," he said. "Mrs. Hazleton is very kind about it, and I dare say will help, for I am quite sure she has got some purpose of her own to serve."

The attorney grinned, but made no answer, and in the space of a quarter of an hour, John Ayliffe was on the road to Mrs. Hazleton's dwelling.

After quarter of an hour's private conversation with the lady of the house, he was admitted to the room in which Emily sat, unconscious of his being there. She was displeased and alarmed at seeing him, but his words and his conduct after he entered, frightened and displeased her still more. He demanded secrecy in a stern and peremptory tone, and threatened with vague, but not ill-devised menaces, to be the ruin of her father and his whole house, if she breathed one word of what had taken place between them. He sought, moreover, to obtain from her a promise of secrecy; but that Emily would on no account give, although he terrified her greatly; and he left her still in doubt as to whether his secret was safe or not.

With Mrs. Hazleton he held another conference, but from her he received better assurances. "Do not be afraid," she said; "I will manage it for you. She shall not betray you--at least for a time. However, you had better proceed as rapidly as possible, and if the means of pursuing your claim be necessary--I mean in point of money--have no scruple in applying to me."

Putting on an air of queenly dignity, Mrs. Hazleton proceeded in search of Emily, as soon as the young man was gone. She found her in tears; and sitting down by her side, she took her hand in a kindly manner, saying, "My dear child, I am very sorry for all this, but it is really in some degree your own fault. Nay, you need not explain any thing. I have just had young Ayliffe with me. He has told me all, and I have dismissed him with a sharp rebuke. If you had confided to me last night that he had proposed to you, and you had rejected him, I would have taken care that he should not have admittance to you. Indeed, I am surprised that he should presume to propose at all, without longer acquaintance. But he seems to have agitated and terrified you much. What did he want?"

"He endeavored to make me promise," replied Emily, "that I would not tell my father, or any one, of what had occurred."

"Foolish boy! he might have taken that for granted," replied Mrs. Hazleton, forgetting for an instant what she had just said. "No woman of any delicacy ever speaks of a matter of this kind, when once she has taken upon herself to reject a proposal unconditionally. If she wishes for advice," continued the lady, recollecting herself, "or thinks that the suit may be pressed improperly, of course she's free to ask counsel and assistance of some female friend, on whom she can depend. But the moment the thing is decided, of course, she is silent for ever; for nothing can be more a matter of honorable confidence than an avowal of honorable love. I will write him a note, and tell him he is in no danger, but warn him not to present himself here again, so long as you are with me."

Emily made no answer, trying to decide in her own mind whether Mrs. Hazleton's reasoning was right; and that lady, choosing to take her assent for granted, from her silence, hurried away, to give her no opportunity for retracting.

CHAPTER XXIII

Before the door of a large brick building, with no windows towards the street, and tall walls rising up till they overtopped the neighboring houses, stood two men, about an hour after night had fallen, waiting for admittance. The great large iron bar which formed the knocker of the door, had descended twice with a heavy thump, but yet no one appeared in answer to the summons. It was again in the hand of Mr. Shanks and ready to descend, when the rattling of keys was heard inside; bolts were withdrawn and bars cast down, and one half of the door opened, displaying a man with a lantern, which he held up to gaze at his visitors. His face was fat and bloated, covered with a good number of spots, and his swollen eyelids made his little keen black eyes look smaller than they even naturally were, while his nose, much in the shape of a horse-chestnut, blushed with the hues of the early morning.

"How are you, Cram, how are you?" asked the attorney. "I haven't been here for a long time, but you know me, I suppose."

"Oh, yes, I know you, Master Shanks," replied the jailer, winking one of his small black eyes; "who have you come to see? Betty Diaper, I'll warrant, who prigged the gentleman's purse at the bottom of the hill. She's as slink a diver as any on the lay; but she's got the shiners and so must have counsel to defend her before the beak, I'll bet a gallon."

"No, no," answered Mr. Shanks, "our old friend Tom Cutter wants to see me on this little affair of his."

"You'll make no hand of that, as sure a my name's Dionysius Cram," replied the jailer. "Can't prove an _alibi_ there, Master Shanks, for I saw him do the job; besides he can't pay. What's the use of meddling with him? He must swing some time you know, and one day's as good as another. But come in, Master Shanks, come in. But who's this here other chap?"

"That's my clerk," replied Mr. Shanks, "I may want him to take instructions."

The man laughed, but demurred, but a crown piece was in those days the key to all jailers' hearts, and after a show of hesitation, Shanks and his young companion were both admitted within the gates. They now found themselves in a small square space, guarded on two sides by tall iron railings, which bent overhead, and were let into the wall somewhat after the manner of a birdcage. On the left-hand side, however, was another brick wall, with a door and some steps leading up to it. By this entrance Mr. Dionysius Cram led them into a small jailer's lodge, with a table and some wooden chairs, in the side of which, opposite to the entrance, was a strong movable grate, between the bars of which might be seen a yawning sort of chasm leading into the heart of the prison.

Again Mr. Cram's great keys were put in motion, and he opened the grate to let them pass, eyeing John Ayliffe with considerable attention as he did so. Locking the grate carefully behind him, he lighted them on with his lantern, muttering as he went in the peculiar prison slang of those days, various sentences not very complimentary to the tastes and habits of young John Ayliffe. "Ay, ay," he said, "clerk be damned! One of Tom's pals, for a pint and a boiled bone--droll I don't know him. He must be twenty, and ought to have been in the stone pitcher often enough before now. Dare say he's been sent to Mill Dol, for some minor. That's not in my department. I shall have the darbies on him some day. He'd look handsome under the tree."

John Ayliffe had a strong inclination to knock him down, but he restrained himself, and at length a large plated iron door admitted the two gentlemen into the penetralia of the temple.

A powerful smell of aqua vitæ and other kinds of strong waters now pervaded the atmosphere, mingled with that close sickly odor which is felt where great numbers of uncleanly human beings are closely packed together; and from some distance was heard the sounds of riotous merriment, ribald song, and hoarse, unfeeling laugh, with curses and execrations not a few. It was a time when the abominations of the prison system were at their height.

"Here, you step in here," said Mr. Cram to the attorney and his companion, "and I'll bring Tom to you in a minute. He's having a lush with some of his pals; though I thought we were going to have a mill, for Jack Perkins, who is to be hanged o' Monday, roused out his slack jaw at him for some quarrel about a gal, and Tom don't bear such like easily. Howsumdever, they made it up and clubbed a gallon. Stay, I'll get you a candle end;" and leaving them in the dark, not much, if the truth must be told, to the satisfaction of John Ayliffe, he rolled away along the passage and remained absent several minutes.

When he returned, a clanking step followed him, as heavy irons were dragged slowly on by unaccustomed limbs, and the moment after, Tom Cutter stood in the presence of his two friends.

The jailer brought them in a piece of candle about two inches long, which he stuck into a sort of socket attached to an iron bar projecting straight from the wall; and having done this he left the three together, taking care to close and lock the door behind him.

Chair or stool in the room there was none, and the only seat, except the floor, which the place afforded was the edge of a small wooden bedstead or trough, as it might be called, scantily furnished with straw.

Both Mr. Shanks and John Ayliffe shook hands with the felon, whose face, though somewhat flushed with drinking, bore traces of deeper and sterner feelings than he chose to show. He seemed glad to see them, however, and said it was very kind of them to come, adding with an inquiring look at Mr. Shanks, "I can't pay you, you know, Master lawyer; for what between my garnish and lush, I shall have just enough to keep me till the 'sizes; I shan't need much after that I fancy."

"Pooh, pooh," cried the attorney, "don't be downhearted, Tom, and as to pay, never mind that. John here will pay all that's needful, and we'll have down counsellor Twistem to work the witnesses. We can't make out an _alibi_, for the folks saw you, but we'll get you up a character, if money can make a reputation, and I never knew the time in England when it could not. We have come to consult with you at once as to what's the best defence to be made, that we may have the story all pat and right from the beginning, and no shifting and turning afterwards."

"I wish I hadn't killed the man," said Tom Cutter, gloomily; "I shan't forget his face in a hurry as he fell over and cried out 'Oh, my poor--!' but the last word choked him. He couldn't get it out; but I fancy he was thinking of his wife--or maybe his children. But what could I do? He gave me a sight of bad names, and swore he would peach about what I wanted him to do. He called me a villain, and a scoundrel, and a cheat, and a great deal more besides, till my blood got up, and having got the stick by the small end, I hit him with the knob on the temple. I didn't know I hit so hard; but I was in a rage."

"That's just what I thought--just what I thought," said Mr. Shanks. "You struck him without premeditation in a fit of passion. Now if we can make out that he provoked you beyond bearing--"

"That he did," said Tom Cutter.

"That's what I say," continued Mr. Shanks, "if we can make out that he provoked you beyond bearing while you were doing nothing unlawful and wrong, that isn't murder, Tom."

"Hum," said Tom Cutter, "but how will you get that up, Mr. Shanks? I've a notion that what I went to him about was devilish unlawful."

"Ay, but nobody knew any thing of that but you and he, and John Ayliffe and I. We must keep that quite close, and get up a likely story about the quarrel. You will have to tell it yourself, you know, Tom, though we'll make counsellor Twistem let the jury see it beforehand in his examinations."

A gleam of hope seemed to lighten the man's face, and Mr. Shanks continued, "We can prove, I dare say, that this fellow Scantling had a great hatred for you."

"No, no, he had not," said Tom Cutter, "he was more civil to me than most, for we had been boys together."

"That doesn't matter," said Mr. Shanks, "we must prove it; for that's your only chance, Tom. If we can prove that you always spoke well of him, so much the better; but we must show that he was accustomed to abuse you, and to call you a damned ruffian and a poacher. We'll do it--we'll do it; and then if you stick tight to your story, we'll get you off."

"But what's the story to be, master Shanks?" asked Tom Cutter, "I can't learn a long one; I never was good at learning by heart."

"Oh, no; it shall be as short and simple as possible," replied Shanks; "you must admit having gone over to see him, and that you struck the blow that killed him. We can't get over that, Tom; but then you must say you're exceedingly sorry, and was so the very moment after."

"So I was," replied Tom Cutter.

"And your story must refer," continued Mr. Shanks, "to nothing but what took place just before the blow was struck. You must say that you heard he accused you of putting wires in Lord Selby's woods, and that you went over to clear yourself; but that he abused you so violently, and insulted you so grossly, your blood got up and you struck him, only intending to knock him down. Do you understand me?"

"Quite well--quite well," replied Tom Cutter, his face brightening; "I do think that may do, 'specially if you can make out that I was accustomed to speak well of him, and he to abuse me. It's an accident that might happen to any man."

"To be sure," replied Mr. Shanks; "we will take care to corroborate your story, only you get it quite right. Now let us hear what you will say."

Tom Cutter repeated the tale he had been taught very accurately; for it was just suited to his comprehension, and Shanks rubbed his hands, saying, "That will do--that will do."

John Ayliffe, however, was still not without his anxieties, and after a little hesitation as to how he should put the question which he meditated, he said, "Of course, Tom, I suppose you have not told any of the fellows here what you came over for?"

The ruffian knew him better than he thought, and understood his object at once.

"No, no, John," he said, "I have'nt peached, and shall not; be you sure of that. If I am to die, I'll die game, depend upon it; but I do think there's a chance now, and we may as well make the best of it."

"To be sure--to be sure," answered the more prudent Shanks; "you don't think, Mr. Ayliffe, that he would be fool enough to go and cut his own throat by telling any one what would be sure to hang him. That is a very green notion."

"Oh, no, nor would I say a word that could serve that Sir Philip Hastings," said Tom Cutter; "he's been my enemy for the last ten years, and I could see he would be as glad to twist my neck as I have been to twist his hares. Perhaps I may live to pay him yet."

"I'm not sure you might not give him a gentle rub in your defence," said John Ayliffe; "he would not like to hear that his pretty proud daughter Emily came down to see me, as I'm sure she did, let her say what she will, when I was ill at the cottage by the park gates. You were in the house, don't you recollect, getting a jug of beer, while I was sitting at the door when she came down?"

"I remember, I remember," replied Tom Cutter, with a malicious smile; "I gave him one rub which he didn't like when he committed me, and I'll do this too."

"Take care," said Mr. Shanks, "you had better not mix up other things with your defence."

"Oh, I can do it quite easily," replied the other with a triumphant look; "I could tell what happened then, and how I heard there that people suspected me of poaching still, though I had quite given it up, and how I determined to find out from that minute who it was accused me."

"That can do no harm," said Shanks, who had not the least objection to see Sir Philip Hastings mortified; and after about half an hour's farther conversation, having supplied Tom Cutter with a small sum of money, the lawyer and his young companion prepared to withdraw. Shanks whistled through the keyhole of the door, producing a shrill loud sound as if he were blowing over the top of a key; and Dionysius Cram understanding the signal, hastened to let them out.

Before we proceed farther, however, with any other personage, we may as well trace the fate of Mr. Thomas Cutter.

The assizes were approaching near at this time, and about a fortnight after, he was brought to trial; not all the skill of counsellor Twistem, however, nor the excellent character which Mr. Shanks tried to procure for him, had any effect; his reputation was too well established to be affected by any scandalous reports of his being a peaceable and orderly man. His violence and irregular life were too well known for the jury to come to any other conclusion than that it would be a good thing to rid the country of him, and whether very legally or not, I cannot say, they brought in a verdict of wilful murder without quitting the box. His defence, however, established for him the name of a very clever fellow, and one portion of it certainly sent Sir Philip Hastings from the Court thoughtful and gloomy. Nevertheless, no recommendation to mercy having issued from the Judge, Tom Cutter was hanged in due form of law, and to use his own words, "died game."

CHAPTER XXIV

We must go back a little, for we have somewhat anticipated our tale. Never did summons strike more joyfully on the ear of mortal than came that of her recall home to Emily Hastings. As so often happens to all in life, the expected pleasure had turned to ashes on the lip, and her visit to Mrs. Hazleton offered hardly one point on which memory could rest happily. Nay, more, without being able definitely to say why, when she questioned her own heart, the character of her beautiful hostess had suffered by close inspection. She was not the same in Emily's esteem as she had been before. She could not point out what Mrs. Hazleton had said or done to produce such an impression; but she was less amiable,--less reverenced. It was not alone that the trappings in which a young imagination had decked her were stripped off; but it was that a baser metal beneath had here and there shown doubtfully through the gilding with which she concealed her real character.

If the summons was joyful to Emily, it was a surprise and an unpleasant one to Mrs. Hazleton. Not that she wished to keep her young guest with her long; for she was too keen and shrewd not to perceive that Emily would not be worked upon so easily as she had imagined; and that under her very youthfulness there was a strength of character which must render one part of the plans against her certainly abortive. But Mrs. Hazleton was taken by surprise. She could have wished to guard against construction of some parts of her conduct which must be the more unpleasant, because the more just. She had fancied she would have time to give what gloss she chose to her conduct in Emily's eyes, and to prevent dangerous explanations between the father and the daughter. Moreover, the suddenness of the call alarmed her and raised doubts. Wherever there is something to be concealed there is something to be feared, and Mrs. Hazleton asked herself if Emily had found means to communicate to Sir Philip Hastings what had occurred with John Ayliffe.

That, however, she soon concluded was impossible. Some knowledge of the facts, nevertheless, might have reached him from other sources, and Mrs. Hazleton grew uneasy. Sir Philip's letter to his daughter, which Emily at once suffered her hostess to see, threw no light upon the subject. It was brief, unexplicit, and though perfectly kind and tender, peremptory. It merely required her to return to the Hall, as some business rendered her presence at home necessary.

Little did Mrs. Hazleton divine the business to which Sir Philip alluded. Had she known it, what might have happened who can say? There were terribly strong passions within that fair bosom, and there were moments when those strong passions mastered even strong worldly sense and habitual self-control.

There was not much time, however, for even thought, and less for preparation. Emily departed, after having received a few words of affectionate caution from Mrs. Hazleton, delicately and skilfully put, in such a manner as to produce the impression that she was speaking of subjects personally indifferent to herself--except in so much as her young friend's own happiness was concerned.

Shall we say the truth? Emily attended but little. Her thoughts were full of her father's letter, and of the joy of returning to a home where days passed peacefully in an even quiet course, very different from that in which the stream of time had flowed at Mrs. Hazleton's. The love of strong emotions--the brandy-drinking of the mind--is an acquired taste. Few, very few have it from nature. Poor Emily, she little knew how many strong emotions were preparing for her.

Gladly she saw the carriage roll onward through scenes more and more familiar at every step. Gladly she saw the forked gates appear, and marked the old well-known hawthorns as they flitted by her; and the look of joy with which she sprang into her fathers arms, might have convinced any heart that there was but one home she loved.

"Now go and dress for dinner at once, my child," said Sir Philip, "we have delayed two hours for you. Be not long."

Nor was Emily long; she could not have been more rapid had she known that Marlow was waiting eagerly for her appearance. Well pleased, indeed, was she to see him, when she entered the drawing-room; but for the first time since she had known him--from some cause or other--a momentary feeling of embarrassment--of timidity, came upon her; and the color rose slightly in her cheek. Her eyes spoke, however, more than her lips could say, and Marlow must have been satisfied, if lovers ever could be satisfied.

Lady Hastings was lying languidly on a couch, not knowing how to intimate to her daughter her disapproval of a suit yet unknown to Emily herself. She could not venture to utter openly one word in opposition; for Sir Philip Hastings had desired her not to do so, and she had given a promise to forbear, but she thought it would be perfectly consistent with that promise, and perfectly fair and right to show in other ways than by words, that Mr. Marlow was not the man she would have chosen for her daughter's husband, and even to insinuate objections which she dare not state directly.

In her manner to Marlow therefore, Lady Hastings, though perfectly courteous and polite--for such was Sir Philip's pleasure--was as cold as ice, always added "Sir" to her replies, and never forgot herself so far as to call him by his name.

Emily remarked this demeanor; but she knew--I should rather have said she was aware; for it was a matter more of sensation than thought,--a conviction that had grown up in her mind without reflection--she was aware that her mother was somewhat capricious in her friendships. She had seen it in the case of servants and of some of the governesses she had had when she was quite young. One day they would be all that was estimable and charming in Lady Hastings' eyes, and another, from some slight offence--some point of demeanor which she did not like--or some moody turn of her own mind, they would be all that was detestable. It, had often been the same, too, with persons of a higher station; and therefore it did not in the least surprise her to find that Mr. Marlow, who had been ever received by Lady Hastings before as a familiar friend, should now be treated almost as a stranger.

It grieved her, nevertheless, and she thought that Marlow must feel her mother's conduct painfully. She would fain have made up for it by any means in her power, and thus the demeanor of Lady Hastings had an effect the direct reverse of that which she intended. Nor did her innuendos produce any better results, for she soon saw that they grieved and offended her husband, while her daughter showed marvellous stupidity, as she thought, in not comprehending them.

Full of love, and now full of hope likewise, Marlow, it must be confessed, thought very little of Lady Hastings at all. He was one of those men upon whom love sits well--they are but few in the world--and whatever agitation he might feel at heart, there was none apparent in his manner. His attention to

Emily was decided, pointed, not to be mistaken by any one well acquainted with such matters; but he was quite calm and quiet about it; there was no flutter about it--no forgetfulness of proprieties; and his conversation had never seemed to Emily so agreeable as that night, although the poor girl knew not what was the additional charm. Delightful to her, however, it was; and in enjoying it she forgot altogether that she had been sent for about business--nay, even forgot to wonder what that business could be.

Thus passed the evening; and when the usual time for retiring came, Emily was a little surprised that there was no announcement of Mr. Marlow's horse, or Mr. Marlow's carriage, as had ever been the case before, but that Mr. Marlow was going to spend some days at the hall.

When Lady Hastings rose to go to rest, and her daughter rose to go with her, another thing struck Emily as strange. Sir Philip, as his wife passed him, addressed to her the single word "Beware!" with a very marked emphasis. Lady Hastings merely bowed her head, in reply; but when she and Emily arrived at her dressing-room, where the daughter had generally stayed to spend a few minutes with her mother alone, Lady Hastings kissed her, and wished her good night, declaring that she felt much fatigue, and would ring for her maid at once.

Lady Hastings was a very good woman, and wished to obey her husband's injunctions to the letter, but she felt afraid of herself, and would not trust herself with Emily alone.

Dear Emily lay awake for half an hour after she had sought her pillow, but not more, and then she fell into a sleep as soft and calm as that of childhood, and the next morning rose as blooming as the flower of June. Sir Philip was up when she went down stairs, and walking on the terrace with Marlow. Lady Hastings sent word that she would breakfast in her own room, when she had obtained a few hours' rest, as she had not slept all night. Thus Emily had to attend to the breakfast-table in her mother's place; but in those days the lady's functions at the morning meal were not so various and important as at present; and the breakfast passed lightly and pleasantly. Still there was no mention of the business which had caused Emily to be summoned so suddenly, and when the breakfast was over, Sir Philip retired to his library, without asking Emily to follow, and merely saying, "You had better not disturb your mother, my dear child. If you take a walk I will join you ere long."

For the first time, a doubt, a notion--for I must not call it a suspicion--came across the mind of Emily, that the business for which she had been sent might have something to do with Mr. Marlow. How her little heart beat! She sat quite still for a minute or two, for she did not know, if she rose, what would become of her.

At length the voice of Marlow roused her from her gently-troubled reverie, as he said. "Will you not come out to take a walk?"

She consented at once, and went away to prepare. Nor was she long, for in less than ten minutes, she and Marlow were crossing the park, towards the older and thicker trees amidst which they had rambled once before. But it was Marlow who now led her on a path which he chose himself. I know not whether it was some memory of his walk with Mrs. Hazleton, or whether it was that instinct which leads love to seek shady places, or whether, like a skilful general, he had previously reconnoitred the ground; but something or other in his own breast induced him to deviate from the more direct track which they had followed on their previous walk, and guide his fair companion across the short dry turf towards the thickest part of the wood, through which there penetrated, winding in and out amongst the trees, a small path, just wide enough for two, bowered overhead by crossing branches, and gaining sweet woodland scenes of light and shade at every step, as the eye dived into the deep green stillness between the large old trunks, carefully freed from underwood, and with their feet carpeted with moss, and flowers, and fern. It was called the deer's track, from the fact that along it, morning and evening, all the bucks and does which had herded on that side of the park might be seen walking stately down to or from a bright, clear-running trout-stream, that wandered along about a quarter of a mile farther on; and often, in the hot weather, a person standing half way down the walk might see a tall antlered fellow standing with his forefeet in the water and his hind-quarters raised upon the bank, gazing at himself in the liquid mirror below, with all his graceful beauties displayed to the uttermost by a burst of yellow light, which towards noon always poured upon the stream at that place.

Marlow and Emily, however, were quite alone upon the walk. Not even a hind or hart was there; and after the first two or three steps, Marlow asked his fair companion to take his arm. She did so, readily; for she needed it, not so much because the long gnarled roots of the trees crossed the path from time to time, and offered slight impediments, for usually her foot was light as air, but because she felt an unaccountable languor upon her, a tremulous, agitated sort of unknown happiness unlike any thing else she had ever before experienced.

Marlow drew her little hand through his arm then, and she rested upon it, not with the light touch of a mere acquaintance, but with a gentle confiding pressure which was very pleasant to him, and yet the capricious man must needs every two or three minutes, change that kindly position as the trees and irregularities of the walk afforded an excuse. Now he placed Emily on the one side, now on the other, and if she had thought at all (but by this time she was far past thought,) she might have fancied that he did so solely for the purpose of once more taking her hand in his to draw it through his arm again.

At the spot where the walk struck the stream, and before it proceeded onward by the bank, there was a little irregular open space not twenty yards broad in any direction, canopied over by the tall branches of an oak, and beneath the shade about twelve yards from the margin of the stream, was a pure, clear, shallow well of exceedingly cold water, which as it quietly flowed over the brink went on to join the rivulet below. The well was taken care of, kept clean, and basined in plain flat stones; but there was, no temple over it, Gothic or Greek. On the side farthest from the stream was a plain wooden bench placed for the convenience of persons who came to drink the waters which were supposed to have some salutary influence, and there by tacit consent Marlow and Emily seated themselves side by side.

They gazed into the clear little well at their feet, seeing all the round variegated pebbles at the bottom glistening like jewels as the branches above, moved by a fresh wind that was stirring in the sky, made the checkered light dance over the surface. There was a green leaf broken by some chance from a bough above which floated about upon the water as the air fanned it gently, now hither, now thither, now gilded by the sunshine, now covered with dim shadow. After pausing in silence for a moment or two, Marlow pointed to the leaf with a light and seemingly careless smile, saying, "See how it floats about, Emily. That leaf is like a young heart full of love."

"Indeed," said Emily, looking full in his face with a look of inquiry, for perhaps she thought that in his smile she might find an interpretation of what was going on in her own bosom. "Indeed! How so?"

"Do you not see," said Marlow, "how it is blown about by the softest breath, which stirs not the less sensitive things around, how it is carried by any passing air now into bright hopeful light, now into dim melancholy shadow?"

"And is that like love?" asked Emily. "I should have thought it was all brightness."

"Ay, happy love--love returned," replied Marlow, "but where there is uncertainty, a doubt, there hope and fear make alternately the light and shade of love, and the lightest breath will bear the heart from the one extreme to the other--I know it from the experience of the last three days, Emily; for since last we met I too have fluctuated between the light and shade. Your father's consent has given a momentary gleam of hope, but it is only you who can make the light permanent."

Emily shook, and her eyes were bent down upon the water; but she remained silent so long that Marlow became even more agitated than herself. "I know not what I feel," she murmured at length,--"it is very strange."

"But hear me, Emily," said Marlow, taking her unresisting hand, "I do not ask an immediate answer to my suit. If you regard me with any favor--if I am not perfectly indifferent to you, let me try to improve any kindly feelings in your heart towards me in the bright hope of winning you at last for my own, my wife. The uncertainty may be painful--must be painful; but--"

"No, no, Marlow," cried Emily, raising her eyes to his face for an instant with her cheek all glowing, "there must be no uncertainty. Do you think I would keep you--you, in such a painful state as you have mentioned? Heaven forbid!"

"Then what am I to think?" asked Marlow pressing closer to her side and gliding his arm round her. "I am almost mad to dream of such happiness, and yet your tone, your look, my Emily, make me so rash. Tell me then--tell me at once, am I to hope or to despair?--Will you be mine?"

"Of course," she answered, "can you doubt it?"

"I can almost doubt my senses," said Marlow; but he had no occasion to doubt them.

They sat there for nearly half an hour; they then wandered on, with marvellous meanderings in their course, for more than an hour and a half more, and when they returned, Emily knew more of love than ever could be learned from books. Marlow drew her feelings forth and gave them definite form and consistency. He presented them to her by telling what he himself felt in a plain and tangible shape, which required no long reverie--none of their deep fits of thoughtfulness to investigate and comprehend. From the rich store of his own imagination, and the treasury of deep feeling in his breast, he poured forth illustrations that brightened as if with sunshine every sensation which had been dark and mysterious in her bosom before; and ere they turned their steps back towards the house, Emily believed-- nay, she felt; and that is much more--that without knowing it, she had loved him long.

CHAPTER XXV

This must be a chapter of rapid action, comprising in its brief space the events of many months--events which might not much interest the reader in minute detail, but which produced important results to all the persons concerned, and drew on the coming catastrophe.

The news that Mr. Marlow was about to be married to Emily, the beautiful heiress of Sir Philip Hastings, spread far and wide over the country; and if joy and satisfaction reigned in the breasts of three persons in Emily's dwelling, discontent and annoyance were felt more and more strongly every hour by Lady Hastings. A Duke, she thought, would not have been too high a match for her daughter, with all the large estates she was to inherit; and the idea of her marrying a simple commoner was in itself very bitter. She was not a woman to bear a disappointment gracefully; and Emily soon had the pain of discovering that her engagement to Marlow was much disapproved by her mother. She consoled herself, however, by the full approval of her father, who was somewhat more than satisfied.

Sir Philip for his part, considering his daughter's youth, required that the marriage should be delayed at least two years, and, in his theoretical way, he soon built up a scheme, which was not quite so successful as he could have wished. Marlow's character was, in most respects, one after his own heart; but as I have shown, he had thought from the first, that there were weak points in it,--or rather points rendered weak by faults of education and much mingling with the world. He wanted, in short, some of that firmness--may I not say hardness of the old Roman, which Sir Philip so peculiarly admired; and the scheme now was, to re-educate Marlow, if I may use the term, during the next two years, to mould him in short after Sir Philip's own idea of perfection. How this succeeded, or failed, we shall have occasion hereafter to show.

Tidings of Emily's engagement were communicated to Mrs. Hazleton, first by rumor, and immediately after by more certain information in a letter from Lady Hastings. I will not dwell upon the effect produced in her. I will not lift up the curtain with which she covered her own breast, and show all the dark and terrible war of passions within. For three days Mrs. Hazleton was really ill, remained shut up in her room, had the windows darkened, admitted no one but the maid and the physician: and well for her was it, perhaps, that the bitter anguish she endured overpowered her corporeal powers, and forced seclusion upon her. During those three days she could not have concealed her feelings from all eyes had she been forced to mingle with society; but in her sickness she had time for thought--space to fight the battle in, and she came forth triumphant.

When she at length appeared in her own drawing-room no one could have imagined that the illness was of the heart. She was a little paler than before, there was a soft and pleasing languor about her carriage, but she was, to all appearance, as calm and cheerful as ever.

Nevertheless she thought it better to go to London for a short time. She did not yet dare to meet Emily Hastings. She feared _herself_.

Yet the letter of Lady Hastings was a treasure to her, for it gave her hopes of vengeance. In it the mother showed but too strongly her dislike of her daughter's choice, and Mrs. Hazleton resolved to cultivate the friendship of Lady Hastings, whom she had always despised, and to use her weakness for her own purposes.

She was destined, moreover, to have other sources of consolation, and that more rapidly than she expected. It was shortly before her return to the country that the trial of Tom Cutter took place; and not long after she came back that he was executed. Many persons at the trial had remarked the effect which some parts of the evidence had produced on Sir Philip Hastings. He was not skilful in concealing the emotions that he felt, and although it was sometimes difficult, from the peculiarities of his character, to discover what was their precise nature, they always left some trace by which it might be seen that he was greatly moved.

Information of the facts was given to Mrs. Hazleton by Shanks the attorney, and young John Ayliffe, who dwelt with pleasure upon the pain his successful artifice had inflicted; and Mrs. Hazleton was well pleased too.

But the wound was deeper than they thought. It was like that produced by the bite of a snake--insignificant in itself, but carrying poison into every vein.

Could his child deceive him? Sir Philip Hastings asked himself. Could Emily have long known this vulgar youth--gone secretly down to see him at a distant cottage--conferred with him unknown to either father or mother? It seemed monstrous to suppose such a thing; and yet what could he believe? She had never named John Ayliffe since her return from Mrs. Hazleton's; and yet it was certain from Marlow's own account, that she had seen him there. Did not that show that she was desirous of concealing the acquaintance from her parents?

Sir Philip had asked no questions, leaving her to speak if she thought fit. He was now sorry for it, and resolved to inquire; as the fact of her having seen the young man, for whom he felt an inexpressible dislike, had been openly mentioned in a court of justice. But as he rode home he began to argue on the other side of the question. The man who had made the assertion was a notorious liar--a convicted felon. Besides, he knew him to be malicious; he had twice before thrown out insinuations which Sir Philip believed to be baseless, and could only be intended to produce uneasiness. Might not these last words of his be traced to the same motive? He would inquire in the first place, he thought, what was the connection between the convict and John Ayliffe, and stopping on the way for that purpose, he, soon satisfied himself that the two were boon companions.

When he reached his own dwelling, he found Emily seated by Marlow in one of her brightest, happiest moods. There was frank candor, graceful innocence, bright open-hearted truth in every look and every word. It was impossible to doubt her; and Sir Philip cast the suspicion from him, but, alas! not for ever. They would return from time to time to grieve and perplex him; and he would often brood for hours over his daughter's character, puzzling himself more and more. Yet he would not say a word--he blamed himself for even thinking of the matter; and he would not show a suspicion. Yet he continued to think and to doubt, while poor unconscious Emily would have been ready, if asked, to solve the whole mystery in a moment. She had been silent from an unwillingness to begin a painful subject herself; and though she had yielded no assent to Mrs. Hazleton's arguments, they had made her doubt whether she ought to mention, unquestioned, John Ayliffe's proposal and conduct. She had made up her mind to tell all, if her father showed the slightest desire to know any thing regarding her late visit; but there was something in the effects which that visit had produced on her mind, which she could not explain to herself.

Why did she love Mrs. Hazleton less? Why had she lost so greatly her esteem for her? What had that lady done or said which justified so great a change of feeling towards her? Emily could not tell. She could fix upon no word, no act, she could entirely blame--but yet there had been a general tone in her whole demeanor which had opened the poor girl's eyes too much. She puzzled herself sadly with her own thoughts; and probably would have fallen into more than one of her deep self-absorbed reveries, had not sweet new feelings, Marlow's frequent presence, kept her awake to a brighter, happier world of thought.

She was indeed very happy; and, could she have seen her mother look brighter and smile upon her, she would have been perfectly so. Her father's occasional moodiness she did not heed; for he often seemed gloomy merely from intense thought. Emily had got a key to such dark reveries in her own heart, and she knew well that they were no true indications either of discontent or grief, for very often when to the eyes of others she seemed the most dull and melancholy, she was enjoying intense delight in the activity of her own mind. She judged her father from herself, and held not the slightest idea that any word, deed or thought of hers had given him the slightest uneasiness.

Notwithstanding the various contending feelings and passions which were going on in the little circle on which our eyes are fixed, the course of life had gone on with tolerable smoothness as far as Emily and Marlow were concerned, for about two months, when, one morning, Sir Philip Hastings received a letter in a hand which he did not know. It reached him at the breakfast table, and evidently affected him considerably with some sort of emotion. His daughters instantly caught the change of his countenance, but Sir Philip did not choose that any one should know he could be moved by any thing on earth, and he instantly repressed all agitation, quietly folded up the letter again, concluded his breakfast, and then retired to his own study.

Emily was not deceived, however. There were moments in Sir Philip's life when he was unable to conceal altogether the strong feelings of his heart under the veil of stoicism--or as he would have termed it--to curb and restrain them by the power of philosophy. Emily had seen such moments, and knew, that whatever were the emotions produced by that letter, whether of anger or grief or apprehension--her father was greatly moved.

In his own study, Sir Philip Hastings seated himself, spread the letter before him, and read it over attentively. But now it did not seem to affect him in the least. He was, in fact, ashamed of the feelings he had experienced and partly shown. "How completely," said he to himself, "does a false and fictitious system of society render us the mere slaves of passion, infecting even those who tutor themselves from early years to resist its influence. Here an insolent young man lays claim to my name, and my inheritance, and coolly assumes not only that he has a title to do so, but that I know it; and this instead of producing calm contempt, makes my heart beat and my blood boil, as if I were the veriest schoolboy."

The letter was all that Sir Philip stated, but it was something more. It was a very artful epistle, drawn up by the joint shrewdness of Mr. Shanks, Mr. John Ayliffe, and Mrs. Hazleton. It concisely stated the claims of the young man who signed it, to all the property of the late Sir John Hastings and to the baronetcy. It made no parade of proofs, but assumed that those in the writer's possession were indisputable, and also that Sir Philip Hastings was well aware that John Ayliffe was his elder brother's legitimate son. The annuity which had been bought for himself and his mother was broadly stated to have been the purchase-money of her silence, negotiated by her father, who had no means to carry on a suit at law. As long as his mother lived, the writer said, he had been silent out of deference to her wishes, but now that she was dead in France, he did not feel himself bound to abide by an arrangement which deprived him at once of fortune and station, and which had been entered into without his knowledge or consent. He then went on to call upon Sir Philip Hastings in the coolest terms to give up possession and acknowledge his right without what the writer called "the painful ceremony of a lawsuit;" and in two parts of the letter allusion was made to secret information which the writer had obtained by the kind confidence of a friend whom he would not name.

It was probably intended to give point to this insinuation at an after period, but if it was aimed at poor Emily, it fell harmless for the time, as no one knew better than Sir Philip that she had never been informed of any thing which could affect the case in question.

Indeed, the subject of the annuity was one which he had never mentioned to any one since the transaction had been completed many years before; and the name of John Ayliffe had never passed his lips till Marlow mentioned having seen that young man at Mrs. Hazleton's house.

When he had read the letter, and as soon as he thought he had mastered the last struggle of passion, he dipped the pen in the ink and wrote the few following words:

"Sir Philip Hastings has received the letter signed John Ayliffe Hastings. He knows no person of that name, but has heard of a young man of the name of John Ayliffe. If that person thinks he has any just claim on Sir Philip Hastings, or his estate, he had better pursue it in the legal and ordinary course, as Sir Philip Hastings begs to disclaim all private communication with him."

He addressed the letter to "Mr. John Ayliffe," and sent it to the post. This done, he rejoined Marlow and Emily, and to all appearance was more cheerful and conversable than he had been for many a previous day. Perhaps it cost him an effort to be cheerful at all, and the effort went a little beyond its mark. Emily was not altogether satisfied, but Lady Hastings, when she came down, which, as usual, was rather late in the day, remarked how gay her husband was.

Sir Philip said nothing to any one at the time regarding the contents of the letter he had received. He consulted no lawyer even, and tried to treat the subject with contemptuous forgetfulness; but his was a brooding and tenacious mind, and he often thought of the epistle, and the menaces it implied, against his own will. Nor could he or any one connected with him long remain unattentive or ignorant of the matter, for in a few weeks the first steps were taken in a suit against him, and, spreading from attorneys' offices in every direction, the news of such proceedings travelled far and wide, till the great Hastings case became the talk of the whole country round.

In the mean time, Sir Philip's reply was very speedily shown to Mrs. Hazleton, and that lady triumphed a good deal. Sir Philip was now in the same position with John Ayliffe, she thought, that she had been in some time before with Mr. Marlow; and already he began to show, in her opinion, a disposition to treat the case very differently in his own instance and in hers.

There he had strongly supported private negotiation; here he rejected it altogether; and she chose to forget that circumstances, though broadly the same, were in detail very different.

"We shall see," she said to herself, "we shall see whether, when the proofs are brought forward, he will act with that rigid sense of justice, which he assumed here."

When the first processes had been issued, however, and common rumor justified a knowledge of the transaction, without private information, Mrs. Hazleton set out at once to visit "poor dear Lady Hastings," and condole with her on the probable loss of fortune. How pleasant it is to condole with friends on such occasions. What an accession of importance we get in our own eyes, especially if the poor people we comfort have been a little bit above us in the world.

But Mrs. Hazleton had higher objects in view; she wanted no accession of importance. She was quite satisfied with her own position in society. She sought to see and prompt Lady Hastings--to sow dissension where she knew there must already be trouble; and she found Sir Philip's wife just in the fit frame of mind for her purpose. Sir Philip himself and Emily had ridden out together; and though Mrs. Hazleton would willingly have found an opportunity of giving Sir Philip a sly friendly kick, and of just reminding him of his doctrines announced in the case between herself and Mr. Marlow, she was not sorry to have Lady Hastings alone for an hour or two. They remained long in conference, and I need not detail all that passed. Lady Hastings poured forth all her grief and indignation at Emily's engagement to Mr. Marlow; and Mrs. Hazleton did nothing to diminish either. She agreed that it was a very unequal match, that Emily with her beauty and talents, and even with her mother's fortune alone, might well marry into the highest family of the land. Nay, she said, could the match be broken off, she might still take her rank among the peeresses. She did not advise, indeed, actual resistance on the part of her friend; she feared Lady Hastings' discretion; but she insinuated that a mother and a wife by unwavering and constant opposition, often obtained her own way, even in very difficult circumstances.

From that hour Mrs. Hazleton was Lady Hastings' best friend.

CHAPTER XXVI

There are seasons in the life of man, as well as in the course of the year; and well, unhappily, have many poets painted them in all their various aspects. But these seasons are subject to variations with different men, as with different years. The summer of one man is all bright and calm--a lapse of tranquil sunshine, and soft airs, and gentle dews. With another, the same season passes in the thunder-storm of passion--the tempests of war or ambition--and often, the gloomy days of autumn or of winter overshadowed the rich land, and spoiled the promised harvest.

It was an autumn-like period during the next three or four months of the family of Sir Philip Hastings. For the first time, uncertainty and doubt fell upon the family generally. There had been differences of temper and of character. There had been slight inconveniences. There had been occasional sickness and anxiety. There had been all those things which in the usual course of events diminished the sum of human happiness even to the most happy. But there had been nothing the least like uncertainty of position. There had been no wavering anxiety from day to day as to what the morrow was to bring forth. There had been none of that poison-drop in which the keenest shafts of fate are dipped, "the looking for of evil."

Now, every day brought some new intelligence, and some new expectation, and the mass was altogether unfavorable. Had the blow fallen at once--had any one been in power to say, "Sir Philip Hastings, you must resign all your paternal estates, and pay back at once the rents for nearly twenty years--you must give up the rank and station which you have hitherto held, and occupy a totally different position in society!" Sir Philip would have submitted at once, and with less discomfort than most of my readers can imagine. But it was the wearing, irritating, exciting, yet stupefying progress of a lawsuit which had a painful and distressing effect upon his mind. One day, he thought he saw the case quite clearly--could track the tricks of his adversary, and expose the insecure foundation of his claim; and then would come two or three days of doubt and discussion, and then disappointment, and a new turn where every thing had to begin again. But gradually proofs swelled up, first giving some show of justice to the pretence that John Ayliffe had some claim, then amounting to a probability in his favor, then seeming, to unlearned eyes, very powerful as to his right.

I am no lawyer, and therefore cannot pursue all the stages of the proceeding; but John Ayliffe had for his assistants unscrupulous men, whose only aims were to succeed, and to shield themselves from danger in case of detection; and their turns, and twists, and new points, were manifold.

Sir Philip Hastings was tortured. It affected his spirits and his temper. He became more gloomy--occasionally irritable, often suspicious. He learned to pore over law papers, to seek out flaws and errors, to look for any thing that might convey a double meaning, to track the tortuous and narrow paths by which that power which bears the name of Justice reaches the clear light of truth, or falls into the thorny deep of error.

All this disturbed and changed him; and these daily anxieties and discomforts affected his family too--Emily, indeed, but little, except inasmuch as she was grieved to see her father grieve. But Lady Hastings was not only pained and mortified herself--she contrived to communicate a share of all she felt to others. She became sad--somewhat sullen--and fancied all the time while she was depressing her husband's spirits, and aggravating all he felt by despondency and murmurs, instead of cheering and supporting him by making light of the threatened evils, that she was but participating sympathetically in his anxieties, and feeling a due share of his sorrows. She had no idea of the duty of cheerfulness, in a wife, and how often it may prove the very blessing that God intended in giving man a helpmate.

Sickness, it is true, had diminished somewhat the light spirits of her youth, but she had assuredly become a creature of repinings--a murmurer by habit--fit to double rather than divide any load of misfortune which fate might cast upon a husband's shoulders.

Lady Hastings strove rather to look sad, Emily Hastings to be gay and cheerful, and both did it perhaps a little too much for the mood and circumstances in which Sir Philip then was. He wondered when he came home, after an anxious day, that Lady Hastings did nothing to cheer him--that every word was gloomy and sad--that she seemed far more affected at the thought of loss of fortune and station than himself. He wondered also that Emily could be so light and playful, so joyous and seemingly unconcerned, when he was suffering such anxiety.

Poor Emily! she was forcing spirits in vain, and playing the kindliest of hypocrites--fashioning every word, and every look, to win him away from painful thought, only to be misunderstood.

But the misunderstanding was heightened and pointed by the hand of malice. The emotion which Sir Philip had displayed in the court had not been forgotten by some whom a spirit of revenge rendered keen and clear-sighted.

It seemed impossible to mingle Emily's name directly with the law proceedings which were taking place; but more than once in accidental correspondence it was insinuated that secret information, which had led to the development of John Ayliffe's claim, had been obtained from some near relation of Sir Philip Hastings, and it became generally rumored and credited in the county, that Emily had indiscreetly betrayed some secrets of her father's. Of course these rumors did not reach her ears, but they reached Sir Philip Hastings, and he thought it strange, and more strange, that Emily had never mentioned to him her several interviews with John Ayliffe, which he had by this time learned were more than one.

Some strange feelings, disguised doubtless by one of those veils which vanity or selfishness are ever ready to cast over the naked emotions of the human heart, withheld him from speaking to his child on the subject which caused him so much pain. Doubtless it was pride--for pride of a peculiar kind was at the bottom of many of his actions. He would not condescend to inquire, he thought, into that which she did not choose to explain herself, and he went on in reality barring the way against confidence, when, in truth, nothing would have given Emily more relief than to open her whole heart to her father.

With Marlow, Sir Philip Hastings was more free and communicative than with any one else. The young man's clear perceptions, and rapid comprehensions on any point in the course of the proceedings going on, his zeal, his anxiety, his thoughtfulness, and his keen sense of what is just and equitable, raised him every day higher in the opinion of Sir Philip Hastings, and he would consult with him for hours, talk the whole matter over in all its bearings, and leave him to solve various questions of conscience in which he found it difficult himself to come to a decision. Only on one point Sir Philip Hastings never spoke to him; and that was Emily's conduct with regard to young Ayliffe. That, the father could not do; and yet, more than once, he longed to do it.

One day, however, towards the end of six months after the first processes had been issued, Sir Philip Hastings, in one of his morning consultations with Marlow, recapitulated succinctly all the proofs which young John Ayliffe had brought forward to establish a valid marriage between his mother and the elder brother of the baronet.

"The case is very nearly complete," said Sir Philip. "But two or three links in the chain of evidence are wanting, and as soon as I become myself convinced that this young man is, beyond all reasonable doubt, the legitimate son of my brother John, my course will be soon taken. It behooves us in the first instance, Marlow, to consider how this may affect you. You have sought the hand of a rich man's daughter, and now I shall be a poor man; for although considerable sums have accumulated since my father's death, they will not more than suffice to pay off the sums due to this young man if his claim be established, and the expenses of this suit must be saved by hard economy. The property of Lady Hastings will still descend to our child, but neither she nor I have the power to alienate even a part of it for our daughter's dowry. It is right, therefore, Marlow, that you should be set free from all engagements."

"When I first asked your daughter's hand, Sir Philip," replied Marlow, "I heartily wished that our fortunes were more equal. Fate has granted that wish, apparently, in making them so; and believe me, I rejoice rather than regret that it is so, as far as I myself am concerned. We shall have enough for comfort, Sir Philip, and not too much for happiness. What need we more? But I cannot help thinking," he continued, "that this suit may turn out differently from that which you expect. I believe that the mind has its instincts, which, though dangerous to trust to, guide us nevertheless, sometimes, more surely than reason. There is an impression on my mind, which all the evidence hitherto brought forward has been unable to shake, that this claim of John Ayliffe is utterly without foundation--that it is, in fact, a trumped up case, supported by proofs which will fall to pieces under close examination."

Sir Philip Hastings shook his head. "But one thing more," he said, "and I am myself convinced. I will not struggle against conviction, Marlow; but the moment I feel morally sure that I am defending a bad cause, that instant I will yield, be the sacrifice what it may. Nothing on earth," he continued, in a stern abstracted tone, "shall ever prevent my doing that which I believe right, and which justice and honor require me to do. Life itself and all that makes life dear were but a poor sacrifice in the eyes of an honest man; what then a few thousand acres, and an empty designation?"

"But, my dear Sir Philip," replied Marlow, "let us suppose for one moment that this claim is a fictitious one, and that it is supported by fraud and forgery, you will allow that more than a few months are required to investigate all the particulars thoroughly, and to detect the knavery which may have been committed?"

"My dear Marlow," replied Sir Philip, "conviction comes to each mind accordingly as it is naturally constituted or habitually regulated. I trust I have studied the nature of evidence well--well enough to be satisfied with much less than mere law will require. In regard to all questions which come under the decision of the law, there are, in fact, two juries who decide upon the merits of the evidence--one, selected from our fellow men--the other in the bosom of the parties before which each man shall scrupulously try the justice of his own cause, and if the verdict be against him, should look upon himself but as an officer to carry the verdict into execution. I will never act against conviction. I will always act with it. My mind will try the cause itself; and the moment its decision is pronounced, that instant I will act upon it."

Marlow knew that it was in vain to argue farther, and could only trust that something would occur speedily to restore Sir Philip's confidence in his own rights.

Sir Philip, however, was now absent very frequently from home. The unpleasant business in which he was engaged, called him continually to the county town, and many a long and happy hour might Marlow and Emily have passed together had not Lady Hastings at this time assumed a somewhat new character--apparently so only--for it was, in fact, merely a phase of the old one. She became--as far as health and indolence would admit--the most prudent and careful mother in the world. She insinuated that it was highly improper for Emily to walk or ride alone with her acknowledged lover, and broadly asserted that their previous rambles had been permitted without her knowledge, and from inadvertence. During all Marlow's afternoon visits, she took especial care to sit with them the whole time, and thus she sought to deprive them of all means of free and unconstrained communication. Such would have been the result, too, indeed, had it not been for a few morning hours snatched now and then; partly from a habit of indulgence, and partly from very delicate health, Lady Hastings was rarely, if ever, down to breakfast, and generally remained in her drawing-room till the hour of noon was past.

The hours of Sir Philip's absence were generally tedious enough to himself. Sometimes a day of weary and laborious business occupied the time; but that was a relief rather than otherwise. In general the day was spent in a visit to the office of his lawyer, in finding the information he wanted, or the case he had desired to be prepared, not ready for him, in waiting for it hour after hour, in tedious gloomy meditation, and very often riding home without it, reflecting on the evils of a dilatory system which often, by the refusal of speedy justice, renders ultimate justice unavailable for any thing but the assertion of an abstract principle. He got tired of this mode of proceeding: he felt that it irritated and disordered him, and after a while, whenever he found that he should be detained in suspense, he mounted his horse again, and rode away to amuse his mind with other things.

The house of Mrs. Hazleton being so near, he more than once paid her a visit during such intervals. His coming frequently was not altogether convenient to her; for John Ayliffe was not an unfrequent visitor at her house, and Mrs. Hazleton had to give the young men a hint to let her see him early in the morning or late in the evening. Nevertheless, Mrs. Hazleton was not at all displeased to cultivate the friendship of Sir Philip Hastings. She had her objects, her purposes, to serve, and with her when she put on her most friendly looks towards the baronet she was not moved merely by that every-day instinctive hypocrisy which leads man to cover the passions he is conscious of, with a veil of the most opposite appearances, but it was a definite hypocrisy, with objects distinctly seen by herself, and full of purpose.

Thus, and for these reasons, she received Sir Philip Hastings on all occasions with the highest distinction--assumed, with a certain chameleon quality which some persons have, the color and tone of his mind to a considerable degree, while yet the general features of her own character were preserved sufficiently to shield her from the charge of affectation. She was easy, graceful, dignified as ever, with a certain languid air, and serious quietness which was very engaging. She never referred in her conversations with Sir Philip to the suit that was going on against him, and when he spoke of it himself, though she assumed considerable interest, and seemed to have a personal feeling in the matter, exclaiming, "If this goes on, nobody's estates will be secure soon!" she soon suffered the subject to drop, and did not recur to it again.

One day after the conversation between Sir Philip and Marlow, part of which has been already detailed, Sir Philip turned his horse's head towards Mrs. Hazleton's at a somewhat earlier hour than usual. It was just half past ten when he dismounted at the door, but he knew her matutinal habits and did not expect to find her occupied. The servant, however, instead of showing him into the small room where she usually sat, took him to the great drawing-room, and as he went, Sir Philip heard the voices of Mrs. Hazleton and another person in quick and apparently eager conversation. There was nothing extraordinary in this, however, and he turned to the window and gazed out into the park. He heard the servant go into the morning room, and then immediately all sound of voices ceased. Shortly after, a horse's feet, beating the ground rapidly, caught the baronet's ear, but the rider must have mounted in the courtyard and taken the back way out of the park; for he came not within Sir Philip's sight. A moment or two after, Mrs. Hazleton appeared, and there was an air of eagerness and excitement about her which was not at all usual. She seated Sir Philip beside her, however, with one of her blandest looks, and then laying her hand on his, said, in a kind and sisterly tone, "Do tell me, Sir Philip--I am not apt to be curious, or meddle with other people's affairs; but in this I am deeply interested. A rumor has just reached me from Hartwell, that you have signified your intention of abandoning your defence against this ridiculous claim upon your property. Do tell me if this is true?"

"Partly, and partly false," replied Sir Philip, "as all rumors are. Who gave you this information?"

"Oh, some of the people from Hartwell," she replied, "who came over upon business."

"The tidings must have spread fast," replied Sir Philip; "I announced to my own legal advisers this morning, and told them to announce to the opposite party, that if they could satisfy me upon one particular point, I would not protract the suit, putting them to loss and inconvenience and myself also."

"A noble and generous proceeding, indeed," said Mrs. Hazleton with an enthusiastic burst of admiration. "Ah, dear Emily, I can see your mediation in this."

Sir Philip started as if a knife had been plunged into him, and with a profound internal satisfaction, Mrs. Hazleton saw the emotion she had produced.

"May I ask," he said, in a dry cold tone, after he had recovered himself a little, "May I ask what my daughter can have to do with this affair?"

"Oh, really--in truth I don't know," said Mrs. Hazleton, stammering and hesitating, "I only thought--but I dare say it is all nonsense. Women are always the peacemakers, you know, Sir Philip, and as Emily knew both parties well, it seemed natural she should mediate between them."

"Well?--" said Sir Philip Hastings to himself, slowly and thoughtfully, but he only replied to Mrs. Hazleton, "No, my dear Madam, Emily has had nothing to do with this. It has never formed a subject of conversation between us, and I trust that she has sufficient respect for me, and for herself, not to interfere unasked in my affairs."

The serpent had done its work; the venom was busy in the veins of Sir Philip Hastings, corrupting the purest sources of the heart's feelings, and Mrs. Hazleton saw it and triumphed.

CHAPTER XXVII

Emily was as gay as a lark. The light of love and happiness was in her eyes, the hue of health was upon her cheek, and a new spirit of hope and joy seemed to pervade all her fair form. So Sir Philip Hastings found her on the terrace with Marlow when he returned from Hartwell. She was dressed in a riding habit, and one word would have explained all the gaiety of her mood. Lady Hastings, never very consequent in her actions, had wished for some one of those things which ladies wish for, and which ladies only can choose. She had felt too unwell to go for it herself; and although she had not a fortnight before expressed her strong disapprobation of her daughter and Mr. Marlow even walking out alone in the park, she had now sent them on horseback to procure what she wanted. They had enjoyed one of those glorious rides over the downs, which seem to pour into the heart fresh feelings of delight at every step, flooding the sense with images of beauty, and making the blood dance freely in the veins. It seemed also, both to her and Marlow, that a part of the prohibition was removed, and though they might not perhaps be permitted to walk out together, Lady Hastings could hardly for the future forbid them to ride. Thus they had come back very well pleased, with light hearts within, and gay hopes fluttering round them.

Sir Philip Hastings, on the other hand, had passed a day of bitterness, and hard, painful thought. On his first visit to the county town, he had, as I have shown, been obliged once more to put off decision. Then came his conference with Mrs. Hazleton. Then he had returned to his lawyer's office, and found that the wanting evidence had been supplied by his opponents. All that he had demanded was there; and no apparent flaw in the case of his adversary. He had always announced his attention of withdrawing opposition if such proofs were afforded, and he did so now, with stern, rigid, and somewhat hasty determination--but not without bitterness and regret. His ride home, too, was troubled with dull and grievous thoughts, and his whole mind was out of tune, and unfit to harmonize with gaiety of any kind. He forgot that poor Emily could not see what had been passing in his bosom, could not know all that had occurred to disturb and annoy him, and her light and cheerful spirits seemed an offence to him.

Sir Philip passed on, after he had spoken a few words to Marlow, and sought Lady Hastings in the room below, where she usually sat after she came down. Sir Philip, as I have shown, had not been nurtured in a tender school, and he was not very apt by gentle preparation to soothe the communication of any bad tidings. Without any circumlocution, then, or prefatory remarks of any kind, he addressed his wife in the following words: "This matter is decided, my dear Rachel. I am no longer Sir Philip Hastings, and it is necessary that we should remove from this house within a month, to your old home--the Court. It will be necessary, moreover, that we should look with some degree of accuracy into the state of our future income, and our expenditure. With your property, and the estate which I inherit from my mother, which being settled on the younger children, no one can take from me, we shall still have more than enough for happiness, but the style of our living must be altered. We shall have plenty of time to think of that, however, and to do what we have to do methodically."

Lady Hastings, or as we should rather call her now, Mistress Hastings, seemed at first hardly to comprehend her husband's meaning, and she replied, "You do not mean to say, Philip, that this horrible cause is decided?"

"As far as I am concerned, entirely," replied Sir Philip Hastings. "I shall offer no farther defence."

Lady Hastings fell into a fit of hysterics, and her husband knowing that it was useless to argue with her in such circumstances, called her maid, and left her.

There was but a dull dinner-party at the Hall that day. Sir Philip was gloomy and reserved, and the news which had spread over the house, as to the great loss of property which he had sustained, soon robbed his daughter of her cheerfulness.

Marlow, too, was very grave; for he thought his friend had acted, not only hastily, but imprudently. Lady Hastings did not come down to dinner, and as soon as the meal was over Emily retired to her mother's dressing-room, leaving Marlow and her father with their wine. Sir Philip avoided the subject of his late loss, however, and when Marlow himself alluded to it, replied very briefly.

"It is done," he said, "and I will cast the matter entirely from my mind, Marlow. I will endeavor, as far as possible, to do in all circumstances what is right, whatever be the anguish it costs me. Having done what is right, my next effort shall be to crush every thing like regret or repining. There is only one thing in life which could give me any permanent pain, and that would be to have an unworthy child."

Marlow did not seem to remark the peculiar tone in which the last words were uttered, and he replied, "There, at least, you are most happy, Sir Philip; for surely Emily is a blessing which may well compensate for any misfortunes."

"I trust so--I think so," said Sir Philip, in a dry and hasty manner, and then changing the subject, he added, "Call me merely Philip Hastings, my good friend. I say with Lord Verulam, 'The Chancellor is gone.' I mean I am no longer a baronet. That will not distress me, however, and as to the loss of fortune, I can bear it with the most perfect indifference."

Mr. Hastings reckoned in some degree without his host, however. He knew not all the petty annoyances that were in store for him. The costs he had to pay, the back-rents which were claimed, the long and complicated accounts that were to be passed, the eager struggle which was made to deprive him of many things undoubtedly his own; all were matters of almost daily trouble and irritation during the next six months. He had greatly miscalculated the whole amount of expenses. Having lived always considerably within his income, he had imagined that he had quite a sufficient amount in ready money to pay all the demands that could be made upon him. But such was far from being the case. Before all the debts were paid, and the accounts closed, he was obliged to raise money upon his life-interest in his mother's property, and to remain dependent, as it were, upon his wife's income for his whole means. These daily annoyances had a much greater effect upon Mr. Hastings than any great and serious misfortune could have had. He became morose, impatient, gloomy. His mind brooded over all that had occurred, and all that was occurring. He took perverted views of many things, and adhered to them with an obstinacy that nothing could shake.

In the mean time all the neighbors and friends of the family endeavored to show their sympathy and kindness by every means in their power. Even before the family quitted the Hall, the visitors were more numerous than they had ever been before, and this was some consolation to Mistress Hastings, though quite the contrary to her husband, who did not indeed appear very frequently amongst the guests, but remained in his own study as much as possible.

It was a very painful day for every one, and for Emily especially, when they passed the door of the old Hall for the last time, and took their way through the park towards the Court. The furniture in great part, the books, the plate, had gone before; the rooms looked vacant and desolate, and as Emily passed through them one by one, ere she went down to the carriage, there was certainly nothing very attractive in their aspect. But there were spots there associated with many dear memories--feelings--fancies--thoughts--all the bright things of early, happy youth; and it was very bitter for her to leave them all, and know that she was never to visit them again.

She might, and probably would, have fallen into one of her deep reveries, but she struggled against it, knowing that both her father and her mother would require comfort and consolation in the coming hours. She exerted herself, then, steadily and courageously to bear up without a show of grief, and she succeeded even too well to satisfy her father. He thought her somewhat light and frivolous, and judged it very strange that his daughter could quit her birth-place, and her early home, without, apparently, one regretful sigh. He himself sat stern, and gloomy, and silent, in the carriage, as it rolled away. Mistress Hastings leaned back, with her handkerchief over her eyes, weeping bitterly. Emily alone was calmly cheerful, and she maintained this demeanor all the way along till they reached the Court, and separated till dinner-time. Then, however, she wept bitterly and long.

Before she had descended to meet her parents at dinner, she did her best to efface all traces of her sad employment for the last hour. She did not succeed completely, and when she entered the drawing-room, and spoke cheerfully to her father, he raised his eyes to her face, and detected, at once, the marks of recent tears on her swollen eyelids.

"She has been weeping," said Mr. Hastings to himself; "can I have been mistaken?"

A gleam of the truth shot through his mind, and comforted him much, but alas, it was soon to be lost again.

From feelings of delicacy, Marlow had absented himself that day, but on the following morning he was there early, and thenceforward was a daily visitor at the Court. He applied himself particularly to cheer Emily's father, and often spent many hours with him, withdrawing Mr. Hastings' mind from all that was painful in his own situation, by leading it into those discussions of abstract propositions of which he was so fond. But Marlow was not the only frequent visitor at the Court. Mrs. Hazleton was there two or three times in the week, and was all kindness, gentleness, and sympathy. She had tutored herself well, and she met Mr. Marlow as Emily's affianced husband, with an ease and indifference which was marvellously well assumed. To Mrs. Hastings she proved the greatest comfort, although it is not be asserted that the counsels which she gave her, proved at all comfortable to the rest of the household, and yet Mrs. Hazleton never committed herself. Mrs. Hastings could not have repeated one word that she said, that any one on earth could have found fault with. She had a mode of insinuating advice without speaking it--of eking out her words by looks and gestures full of significance to the person who beheld them, but perfectly indescribable to others.

She was not satisfied, however, with being merely the friend and confidante of Mrs. Hastings. She must win Emily's father also, and she succeeded so well that Mr. Hastings quite forgot all doubts and suspicions, and causes of offence, and learned to look upon Mrs. Hazleton as a really kind and amiable person, and as consistent as could be expected of any woman.

Not one word, however, did Mrs. Hazleton say in the hearing of Emily's father which could tend in any degree to depreciate the character of Mr. Marlow, or be construed into a disapproval of the proposed marriage. She was a great deal too wise for that, knowing the character of Mr. Hastings sufficiently to see that she could effect no object, and only injure herself by such a course.

To Emily she was all that was kind and delightful. She was completely the Mrs. Hazleton of former days; but with the young girl she was less successful than with her parents. Emily could never forget the visit to her house, and what had there occurred, and the feelings which she entertained towards Mrs. Hazleton were always those of doubt. Her character was a riddle to Emily, as well it might be. There was nothing upon which she could definitely fix as an indication of a bad heart, or of duplicity of nature, and yet she doubted; nor did Marlow at all assist in clearing her mind; for although they often spoke of Mrs. Hazleton, and Marlow admitted all her bright and shining qualities, yet he became very taciturn when Emily entered more deeply into that lady's character. Marlow likewise had his doubts, and to say sooth, he was not at all well pleased to see Mrs. Hazleton so frequently with Mrs. Hastings. He did not well know what it was he feared, but yet there was a something which instinctively told him that his interests in Emily's family would not find the most favorable advocate in Mrs. Hazleton.

Such was the state of things when one evening there was assembled at the house of Mr. Hastings, a small dinner party--the first which had been given since his loss of property. The summer had returned, the weather was beautiful, the guests were cheerful and intellectual, and the dinner passed off happily enough. There were several gentlemen and several ladies present, and amongst the latter was Mrs. Hazleton. Politics at that time ran high: the people were not satisfied altogether with the King whom they had themselves chosen, and several acts of intolerance had proved that promises made before the attainment of power are not always very strictly maintained when power has been reached. Mr. Hastings had never meddled in the strife of party. He had a thorough contempt for policy and politicians, but he did not at all object to argue upon the general principles of government, in an abstract manner, and very frequently startled his hearers by opinions, not only unconstitutional, and wide and far from any of the received notions of the day, but sometimes also, very violent, and sometimes, at first sight, irreconcilable with each other. On the present occasion the conversation after dinner took a political turn, and straying away from their wine, the gentlemen walked out into the gardens, which were still beautifully kept up, and prolonged their discussion in the open air. The ladies too--as all pictures show they were fond of doing in those days--were walking amongst the flowers, not in groups, but scattered here and there. Marlow was naturally making his way to the side of Emily, who was tying up a shrub at no great distance from the door, but Mrs. Hazleton unkindly called him to her, to tell her the name of a flower which she did not know. In the mean time Mr. Hastings took his daughter by the arm, leaning gently upon her, and walking up and down the terrace, while he continued his discussion with a Northumberland gentleman known in history as Sir John Fenwick. "The case seems to be this," said Mr. Hastings, in reply to some question or the other; "all must depend upon the necessity. Violent means are bad as a remedy for any thing but violent evils, but the greatness of the evil will often justify any degree of vigor in the means. Will any one tell me that Brutus was not justified in stabbing Cæsar? Will any one tell me that William Tell was not justified in all that he did against the tyrant of his country? I will not pretend to justify the English regicides, not only because they condemned a man by a process unknown to our laws, and repugnant to all justice, but because they committed an act for which there was no absolute necessity. Where an absolute necessity is shown, indeed--where no other means can be found of obtaining freedom, justice and security, I see no reason why a King should not be put to death as well as any other man. Nay more, he who does the deed with a full appreciation of its importance, a conscience clear of any private motives, and a reasoning sense of all the bearings of the act he commits, merits a monument rather than a gibbet, though in these days he is sure to obtain the one and not the other."

"Hush, hush, do not speak so loud, my dear sir," said Sir John Fenwick; "less than those words brought Sidney's head to the block."

"I am not afraid of mine," replied Mr. Hastings, with a faint smile; "mine are mere abstract notions with regard to such things; very little dangerous to any crowned heads, and if they thought fit to put down such opinions, they would have to burn more than one half of all the books we have derived from Rome."

Sir John Fenwick would not pursue the subject, however, and turned the conversation in another course. He thought indeed that it had gone far enough, especially when a young lady was present; for he was one of those men who have no confidence in any woman's discretion, and he knew well, though he did not profit much by his knowledge, that things very slight, when taken abstractedly, may become very dangerous if forced into connection with events. Philip Hastings would have said what he did say, before any ears in Europe, without the slightest fear, but as it proved, he had said too much for his own safety. No one indeed seemed to have noticed the very strong opinions he had expressed except Sir John Fenwick himself, and shortly after the party gathered together again, and the conversation became general and not very interesting.

CHAPTER XXVIII

Men have lived and died in the pursuit of two objects the least worthy, on which the high mind of man could ever fix, out of all the vain illusions that lead us forward through existence from youth to old age: the philosopher's stone, and the elixir of life. Gold, gold, sordid gold--not competence--not independence, but wealth--profuse, inexhaustible wealth--the hard food of Crœsus; strange that it should ever form the one great object of an immortal spirit! But stranger still, that a being born to higher destinies should seek to pin itself down to this dull earth forever--to dwell in a clay hut, when a palace gates are open--to linger in a prison, when freedom may be had--to outlive affections, friendships, hope and happiness--to remain desolate in a garden where every flower has withered. To seek the philosopher's stone--even could it have been found--was a madness: but to desire the elixir of life was a worse insanity.

There was once, however, in the world's history a search--an eager search, for that which at first sight may seem nearly the same as the great elixir; but which was in reality very, very different.

We are told by the historians of America, that a tradition prevailed amongst the Indians of Puerto Rico, that in one of the islands on the coast, there was a fountain which possessed the marvellous power of restoring, to any one who bathed in its waters, all the vigor and freshness of youth, and that some of the Spanish adventurers sought it anxiously, but sought in vain. Here indeed was an object worthy of desire--here, what the heart might well yearn for, and mourn to find impossible.

Oh, that fountain of youth, what might it not give back! The easy pliancy of limb: the light activity of body: the calm, sweet sleep: the power of enjoyment and acquisition: the freshness of the heart: the brightness of the fancy: the brilliant dreams: the glorious aspirations: the beauty and the gentleness: the innocence: the love. We, who stand upon the shoal of memory, and look back in our faint dreams, to the brighter land left far behind, may well long for that sweet fountain which could renew--not life--but youth.

Oh youth--youth! Give me but one year of youth again. And it shall come. I see it there, beyond the skies, that fountain of youth, in the land where all flowers are immortal.

It is very strange, however, that with some men, when youth is gone, its very memories die also. They can so little recollect the feelings of that brighter time, that they cannot comprehend them in others: that they become a mystery--a tale written in a tongue they have forgotten.

It was so with Philip Hastings, and so also with his wife. Neither seemed to comprehend the feelings of Marlow and Emily; but her father understood them least. He had consented to their union: he approved of her choice; but yet it seemed strange and unpleasant to him, that her thoughts should be so completely given to her lover. He could hardly believe that the intense affection she felt for another, was compatible with love towards her parent. He knew not, or seemed to have forgotten that the ordinance to leave all and cleave unto her husband, is written in woman's heart as plainly as in the Book.

Nevertheless, that which he felt was not the least like jealousy--although I have seen such a thing even in a parent towards a child. It was a part of the problem of Emily's character, which he was always trying to solve without success.

"Here," he thought, "she has known this young man, but a short time-- no years--not very many months; and yet, it is clear, that in that short space, she has learned to love him better than those to whom she is bound by every tie of long enduring affection and tenderness."

Had he thought of comparing at all, her conduct and feelings with those of his own youth, he would still have marvelled; for he would have said, "I had no tenderness shown me in my young days--I was not the companion, the friend, the idol, the peculiar loved one of father or mother, so long as my elder brother lived. I loved her who first really loved me. From _my parents_, I had met small affection, and but little kindness. It was therefore natural that I should fix my love elsewhere, as they had fixed theirs. But with my child, the case is very different."

Yet he loved Marlow well--was fond of his society--was well pleased that he was to be his daughter's husband; but even in his case, Mr. Hastings was surprised in a certain degree; for Marlow did not, and could not conceal that he loved Emily's society better than her father's--that he would rather a great deal be with her than with Brutus himself or Cato.

This desire on the part of Marlow to be ever by her side, was a great stumbling-block in the way of Mr. Hastings' schemes for re-educating Marlow, and giving that strength and vigor to his character of which his future father-in-law had thought it susceptible. He made very little progress, and perhaps Marlow's society might even have had some influence upon him--might have softened--mitigated his character; but that there were counteracting influences continually at work.

All that had lately happened--the loss of fortune and of station--the dark and irritating suspicions which had been instilled into his mind in regard to his child's conduct--the doubts which had been produced of her frankness and candor--the fact before his eyes, that she loved another better, far better, than himself, with a kind word, now and then, from Mrs. Hazleton, spoken to drive the dart deeper into his heart, had rendered him somewhat morose and gloomy,--apt to take a bad view of other people's actions, and to judge less fairly than he always wished to judge. When Marlow hastened away from him to rejoin Emily, and paint, with her, in all the brightest colors of imagination, a picture of the glowing future, her father would walk solitary and thoughtful, giving himself up to dark and unprofitable reveries.

Mrs. Hastings in the mean time would take counsel with Mrs. Hazleton, and they would settle between them that the father was already dissatisfied with the engagement he had aided to bring about, and that a little persevering opposition on the part of the mother, would ultimately bring that engagement to an end.

Mrs. Hastings, too, thought--or rather seemed to feel, for she did not reduce it to thought--that she had now a greater right to exercise some authority in regard to her daughter's marriage, as Emily's whole fortune must proceed from her own property. She ventured to oppose more boldly, and to express her opinion against the marriage, both to her husband and her child. It was against the advice of Mrs. Hazleton that she did so; for that lady knew Mr. Hastings far better than his own wife knew him; and while Emily's cheek burned, and her eye swam in tears, Mr. Hastings replied in so stern and bitter a tone that Mrs. Hastings shrunk back alarmed at what she herself had done.

But the word had been spoken: the truth revealed. Both Mr. Hastings and Emily were thenceforth aware that she wished the engagement between her daughter and Marlow broken off--she was opposed to the marriage; and would oppose it.

The effect of this revelation of her views upon her child and her husband, was very different. Emily had colored with surprise and grief--not, as her father thought, with anger; and she resolved thenceforth to endeavor to soften her mother's feelings towards him she loved, and to win her consent to that upon which all her own happiness depended; but in which her own happiness could not be complete without a mother's approbation.

Mr. Hastings, on the contrary, entertained no expectation that his wife would ever change her views, even if she changed her course. Some knowledge--some comprehension of her character had been forced upon him during the many years of their union; and he believed that, if all open remonstrance, and declared opposition had been crushed by his sharp and resolute answer, there would nevertheless be continual or ever recurring efforts on Mrs. Hastings' part, to have her own way, and thwart both his purposes and Emily's affection. He prepared to encounter that sort of irritating guerrilla warfare of last words, and sneers, and innuendoes, by which a wife sometimes endeavors to overcome a husband's resolutions; and he hardened himself to resist. He knew that she could not conquer in the strife; but he determined to put an end to the warfare, either by some decided expression of his anger at such proceedings, or by uniting Emily to Marlow, much sooner than he had at first proposed.

The latter seemed the easiest method, and there was a great chance of the marriage, which it had been agreed should be delayed till Emily was nineteen, taking place much earlier, when events occurred which produced even a longer delay.

One of the first steps taken by Mr. Hastings to show his wife that her unreasonable opposition would have no effect upon him, was not only to remove the prohibition of those lovers' rambles which Mrs. Hastings had forbidden, but to send his daughter and her promised husband forth together on any pretext that presented itself. He took the opportunity of doing so, first, when his wife was present, and on the impulse of the moment, she ventured to object. One look--one word from her husband, however, silenced her; for they were a look and word too stern to be trifled with, and Emily went to dress for her walk; but she went with the tears in her eyes. She was grieved to find that all that appertained to her happiness was likely to become a cause of dissension between her father and her mother. Had Marlow not been concerned--had his happiness not been also at stake--she would have sacrificed any thing--every thing--to avoid such a result; but she felt she had no right to yield to caprice, where he was to suffer as well as herself.

The walk took place, and it might have been very sweet to both, had not the scene which had immediately preceded poured a drop of bitterness into their little cup of joy. Such walks were often renewed during the month that followed; but Emily was not so happy as she might have been; for she saw that her father assumed a sterner, colder tone towards his wife, and believed that she might be the unwilling cause of this painful alienation. She knew not that it proceeded partly from another source--that Mr. Hastings had discovered, or divined, that his wife had some feeling of increased power and authority from the fact of his having lost his large estates, and of her property being all that remained to them both.

Poor Emily! Marlow's love, that dream of joy, seemed destined to produce, for a time at least, nothing but grief and anxiety. Her reveries became more frequent, and more deep, and though her lover could call her from them in a moment, no one else had the power.

One day, Marlow and his Emily--for whom every day his love increased; for he knew and comprehended her perfectly, and he was the only one--had enjoyed a more happy and peaceful ramble than usual, through green lanes, and up the hill, and amidst the bright scenery which lay on the confines of the two counties, and they returned slowly towards the house, not anticipating much comfort there. As they approached, they saw from the road a carriage standing before the door, dusty, as if from a long journey, but with the horses still attached. There were three men, too, with the carriage, besides the driver, and they were walking their horses up and down the terrace, as if their stay was to be but short. It was an unusual number of attendants, even in those days, to accompany a carriage in the country, except upon some visit of great ceremony; and the vehicle itself--a large, old, rumbling coach, which had seen better days--gave no indication of any great state or dignity on the part of its owner.

Why, she knew not, but a feeling of fear, or at least anxiety, came over Emily as she gazed, and turning to Marlow, she said, "Who can these visitors be?"

"I know not, indeed, dear love," he answered, "but the equipage is somewhat strange. Were we in France," he added, with a laugh, "I should think it belonged to an exempt, bearing a _lettre de cachet_."

Emily smiled also, for the idea of her, father having incurred the anger of any government or violated any law seemed to her quite out of the question.

When they approached the door, however, they were met by a servant, with a grave and anxious countenance, who told her that her father wished to see her immediately in the dining hall.

"Is there any one with him?" asked Emily, in some surprise.

"Yes, Mistress Emily," replied the man, "there is a strange gentleman with him. But you had better go in at once; for I am afraid things are not going well."

Marlow drew her arm through his, and pressed it gently to make her feel support; and then went into the eating-room, as it was usually called, by her side.

When they entered they found the scene a strange and painful one. Mr. Hastings was seated near a window, with his hat on, and his cloak cast down on a chair beside him. His wife was placed near him, weeping bitterly; and at the large table in the middle of the room was a coarse-looking man, in the garb of a gentleman, but with no other indication but that of dress of belonging to a superior class. He was very corpulent, and his face, though shadowed by an enormous wig, was large and bloated. There was food and wine before him, and to both he seemed to be doing ample justice, without taking any notice of the master of the house or his weeping lady.

Mr. Hastings, however, rose and advanced towards his daughter, as soon as she entered, and in an instant the eye of the gormandizing guest was raised from his plate and turned towards the party, with a look of eager suspicion.

"Oh, my dear father, what is this?" exclaimed Emily, running towards him.

"One of those accidents of life, my child," replied Mr. Hastings, "from which I had hoped to be exempt--most foolishly. But it seems," he continued, "no conduct, however reserved, can shield one from the unjust suspicions of princes and governments."

"Very good cause for suspicion, sir," said the man at the table, quaffing a large glass of wine. "Mr. Secretary would not have signed a warrant without strong evidence. Vernon is a cautious man, sir, a very cautious man."

"And who is this person?" asked Marlow pointing to the personage who spoke.

"A messenger of the powers that be," replied Mr. Hastings; "it seems that because Sir John Fenwick dined here a short time ago, and has since been accused of some practices against the state, his Majesty's advisers have thought fit to connect me with his doings, or their own suspicions, though they might as well have sent down to arrest my butler or my footman, and I am now to have the benefit of a journey to the Tower of London under arrest."

"Or to Newgate," said the messenger, significantly.

"To London, at all events," replied Mr. Hastings.

"I will go with you," said Marlow, at once; but before the prisoner could answer, the messenger interfered, saying, "That I cannot allow."

"I am afraid you must allow it," replied Marlow, "whether it pleases you or not."

"I will have no one in the carriage with my prisoner," said the messenger, striking the table gently with the haft of his knife.

"That may be," answered Marlow; "but you will not, I presume, pretend to prevent my going where I please in my own carriage; and when once in London, I shall find no difficulty, knowing Mr. Vernon well."

The latter announcement made a great change in the messenger's demeanor, and he became much more tame and docile from the moment it struck his ear.

Mr. Hastings indeed would fain have persuaded his young friend to remain where he was, and looked at Emily with some of that tenderer feeling of a parent which so often prompts to every sacrifice for a child's sake. But Emily thanked Marlow eagerly for proposing to go; and Mrs. Hastings, even, expressed some gratitude.

The arrangements were soon made. There being no time to send for Marlow's own carriage and horses, it was agreed that he should take a carriage belonging to Mr. Hastings, with his horses, for the first stage; the prisoner's valet was to accompany his friend, and immediate orders were given for the necessary preparations.

When all was ready, Emily asked some question of her father, in a low tone, to which he replied, "On no account, my child. I will send for you and your mother should need be; but do not stir before I do. This is a mere cloud- -a passing shower, which will soon be gone, and leave the sky as bright as ever. We do not live in an age when kings of England can play at foot-ball with the heads of innocent men, and I, as you all know, am innocent."

He then embraced his wife and child with more tenderness than he was wont to show, and entering the carriage first, was followed by the messenger. The other men mounted their horses, and Marlow did not linger long behind the sad cavalcade.

CHAPTER XXIX

Philip Hastings had calculated much upon his Roman firmness; and he could have borne death, or any great and sudden calamity, with fortitude; but small evils often affect us more than great ones. He knew not what it is to suffer long imprisonment, to undergo the wearing, grinding process of life within a prison's walls. He knew not the effect of long suspense either, of the fretful impatience for some turn in our fate, of the dull monotony of long continued expectation and protracted disappointment, of the creeping on of leaden despair, which craves nothing in the end but some change, be it for better or for worse.

They took him to Newgate--the prison of common felons, and there, in a small room, strictly guarded, he remained for more than two months. At first he would send for no lawyer, for he fancied that there must either be some error on the part of the government, or that the suspicion against him must be so slight as to be easily removable. But day went by on day, and hour followed hour, without any appearance of a change in his fate. There came a great alteration, however, in his character. He became morose, gloomy, irritable. Every dark point in his own fate and history--every painful event which had occurred for many years--every doubt or suspicion which had spread gloom and anxiety through his mind, was now magnified a thousand-fold by long, brooding, solitary meditation. He pondered such things daily, hourly, in the broad day, in the dead, still night, when want of exercise deprived him of sleep, till his brain seemed to turn, and his whole heart was filled with stern bitterness.

Marlow, who visited him every day by permission of the Secretary of State, found him each day much changed, both in appearance and manner; and even his conversation gave but small relief. He heard with small emotion the news of the day, or of his own family. He read the letters of his wife and daughter coldly. He heard even the intelligence that Sir John Fenwick was condemned for high treason, and to die on a scaffold, without any appearance of interest. He remained self-involved and thoughtful.

At length, after a long interval--for the government was undecided how to proceed in his and several other cases connected with that famous conspiracy--a day was appointed for his first examination by the Secretary of State; for matters were then conducted in a very different manner from that in which they are treated at present; and he was carried under guard to Whitehall.

Vernon was a calm and not unamiable man; and treating the prisoner with unaffected gentleness, he told him that the government was very anxious to avoid the effusion of any more blood, and expressed a hope that Mr. Hastings would afford such explanations of his conduct as would save the pain of proceeding against him. He did not wish by any means, he said, to induce him to criminate himself; but merely to give such explanations as he might think fit.

Philip Hastings replied, with stern bitterness, that before he could give any explanations, he must learn what there was in his conduct to explain. "It has ever been open, plain, and straightforward," he said. "I have taken no part in conspiracies, very little part in politics. I have nothing to fear from any thing I myself can utter; for I have nothing to conceal. Tell me what is the charge against me, and I will answer it boldly. Ask what questions you please; and I will reply at once to those to which I can find a reply in my own knowledge."

"I thought the nature of the charge had been made fully known to you," replied Vernon. "However, it is soon stated. You are charged, Mr. Hastings, with having taken a most decided part in the criminal designs, if not in the criminal acts, of that unfortunate man Sir John Fenwick. Nay, of having first suggested to him the darkest of all his designs, namely, the assassination of his Majesty."

"I suggest the assassination of the King!" exclaimed Mr. Hastings. "I propose such an act! Sir, the charge is ridiculous. Has not the only share I ever took in politics been to aid in placing King William upon the throne, and consistently to support his government since? What the ministers of the crown can seek by bringing such a charge against me, I know not; but it is evidently fictitious, and of course has an object."

Vernon's cheek grew somewhat red, and he replied warmly, "That is an over-bold assertion, sir. But I will soon satisfy you that it is unjust, and that the crown has not acted without cause. Allow me, then, to tell you, that no sooner had the conspiracy of Sir John Fenwick been detected, and his apprehension been made known, than information was privately given--from your own part of the country--to the following effect;" and he proceeded try to read from a paper, which had evidently been folded in the form of a letter, the ensuing words: "That on the ---- day of May last, when walking in the gardens of his own house, called 'The Court,' he--that is yourself, sir--used the following language to Sir John Fenwick: 'When no other means can be found of obtaining justice, freedom, and security, I see no reason why a king should not be put to death as well as any other man. He who does the deed merits a monument rather than a gibbet.' Such was the information, sir, on which government first acted in causing your apprehension."

The Secretary paused, and for a few moments Mr. Hastings remained gazing down in silence, like a man utterly confounded. Vernon thought he had touched him home; but the emotions in the prisoner's bosom, though very violent, were very different from those which the Secretary attributed to him. He remembered the conversation well, but he remembered also that the only one who, besides Sir John Fenwick, was with him at the moment, was his own child. I will not dwell upon his feelings, but they absorbed him entirely, till the Secretary went on, saying--"Not satisfied with such slender information, Mr. Hastings, the government caused that unhappy criminal, Sir John Fenwick, to be asked, after his fate was fixed, if he recollected your having used those words to him, and he replied, something very like them.'"

"And I reply the same," exclaimed Philip Hastings, sternly. "I did use those words, or words very like them. But, sir, they were in connection with others, which, had they been repeated likewise, would have taken all criminal application from them. May I be permitted to look at that letter in your hand, to see how much was really told, how much suppressed?"

"I have read it all to you," said Mr. Vernon, "but you may look at it if you please," and he handed it to him across the table. Philip Hastings spread it out before him, trembling violently, and then drew another letter from his pocket, and laid them aide by side. He ran his eye from one to the other for a moment or two, and then sunk slowly down, fainting upon the floor.

While a turnkey and one of the messengers raised him, and some efforts were made to bring him back to consciousness, Mr. Vernon walked round the table and looked at the two letters which were still lying on it. He compared them eagerly, anxiously. The handwriting of the one was very similar to that of the other, and in the beginning of that which Mr. Hastings had taken from his pocket, the Secretary found the words, "My dear father."

It was signed, "Emily Hastings;" and Vernon instantly comprehended the nature of the terrible emotion he had witnessed.

He was really, as I have said, a kind and humane man, and he felt very much for the prisoner, who was speedily brought to himself again, and seated in a chair before the table.

"Perhaps, Mr. Hastings," said Vernon, "we had better not protract this conversation today. I will see you again to-morrow, at this hour, if you would prefer that arrangement."

"Not at all, sir," answered the prisoner, "I will answer now, for though the body be weak, the spirit is strong. Remember, however, that I am not pleading for life. Life is valueless to me. The block and axe would be a relief. I am only pleading to prevent my own character from being stained, and to frustrate this horrible design. I used the words imputed to me; but if I recollect right, with several qualifications, even in the sentence which has been extracted. But before that, many other words had passed which entirely altered the whole bearing of the question. The conversation began about the regicides of the great rebellion, and although my father was of the party in arms against the King, I expressed my unqualified disapprobation of their conduct in putting their sovereign to death. I then approached as a mere matter of abstract reasoning, in which, perhaps, I am too apt to indulge, the subject of man's right to resist by any means an unendurable tyranny, and I quoted the example of Brutus and William Tell; and it was in the course of these abstract remarks, that I used the words which have been cited. I give you my word, however, and pledge my honor, that I entertained no thought, and had no cause whatever to believe that Sir John Fenwick who was dining with me as an old acquaintance, entertained hostile designs against the government of his native land."

"Your admitted opinions, Mr. Hastings," said Vernon, "seem to me to be very dangerous ones."

"That may be," replied the prisoner, "but in this country at least, sir, you cannot kill a man for opinions."

"No; but those opinions, expressed in conversation with others who proceed to acts," replied Vernon, "place a man in a very dangerous position, Mr. Hastings. I will not conceal from you that you are in some peril; but at the same time I am inclined to think that the evidence, without your admissions this day, might prove insufficient, and it is not my intention to take advantage of any thing you have said. I shall report to his Majesty accordingly; but the proceedings of the government will be guided by the opinion of the law officers of the crown, and not by mine. I therefore can assure you of nothing except my sincere grief at the situation in which you are placed."

"I little heed the result of your report, sir," replied Mr. Hastings; "life, I say, is valueless to me, and if I am brought to trial for words very innocently spoken, I shall only make the same defence I have done this day, and I shall call no witness; the only witness of the whole," he added with stern, concentrated bitterness, "is probably on the side of the crown."

Mr. Hastings was then removed to Newgate, leaving the two letters on the table behind him, and as soon as he was gone, Mr. Vernon sent a messenger to an inn near Charing Cross, to say he should be glad to speak for a few moments with Mr. Marlow. In about half an hour Marlow was there, and was received by Vernon as an old acquaintance. The door was immediately closed, and Marlow seated himself near the table, turning his eyes away, however, as an honorable man from the papers which lay on it.

"I have had an interview with your friend, Mr. Marlow," said the Secretary, "and the scene has been a very gainful one. Mr. Hastings has been more affected than I expected, and actually fainted."

Marlow's face expressed unutterable astonishment, for the idea of Philip Hastings fainting under any apprehension whatever, could never enter into the mind of any one who knew him.

"Good God!" he exclaimed, "what could be the cause of that! Not fear, I am sure."

"Something more painful than even fear, I believe," replied Mr. Vernon; "Mr. Hastings has a daughter, I believe?"

"Yes, sir, he has," replied Marlow, somewhat stiffly.

"Do you know her handwriting?" asked the Secretary.

"Yes, perfectly well," answered Marlow.

"Then be so good as to take up that letter next you," said Vernon, "and tell me if it is in her hand."

Marlow took up the paper, glanced at it, and at once said, "Yes;" but the next instant he corrected himself, saying, "No, no--it is very like Emily's hand--very, very like; but more constrained."

"May not that proceed from an attempt to disguise her hand?" asked Vernon.

"Or from an attempt on the part of some other to imitate it," rejoined Marlow; "but this is very strange, Mr. Vernon; may I read this through?"

"Certainly," replied the Secretary, and Marlow read every word three or four times over with eager attention. They seemed to affect him very much, for notwithstanding the Secretary's presence, he started up and paced the room for a minute or two in thought.

"I must unravel this dark mystery," he said at length. "Mr. Vernon, there have been strange things taking place lately in the family of Mr. Hastings. Things which have created in my mind a suspicion that some secret and external agency is at work to destroy his peace as well as to ruin his happiness, and still more, I fear, to ruin the happiness of his daughter. This letter is but one link in a long chain of suspicious facts, and I am resolved to sift the whole matter to the bottom. The time allowed me to do so, must depend upon the course you determine to pursue towards Mr. Hastings. If you resolve to proceed against him I must lose no time--although I think I need hardly say, there is small chance of your success upon such evidence as this;" and he struck the letter with his fingers.

"We have more evidence, such as it is," replied Vernon, "and he himself admits having used those words."

Marlow paused thoughtfully, and then replied, "He may have used them--he is very likely to have used them; but it must have been quite abstractedly, and with no reference to any existing circumstance. I remember the occasion on which Sir John Fenwick dined with him, perfectly. I was there myself. Now let me see if I can recall all the facts. Yes, I can, distinctly. During the whole of dinner--during the short time we sat after dinner, those words were never used; nor were conspiracies and treason ever thought of. I remember, too, from a particular circumstance, that when we went out into the gardens Mr. Hastings took his daughter's arm, and walked up and down the terrace with Sir John Fenwick at his side. That must have been the moment. But I need hardly point out to you, Mr. Vernon, that such was not a time when any man in his senses, and especially a shrewd, cunning, timid man, like Sir John Fenwick, would have chosen for the development of treasonable designs."

"Were any other persons near?" asked Vernon; "the young lady might have been in the conspiracy as well as her father."

Marlow laughed. "There were a dozen near," he answered; "they were subject to interruption at any moment--nay, they could not have gone on for three minutes; for that space of time did not elapse after the gentlemen entered the garden where the ladies were, before I was at Emily's side, and not one word of this kind was spoken afterwards."

"Then what could have induced her to report those words to the government?" asked Mr. Vernon.

"She never did so," replied Marlow, earnestly; "this is not her handwriting, though the imitation is very good--and now, sir," he continued, "if it be proper, will you explain to me what course you intend to pursue, that I may act accordingly? For as I before said, I am resolved to search this mystery out into its darkest recesses. It has gone on too long already."

Vernon smiled. "You are asking a good deal," he said, "but yet my views are so strong upon the subject, that I think I may venture to state them, even if the case against Mr. Hastings should be carried a step or two farther--which might be better, in order to insure his not being troubled on an after occasion. I shall strongly advise that a _nolle prosequi_ be entered, and I think I may add that my advice will be taken."

"You think I have asked much already, Mr. Vernon," said Marlow, "but I am now going to ask more. Will you allow me to have this letter? I give you my word of honor that it shall only be used for the purposes of justice. You have known me from my boyhood, my dear sir; you can trust me."

"Perfectly, my young friend," replied Vernon, "but you must not take the letter to-day. In two days the action of the government will be determined, and if it be such as I anticipate you shall have the paper, and I trust it will lead to some discovery of the motives and circumstances of this strange transaction. Most mysterious it certainly is; for one can hardly suppose any one but a fiend thus seeking to bring a father's life into peril."

"A fiend!" exclaimed Marlow, with a scoff, "much more like an angel, my dear sir."

"You seem to think so," said Vernon, smiling, "and I trust, though love is blind, he may have left you clear-sighted in this instance."

"I think he has," answered Marlow, "and as this young lady's fate is soon to be united to mine, it is very necessary I should see clearly. I entertain no doubt, indeed, and I say boldly, that Emily never wrote this letter. It will give me, however, a clue which perhaps may lead me to the end of the labyrinth, though as yet I hardly see my way. But a strong resolution often does much.

"Might it not be better for you," asked Vernon, "to express your doubts in regard to this letter to Mr. Hastings himself? He was terribly affected, as well he might be, when he saw this document, and believed it to be his own child's writing."

Marlow mused for some time ere he replied. "I think not," he answered at length; "he is a man of peculiar disposition; stern, somewhat gloomy, but honorable, upright, and candid. Now what I am going to say may make me appear as stern as himself, but if he is suffering from doubts of that dear girl, knowing her as well as he does, he is suffering from his own fault, and deserves it. However, my object is not to punish him, but thoroughly, completely, and for ever to open his eyes, and to show him so strongly that he has done his child injustice, as to prevent his ever doing the like again. This can only be done by bringing all the proofs upon him at once, and my task is now to gather them together. To my mere opinion regarding the handwriting, he would not give the slightest heed, but he will not shut his eyes to proofs. May I calculate upon having the letter in two days?"

"I think you may," replied Vernon.

"Then when will Mr. Hastings be set free?" asked Marlow; "I should wish to have some start of him into the country."

"That will depend upon various circumstances," replied the Secretary; "I think we shall take some steps towards the trial before we enter the _nolle prosequi_. It is necessary to check in some way the expression of such very dangerous opinions as he entertains."

Marlow made no reply but by a smile, and they soon after parted.

CHAPTER XXX

Mrs. Hazleton was very consoling. She was with Mrs. Hastings two or three times in the week, and poor Mrs. Hastings required a considerable degree of consolation; for the arrest of her husband, coming so close upon the bitter mortification of loss, and abatement of dignity, and at the end of a long period of weak health, had made her seriously ill. She now kept her bed the whole day long, and lay, making herself worse by that sort of fretful anxiety which was constitutional with her as well as with many other people. Mrs. Hazleton's visits were a great comfort to her, and yet, strange to say, Emily almost always found her more irritable after that lady had left her.

Poor Emily seemed to shine under the cloud of misfortune. Her character came out and acted nobly in the midst of disasters. She was her mother's nurse and constant attendant; she kept her father informed of every thing that passed--not an opportunity was missed of sending him a letter; and although she would have made any sacrifice to be with him in prison, to comfort and support him in the peril and sorrow of his situation, she was well satisfied that he had not taken her, when she found the state into which her mother had fallen.

Often, after Mrs. Hazleton had sat for an hour or two with her sick friend, she would come down and walk upon the terrace for a while with Emily, and comfort her much in the same way that she did Mrs. Hastings. She would tell her not to despond about her mother: that though she was certainly very ill, and in a dangerous state, yet people had recovered who had been quite as ill as she was. Then she would talk about lungs, and nerves, and humors, and all kinds of painful and mortal diseases, as if she had studied medicine all her life; and she did it, too, with a quiet, dignified gravity which made it more impressive and alarming. Then again, she would turn to the situation of Mr. Hastings, and wonder what they would do with him. She would also bring every bit of news that she could collect, regarding the case of Sir John Fenwick, especially when the intelligence was painful and disastrous; but she hinted that, perhaps, after all, they might not be able to prove any thing against Mr. Hastings, and that even if they did--

although the Government were inclined to be severe--they might, perhaps, commute his sentence to transportation for the colonies, or imprisonment in the Tower for five or six years.

It is thus our friends often console us; some of them, from a dark and gloomy turn of mind, and some of them from the satisfaction many people feel in meddling with the miseries of others. But it was neither natural despondency of character, nor any general love of sorrowful scenes or thoughts, that moved Mrs. Hazleton in the present instance. She had a peculiar and especial pleasure in the wretchedness of the Hastings family, and particularly in that of Emily. The charming lady fancied that if Marlow were free from his engagement with Emily the next day, and a suitor for her own hand, she would never think of marrying him. I am not quite sure of that fact, but that is no business of ours, dear reader, and one thing is certain, that she would have very willingly sacrificed one half of her whole fortune, nay more, to have placed an everlasting barrier between Emily and Marlow.

She was thus walking with her dear Emily, as she called her, one day on that terrace at the back of the house where the memorable conversation had taken place between Mr. Hastings and Sir John Fenwick, and was treating Emily to a minute and particular account of the death of the latter, when Marlow suddenly arrived from London, and entered the house by the large glass door in front. He found a servant in the hall who informed him that Mrs. Hastings was still in bed, and that Emily was walking on the terrace with Mrs. Hazleton. Marlow paused, and considered for a moment. "Any thing not dishonorable," he said to himself, "is justifiable to clear up such a mystery;" and passing quietly through the house into the dining-room, which had one window opening as a door upon the terrace, he saw his fair Emily and her companion pass along towards the other end of the walk without being himself perceived. He then approached the window, and calculating the distances nicely, so as to be sure that Mrs. Hazelton was fully as far distant from himself as she could have been from Sir John Fenwick and Mr. Hastings on the evening when they walked there together, he pronounced her name in an ordinary tone, somewhat lower than that which Mr. Hastings usually employed.

Mrs. Hazleton instantly started, and looked round towards the spot where Marlow was now emerging from the room.

The lady could not miss an occasion, and the moment she saw him she exclaimed, "Dear me! there is Mr. Marlow; I am afraid he brings bad tidings, Emily."

Emily paused not to consider, but with her own wild grace ran forward and cast herself into his arms.

Fortunately Mrs. Hazleton had no dagger with her. Her face was benevolent and smiling when she joined them; for the joy there was upon Emily's countenance forbade any affectation of apprehension. It said as plainly as possible, "All is well;" but she added the words too, stretching forth her hand to her supposed friend, and saying, "Dear Mrs. Hazleton, Charles brings me word that my father is safe--that the Government have declared they will not prosecute."

"I congratulate you with my whole heart, Emily," replied the lady; "and I do sincerely hope that ministers may keep their word better in this instance than they have done in some others."

"There is not the slightest doubt of it, my dear madam," said Marlow; "for I have the official announcement under the hand of the Secretary of State."

"I must fly and tell my mother," said Emily, and without waiting for a reply she darted away.

Mrs. Hazleton took a turn or two up and down the terrace with Marlow, considering whether it was at all possible for her to be of any further comfort to her friends at the Court. As she could not stay all night, however, so as to prevent Emily and Marlow from having any happy private conversation together, and as she judged that, in their present joy, they would a good deal forget conventional restraints, and give way to their lover-like feelings even in her presence, which would be exceedingly disagreeable to her, she soon re-entered the house, and ordered her carriage. It must be acknowledged that both Emily and Marlow were well satisfied to see her depart, and it is not to be wondered at if they gave themselves up for half an hour to the pleasure of meeting again.

At the end of that time, however, Marlow drew forth a letter from his pocket, carefully folded, so that a line or two only was apparent, and placing it before Emily, inquired if she knew the hand.

"It is mine," said Emily, at first; but the moment after she exclaimed "No!--it is not; it is Mrs. Hazleton's. I know it by the peculiar way she forms the _g_ and the _y_.--Stay, let me see, Marlow. She has not done so always; but that _g_, and that _y_, I am quite certain of. Why do you ask, Marlow?"

"For reasons of the utmost importance, dear Emily," he answered, "have you any letters or notes of Mrs. Hazleton's?"

"Yes, there is one which came yesterday," replied Emily; "it is lying on my table upstairs."

"Bring it--bring it, dearest girl," he said; "I wish very much to see it."

When he had got, he examined it with a well-pleased smile, and then said, with a laugh, "I must impound this, my love. I am now on the right track, and will not leave it till I have arrived at perfect certainty."

"You are very strange and mysterious to-day, Marlow," said the beautiful girl, "what does all this mean?"

"It means, my love," replied Marlow, "that I have very dark doubts and suspicions of Mrs. Hazleton,--and all I have seen and heard to-day confirms me. Now sit down here by me, dear Emily, and tell me if, to your knowledge, you have ever given to Mrs. Hazleton cause of offence."

"Never!" answered Emily, firmly and at once. "Never in my life."

Marlow mused, and then, with his arms round her waist, he continued, "Bethink yourself, my love. Within the course of the last two or three years, have you ever seen reason to believe that Mrs. Hazleton's affection for you is not so great as it appears?--Has it ever wavered?--Has it ever become doubtful to you from any stray word or accidental circumstance?"

Emily was silent for a moment, and then replied, thoughtfully, "Perhaps I did think so, once or twice, when I was staying at her house, last year."

"Well, then, now, dear Emily," said Marlow, "tell me every thing down to the most minute circumstance that occurred there."

Emily hesitated. "Perhaps I ought not," she said; "Mrs. Hazleton showed me, very strongly, that I ought not, except under an absolute necessity."

"That necessity is now, my love," replied Marlow; "love cannot exist without confidence, Emily; and I tell you, upon my honor and my faith, that your happiness, my happiness, and even your father's safety, depends in a great degree upon your telling me all. Do you believe me, Emily?"

"Fully," she answered; "and I will tell you all."

Thus seated together, she poured forth the whole tale to her lover's ears, even to the circumstances which had occurred in her own room, when Mrs.

Hazleton had entered it, walking in her sleep. The whole conduct of John Ayliffe, now calling himself Sir John Hastings, was also displayed; and the dark and treacherous schemes which had been going on, began gradually to evolve themselves to Marlow's mind. Obscure and indistinct they still were; but the gloomy shadow was apparent, and he could trace the outline though he could not fill up the details.

"Base, treacherous woman!" he murmured to himself, and then, pressing Emily more closely to his heart, he thanked her again and again for her frankness. "I will never misuse it, my Emily," he said; "and no one shall ever know what you have told me except your father: to him it must be absolutely revealed."

"I would have told him myself," said Emily, "if he had ever asked me any questions on the subject; but as he did not, and seemed very gloomy just then, I thought it better to follow Mrs. Hazleton's advice."

"The worst and the basest she could have given you," said Marlow; "I have had doubts of her for a long time, Emily, but I have no doubts now; and, moreover, I firmly believe that the whole case of this John Ayliffe--his claim upon your father's estate and title--is all false and factitious together, supported by fraud, forgery, and crime. Have you preserved this young man's letter, or have you destroyed it, Emily?"

"I kept it," she replied, "thinking that, some time or another, I might have to show it to my father."

"Then one more mark of confidence, my love," said Marlow; "let me have that letter. I do not wish to read it; therefore you had better fold it up and seal it; but it may be necessary as a link in the chain of evidence which I wish to bring forward for your father's satisfaction."

"Read it, if you will, Marlow," she answered; "I have told you the contents, but it may be as well that you should see the words: I will bring it to you in a moment."

They read the letter over together, and when Marlow had concluded, he laid his hand upon it, saying, "This is Mrs. Hazleton's composition."

"I'm almost inclined to fancy so, myself," answered Emily.

"He is incapable of writing this," replied her lover; "I have seen his letters on matters of business, and he cannot write a plain sentence in English to an end without making some gross mistake. This is Mrs. Hazleton's doing, and there is some dark design underneath it. Would to God that visit had never taken place!"

"There has been little happiness in the house since," said Emily, "except what you and I have known together, Marlow; and that has been sadly checkered by many a painful circumstance."

"The clouds are breaking, dear one," replied Marlow, rising; "but I will not pause one moment in my course till all this is made clear--no, not even for the delight of sitting here by you, my love. I will go home at once, Emily; mount my horse, and ride over to Hartwell before it be dark."

"What is your object there?" asked Emily.

"To unravel one part of this mystery," replied her lover. "I will ascertain, by some means, from whom, or in what way, this young man obtained sufficient money to commence and carry on a very expensive suit at law. That he had it not himself, I am certain. That his chances were not sufficiently good, when first he commenced, to induce any lawyer to take the risk, I am equally certain. He must have had it from some one, and my suspicions point to Mrs. Hazleton. Her bankers are mine, and I will find means to know. So, now, farewell, my love; I will see you again early to-morrow."

He lingered yet for a moment or two, and then left her.

CHAPTER XXXI

Marlow was soon on horseback, and riding on to the country town. But he had lingered longer with Emily than he imagined, and the day declined visibly as he rode along.

"The business hours are over," he thought; "bankers and lawyers will have abandoned the money-getting and mischief-making toils of the day; and I must stay at the inn till to-morrow."

He had been riding fast; but he now drew in his rein, and suffered his horse to walk. The sun was setting gloriously, and the rich, rosy light, diffused through the air, gave every thing an aspect of warmth, and richness, and cheerfulness. But Marlow's heart was any thing but gay. Whether it was that the scenes which he had passed through in London, his visits to a prison, his dealings with hard official men, the toiling, moiling crowds that had surrounded him; the wearisome, eternal, yet ever-changing struggle of life displayed in the streets and houses of a capital, the infinite varieties of selfishness, and folly, and vice, and crime, had depressed his spirits, or that his health had somewhat suffered in consequence of anxious waiting for events in the foul air of the metropolis, I cannot tell. But certain, he was sadder than was usual with him. His was a spirit strong and active, naturally disposed to bright views and happy hopes, too firm to be easily depressed, too elastic to be long kept down. But yet, as he rode along, there was a sort of feeling of apprehension upon his mind that oppressed him mightily. He revolved all that had lately passed. He compared the state of Mr. Hastings' family, as it actually was, with what it had been when he first knew it, and there seemed to be a strange mystery in the change. It had then been all happiness and prosperity with that household; a calm, grave, thoughtful, but happy father and husband; a bright, amiable, affectionate mother and wife; a daughter, to his mind the image of every thing that was sweet, and gentle, and tender--of every thing that was gay, and sparkling, and cheerful; full of light and life, and fancy, and hope. Now, there was a father in prison, deprived of his greatest share of worldly prosperity, cast down from his station in society, gloomy, desponding, suspicious, and, as it seemed to him, hardly sane: a mother, irritable, capricious, peevish, yielding to calamity, and lying on a bed of sickness, while the bright angel of his love remained to nurse, and tend, and soothe the one parent, with a heart torn and bleeding for the distresses of the other. "What have they done to merit all this?" he asked himself. "What fault, what crime have they committed to draw down such sorrows on their heads? None--none whatever. Their lives had been spent in kindly acts and good deeds; they had followed the precepts of the religion they professed; their lives had been spent in doing service to their fellow-creatures, and making all happy around them."

Then again, on the other hand, he saw the coarse, and the low, and the base, and the licentious prosperous and successful, rising on the ruins of the pure and the true. Wily schemes and villanous intrigues obtaining every advantage, and honesty of purpose and rectitude of action frustrated and cast down.

Marlow was no unbeliever--he was not even inclined to skepticism--but his mind labored, not without humility and reverence, to see how it could reconcile such facts with the goodness and providence of God.

"He makes the sun shine upon the just and the unjust, we are told," said Marlow to himself; "but here the sun seems to shine upon the unjust alone, and clouds and tempests hang about the just. It is very strange, and even discouraging; and yet, all that we see of these strange, unaccountable dispensations may teach us lessons for hereafter--may give us the grandest confirmation of the grandest truth. There must be another world, in which these things will be made equal--a world where the wicked cease from troubling, and the weary are at rest. We only see in part, and the part we do not see must be the part which will reconcile all the seeming contradictions between the justice and goodness of God and the course of this mortal life."

This train pursued him till he reached the town, and put up his horse at the inn. By that time it was quite dark, and he had tasted nothing since early in the morning. He therefore ordered supper, and the landlord, by whom he was now well known--a good, old, honest, country landlord of the olden time--brought in the meal himself, and waited on his guest at table. It was so much the custom of gentlemen, in those days, to order wine whenever they stopped at an inn--it was looked upon so much as a matter of course that this should be done for the good of the house--that the landlord, without any direct commands to that effect, brought in a bottle of his very best old sherry, always a favorite wine with the English people, though now hardly to be got, and placed it by the side of his guest. Marlow was by habit no drinker of much wine. He avoided, as much as in him lay, the deep potations then almost universal in England; but, not without an object, he that night gave in to a custom which was very common in England then, and for many years afterwards, and requested the landlord, after the meal was over, to sit down, and help him with his bottle.

"You'll need another bottle, if I once begin, Master Marlow," said the jolly landlord, who was a wag in his way.

Marlow nodded his head significantly, as if he were prepared for the infliction, replying quietly, "Under the influence of your good chat, Mr. Cherrydew, I can bear it, I think."

"Well, that's hearty," said the landlord, drawing a chair sideways to the table; for his vast rotundity prevented him from approaching it full front. "Here's to your very good health, sir, and may you never drink worse wine, sit in a colder room, or have a sadder companion."

Now I have said that Marlow did not invite the landlord to join him, without an object. That object was to obtain information, and it had struck him even while the trout, which formed the first dish at his supper, was being placed on the table, that he might be able, if willing, to afford it.

Landlords in England at that time--I mean, of course, in country towns--were very different in many respects, and of a different class from what they are at present. In the first place, they were not fine gentlemen: in the next place, they were not discharged valets de chambre, or butlers, who, having cheated their masters handsomely, and perhaps laid them under contribution in many ways, retire to enjoy the fat things at their ease in their native town. Then, again, they were on terms of familiar intercourse with two or three classes, completely separate and distinct from each other--a sort of connecting link between them. At their door the justice of the peace, the knight of the shire, the great man of the neighborhood, dismounted from his horse, and had his chat with mine host. There came the village lawyer when he had gained a cause, or won a large fee, or had been paid a long bill, to indulge in his pint of sherry, and gossiped, as he drank it, of all the affairs of his clients. There sneaked in the Doctor to get his glass of eau de vie, or plague water, or aqua mirabilis, or strong spirits, in short of any other denomination, and tell little dirty anecdotes of his cases, and his patients. There the alderman, the wealthy shop-keeper, and the small proprietor, or the large farmer, came to take his cheerful cup on Saturdays or on market-day. But, besides these, the inn was the resort, though approached by another door, of a lower and a poorer class, with whom the landlord was still upon as good terms as with the others. The wagoner, the carter, the lawyer's and the banker's clerk, the shopman, the porter even, all came there; and it mattered not to Mr. Cherrydew or his confraternity, whether it was a bowl of punch, a draught of ale, a glass of spirits, or a bottle of old wine that his guests demanded; he was civil, and familiar, and chatty with them all.

Thus under the rosy and radiant face of Mr. Cherrydew, and in that good, round, fat head, was probably accumulated a greater mass of information, regarding the neighborhood in which he lived, and all that went on therein, than in any other head, in the whole town, and the only difficulty was to extract that part of the store which was wanted.

Marlow knew that it would not do to approach the principal subject of inquiry rashly; for Mr. Cherrydew, like most of his craft, was somewhat cautious, and would have shut himself up in silent reserve, or enveloped himself in intangible ambiguities, if he had known that his guest had any distinct and important object in his questions--having a notion that a landlord should be perfectly cosmopolitan in all his feelings and his actions, and should never commit himself in such a manner as to offend any one who was, had been, or might be his guest. He was fond of gossip, it is true, loved a jest, and was not at all blind to the ridiculous in the actions of his neighbors; but habitual caution was in continual struggle with his merry, tattling disposition, and he was generally considered a very safe man.

Marlow, therefore, began at a great distance, saying, "I have just come down from London, Mr. Cherrydew, and rode over, thinking that I should arrive in time to catch my lawyer in his office."

"That is all over now, sir, for the night," replied the landlord. "In this, two-legged foxes differ from others: they go to their holes at sunset, just when other foxes go out to walk. They divide the world between them, Master Marlow; the one preys by day, the other by night.--Well, I should like to see Lunnun. It must be a grand place, sir, though somewhat of a bad one. Why, what a number of executions I have read of there lately, and then, this Sir John Fenwick's business. Why, he changed horses here, going to dine with Sir Philip, as I shall call him to the end of my days. Ah, poor gentleman, he has been in great trouble! But I suppose, from what I hear, he'll get clear now?"

"Beyond all doubt," said Marlow; "the Government have no case against him. But you say very true, Mr. Cherrydew, there has been a sad number of executions in London--seven and twenty people hanged, at different times, while I was there."

"And the town no better," said Mr. Cherrydew.

"By the way," said Marlow, "were you not one of the jury at the trial of that fellow, Tom Cutter?--Fill your glass, Mr. Cherrydew."

"Thank you, sir.--Yes I was, to be sure," answered the landlord; "and I'll tell you the funniest thing in the world that happened the second day. Lord bless you, sir, I was foreman,--and on the first day the judge suffered the case to go on till his dinner was quite cold, and we were all half starved; but he saw that he could not hang him that night, at all events--here's to your health, sir!--so he adjourned the Court, and called for a constable, and ordered all of us, poor devils, to be locked up tight in Jones's public-house till the next day; for the jury room is so small, that there is not standing-room for more than three such as me. Well, the other men did not much like it, though I did not care,--for I had my boots full of ham, and a brandy-bottle in my breeches-pocket. One of them asked the judge, for all his great black eyebrows, if he could'nt go on that night; but his lordship answered, with a snort like a cart horse, and told us to hold our tongues, and mind our own business, and only to take care and keep ourselves together. Well, sir, we had to walk up the hill, you know, and there was the constable following us with his staff in his hand; so I had compassion on my poor fellow-sufferers, and I whispered, first to one, then to another, that this sort of jog would never do, but I would manage to tell them how to have a good night's rest. You see, says I, here's but one constable to thirteen people, so when you get to the cross-roads, let every man take up his legs and run, each his own way. He can but catch one, and the slowest runner will have the chance. Now, I was the fattest of them all, you see, so that every one of them thought that I should be the man. Well, sir, they followed my advice; but it's a different thing to give advice, and take it. No sooner did we get to the cross-roads, than they scattered like a heap of dust in the wind, some down the roads and lanes, some over the styles and gates, some through the hedges. Little Sninkum, the tailor, stuck in the hedge by the way, and was the man caught, for he was afraid of his broadcloth; but I stood stock still, with a look of marvellous astonishment, crying out, 'For God's sake catch them, constable, or what will my lord say to you and me?' Off the poor devil set in a moment, one man to catch twelve, all over the face of the country. He thought he was sure enough of me; but what did I do I why, as soon as he was gone, I waddled home to my own house, and got my wife to put me to bed up-stairs, and pass me for my grandfather. Well, sir, that's not the best of it yet. We were all in Court next day at the right hour, and snug in the jury-box before the judge came in; but I have a notion he had heard something of the matter. He looked mighty hard at Sninkum, whose face was all scratched to pieces, and opening his mouth with a pop, like the drawing of a cork, he said, 'Why, man, you look as if you and your brethren had been fighting!' and then he looked as hard at me, and roared, 'I hope, gentlemen, you have kept yourselves together?' Thereupon, I laid my two hands upon my stomach, sir,--it weighs a hundred and a half, if it were cut off to-morrow, as I know to my cost, who carry it--and I answered quite, respectful, 'I can't answer for the other gentlemen, my lord, but I'll swear I've kept myself together.' You should have heard how the Court rang with the people laughing, while I remained as grave as a judge, and much graver than the one who was there; for I thought he would have burst before he was done, and a fine mess that would have made."

Serious as his thoughts were, Marlow could not refrain from smiling; but he did not forget his object, and remarked, "There were efforts made to save that scoundrel, and the present Sir John Hastings certainly did his best for his friend."

"Call him John Ayliffe, sir, call him John Ayliffe," said the host. "Here's to you, sir,--he's never called any thing else here."

"I wonder," said Marlow, musingly, "if there was any relationship between this Tom Cutter and John Ayliffe's mother?"

"Not a pin's point of it, sir," replied the landlord. "They were just two bad fellows together; that was the connection between them, and nothing else."

"Well, John stood by his friend, at all events," said Marlow; "though where he got the money to pay the lawyers in that case, or in his suit against Sir Philip, is a marvel to me."

Mine host winked his eye knowingly, and gave a short laugh.

That did not entirely suit Marlow's purpose, and he added in a musing tone, "I know that he wanted to borrow ten pounds two or three months before, but was refused, because he had not repaid what he had borrowed of the same party, previously."

"Ay, ay, sir," said the landlord; "there are secrets in all things. He got money, and money enough, somehow, just about that time. He has not repaid it yet, either, but he has given a mortgage, I hear, for the amount; and if he don't mortgage his own carcase for it too, I am very much mistaken, before he has done."

"Mortgage his own carcase! I do not understand what you mean," replied Marlow. "I am sure I would not give a shilling for that piece of earth."

"A pretty widow lady, not a hundred miles off, may think differently," replied the landlord, grinning again, and filling his glass once more.

"Ah, ha," said Marlow, trying to laugh likewise; "so you think she advanced the money, do you?"

"I am quite sure of it, sir," said Mr. Cherrydew, nodding his head profoundly. "I did not witness the mortgage, but I know one who did."

"What! Shanks' clerk, I suppose," said Marlow.

"No, sir, no," replied the landlord; "Shanks did not draw the mortgage, either; for he was lawyer to both parties, and Mrs. Hazleton didn't like that;--O, she's cute enough!"

"I think you must be mistaken," said Marlow, in a decided tone; "for Mrs. Hazleton assured me, when there was a question between herself and me, that she was not nearly as rich as she was supposed, and that if the law should award me back rents, it would ruin her."

"Gammon, sir!" replied the landlord, who had now imbibed a sufficient quantity of wine, in addition to sundry potations during the day. "I should not have thought you a man to be so easily hooked, Mr. Marlow; but if you will ask the clerk of Doubledoo and Kay, who was down here, staying three or four days about business, you'll find that she advanced every penny, and got a mortgage for upwards of five thousand pounds;--but I think we had better have that other bottle, sir?"

"By all means," said Marlow, and Mr. Cherrydew rolled away to fetch it.

"By the way, what was that clerk's name you mentioned?"

"Sims, sir, Sims," said the landlord, drawing the cork; and then setting down the bottle on the table, he added, with a look of great contempt, "he's the leetlest little man you ever saw, sir, not so tall as my girl Dolly, and with no more stomach than a currycomb, a sort of cross breed between a monkey and a penknife. He's as full of fun as the one, too, and as sharp as the other. He will hold a prodigious quantity of punch, though, small as he is. I could not fancy where he put it all, it must have gone into his shoes."

"Come, come, Mr. Cherrydew," said Marlow, laughing, "do not speak disrespectfully of thin people--I am not very fat myself."

"Lord bless you, sir, you are quite a fine, personable man; and in time, with a few butts, you would be as fine a man as I am."

Marlow devoutly hoped not, but he begged Mr. Cherrydew to sit down again, and do his best to help him through the wine he had brought; and out of that bottle came a great many things which Marlow wanted much more than the good sherry which it contained.

CHAPTER XXXII

It was about ten o'clock in the day when Marlow returned to the Court, as it was called. The butler informed him that Miss Emily was not down--a very unusual thing with her, as she was exceedingly matutinal in her habits; but he found, on inquiry, that she had sat up with her mother during the greater part of the night. Marlow looked at his watch, then at the gravelled space before the house, where his own horse was being led up and down by his groom, and a stranger who had come with him was sitting quietly on horseback, as if waiting for him. "I fear," said Marlow, after a moment's musing, "I must disturb your young lady. Will you tell her maid to go up and inform her that I am here, and wish to speak with her immediately, as I have business which calls me to London without delay." The man retired, and Marlow entered what was then called the withdrawing room, walking up and down in thought. He had not remained many minutes, however, when Emily herself appeared, with her looks full of surprise and anxiety. "What is the matter, Marlow?" she said. "Has any new evil happened?"

"Nay, nay, my love," said Marlow, embracing her tenderly. "You must not let the few ills that have already befallen you, my Emily, produce that apprehensiveness which long years of evil and mischance but too often engender. Brighter days are coming, I trust, my love; so far from new evils having arisen, I have been very fortunate in my inquiries, and have got information which must lead to great results. I must pursue the clue that has been afforded me without a moment's delay or hesitation; for once the thread be broken I may have difficulty in uniting it again. But if I judge rightly, my Emily, it will lead me to the following results. To the complete exposure of a base conspiracy; to the punishment of the offenders; to the restoration of your father's property, and of his rank."

He held her hand in his while he spoke, and gazed into her beautiful eyes; but Emily did not seem very much overjoyed. "For my own part," she said, "I care little as to the loss of property or station, Marlow, and still less do I care to punish offenders; but I think my father and mother will be very glad of the tidings you give me. May I tell them what you say?"

Marlow mused for a moment or two. He was anxious to give any comfort to Mrs. Hastings, but yet he doubted her discretion, and he replied, "Not the whole, dear Emily, except in case of urgent need. You may tell your mother that I think I have obtained information which will lead to the restoration of your father's property, and you may assure her that no effort shall be wanting on my part to attain that object. Say that I am, even now, setting out for London for the purpose, and that I am full of good hopes. I believe I can prove," he added, after a moment's consideration, and in reality more to lead Mrs. Hastings away from the right track than from any other consideration, although the point he was about to state was a fact, "I believe I can prove that the missing leaf of the marriage register, which was supposed to have been torn out by your grandfather's orders, was there not two years ago, and that I can show by whose hands it was torn out at a much later date. Assure her, however, that I will do every thing in my power, and bid her be of good hope."

"I do not understand the matter," answered Emily, "and never heard of this register, but I dare say my mother has, and will comprehend your meaning better than I do. I know the very hope will give her great pleasure."

"Remember one thing, however, dear Emily," replied Marlow, "on no account mention to her my suspicions of Mrs. Hazleton, nor show any suspicions of that good lady yourself. It is absolutely necessary that she should be kept in ignorance of our doubts, till those doubts, become certainties. However, in case of any painful and unpleasant circumstances occurring while I am absent, I must leave these papers with you. They consist of the note sent you by Mrs. Hazleton which you showed me, a paper which I feel confident is in her handwriting, but which imitates your hand very exactly, and which has led to wrong impressions, and the letter of young John Ayliffe--or at least that which he wrote under Mrs. Hazleton's direction. I have added a few words of my own, on a separate sheet of paper, stating the impression which I have in regard to all these matters, and which I will justify whenever it may be needful."

"But what am I to do with them?" asked Emily, simply.

"Keep them safely, and ever at hand, dear girl," replied Marlow, in a grave tone. "You will find your father on his return a good deal altered--moody and dissatisfied. It will be as well for you to take no notice of such demeanor, unless he expresses plainly some cause of discontent. If he do so--if he should venture upon any occasion to reproach you, my Emily--"

"For what?" exclaimed Emily, in utter surprise.

"It would be too long and too painful to explain all just now, dear one," answered her lover. "But such a thing may happen, my Emily. Deceived, and in error, he may perhaps reproach you for things you never dreamt of. He may also judge wrongly of your conduct in not having told him of this young scoundrel's proposal to you. In either case put that packet of papers in his hands, and tell him frankly and candidly every thing."

"He is sometimes so reserved and grave," said Emily, "that I never like to speak to him on any subject to which he does not lead the way. I sometimes think he does not understand me, Marlow, and dread to open my whole heart to him, as I would fain do, lest he should mistake me still more."

"Let no dread stop you in this instance, my own dear girl," Marlow answered. "That there have been dark plots against you, Emily, I am certain. The only way to meet and frustrate them is to place full and entire confidence in your father. I do not ask you to speak to him on the subject unless he speaks to you till I have obtained the proofs which will make all as clear as daylight. Then, every thing must be told, and Sir Philip will find that had he been more frank himself he would have met with no want of candor in his daughter. Now, one more kiss, dear love, and then to my horse's back."

I will not pursue Marlow's journey across the fair face of merry England, nor tell the few adventures that befell him on the way, nor the eager considerations that pressed, troop after troop, upon his mind, neither will I dwell long upon his proceedings in London, which occupied but one brief day. He went to the house of his banker, sought out the little clerk of Messrs. Doubledoo and Kay, and contrived from both to obtain proof positive that Mrs. Hazleton had supplied a large sum of money to young John Ayliffe to carry on his suit against Sir Philip Hastings. He also obtained a passport for France, and one or two letters for influential persons in Paris, and returning to the inn where he had left the man who had accompanied him from the country, set out for Calais, without pausing even to take rest himself. Another man, a clerk from his own lawyer's house, accompanied him, and though the passage was somewhat long and stormy, he reached Calais in safety.

Journeys to Paris were not then such easy things as now. Three days passed ere Marlow reached the French capital, and then both his companions were inclined to grumble not a little at the rapidity with which he travelled, and the small portion of rest he allowed them or himself. In the capital, however, they paused for two days, and, furnished with an interpreter and guide, amused themselves mightily, while Marlow passed his time in government offices, and principally with the lieutenant of police, or one of his commissaries.

At length the young gentleman notified his two companions that they must prepare to accompany him at nine o'clock in the morning to St. Germain en Laye, where he intended to reside for some days. A carriage was at the door to the moment, and they found in it a very decent and respectable gentleman in black, with a jet-hilted sword by his side, and a certain portion of not very uncorrupt English. The whole party jogged on pleasantly up the steep ascent, and round the fine old palace, to a small inn which was indicated to the driver by the gentleman in black, for whom that driver seemed to entertain a profound reverence. When comfortably fixed in the inn, Marlow left his two English companions, and proceeded, as it was the hour of promenade, to take a walk upon the terrace with his friend in black. They passed a great number of groups, and a great number of single figures, and Marlow might have remarked, if he had been so disposed, that several of the persons whom they met seemed to eye his companion with a suspicious and somewhat anxious glance. All Marlow's powers of observation, however, were directed in a different way. He examined every face that he saw, every group that he came near; but at length, as they passed a somewhat gayly dressed woman of the middle age, who was walking alone, the young Englishman touched the arm of the man in black, saying, "According to the description I have had of her, that must be very like the person."

"We will follow her, and see," said the man in black.

Without appearing to notice her particularly, they kept near the lady who had attracted their attention, as long as she continued to walk upon the terrace, and then followed her when she left it, through several streets which led away in the direction of the forest. At length she stopped at a small house, opened the door, and went in.

The man in black took out a little book from his pocket, closely written with long lists of names.

"Monsieur et Madame Jervis," he said, after having turned over several pages. "Here since three years ago."

"That cannot be she, then," answered Marlow.

"Stay, stay," said his companion, "that is _au premier_. On the second floor lodges Monsieur Drummond. Old man of sixty-eight. He has been here two years; and above Madame Dupont, an old French lady whom I know quite well. You must be mistaken, Monsieur, but we will go into this _charcutier's_ just opposite, and inquire whether that is Madame Jervis who went in."

It proved to be so. The pork butcher had seen her as she passed the window, and Marlow's search had to begin again. When he and his companion returned to their inn, however, the man whom he had brought up from the country met him eagerly, saying, "I have seen her, sir! I have seen her! She passed by here not ten minutes ago, dressed in weeds like a widow, and walking very fast. I would swear to her."

"Oh, he," said the man in black, "we will soon find her now," and calling to the landlord, who was as profoundly deferential towards him as the coachman had been, he said in the sweetest possible tone, "Will you have the goodness to let Monsieur Martin know that the _bon homme grivois_ wishes to speak with him for a moment?"

It was wonderful with what rapidity Monsieur St. Martin, a tall, dashing looking personage, with an infinite wig, obeyed the summons of the _bon homme grivois_.

"Ah, _bon jour_, St. Martin," said the man in black.

"_Bon jour, Monsieur_," replied the other with a profound obeisance.

"A lady of forty--has been handsome, fresh color, dark eyes, middle height, hair brown, hardly gray," said the man in black. "Dressed like an English widow, somewhat common air and manner, has come here within a year. Where is she to be found, St. Martin?"

The other, who had remained standing, took out his little book, and after consulting its pages diligently, gave a street and a number.

"What's her name?" asked the man in black.

"Mistress Brown," replied Monsieur St. Martin.

"Good," said the man in black, "but we must wait till to-morrow morning, as it is now growing dark, and there must be no mistake; first, lest we scare the real bird in endeavoring to catch one we don't want, and next, lest we give annoyance to any of his Majesty's guests, which would reduce the king to despair."

The next morning, at an early hour, the party of four proceeded to the street which had been indicated, discovered the number, and then entered a handsome hotel, inhabited by an old French nobleman. The man in black seemed unknown to either the servants or their master, but a very few words spoken in the ear of the latter, rendered him most civil and accommodating. A room in the front of the house, just over that of the porter, was put at the disposal of the visitors, and the man who had accompanied Marlow from the country was placed at the window to watch the opposite dwelling. It was a balmy morning, and the house was near the outskirts of the town, so that the fresh air of the country came pleasantly up the street. The windows of the opposite house were, however, still closed, and it was not till Marlow and his companions had been there near three quarters of an hour, that a window on the first floor was opened, and a lady looked out for a moment, and then drew in her head again.

"There she is!" cried the man who was watching, "there she is, sir."

"Are you quite certain?" asked the man in black.

"Beyond all possible doubt, sir," replied the other. "Lord bless you, I know her as well as I know my own mother. I saw her almost every day for ten years."

"Very well, then," said the man in black, "I wilt go over first alone, and as soon as I have got in, you, Monsieur Marlow, with these two gentlemen, follow me thither. She won't escape me when once I'm in, but the house may have a back way, and therefore we will not scare her by too many visitors at this early hour."

He accordingly took his departure, and Marlow and his companions saw him ring the bell at the opposite house. But the suspicion of those within fully justified the precautions he had taken. Before he obtained admission, he was examined very narrowly by a maid-servant from the window above. It is probable that he was quite conscious of this scrutiny, but he continued quietly humming an opera air for a minute or two, and then rang the bell again. The door was then opened. He entered, and Marlow and his companions ran across, and got in before the door was shut. The maid gave a little scream at the sudden ingress of so many men, but the gentleman in black told her to be silent, to which she replied, "Oh, Monsieur, you have cheated me. You said you wanted lodgings."

"Very good, my child," replied the man, "but the lodgings which I want are those of Madame Brown, and you will be good enough to recollect that

I command all persons, in the king's name, now in this house, to remain in it, and not to go out on any pretence whatever till they have my permission. Lock that door at the back, and then bring me the key."

The maid, pale and trembling, did as she was commanded, and the French gentleman then directed the man who had accompanied Marlow to precede the rest up the stairs, and enter the front room of the first floor. The others followed close, and as soon as the door of the room was open, it was evident that the lady of the house had been alarmed by the noise below; for she stood looking eagerly towards the top of the stairs, with cheeks very pale indeed. At the same moment that this sight was presented to them, they heard the man who had gone on exclaim in English, "Ah, Mistress Ayliffe, how do you do? I am very glad to see you. Do you know they said you were dead--ay, and swore to it."

John Ayliffe's mother sank down in a seat, and hid her face with her hands.

CHAPTER XXXIII

Marlow could not be hard-hearted with a woman, and he felt for the terrible state of agitation and alarm, to which John Ayliffe's mother was reduced.

"We must be gentle with her," he said in French to the Commissary of Police, who was with him, and whom we have hitherto called the man in black.

"_Oui, monsieur_," replied the other, taking a pinch of snuff, and perfectly indifferent whether he was gentle or not,--for the Commissary had the honor, as he termed it, of assisting at the breaking of several gentlemen on the wheel, to say nothing of sundry decapitations, hangings, and the question, ordinary and extraordinary, all of which have a certain tendency, when witnessed often, slightly to harden the human heart, so that he was not tender.

Marlow was approaching to speak to the unfortunate woman, when removing her hands from her eyes, she looked wildly round, exclaiming, "Oh! have you come to take me, have you come to take me?"

"That must depend upon circumstances, madam," replied Marlow, in a quiet tone. "I have obtained sufficient proofs of the conspiracy in which your son has been engaged with yourself and Mr. Shanks, the attorney, to justify me in applying to the Government of his most Christian Majesty for your apprehension and removal to England. But I am unwilling to deal at all harshly with you, if it can be avoided."

"Oh! pray don't, pray don't!" she exclaimed vehemently; "my son will kill me, I do believe, if he knew that you had found me out; for he has told me, and written to me so often to hide myself carefully, that he would think it was my fault."

"It is his own fault in ordering your letters to him to be sent to the Silver Cross at Hartwell," replied Marlow. "Every body in the house knew the handwriting, and became aware that you were not dead, as had been pretended. But your son will soon be in a situation to kill nobody; for the very fact of your being found here, with the other circumstances we know, is sufficient to convict him of perjury."

"Then he'll lose the property and the title, and not be Sir John any more," said the unhappy woman.

"Beyond all doubt," replied Marlow. "But to return to the matter before us; my conduct with regard to yourself must be regulated entirely by what you yourself do. If you furnish me with full and complete information in regard to this nefarious business, in which I am afraid you have been a participator, as well as a victim, I will consent to your remaining where you are, under the superintendence of the police, of which this gentleman is a Commissary."

"O, I have been a victim, indeed," answered Mrs. Ayliffe, weeping. "I declare I have not had a moment's peace, or a morsel fit to eat since I have been in this outlandish country, and I can hardly get any body, not even a servant girl, who understands a word of English, to speak to."

Marlow thought that he saw an inclination to evade the point of his questions, in order to gain time for consideration, and the Commissary thought so too: though both of them were, I believe, mistaken; for collaterality, if I may use such a word, was a habit of the poor woman's mind.

The Commissary interrupted her somewhat sharply in her catalogue of the miseries of France, by saying, "I will beg you to give me your keys, madame, for we must have a visitation of your papers."

"My keys, my keys!" she said, putting her hands in the large pockets then worn. "I am sure I do not know what I have done with them, or where they are."

"O, we will soon find keys that will open any thing," replied the Commissary. "There are plenty of hammers in St. Germain."

"Stay, stay a moment," said Marlow; "I think Mrs. Ayliffe will save us the trouble of taking any harsh steps."

"O yes, don't; I will do any thing you please," she said, earnestly.

"Well then, madame," said Marlow, "will you have the goodness to state to this gentleman, who will take down your words, and afterwards authenticate the statement, what is your real name, and your ordinary place of residence in England?"

She hesitated, and he added more sternly, "You may answer or not, as you like, madame; we have proof by the evidence of Mr. Atkinson here, who has known you so many years, that you are living now in France, when your son made affidavit that you were dead. That is the principal point; but at the same time I warn you, that if you do not frankly state the truth in every particular, I must demand that you be removed to England."

"I will indeed," she said, "I will indeed;" and raising her eyes to the face of the Commissary, of whom she seemed to stand in great dread, she stated truly her name and place of abode, adding, "I would not, indeed I would not have taken a false name, or come here at all, if my son had not told me that it was the only way for him to get the estate, and promised that I should come back directly he had got it. But now, he says I must remain here forever, and hide myself;" and she wept bitterly.

In the mean while, the Commissary continued to write actively, putting down all she said. She seemed to perceive that she was committing herself, but, as is very common in such cases, she only rendered the difficulties worse, adding, in a low tone, "After all, the estate ought to have been his by right."

"If you think so, madame," replied Marlow, "you had better return to England, and prove it; but I can hardly imagine that your son and his sharp lawyer would have had recourse to fraud and perjury in order to keep you concealed, if they judged that he had any right at all."

"Ay, he might have a right in the eyes of God," replied the unhappy woman, "not in the eyes of the law. We were as much married before heaven as any two people could be, though we might not be married before men."

"That is to say, you and your husband," said the Commissary in an insinuating tone.

"I and Mr. John Hastings, old Sir John's son," she answered; and the Commissary drawing Marlow for a moment aside, conversed with him in a whisper.

What they said she could not hear, and could not have understood had she heard, for they spoke in French; but she grew alarmed as they went on, evidently speaking about her, and turning their eyes towards her from time to time. She thought they meditated at least sending her in custody to England, and perhaps much worse. Tales of bastiles, and dungeons, and wringing confessions from unwilling prisoners by all sorts of tortures, presented themselves to her imagination, and before they had concluded, she exclaimed in a tone of entreaty, "I will tell all, indeed I will tell all, if you will not send me any where."

"The Commissary thinks, madame," said Marlow, "that the first thing we ought to do is to examine your papers, and then to question you from the evidence they afford. The keys must, therefore, be found, or the locks must be broken open."

"Perhaps they may be in that drawer," said Mrs. Ayliffe, pointing across to an escrutoire; and there they were accordingly found. No great search for papers was necessary; for the house was but scantily furnished, and the escrutoire itself contained a packet of six or seven letters from John Ayliffe to his mother, with two from Mr. Shanks, each of them ending with the words "_read and burn_;" an injunction which she had religiously failed to comply with. These letters formed a complete series from the time of her quitting England up to that day. They gave her information of the progress of the suit against Sir Philip Hastings, and of its successful termination by his withdrawing from the defence. The first letters held out to her, every day, the hope of a speedy return to England. The later ones mentioned long fictitious consultations with lawyers in regard to her return, and stated that it was found absolutely necessary that she should remain abroad under an assumed name. The last letter, however, evidently in answer to one of remonstrance and entreaty from her, was the most important in Marlow's eyes. It was very peremptory in its tone, asked if she wanted to ruin and destroy her son, and threatened all manner of terrible things if she suffered her retreat to be discovered. As some compensation, however, for her disappointment, John Ayliffe promised to come and see her speedily, and secure her a splendid income, which would enable her to keep carriages and horses, and "live like a princess." He excused his not having done so earlier, on the ground that his friend Mrs. Hazleton had advanced him a very large sum of money to carry on the suit, which he was obliged to pay immediately. The letter ended with these words, "She is as bitter against all the Hastings' as ever; and nothing will satisfy her till she has seen the last of them all, especially that saucy girl; but she is cute after her money, and will be paid. As for my part, I don't care what she does to Mistress Emily; for I now hate her as much as I once liked her,--but you will see something there, I think, before long."

"In the name of Heaven," exclaimed Marlow, as he read that letter, "what can have possessed the woman with so much malice towards poor Emily Hastings?"

"Why, John used always to think," said Mistress Ayliffe, with a weak smile coming upon her face in the midst of her distress, "that it was because Madame Hazleton wanted to marry a man about there, called Marlow, and Mistress Emily carried him off from her."

The Commissary laughed, and held out his snuff-box to Marlow, who did not take the snuff, but fell into a deep fit of thought, while the Commissary continued his perquisitions.

Only two more papers of importance were found, and they were of a date far back. The one fresh, and evidently a copy of some other letter, the other yellow, and with the folds worn through in several places. The former was a copy of a letter of young John Hastings to the unfortunate girl whom he had seduced, soothing her under her distress of mind, and calling her his "dear little wife." It was with the greatest difficulty she could be induced to part with the original, it would seem, and had obtained a copy before she consented to do so. The latter was the antidote to the former. It was a letter from old Sir John Hastings to her father, and was to the following effect:

"Sir:

"As you have thought fit distinctly to withdraw all vain and fraudulent pretences of any thing but an illicit connection between your daughter and my late son, and to express penitence for the insolent threats you used, I will not withhold due support from my child's offspring, nor from the unfortunate girl to whom he behaved ill. I therefore write this to inform you that I will allow her the sum of two hundred pounds per annum, as long as she demeans herself with propriety and decorum. I will also leave directions in my will for securing to her and her son, on their joint lives, a sum of an equal amount, which may be rendered greater if her behavior for the next few years is such as I can approve.

"I am, sir, your obedient servant,

"JOHN HASTINGS."

Marlow folded up the letter with a smile, and the Commissary proceeded, with all due formalities, to mark and register the whole correspondence as found in the possession of Mrs. Ayliffe.

When this was done, what may be called the examination of that good lady was continued, but the sight of those letters in the hands of Marlow, and the well-satisfied smile with which he read them, had convinced her that all farther attempt at concealment would be vain. Terror had with her a great effect in unloosing the tongue, and, as is very common in such cases, she flew into the extreme of loquacity, told every thing she knew, or thought, or imagined, and being, as is common with very weak people, of a prying and inquisitive turn, she could furnish ample information in regard to all the schemes and contrivances by which her son had succeeded in convincing even Sir Philip Hastings himself of his legitimacy.

Her statements involved Mr. Shanks the lawyer in the scheme of fraud as a principal, but they compromised deeply Mrs. Hazleton herself as cognizant of all that was going on, and aiding and abetting with her personal advice. She detailed the whole particulars of the plan which had been formed for bringing Emily Hastings to Mrs. Hazleton's house, and frightening her into a marriage with John Ayliffe; and she dwelt particularly on the tutoring he had received from that lady, and his frantic rage when the scheme was frustrated. The transactions between him and the unhappy man Tom Cutter she knew only in part; but she admitted that her eon had laughed triumphantly at the thought of how Sir Philip would be galled when he was made to believe that his beloved Emily had been to visit her young reprobate son at the cottage near the park, and that, too, at a time when he had been actually engaged in poaching.

All, in fact, came forth with the greatest readiness, and indeed much more was told than any questions tended to elicit. She seemed indeed to have now lost all desire for concealment, and to found her hopes and expectations on the freest discovery. Her only dread, apparently, being that she might be taken to England, and confronted with her son. On this point she dwelt much, and Marlow consented that she should remain in France, under the supervision of the police, for a time at least, though he would not promise her, notwithstanding all her entreaties, that she should never be sent for. He endeavored, however, to obviate the necessity of so doing, by taking every formal step that could be devised to render the evidence he had obtained available in a court of law, as documentary testimony. A magistrate was sent for, her statements were read over to her in his presence by the commissary of police, and though it cannot be asserted that either the style or the orthography of the worthy commissary were peculiarly English, yet Mrs. Ayliffe signed them, and swore to them in good set form, and in the presence of four witnesses.

To Marlow, the scene was a very painful one; for he had a natural repugnance to seeing the weakness and degradation of human nature so painfully exhibited by any fellow-creature, and he left her with feelings of pity, but still stronger feelings of contempt.

All such sensations, however, vanished when he reached the inn again, and he found himself in possession of evidence which would clear his beloved Emily of the suspicions which had been instilled into her father's mind, and which he doubted not in the least would effect the restoration of Sir Philip Hastings to his former opulence and to his station in society.

The mind of man has a sun in its own sky, which pours forth its sunshine, or is hidden by clouds, irrespective of the atmosphere around. In fact we always see external objects through stained glass, and the hues imparted are in our windows, not in the objects themselves. It is wonderful how different the aspect of every thing was to the eyes of Marlow as he returned towards Paris, from that which the scene had presented as he went. All seemed sunshine and brightness, from the happiness of his own heart. The gloomy images, which, as I have shown, had haunted him on his way from his own house to Hartwell--the doubts, if they can be so called-- the questionings of the unsatisfied heart in regard the ways of Providence- -the cloudy dreads which almost all men must have felt as to the real, constant, minute superintendence of a Supreme Power being but a sweet vision, the child of hope and veneration, were all dispelled. I do not mean to say that they were dissipated by reason or by thought, for his was a strong mind, and reason and thought with him were always on the side of faith; but those clouds and mists were suddenly scattered by the success which he had obtained, and the cheering expectation which might be now well founded upon that success. Is was not enough for him that he knew, and understood, and appreciated to the full the beauty and excellence of his Emily's character. He could not be contented unless every one connected with her understood and appreciated it also. He cared little what the world thought of himself, but he would have every one think well of her, and the deepest pang he had perhaps ever felt in life had been experienced when he first found that Sir Philip Hastings doubted and suspected his own child. Now, all must be clear--all must be bright. The base and the fraudulent will be punished and exposed, the noble and the good honored and justified. It was his doing; and as he alighted from the carriage, and mounted the stairs of the hotel in Paris, his step was as triumphant as if he had won a great victory.

Fate will water our wine, however--I suppose lest we should become intoxicated with the delicious draught of joy. Marlow longed and hoped to fly back to England with the tidings without delay, but certain formalities had to be gone through, official seals and signatures affixed to the papers he had obtained, in order to leave no doubt of their authenticity. Cold men of office could not be brought to comprehend or sympathize with, his impetuous eagerness, and five whole days elapsed before he was able to quit the French capital.

CHAPTER XXXIV

John Ayliffe, as we may now once more very righteously call him, was seated in the great hall of the old house of the Hastings family. Very different indeed was the appearance of that large chamber now from that which it had presented when Sir Philip Hastings was in possession. All the old, solid, gloomy-looking furniture, which formerly had given it an air of baronial dignity, and which Sir Philip had guarded as preciously as if every antique chair and knotted table had been an heir-loom, was now removed, and rich flaunting things of gaudy colors substituted. Damask, and silk, and velvet, and gilt ornaments in the style of France, were there in abundance, and had it not been for the arches overhead, and the stone walls and narrow windows around, the old hall might have passed for the saloon of some newly-enriched financier of Paris.

The young man sat at table alone--not that he was by any means fond of solitude, for on the contrary he would have fain filled his house with company--but for some reason or another, which he could not divine, he found the old country gentlemen in the neighborhood somewhat shy of his society. His wealth, his ostentation, his luxury--for he had begun his new career with tremendous vehemence--had no effect upon them. They looked upon him as somewhat vulgar, and treated him with mere cold, supercilious civility as an upstart. There was one gentleman of good family, indeed, at some distance, who had hung a good deal about courts, had withered and impoverished himself, and reduced both his mind and his fortune in place-hunting, and who had a large family of daughters, to whom the society of John Ayliffe was the more acceptable, and who not unfrequently rode over and dined with him--nay, took a bed at the Hall. But that day he had not been over, and although upon the calculation of chances, one might have augured two to one John Ayliffe would ultimately marry one of the daughters, yet at this period he was not very much smitten with any of them, and was contemplating seriously a visit to London, where he thought his origin would be unknown, and his wealth would procure him every sort of enjoyment.

Two servants were in the Hall, handing him the dishes. Well-cooked viands were on the table, and rich wine. Every thing which John Ayliffe in his sensual aspirations had anticipated from the possession of riches was there--except happiness, and that was wanting. To sit and feed, and feel one's self a scoundrel--to drink deep draughts, were it of nectar, for the purpose of drowning the thought of our own baseness--to lie upon the softest bed, and prop the head with the downiest pillow, with the knowledge that all we possess is the fruit of crime, can never give happiness--surely not, even to the most depraved.

That eating and drinking, however, was now one of John Ayliffe's chief resources--drinking especially. He did not actually get intoxicated every night before he went to bed, but he always drank to a sufficient excess to cloud his faculties, to obfuscate his mind. He rather liked to feel himself in that sort of dizzy state where the outlines of all objects become indistinct, and thought itself puts on the same hazy aspect.

The servants had learned his habits already, and were very willing to humor them; for they derived their own advantage therefrom. Thus, on the present occasion, as soon as the meal was over, and the dishes were removed, and the dessert put upon the table--a dessert consisting principally of sweetmeats, for which he had a great fondness, with stimulants to thirst. Added to these were two bottles of the most potent wine in his cellar, with a store of clean glasses, and a jug of water, destined to stand unmoved in the middle of the table.

After this process it was customary never to disturb him, till, with a somewhat wavering step, he found his way up to his bedroom. But on the night of which I am speaking, John Ayliffe had not finished his fourth glass after dinner, and was in the unhappy stage, which, with some men, precedes the exhilarating stage of drunkenness, when the butler ventured to enter with a letter in his hand.

"I beg pardon for intruding, sir," he said, "but Mr. Cherrydew has sent up a man on horseback from Hartwell with this letter, because there is marked upon it, 'to be delivered with the greatest possible haste.'"

"Curse him!" exclaimed John Ayliffe, "I wish he would obey the orders I give him. Why the devil does he plague me with letters at this time of night?--there, give it to me, and go away," and taking the letter from the man's hand, he threw it down on the table beside him, as if it were not his intention to read it that night. Probably, indeed, it was not; for he muttered as he looked at the address, "She wants more money, I dare say, to pay for some trash or another. How greedy these women are. The parson preached the other day about the horse-leech's daughter. By ---- I think I have got the horse-leech's mother!" and he laughed stupidly, not perceiving that the point of his sarcasm touched himself.

He drank another glass of wine, and then looked at the letter again; but at length, after yet another glass, curiosity got the better of his moodiness, and he opened the epistle.

The first sight of the contents dispelled not only his indifference but the effects of the wine he had taken, and he read the letter with an eager and a haggard eye. The substance was as follows:

"My dearest boy:

"All is lost and discovered. I can but write you a very short account of the things that have been happening here, for I am under what these people call the surveillance of the police. I have got a few minutes, however, and I will pay the maid secretly to give this to the post. Never was such a time as I have had this morning. Four men have been here, and among them Atkinson, who lived just down below at the cottage with the gray shutters. He knew me in a minute, and told everybody who I was. But that is not the worst of it, for they have got a commissioner of police with him--a terrible looking man, who took as much snuff as Mr. Jenkins, the justice of peace. They had got all sorts of information in England about me, and you, and every body, and they came to me to give them more, and cross-questioned me in a terrible manner; and that ugly old Commissioner, in his black coat and great wig, took my keys, and opened all the drawers and places. What could I do to stop them? So they got all your letters to me; because I could not bear to burn my dear boy's letters, and that letter from old Sir John to my poor father, which I once showed you. So when they got all those, there was no use of trying to conceal it any more, and, besides, they might have sent me to the Bastile or the Tower of London. So every thing has come out, and the best thing you can do is to take whatever money you have got, or can get, and run away as fast as possible, and come over here and take me away. One of them was as fine a man as ever I saw, and quite a gentleman, though very severe.

"Pray, my dear John, don't lose a moment's time, but run away before they catch you; for they know every thing now, depend upon it, and nothing will stop them from hanging you or sending you to the colonies that you can do; for they have got all the proofs, and I could see by their faces that they wanted nothing more; and if they do, my heart will be quite broken, that is, if they hang you or send you to the colonies, where you will have to work like a galley-slave, and a man standing over you with a whip, beating your bare back very likely. So run away, and come to your afflicted mother."

She did not seem to have been quite sure what name to sign, for she first put "Brown," but then changed the word to "Hastings," and then again to "Ayliffe." There were two or three postscripts, but they were of no great importance, and John Ayliffe did not take the trouble of reading them. The terms he bestowed upon his mother--not in the secrecy of his heart, but aloud and fiercely--were any thing but filial, and his burst of rage lasted full five minutes before it was succeeded by the natural fear and trepidation which the intelligence he had received might well excite. Then, however, his terror became extreme. The color, usually high, and now heightened both by rage and wine, left his cheeks, and, as he read over some parts of his mother's letter again, he trembled violently.

"She has told all," he repeated to himself, "she has told all--and most likely has added from his own fancy. They have got all my letters too which the fool did not burn. What did say, I wonder? Too much--too much, I am sure. Heaven and earth, what will come of it! Would to God I had not listened to that rascal Shanks! Where should I go now for advice? It must not be to him. He would only betray and ruin me--make me the scape-goat--pretend that I had deceived him, I dare say. Oh, he is a precious villain, and Mrs. Hazleton knows that too well to trust him even with a pitiful mortgage-- Mrs. Hazleton--I will go to her. She is always kind to me, and she is devilish clever too--knows a good deal more than Shanks if she did but understand the law--I will go to her---she will tell me how to manage."

No time was to be lost. Ride as hard as he could it would take him more than an hour to reach Mrs. Hazleton's house, and it was already late. He ordered a horse to be saddled instantly, ran to his bedroom, drew on his boots, and then, descending to the hall, stood swearing at the slowness of the groom till the sound of hoofs made him run to the door. In a moment he was in the saddle and away, much to the astonishment of the servants, who puzzled themselves a little as to what intelligence their young master could have received, and then proceeded to console themselves according to the laws and ordinances of the servants' hall in such cases made and provided. The wine he had left upon the table disappeared with great celerity, and the butler, who was a man of precision, arrayed a good number of small silver articles and valuable trinkets in such a way as to be packed up and removed with great facility and secrecy.

In the meanwhile John Ayliffe rode on at a furious pace, avoiding a road which would have led him close by Mr. Shanks's dwelling, and reached, Mrs. Hazleton's door about nine o'clock.

That lady was sitting in a small room behind the drawing-room, which I have already mentioned, where John Ayliffe was announced once more as Sir John Hastings. But Mrs. Hazleton, in personal appearance at least, was much changed since she was first introduced to the reader. She was still wonderfully handsome. She had still that indescribable air of calm, high-bred dignity which we are often foolishly inclined to ascribe to noble feelings and a high heart; but which--where it is not an art, an acquirement--only indicates, I am inclined to believe, when it has any moral reference at all, strength of character and great self-reliance. But Mrs. Hazleton was older--looked older a good deal--more so than the time which had passed would alone account for. The passions of the last two or three years had worn her sadly, and probably the struggle to conceal those passions had worn her as much. Nevertheless, she had grown somewhat fat under their influence, and a wrinkle here and there in the fair skin was contradicted by the plumpness of her figure.

She rose with quiet, easy grace to meet her young guest, and held out her hand to him, saying, "Really, my dear Sir John, you must not pay me such late visits or I shall have scandal busying herself with my good name."

But even as she spoke she perceived the traces of violent agitation which had not yet departed from John Ayliffe's visage, and she added, "What is the matter? Has any thing gone wrong?"

"Every thing is going to the devil, I believe," said John Ayliffe, as soon as the servant had closed the door. "They have found out my mother at St. Germain."

He paused there to see what effect this first intelligence would produce, and it was very great; for Mrs. Hazleton well knew that upon the concealment of his mother's existence had depended one of the principal points in his suit against Sir Philip Hastings. What was going on in her mind, however, appeared not in her countenance. She paused in silence, indeed, for a moment or two, and then said in her sweet musical voice, "Well, Sir John, is that all?"

"Enough too, dear Mrs. Hazleton!" replied the young man. "Why you surely remember that it was judged absolutely necessary she should be supposed dead--you yourself said, when we were talking of it, 'Send her to France.' Don't you remember?"

"No I do not," answered Mrs. Hazleton, thoughtfully; "and if I did it could only be intended to save the poor thing from all the torment of being cross-examined in a court of justice."

"Ay, she has been cross-examined enough in France nevertheless," said the young man bitterly, "and she has told every thing, Mrs. Hazleton--all that she knew, and I dare say all that she guessed."

This news was somewhat more interesting than even the former; it touched Mrs. Hazleton personally to a certain extent, for all that Jane Ayliffe knew and all that she guessed might comprise a great deal that Mrs. Hazleton would not have liked the world to know or guess either. She retained all her presence of mind however, and replied quite quietly "Really, Sir John, I cannot at all form a judgment of these things, or give you either assistance or advice, as I am anxious to do, unless you explain the whole matter fully and clearly. What has your mother done which seems to have affected you so much? Let me hear the whole details, then I can judge and speak with some show of reason. But calm yourself, calm yourself, my dear sir. We often at the first glance of any unpleasant intelligence take fright, and thinking the danger ten times greater than it really is, run into worse dangers in trying to avoid it. Let me hear all, I say, and then I will consider what is to be done."

Now Mrs. Hazleton had already, from what she had just heard, determined precisely and entirely what she would do. She had divined in an instant that the artful game in which John Ayliffe had been engaged, and in which she herself had taken a hand, was played out, and that he was the loser; but it was a very important object with her to ascertain if possible how far she herself had been compromised by the revelations of Mrs. Ayliffe. This was the motive of her gentle questions; for at heart she did not feel the least gentle.

On the other hand John Ayliffe was somewhat angry. All frightened people are angry when they find others a great deal less frightened than themselves. Drawing forth his mother's letter then, he thrust it towards Mrs. Hazleton, almost rudely, saying, "Read that, madam, and you'll soon see all the details, that you could wish for."

Mrs. Hazleton did read it from end to end, postscript and all, and she saw with infinite satisfaction and delight, that her own name was never once mentioned in the whole course of that delectable epistle. As she read that part of the letter, however, in which Mrs. Ayliffe referred to the very handsome gentlemanly man who had been one of her unwished for visitors, Mrs. Hazleton said within herself, "This is Marlow; Marlow has done this!" and tenfold bitterness took possession of her heart. She folded up the letter with neat propriety, however, and handed it back to John Ayliffe, saying, in her very sweetest tones, "Well, I do not think this so very bad as you seem to imagine. They have found out that your mother is still living, and that is all. They cannot make much of that."

"Not much of that!" exclaimed John Ayliffe, now nearly driven to frenzy, "what if they convict one of perjury for swearing she was dead?"

"Did you swear she was dead?" exclaimed Mrs. Hazleton with an exceedingly well assumed look of profound astonishment.

"To be sure I did," he answered. "Why you proposed that she should be sent away yourself, and Shanks drew out the affidavit."

A mingled look of consternation and indignation came into Mrs. Hazleton's beautiful face; but before she could make any reply he went on, thinking he had frightened her; which was in itself a satisfaction and a sort of triumph.

"Ay, that you did," he said, "and not only that, but you advanced me all the money to carry on the suit, and I am told that that is punishable by law. Besides, you knew quite well of the leaf being torn out of the register, so we are in the same basket I can tell you, Mrs. Hazleton."

"Sir, you insult me," said the lady, rising with an air of imperious dignity. "The charity which induced me to advance you different sums of money, without knowing what they were to be applied to--and I can prove that some of them were applied to very different purposes than a suit at law--has been misunderstood, I see. Had I advanced them to carry on this suit, they would have been paid to your and my lawyer, not to yourself. Not a word more, if you please! You have mistaken my character as well as my motives, if you suppose that I will suffer you to remain here one moment after you have insulted me by the very thought that I was any sharer in your nefarious transactions." She spoke in a loud shrill tone, knowing that the servants were in the hall hard by, and then she added, "Save me the pain, sir, of ordering some of the men to put you out of the house by quitting it directly."

"Oh, yes, I will go, I will go," cried John Ayliffe, now quite maddened, "I will go to the devil, and you too, madam," and he burst out of the room, leaving the door open behind him.

"I can compassionate misfortune," cried Mrs. Hazleton, raising her voice to the very highest pitch for the benefit of others, "but I will have nothing to do with roguery and fraud," and as she heard his horse's feet clatter over the terrace, she heartily wished he might break his neck before he passed the park gates. How far she was satisfied, and how far she was not, must be shown in another chapter.

CHAPTER XXXV

John Ayliffe got out of the park gates quite safely, though he rode down the slope covered with loose stones, as if he had no consideration for his own neck or his horse's knees. He was in a state of desperation, however, and feared little at that moment what became of himself or any thing else. With fierce and angry eagerness he revolved in his own mind the circumstances of his situation, the conduct of Mrs. Hazleton, the folly, as he was pleased to term it, of his mother, the crimes which he had himself committed, and he found no place of refuge in all the dreary waste of thought. Every thing around looked menacing and terrible, and the world within was all dark and stormy.

He pushed his horse some way on the road which he had come, but suddenly a new thought struck him. He resolved to seek advice and aid from one whom he had previously determined to avoid. "I will go to Shanks," he said to himself, "he at least is in the same basket with myself. He must work with me, for if my mother has been fool enough to keep my letters, I have been wise enough to keep his--perhaps something may be done after all. If not, he shall go along with me, and we will try if we cannot bring that woman in too. He can prove all her sayings and doings." Thus thinking, he turned his horse's head towards the lawyer's house, and rode as hard as he could go till he reached it.

Mr. Shanks was enjoying life over a quiet comfortable bowl of punch in a little room which looked much more tidy and comfortable, than it had done twelve or eighteen months before. Mr. Shanks had been well paid. Mr. Shanks had taken care of himself. No small portion of back rents and costs had gone into the pockets of Mr. Shanks. Mr. Shanks was all that he had ever desired to be, an opulent man. Moreover, he was one of those happily constituted mortals who know the true use of wealth--to make it a means of enjoyment. He had no scruples of conscience--not he. He little cared how the money came, so that it found its way into his pocket. He was not a man to let his mind be troubled by any unpleasant remembrances; for he had a maxim that every man's duty was to do the very best he could for his client, and that every man's first client was himself.

He heard a horse stop at his door, and having made up his mind to end the night comfortably, to finish his punch and go to bed, he might perhaps have been a little annoyed, had he not consoled himself with the thought that the call must be upon business of importance, and he had no idea of business of importance unconnected with that of a large fee.

"To draw a will, I'll bet any money," said Mr. Shanks to himself; "it is either old Sir Peter, dying of indigestion, and sent for me when he's no longer able to speak, or John Ayliffe broken his neck leaping over a five-barred gate--John Ayliffe, bless us all, Sir John Hastings I should have said."

But the natural voice of John Ayliffe, asking for him in a loud impatient tone, dispelled these visions of his fancy, and in another moment the young man was in the room.

"Ah, Sir John, very glad to see you, very glad to see you," said Mr. Shanks, shaking his visitor's hand, and knocking out the ashes of his pipe upon the hob; "just come in pudding time, my dear sir--just in time for a glass of punch--bring some more lemons and some sugar, Betty. A glass of punch will do you good. It is rather cold to-night."

"As hot as h--l," answered John Ayliffe, sharply; "but I'll have the punch notwithstanding," and he seated himself while the maid proceeded to fulfil her master's orders.

Mr. Shanks evidently saw that something had gone wrong with his young and distinguished client, but anticipating no evil, he was led to consider whether it was any thing referring to a litter of puppies, a favorite horse, a fire at the hall, a robbery, or a want of some more ready money.

At length, however, the fresh lemons and sugar were brought, and the door closed, before which, time John Ayliffe had helped himself to almost all the punch which he had found remaining in the bowl. It was not much, but it was strong, and Mr. Shanks applied himself to the preparation of some more medicine of the same sort. John Ayliffe suffered him to finish before he said any thing to disturb him, not from any abstract reverence for the office which Mr. Shanks was fulfilling, or for love of the beverage he was brewing, but simply because John Ayliffe began to find that he might as well consider his course a little. Consideration seldom served him very much, and in the present instance, after he had labored hard to find out the best way of breaking the matter, his impetuosity as usual got the better of him, and he thrust his mother's letter into Mr. Shanks's hand, out of which as a preliminary he took the ladle and helped himself to another glass of punch.

The consternation of Mr. Shanks, as he read Mrs. Ayliffe's letter, stood out in strong opposition to Mrs. Hazleton's sweet calmness. He was evidently as much terrified as his client; for Mr. Shanks did not forget that he had written Mrs. Ayliffe two letters since she was abroad, and as she had kept her son's epistles, Mr. Shanks argued that it was very likely she had kept his also. Their contents, taken alone, might amount to very little, but looked at in conjunction with other circumstances might amount to a great deal.

True, Mr. Shanks had avoided, as far as he could, any discussions in regard to the more delicate secrets of his profession in the presence of Mrs. Ayliffe, of whose discretion he was not as firmly convinced as he could have desired; but it was not always possible to do so, especially when he had been obliged to seek John Ayliffe in haste at her house; and now the memories of many long and dangerous conversations which had occurred in her presence, spread themselves out before his eyes in a regular row, like items on the leaves of a ledger.

"Good God!" he cried, "what has she done?"

"Every thing she ought not to have done, of course!" replied John Ayliffe, replenishing his glass, "but the question now, is, Shanks, what are we to do? That is the great question just now."

"It is indeed," answered Mr. Shanks, in great agitation; "this is very awkward, very awkward indeed."

"I know that," answered John Ayliffe, laconically.

"Well but, sir, what is to be done?" asked Mr. Shanks, fidgeting uneasily about the table.

"That is what I come to ask you, not to tell you," answered the young man; "you see, Shanks, you and I are exactly in the same case, only I have more to lose than you have. But whatever happens to me will happen to you, depend upon it. I am not going to be the only one, whatever Mrs. Hazleton may think."

Shanks caught at Mrs. Hazleton's name; "Ay, that's a good thought," he said, "we had better go and consult her. Let us put our three heads together, and we may beat them yet--perhaps."

"No use of going to her," answered John Ayliffe, bitterly; "I have been to her, and she is a thorough vixen. She cried off having any thing to do with me, and when I just told her quietly that, she ought to help me out of the scrape because she had a hand in getting me into it, she flew at my throat like a terrier bitch with a litter of puppies, barked me out of the house as if I had been a beggar, and called me almost rogue and swindler in the hearing of her own servants."

Mr. Shanks smiled--he could not refrain from smiling with a feeling of admiration and respect, even in that moment of bitter apprehension, at the decision, skill, and wisdom of Mrs. Hazleton's conduct. He approved of her highly; but he perceived quite plainly that it would not do for him to play the same game. A hope--a feeble hope--light through a loop-hole, came in upon him in regard to the future, suggested by Mrs. Hazleton's conduct. He thought that if he could but clear away some difficulties, he too might throw all blame upon John Ayliffe, and shovel the load of infamy from his own shoulders to those of his client; but to effect this, it was not only necessary that he should soothe John Ayliffe, but that he should provide for his safety and escape. Recriminations he was aware were very dangerous things, and that unless a man takes care that it shall not be in the power or for the interest of a fellow rogue to say _tu quoque_, the effort to place the burden on his shoulders only injures him without making our own case a bit better. It was therefore requisite for his purposes that he should deprive John Ayliffe of all interest or object in criminating him; but foolish knaves are very often difficult to deal with, and he knew his young client to be eminent in that class. Wishing for a little time to consider, he took occasion to ask one or two meaningless questions, without at all attending to the replies.

"When did this letter arrive here?" he inquired.

"This very night," answered John Ayliffe, "not three hours ago."

"Do you think she has really told all?" asked Mr. Shanks.

"All, and a great deal more," replied the young man.

"How long has she been at St. Germain?" said the lawyer.

"What the devil does that signify?" said John Ayliffe, growing impatient.

"A great deal, a great deal," replied Mr. Shanks, sagely. "Take some more punch. You see perhaps we can prove that you and I really thought her dead at the time the affidavit was made."

"Devilish difficult that," said John Ayliffe, taking the punch. "She wrote to me about some more money just at that time, and I was obliged to answer her letter and send it, so that if they have got the letters that won't pass."

"We'll try at least," said Mr. Shanks in a bolder tone.

"Ay, but in trying we may burn our fingers worse than ever," said the young man. "I do not want to be tried for perjury and conspiracy, and sent to the colonies with the palm of my hand burnt out, whatever you may do, Shanks."

"No, no, that would never do," replied the lawyer. "The first thing to be done, my dear Sir John, is to provide for your safety, and that can only be done by your getting out of the way for a time. It is very natural that a young gentleman of fortune like yourself should go to travel, and not at all unlikely that he should do so without letting any one know where he is for a few months. That will be the best plan for you you must go and travel. They can't well be on the look-out for you yet, and you can get away quite safely to-morrow morning. You need not say where you are going, and by that means you will save both yourself and the property too; for they can't proceed against you in any way when you are absent."

John Ayliffe was not sufficiently versed in the laws of the land to perceive that Mr. Shanks was telling him a falsehood. "That's a good thought," he said; "if I can live abroad and keep hold of the rents we shall be safe enough."

"Certainly, certainly," said Mr. Shanks, "that is the only plan. Then let them file their bills, or bring their actions or what not. They cannot compel you to answer if you are not within the realm."

Mr. Shanks was calling him all the time, in his own mind, a jolter-headed ass, but John Ayliffe did not perceive it, and replied with a touch of good feeling, perhaps inspired by the punch, "But what is to become of you, Shanks?"

"Oh, I will stay and face it out," replied the lawyer, "with a bold front. If we do not peach of each other they cannot do much against us. Mrs. Hazleton dare not commit us, for by so doing she would commit herself; and your mother's story will not avail very much. As to the letters, which is the worst part of the business, we must try and explain those away; but clearly the first thing for you to do is to get out of England as soon as possible. You can go and see your mother secretly, and if you can but get her to prevaricate a little in her testimony it will knock it all up."

"Oh, she'll prevaricate enough if they do but press her hard," said John Ayliffe. "She gets so frightened at the least thing she doesn't know what she says. But the worst of it is, Shanks, I have not got money enough to go. I have not got above a hundred guineas in the house."

Mr. Shanks paused and hesitated. It was a very great object with him to get John Ayliffe out of the country, in order that he might say any thing he liked of John Ayliffe when his back was turned, but it was also a very great object with him to keep all the money he had got. He did not like to part with one sixpence of it. After a few moments' thought, however, he recollected that a thousand pounds' worth of plate had come down from London for the young man within the last two months, and he thought he might make a profitable arrangement.

"I have got three hundred pounds in the house," he said, "all in good gold, but I can really hardly afford to part with it. However, rather than injure you, Sir John, I will let you have it if you will give me the custody of your plate till your return, just that I may have something to show if any one presses me for money."

The predominant desire of John Ayliffe's mind, at that moment, was to get out of England as fast as possible, and he was too much blinded by fear and anxiety to perceive that the great desire of Mr. Shanks was to get him out. But there was one impediment. The sum of four hundred pounds thus placed at his command would, some years before, have appeared the Indies to him, but now, with vastly expanded ideas with regard to expense, it seemed a drop of water in the ocean. "Three hundred pounds, Shanks," he said, "what's the use of three hundred pounds? It would not keep me a month."

"God bless my soul!" said Mr. Shanks, horrified at such a notion, "why it would keep me a whole year, and more too. Moreover, things are cheaper there than they are here; and besides you have got all those jewels, and knick-knacks, and things, which cost you at least a couple of thousand pounds. They would sell for a great deal."

"Come, come, Shanks," said the young man, "you must make it five hundred guineas. I know you've got them in your strong box here."

Shanks shook his head, and John Ayliffe added sullenly, "Then I'll stay and fight it out too. I won't go and be a beggar in a foreign land."

Shanks did not like the idea of his staying, and after some farther discussion a compromise was effected. Mr. Shanks agreed to advance four hundred pounds. John Ayliffe was to make over to him, as a pledge, the whole of his plate, and not to object to a memorandum to that effect being drawn up immediately, and dated a month before. The young man was to set off the very next day, in the pleasant gray of the morning, driving his own carriage and horses, which he was to sell as soon as he got a convenient distance from his house, and Mr. Shanks was to take the very best possible care of his interests during his absence.

John Ayliffe's spirits rose at the conclusion of this transaction. He calculated that with one thing or another he should have sufficient money to last him a year, and that was quite as far as his thoughts or expectations went. A long, long year! What does youth care for any thing beyond a year? It seems the very end of life to pant in expectation, and indeed, and in truth, it is very often too long for fate.

"Next year I will"-- Pause, young man! there is a deep pitfall in the way. Between you and another year may lie death. Next year thou wilt do nothing--thou wilt be nothing.

His spirits rose. He put the money into his pocket, and, with more wit than he thought, called it "light heaviness," and then he sat down and smoked a pipe, while Mr. Shanks drew up the paper; and then he drank punch, and made more, and drank that too, so that when the paper giving Mr. Shanks a lien upon the silver was completed, and when a dull neighbor had been called in to see him sign his name, it needed a witness indeed to prove that that name was John Ayliffe's writing.

By this time he would very willingly have treated the company to a song, so complete had been the change which punch and new prospects had effected; but Mr. Shanks besought him to be quiet, hinting that the neighbor, though as deaf as a post and blind as a mole, would think him as the celebrated sow of the psalmist. Thereupon John Ayliffe went forth and got his horse out of the stable, mounted upon his back, and rode lolling at a sauntering pace through the end of the town in which Mr. Shanks's house was situated. When he got more into the Country he began to trot, then let the horse fall into a walk again, and then he beat him for going slow. Thus alternately galloping, walking, and trotting, he rode on till he was two or three hundred yards past the gates of what was called the Court, where the family of Sir Philip Hastings now lived. It was rather a dark part of the road, and there was something white in the hedge--some linen put out to dry, or a milestone. John Ayliffe was going at a quick pace at that moment, and the horse suddenly shied at this white apparition--not only shied, but started, wheeled round, and ran back. John Ayliffe kept his seat, notwithstanding his tipsiness, but he struck the furious horse over the head, and pulled the rein violently. The annual plunged--reared--the young man gave the rein a furious tug, and over went the horse upon the road, with his driver under him.

CHAPTER XXXVI

There was a man lay upon the road in the darkness of the night for some five or six minutes, and a horse galloped away snorting, with a broken bridle hanging at his head, on the way towards the park of Sir Philip Hastings. Had any carriage come along, the man who was lying there must have been run over; for the night was exceedingly dark, and the road narrow. All was still and silent, however. No one was seen moving--not a sound was heard except the distant clack of a water-mill which lay further down the valley. There was a candle in a cottage window at about a hundred yards' distance, which shot a dim and feeble ray athwart the road, but shed no light on the spot where the man lay. At the end of about six minutes, a sort of convulsive movement showed that life was not yet extinct in his frame--a sort of heave of the chest, and a sudden twitch of the arm; and a minute or two after, John Ayliffe raised himself on his elbow, at put his hand to his head.

"Curse the brute," he said, in a wandering sort of way, "I wonder, Shanks, you don't--damn it, where am I?--what's the matter? My side and leg are cursed sore, and my head all running round."

He remained in the same position for a moment or two more, and then got upon his feet; but the instant he did so he fell to the ground again with a deep groan, exclaiming, "By--, my leg's broken, and I believe my ribs too. How the devil shall I get out of this scrape? Here I may lie and die, without any body ever coming near me. That is old Jenny Best's cottage, I believe. I wonder if I could make the old canting wretch hear," and he raised his voice to shout, but the pain was two great. His ribs were indeed broken, and pressing upon his lungs, and all that he could do was to lie still and groan.

About a quarter of an hour after, however, a stunt, middle-aged man--rather, perhaps, in the decline of life--came by, carrying a hand-basket, plodding at a slow and weary pace as if he had had a long walk.

"Who's that? Is any one there?" said a feeble voice, as he approached; and he ran up, exclaiming, "Gracious me, what is the matter? Are you hurt, sir? What has happened?"

"Is that you, Best?" said the feeble voice of John Ayliffe, "my horse has reared and fallen over with me. My leg is broken, and the bone poking through, and my ribs are broken too, I think."

"Stay a minute, Sir John," said the good countryman, "and I'll get help, and we'll carry you up to the Hall."

"No, no," answered John Ayliffe, who had now had time for thought, "get a mattress, or a door, or something, and carry me into your cottage. If your son is at home, he and you can carry me. Don't send for strangers."

"I dare say he is at home, sir," replied the man. "He's a good lad, sir, and comes home as soon as his work's done. I will go and see. I won't be a minute."

He was as good as his word, and in less than a minute returned with his son, bringing a lantern and a straw mattress.

Not without inflicting great pain, and drawing forth many a heavy groan, the old man and the young one placed John Ayliffe on the paliasse, and carried him into the cottage, where he was laid upon young Best's bed in the back room. Good Jenny Best, as John Ayliffe had called her--an excellent creature as ever lived--was all kindness and attention, although to say truth the suffering man had not shown any great kindness to her and hers in his days of prosperity. She was eager to send off her son immediately for the surgeon, and did so in the end; but to the surprise of the whole of the little cottage party, it was not without a great deal of reluctance and hesitation that John Ayliffe suffered this to be done. They showed him, however, that he must die or lose his limb if surgical assistance was not immediately procured, and he ultimately consented, but told the young man repeatedly not to mention his name even to the surgeon on any account, but simply to say that a gentleman had been thrown by his horse, and brought into the cottage with his thigh broken. He cautioned father and mother too not to mention the accident to any one till he was well again, alluding vaguely to reasons that he had for wishing to conceal it.

"But, Sir John," replied Best himself, "your horse will go home, depend upon it, and your servants will not know where you are, and there will be a fuss about you all over the country."

"Well, then, let them make a fuss," said John Ayliffe, impatiently. "I don't care--I will not have it mentioned."

All this seemed very strange to the good wan and his wife, but they could only open their eyes and stare, without venturing farther to oppose the wishes of their guest.

It seemed a very long time before the surgeon made his appearance, but at length the sound of a horse's feet coming fast, could be distinguished, and two minutes after the surgeon was in the room. He was a very good man, though not the most skilful of his profession, and he was really shocked and confounded when he saw the state of Sir John Hastings, as he called him. Wanting confidence in himself, he would fain have sent off immediately for farther assistance, but John Ayliffe would not hear of such a thing, and the good man went to work to set the broken limb as best he might, and relieve the anguish of the sufferer. So severe, however, were the injuries which had been received, that notwithstanding a strong constitution, as yet but little impaired by debauchery, the patient was given over by the surgeon in his own mind from the first. He remained with him, watching him all night, which passed nearly without sleep on the part of John Ayliffe; and in the course of the long waking hours he took an opportunity of enjoining secrecy upon the surgeon as to the accident which had happened to him, and the place where he was lying. Not less surprised was the worthy man than the cottager and his wife had been at the young gentleman's exceeding anxiety for concealment, and as his licentious habits were no secret in the country round, they all naturally concluded that the misfortune which had overtaken him had occurred in the course of some adventure more dangerous and disgraceful than usual.

Towards morning John Ayliffe fell into a sort of semi-sleep, restless and perturbed, speaking often without reason having guidance of his words, and uttering many things which, though disjointed and often indistinct, showed the good man who had watched by him that the mind was as much affected as the body. He woke confused and wandering about eight o'clock, but speedily returned to consciousness of his situation, and insisted, notwithstanding the pain he was suffering, upon examining the money which was in his pockets to see that it was all right. Vain precaution! He was never destined to need it more.

Shortly after the surgeon left him, but returned at night again to watch by his bedside. The bodily symptoms which he now perceived would have led him to believe that a cure was possible, but there was a deep depression of mind, a heavy irritable sombreness, from the result of which the surgeon augured much evil. He saw that there was some terrible weight upon the young man's heart, but whether it was fear or remorse or disappointment he could not tell, and more than once he repeated to himself, "He wants a priest as much as a physician."

Again the surgeon would often argue with himself in regard to the propriety of telling him the very dangerous state in which he was. "He may at any time become delirious," he said, "and lose all power of making those dispositions and arrangements which, I dare say, have never been thought of in the time of health and prosperity. Then, again, his house and all that it contains is left entirely in the hands of servants-a bad set too, as ever existed, who are just as likely to plunder and destroy as not; but on the other hand, if I tell him it may only increase his dejection and cut off all hope of recovery. Really I do not know what to do. Perhaps it would be better to wait awhile, and if I should see more unfavorable symptoms and no chance left, it will then be time enough to tell him his true situation and prepare his mind for the result."

Another restless, feverish night passed, another troubled sleep towards morning, and then John Ayliffe woke with a start, exclaiming, "You did not tell them I was here--lying here unable to stir, unable to move--I told you not, I told you not. By--" and then he looked round, and seeing none but the surgeon in the room, relapsed into silence.

The surgeon felt his pulse, examined the bandages, and saw that a considerable and unfavorable change had taken place; but yet he hesitated. He was one of those men who shrink from the task of telling unpleasant truths. He was of a gentle and a kindly disposition, which even the necessary cruelties of surgery had not been able to harden.

"He may say what he likes," he said, "I must have some advice as to how I should act. I will go and talk with the parson about the matter. Though a little lacking in the knowledge of the world, yet Dixwell is a good man and a sincere Christian. I will see him as I go home, but make him promise secrecy in the first place, as this young baronet is so terribly afraid of the unfortunate affair being known. He will die, I am afraid, and that before very long, and I am sure he is not in a fit state for death." With this resolution he said some soothing words to his patient, gave him what he called a composing draught, and sent for his horse from a neighboring farm-house, where he had lodged it for the night. He then rode at a quiet, thoughtful pace to the parsonage house at the gates of the park, and quickly walked in. Mr. Dixwell was at breakfast, reading slowly one of the broad sheets of the day as an especial treat, for they seldom found their way into his quiet rectory; but he was very glad to see the surgeon, with whom he often contrived to have a pleasant little chat in regard to the affairs of the neighborhood.

"Ah, Mr. Short, very glad to see you, my good friend. How go things in your part of the world? We are rather in a little bustle here, though I think it is no great matter."

"What is it, Mr. Dixwell?" asked the surgeon.

"Only that wild young man, Sir John Hastings," said the clergyman, "left his house suddenly on horseback the night before last, and has never returned. But he is accustomed to do all manner of strange things, and has often been out two or three nights before without any one knowing where he was. The butler came down and spoke to me about it, but I think there was a good deal of affectation in his alarm, for when I asked him he owned his master had once been away for a whole week."

"Has his horse come back?" asked the surgeon.

"Not that I know of," replied Mr. Dixwell. "I suppose the man would have mentioned it if such had been the case. But what is going on at Hartwell?"

"Nothing particular," said the surgeon, "only Mrs. Harrison brought to bed of twins on Saturday night at twenty minutes past eleven. I think all those Harrisons have twins--but I have something to talk to you about, my good friend, a sort of case of conscience I want to put to you. Only you must promise me profound secrecy."

Mr. Dixwell laughed--"What, under the seal of confession?" he said. "Well, well, I am no papist, as you know, Short, but I'll promise and do better than any papist does, keep my word when I have promised without mental reservation."

"I know you will, my good friend," answered the surgeon, "and this is no jesting matter, I can assure you. Now listen, my good friend, listen. Not many evenings ago, I was sent for suddenly to attend a young man who had met with an accident, a very terrible accident too. He had a compound fracture of the thigh, three of his ribs broken, and his head a good deal knocked about, but the cranium uninjured. I had at first tolerable hope of his recovery; but he is getting much worse and I fear that he will die."

"Well, you can't help that," said Mr. Dixwell, "men will die in spite of all you can do, Short, just as they will sin in spite of all I can say."

"Ay, there's the rub," said the surgeon, "I fear he has sinned a very tolerably sufficient quantity, and I can see that there is something or another weighing very heavy on his mind, which is even doing great harm to his body."

"I will go and see him, I will go and see him," said Mr. Dixwell, "it will do him good in all ways to unburden his conscience, and to hear the comfortable words of the gospel."

"But the case is, Mr. Dixwell," said Short, "that he has positively forbidden me to let any of his friends know where he lies, or to speak of the accident to any one."

"Pooh, nonsense," said the clergyman, "if a man has fractured his skull and you thought it fit to trepan him, would you ask him whether he liked it or not? If the young man is near death, and his conscience is burdened, I am the physician who should be sent for rather than you."

"I fancy his conscience is burdened a good deal," said Mr. Short, thoughtfully; "nay, I cannot help thinking that he was engaged in some very bad act at the time this happened, both from his anxiety to conceal from every body where he now lies, and from various words he has dropped, sometimes in his sleep, sometimes when waking confused and half delirious. What puzzles me is, whether I should tell him his actual situation or not."

"Tell him, tell him by all means," said Mr. Dixwell, "why should you not tell him?"

"Simply because I think that it will depress his mind still more," replied the surgeon, "and that may tend to deprive him even of the very small chance that exists of recovery."

"The soul is of more value than the body," replied the clergyman, earnestly; "if he be the man you depict, my friend, he should have as much time as possible to prepare--he should have time to repent--ay, and to atone. Tell him by all means, or let me know where he is to be found, and I will tell him."

"That I must not do," said Mr. Short, "for I am under a sort of promise not to tell; but if you really think that I ought to tell him myself, I will go back and do it."

"If I really think!" exclaimed Mr. Dixwell, "I have not the slightest doubt of it. It is your bounden duty if you be a Christian. Not only tell him, my good friend, but urge him strongly to send for some minister of religion. Though friends may fail him, and he may not wish to see them--though all worldly supports may give way beneath him, and he may find no strengthening--though all earthly hopes may pass away, and give him no mortal cheer, the gospel of Christ can never fail to support, and strengthen, and comfort, and elevate. The sooner he knows that his tenement of clay is falling to the dust of which it was raised, the better will be his readiness to quit it, and it is wise, most wise, to shake ourselves free altogether from the dust and crumbling ruins of this temporal state, ere they fall upon our heads and bear us down to the same destruction as themselves."

"Well, well, I will go back and tell him," said Mr. Short, and bidding the good rector adieu, he once more mounted his horse and rode away.

Now Mr. Dixwell was an excellent good man, but he was not without certain foibles, especially those that sometimes accompany considerable simplicity of character. "I will see which way he takes," said Mr. Dixwell, "and go and visit the young man myself if I can find him out;" and accordingly he marched up stairs to his bedroom, which commanded a somewhat extensive prospect of the country, and traced the surgeon, as he trotted slowly and thoughtfully along. He could not actually see the cottage of the Bests, but he perceived that the surgeon there passed over the brow of the hill, and after waiting for several minutes, he did not catch any horseman rising upon the opposite slope over which the road was continued. Now there was no cross road in the hollow and only three houses, and therefore Mr. Dixwell naturally concluded that to one of those three houses the surgeon had gone.

In the mean while, Mr. Short rode on unconscious that his movements were observed, and meditating with a troubled mind upon the best means of conveying the terrible intelligence he had to communicate. He did not like the task at all; but yet he resolved to perform it manfully, and dismounting at the cottage door, he went in again. There was nobody within but the sick man and good old Jenny Best. The old woman was at the moment in the outer room, and when she saw the surgeon she shook her head, and said in a low voice, "Ah, dear, I am glad you have come back again, sir, he does not seem right at all."

"Who's that?" said the voice of John Ayliffe; and going in, Mr. Short closed the doors between the two rooms.

"There, don't shut that door," said John Ayliffe, "it is so infernally close--I don't feel at all well, Mr. Short--I don't know what's the matter with me. It's just as if I had got no heart. I think a glass of brandy would do me good."

"It would kill you," said the surgeon.

"Well," said the young man, "I'm not sure that would not be best for me--come," he continued sharply, "tell me how long I am to lie here on my back?"

"That I cannot tell, Sir John," replied the surgeon, "but at all events, supposing that you do recover, and that every thing goes well, you could not hope to move for two or three months."

"Supposing I was to recover!" repeated John Ayliffe in a low tone, as if the idea of approaching death had then, for the first time, struck him as something real and tangible, and not a mere name. He paused silently for an instant, and then asked almost fiercely, "what brought you back?"

"Why, Sir John, I thought it might be better for us to have a little conversation," said the surgeon. "I can't help being afraid, Sir John, that you may have a great number of things to settle, and that not anticipating such a very severe accident, your affairs may want a good deal of arranging. Now the event of all sickness is uncertain, and an accident such as this especially. It is my duty to inform you," he continued, rising in resolution and energy as he proceeded, "that your case is by no means free from danger--very great danger indeed."

"Do you mean to say that I am dying?" asked John Ayliffe, in a hoarse voice.

"No, no, not exactly dying," said the surgeon, putting his hand upon his pulse, "not dying I trust just yet, but--"

"But I shall die, you mean?" cried the other.

"I think it not at all improbable," answered the surgeon, gravely, "that the case may have a fatal result."

"Curse fatal results," cried John Ayliffe, giving way to a burst of fury; "why the devil do you come back to tell me such things and make me wretched? If I am to die, why can't you let me die quietly and know nothing about it?"

"Why, Sir John, I thought that you might have many matters to settle," answered the surgeon somewhat irritated, "and that your temporal and your spiritual welfare also required you should know your real situation."

"Spiritual d----d nonsense!" exclaimed John Ayliffe, furiously; "I dare say it's all by your folly and stupidity that I am likely to die at all. Why I hear of men breaking their legs and their ribs every day and being none the worse for it."

"Why, Sir John, if you do not like my advice you need not have it," answered the surgeon; "I earnestly wished to send for other assistance, and you would not let me."

"There, go away, go away and leave me," said John Ayliffe; but as the surgeon took up his hat and walked towards the door, he added, "come again at night. You shall be well paid for it, never fear."

Mr. Short made no reply, but walked out of the room.

CHAPTER XXXVII

Solitude and silence, and bitter thought are great tamers of the human heart. "As ye sow, so shall ye reap," says the Apostle, and John Ayliffe was now forced to put in the sickle. Death was before his eyes, looming large and dark and terrible, like the rock of adamant in the fairy tale, against which the bark of the adventurous mariner was sure to be dashed. Death for the first time presented itself to his mind in all its grim reality. Previously it had seemed with him a thing hardly worth considering--inevitable-- appointed to all men--to every thing that lives and breathes--no more to man than to the sheep, or the ox, or any other of the beasts that perish. He had contemplated it merely as death--as the extinction of being--as the goal of a career--as the end of a chase where one might lie down and rest, and forget the labor and the clamor and the trouble of the course. He had never in thought looked beyond the boundary--he had hardly asked himself if there was aught beyond. He had satisfied himself by saying, as so many men do, "Every man must die some time or another," and had never asked his own heart, "What is it to die?"

But now death presented itself under a new aspect; cold and stern, relentless and mysterious, saying in a low solemn tone, "I am the guide. Follow me there. Whither I lead thou knowest not, nor seest what shall befall thee. The earth-worm and the mole fret but the earthly garment of the man; the flesh, and the bones, and the beauty go down to dust, and ashes, and corruption. The man comes with me to a land undeclared--to a presence infinitely awful--to judgment and to fate; for on this side of the dark portal through which I am the guide, there is no such thing as fate. It lies beyond the grave, and thither thou must come without delay."

He had heard of immortality, but he had never thought of it. He had been told of another world, but he had never rightly believed in it. The thought of a just judge, and of an eternal doom, had been presented to him in many shapes, but he had never received it; and he had lived and acted, and thought and felt, as if there were neither eternity, nor judgment, nor punishment. But in that dread hour the deep-rooted, inexplicable conviction of a God and immortality, implanted in the hearts of all men, and only crushed down in the breasts of any by the dust of vanity and the lumber of the world, rose up and bore its fruits according to the soil. They were all bitter. If there were another life, a judgment, an eternity of weal or woe, what was to be his fate? How should he meet the terrors of the judgment-seat--he who had never prayed from boyhood--he who through life had never sought God--he who had done in every act something that conscience reproved, and that religion forbade?

Every moment as he lay there and thought, the terrors of the vast unbounded future grew greater and more awful. The contemplation almost drove him to frenzy, and he actually made an effort to rise from his bed, but fell back again with a deep groan. The sound caught the ear of good Jenny Best, and running in she asked if he wanted any thing.

"Stay with me, stay with me," said the unhappy young man, "I cannot bear this--it is very terrible--I am dying, Mrs. Best, I am dying."

Mrs. Best shook her head with a melancholy look; but whether from blunted feelings, from the hard and painful life which they endured, or from a sense that there is to be compensation somewhere, and that any change must be for the better, or cannot be much worse than the life of this earth, or from want of active imagination, the poorer and less educated classes I have generally remarked view death and all its accessories with less of awe, if not of dread, than those who have been surrounded by luxuries, and perhaps have used every effort to keep the contemplation of the last dread scene afar, till it is actually forced upon their notice. Her words were homely, and though intended to comfort did not give much consolation to the dying man.

"Ah well, sir, it is very sad," she said, "to die so young; though every one must die sooner or later, and it makes but little difference whether it be now or then. Life is not so long to look back at, sir, as to look forward to, and when one dies young one is spared many a thing. I recollect my poor eldest son who is gone, when he lay dying just like you in that very bed, and I was taking on sadly, he said to me, 'Mother don't cry so. It's just as well for me to go now when I've not done much mischief or suffered much sorrow.' He was as good a young man as ever lived; and so Mr. Dixwell said; for the parson used to come and see him every day, and that was a great comfort and consolation to the poor boy."

"Was it?" said John Ayliffe, thoughtfully. "How long did he know he was dying?"

"Not much above a week, sir," said Mrs. Best; "for till Mr. Dixwell told him, he always thought he would get better. We knew it a long time however, for he had been in a decline a year, and his father had been laying by money for the funeral three months before he died. So when it was all over we put him by quite comfortable."

"Put him by!" said John Ayliffe.

"Yes, sir, we buried him, I mean," answered Mrs. Best. "That's our way of talking. But Mr. Dixwell had been to see him long before. He knew that he was dying, and he wouldn't tell him as long as there was any hope; for he said it was not necessary--that he had never seen any one better prepared to meet his Maker than poor Robert, and that it was no use to disturb him about the matter till it came very near."

"Ah, Dixwell is a wise man and a good man," said John Ayliffe. "I should very much like to see him."

"I can run for him in a minute sir," said Dame Best, but John Ayliffe replied, in a faint voice, "No, no, don't, don't on any account."

In the mean while, the very person of whom they were speaking had descended from the up-stairs room, finished his breakfast in order to give the surgeon time to fulfil his errand, and then putting on his three-cornered hat had walked out to ascertain at what house Mr. Short had stopped. The first place at which he inquired was the farm-house at which the good surgeon had stabled his horse on the preceding night. Entering by the kitchen door, he found the good woman of the place bustling about amongst pots and pans and maidservants, and other utensils, and though she received him with much reverence, she did not for a moment cease her work.

"Well, Dame," he said, "I hope you're all well here."

"Quite well, your reverence----Betty, empty that pail."

"Why, I've seen Mr. Short come down here," said the parson, "and I thought somebody might be ill."

"Very kind, your reverence--mind yen don't spill it.--No, it warn't here. It's some young man down at Jenny Best's, who's baddish, I fancy, for the Doctor stabled his horse here last night."

The Man In Black | 263

"I am glad to hear none of you are ill," said Mr. Dixwell, and bidding her good morning, he walked away straight to the cottage where John Ayliffe lay. There was no one in the outer room, and the good clergyman, privileged by his cloth, walked straight on into the room beyond, and stood by the bedside of the dying man before any one was aware of his presence.

Mr. Dixwell was not so much surprised to see there on that bed of death the face of him he called Sir John Hastings, as might be supposed. The character which the surgeon had given of his patient, the mysterious absence of the young man from the Hall, and the very circumstance of his unwillingness to have his name and the place where he was lying known, had all lent a suspicion of the truth. John Ayliffe's eyes were shut at the moment he entered, and he seemed dozing, though in truth sleep was far away. But the little movement of Mr. Dixwell towards his bedside, and of Mrs. Best giving place for the clergyman to sit down, caused him to open his eyes, and his first exclamation was, "Ah, Dixwell! so that damned fellow Short has betrayed me, and told when I ordered him not."

"Swear not at all," said Mr. Dixwell. "Short has not betrayed you, Sir John. I came here by accident, merely hearing there was a young man lying ill here, but without knowing actually that it was you, although your absence from home has caused considerable uneasiness. I am very sorry to see you in such a state. How did all this happen?"

"I will not tell you, nor answer a single word," replied John Ayliffe, "unless you promise not to say a word of my being here to any one. I know you will keep your word if you say so, and Jenny Best too--won't you, Jenny?--but I doubt that fellow Short."

"You need not doubt him, Sir John," said the clergyman; "for he is very discreet. As for me, I will promise, and will keep my word; for I see not what good it could be to reveal it to any body if you dislike it. You will be more tenderly nursed here, I am sure, than you would be by unprincipled, dissolute servants, and since your poor mother's death--"

John Ayliffe groaned heavily, and the clergyman stopped. The next moment, however, the young man said, "Then you do promise, do you?"

"I do," replied Mr. Dixwell. "I will not at all reveal the facts without your consent."

"Well, then, sit down, and let us be alone together for a bit," said John Ayliffe, and Mrs. Best quietly quitted the room and shut the door.

John Ayliffe turned his languid eyes anxiously upon the clergyman, saying, "I think I am dying, Mr. Dixwell."

He would fain have had a contradiction or even a ray of earthly hope; but he got none; for it was evident to the eyes of Mr. Dixwell, accustomed as he had been for many years to attend by the bed of sickness and see the last spark of life go out, that John Ayliffe was a dying man--that he might live hours, nay days; but that the irrevocable summons had been given, that he was within the shadow of the arch, and must pass through!

"I am afraid you are, Sir John," he replied, "but I trust that God will still afford you time to make preparation for the great change about to take place, and by his grace I will help you to the utmost in my power."

John Ayliffe was silent, and closed his eyes again. Nor was he the first to speak; for after having waited for several minutes, Mr. Dixwell resumed, saying in a grave but kindly tone, "I am afraid, Sir John, you have not hitherto given much thought to the subject which is now so sadly fixed upon you. We must make haste, my good sir; we must not lose a moment."

"Then do you think I am going to die so soon?" asked the young man with a look of horror; for it cost him a hard and terrible struggle to bring his mind to grasp the thought of death being inevitable and nigh at hand. He could hardly conceive it--he could hardly believe it--that he who had so lately been full of life and health, who had been scheming schemes, and laying out plans, and had looked upon futurity as a certain possession--that, he was to die in a few short hours; but whenever the wilful heart would have rebelled against the sentence, and struggle to resist it, sensations which he had never felt before, told him in a voice not to be mistaken, "It must be so!"

"No one can tell," replied Mr. Dixwell, "how soon it may be, or how long God may spare you; but one thing is certain, Sir John, that years with you have now dwindled down into days, and that days may very likely be shortened to hours. But had you still years to live, I should say the same thing, that no time is to be lost; too much has been lost already."

John Ayliffe did not comprehend him in the least. He could not grasp the idea as yet of a whole life being made a preparation for death, and looked vacantly in the clergyman's face, utterly confounded at the thought.

Mr. Dixwell had a very difficult task before him--one of the most difficult he had ever undertaken; for he had not only to arouse the conscience, but to awaken the intellect to things importing all to the soul's salvation, which had never been either felt or believed, or comprehended before. At first too, there was the natural repugnance and resistance of a wilful, selfish, over-indulged heart to receive painful or terrible truths, and even when the obstacle was overcome, the young man's utter ignorance of religion and want of moral feeling proved another almost insurmountable. He found that the only access to John Ayliffe's heart was by the road of terror, and without scruple he painted in stern and fearful colors the awful state of the impenitent spirit called suddenly into the presence of its God. With an unpitying hand he stripped away all self-delusions from the young man's mind and laid his condition before him, and his future state in all their dark and terrible reality.

This is not intended for what is called a religious book, and therefore I must pass over the arguments he used, and the course he proceeded in. Suffice it that he labored earnestly for two hours to awaken something like repentance in the bosom of John Ayliffe, and he succeeded in the end better than the beginning had promised. When thoroughly convinced of the moral danger of his situation, John Ayliffe began to listen more eagerly, to reply more humbly, and to seek earnestly for some consolation beyond the earth. His depression and despair, as terrible truths became known to him were just in proportion to his careless boldness and audacity while he had remained in wilful ignorance, and as soon as Mr. Dixwell saw that all the clinging to earthly expectations was gone--that every frail support of mortal thoughts was taken away, he began to give him gleams of hope from another world, and had the satisfaction of finding that the doubts and terrors which remained arose from the consciousness of his own sins and crimes, the heavy load of which he felt for the first time. He told him that repentance was never too late--he showed him that Christ himself had stamped that great truth with a mark that could not be mistaken in his pardon of the dying thief upon the cross, and while he exhorted him to examine himself strictly, and to make sure that what he felt was real repentance, and not the mere fear of death which so many mistake for it in their last hours, he assured him that if he could feel certain of that fact, and trust in his Saviour, he might comfort himself and rest in good hope. That done, he resolved to leave the young man to himself for a few hours that he might meditate and try the great question he had propounded with his own heart. He called in Mistress Best, however, and told her that if during his absence Sir John wished her to read to him, it would be a great kindness to read certain passages of Scripture which he pointed out in the house Bible. The good woman very willingly undertook the task, and shortly after the clergyman was gone John Ayliffe applied to hear the words of that book against which he had previously shut his ears. He found comfort and consolation and guidance therein; for Mr. Dixwell, who, on the one subject which had been the study of his life was wise as well as learned, had selected judiciously such passages as tend to inspire hope without diminishing penitence.

CHAPTER XXXVIII

We must now turn on more to Sir Philip Hastings as he sat in his lonely room in prison. Books had been allowed him, paper, pen, and ink, and all that could aid to pass the time; but Sir Philip had matter for study in his own mind, and the books had remained unopened for several days. Hour after hour, since his interview with Secretary Vernon, and day after day he had paced that room to and fro, till the sound of his incessant footfall was a burthen to those below. His hair had grown very white, the wrinkles on his brow had deepened and become many, and his head was bowed as if age had pressed it down. As he walked, his eye beneath his shaggy eyebrow was generally bent upon the floor, but when any accidental circumstance caused him to raise it--a distant sound from without, or some thought passing through his own mind--there was that curious gleam in it which I have mentioned when describing him in boyhood, but now heightened and rendered somewhat more wild and mysterious. At those moments the expression of his eyes amounted almost to fierceness, and yet there was something grand, and fixed, and calm about the brow which seemed to contradict the impatient, irritable look.

At the moment I now speak of there was an open letter on the table, written in his daughter's hand, and after having walked up and down for more than one hour, he sat down as if to answer it. We must look over his shoulder and see what he writes, as it may in some degree tend to show the state of his mind, although it was never sent.

"MY CHILD" (it was so he addressed the dear girl who had once been the joy of his heart): "The news which has been communicated to you by Marlow has been communicated also to me, but has given small relief. The world is a prison, and it is not very satisfactory to leave one dungeon to go into a larger.

"Nevertheless, I am desirous of returning to my own house. Your mother is very ill, with nobody to attend upon her but yourself--at least no kindred. This situation does not please me. Can I be satisfied that she will be well and properly cared for? Will a daughter who has betrayed her father show more piety towards a mother? Who is there that man can trust?"

He was going on in the same strain, and his thoughts becoming more excited, his language more stern and bitter every moment, when suddenly he paused, read over the lines he had written with a gleaming eye, and then bent his head, and fell into thought. No one can tell, no pen can describe the bitter agony of his heart at that moment. Had he yielded to the impulse--had he spoken ever so vehemently and fiercely, it would have been happier for him and for all. But men will see without knowing it in passing through the world, conventional notions which they adopt as principles. They fancy them original thoughts, springing from their own convictions, when in reality they are bents--biases given to their minds by the minds of other men. The result is very frequently painful, even where the tendency of the views received is good. Thus a shrub forced out of its natural direction may take a more graceful or beautiful form, but there is ever a danger that the flow of the sap may be stopped, or some of the branches injured by the process.

"No," said Sir Philip Hastings, at length, with a false sense of dignity thus acquired, "no, it is beneath me to reproach her. Punish her I might, and perhaps I ought; for the deed itself is an offence to society and to human nature more than to me. To punish her would have been a duty, even if my own heart's blood had flowed at the same time, in those ancient days of purer laws and higher principles; but I will not reproach without punishing. I will be silent. I will say nothing. I will leave her to her own conscience," and tearing the letter he had commenced to atoms, he resumed his bitter walk about the room.

It is a terrible and dangerous thing to go on pondering for long solitary hours on any one subject of deep interest. It is dangerous even in the open air, under the broad, ever-varying sky, with the birds upon the bough, and the breeze amongst the trees, and a thousand objects in bright nature to breathe harmonies to the human heart. It is dangerous in the midst of crowds and gay scenes of active life so to shut the spirit up with one solitary idea, which, like the fabled dragon's egg, is hatched into a monster by long looking at it. But within the walls of a prison, with nothing to divert the attention, with nothing to solicit or compel the mind even occasionally to seek some other course, with no object in external nature, with the companionship of no fellow being, to appeal to our senses or to awake our sympathies, the result is almost invariable. An innocent man--a man who has no one strong passion, or dark, all-absorbing subject of contemplation, but who seeks for and receives every mode of relief from the monotony of life that circumstances can afford may endure perfect solitude for years and live sane, but whoever condemns a criminal--a man loaded with a great offence--to solitary confinement, condemns him to insanity--a punishment far more cruel than death or the rack. Hour after hour again, day after day, Sir Philip Hastings continued to beat the floor of the prison with untiring feet. At the end of the third day, however, he received formal notice that he would be brought into court on the following morning, that the indictment against him would be read, and that the attorney-general would enter a _nolle prosequi_. Some of these forms were perhaps unnecessary, but it was the object of the government at that time to make as strong an impression on the public mind as possible without any unnecessary effusion of blood.

The effect upon the mind of Sir Philip Hastings, however, was not salutary. The presence of the judges, the crowd in the court, the act of standing in the prisoners' dock, even the brief speech of the lawyer commending the lenity and moderation of government, while he moved the recording of the _nolle prosequi_, all irritated and excited the prisoner. His irritation was shown in his own peculiar way, however; a smile, bitter and contemptuous curled his lip. His eye seemed to search out those who gazed at him most and stare them down, and when he was at length set at liberty, he turned away from the dock and walked out of the court without saying a word to any one. The governor of the jail followed him, asking civilly if he would not return to his house for a moment, take some refreshment, and arrange for the removal of his baggage. It seemed as if Sir Philip answered at all with a great effort; but in the end he replied laconically, "No, I will send."

Two hours after he did send, and towards evening set out in a hired carriage for his own house. He slept a night upon the road, and the following day reached the Court towards evening. By that time, however, a strange change had come over him. Pursuing the course of those thoughts which I have faintly displayed, he had waged war with his own mind--he had struggled to banish all traces of anger and indignation from his thoughts--in short, fearing from the sensations experienced within, that he would do or say something contrary to the rigid rule he had imposed upon himself, he had striven to lay out a scheme of conduct which would guard against such a result. The end of this self-tutoring was satisfactory to him. He had fancied he had conquered himself, but he was very much mistaken. It was only the outer man he had subdued, but not the inner.

When the carriage drew up at his own door, and Sir Philip alighted, Emily flew out to meet him. She threw her arms around his neck and kissed his cheek, and her heart beat with joy and affection.

For an instant Sir Philip remained grave and stern, did not repel her, but did not return her embrace. The next instant, however, his whole manner changed. A sort of cunning double-meaning look came into his eyes. He smiled, which was very unusual with him, assumed a sort of sportiveness, which was not natural, called her "dainty Mistress Emily," and asked after the health of "his good wife."

His coldness and his sternness might not have shocked Emily at all, but his apparent levity pained and struck her with terror. A cold sort of shudder passed over her, and unclasping her arms from his neck, she replied, "I grieve to say mamma is very ill, and although the news of your safety cheered her much, she has since made no progress, but rather fallen back."

"Doubtless the news cheered you too very much, my sweet lady," said Sir Philip in an affected tone, and without waiting for reply, he walked on and ascended to his wife's room.

Emily returned to the drawing-room and fell into one of her profound fits of meditation; but this time they were all sad and tending to sadness. There Sir Philip found her when he came down an hour after. She had not moved, she had not ordered lights, although the sun was down and the twilight somewhat murky. She did not move when he entered, but remained with her head leaning on her hand, and her eyes fixed on the table near which she sat. Sir Philip gazed at her gloomily, and said to himself, "Her heart smites her. Ha, ha, beautiful deceitful thing. Have you put the canker worm in your own bosom? Great crimes deserve great punishments. God of heaven! keep me from such thoughts. No, no, I will never avenge myself on the plea of avenging society. My own cause must not mingle with such vindications."

"Emily," he said in a loud voice, which startled her suddenly from her reverie, "Emily, your mother is very ill."

"Worse? worse?" cried Emily with a look of eager alarm; "I will fly to her at once. Oh, sir, send for the surgeon."

"Stay," said Sir Philip, "she is no worse than when you left her, except insomuch as a dying person becomes much worse every minute. Your mother wishes much to see Mrs. Hazleton, who has not been with her for two days, she says. Sit down and write that lady a note asking her to come here to-morrow, and I will send it by a groom."

Emily obeyed, though with infinite reluctance; for she had remarked that the visits of Mrs. Hazleton always left her mother neither improved in temper nor in health.

The groom was dispatched, and returned with a reply from Mrs. Hazleton to the effect that she would be there early on the following day. During his absence, Sir Philip had been but little with his daughter. Hardly had the note been written when he retired to his own small room, and there remained shut up during the greater part of the evening. Emily quietly stole into her mother's room soon after her father left her, fearing not a little that Lady Hastings might have remarked the strange change which had come upon her husband during his absence. But such was not the case. She found her mother calmer and gentler than she had been during the last week or ten days. Her husband's liberation, and the certainty that all charge against him was at an end, had afforded her great satisfaction; and although she was still evidently very ill, yet she conversed cheerfully with her daughter for nearly an hour.

"As I found you had not told your father the hopes that Mr. Marlow held out when he went away, I spoke to him on the subject," she said. "He is a strange cynic, my good husband, and seemed to care very little about the matter. He doubt's Marlow's success too, I think, but all that he said was, that if it pleased me, that was enough for him. Mrs. Hazleton will be delighted to hear the news."

Emily doubted the fact, but she did not express her doubt, merely telling her mother she had written to Mrs. Hazleton, and that the servant had been sent with the note.

"She has not been over for two days," said Lady Hastings. "I cannot think what has kept her away."

"Some accidental circumstance, I dare say," said Emily, "but there can be no doubt she will be here to-morrow early."

They neither of them knew that on the preceding night but one Mrs. Hazleton had received a visit from John Ayliffe, which, notwithstanding all her self-command and assumed indifference, had disturbed her greatly.

Mrs. Hazleton nevertheless was, as Emily anticipated, very early at the house of Sir Philip Hastings. She first made a point of seeing that gentleman himself; and though her manner was, as usual, calm and lady-like, yet every word and every look expressed the greatest satisfaction at seeing him once more in his home and at liberty. To Emily also she was all tenderness and sweetness; but Emily, on her part, shrunk from her with a feeling of dread and suspicion that she could not repress, and hardly could conceal. She had not indeed read any of the papers which Marlow had left with her, for he had not told her to read them; but he had directed her thoughts aright, and had led her to conclusions in regard to Mrs. Hazleton which were very painful, but no less just.

That lady remarked a change in Emily's manner--she had seen something of it before;--but it now struck her more forcibly, and though she took no notice of it whatever, it was not a thing to be forgotten or forgiven; for to those who are engaged in doing ill there cannot be a greater offence than to be suspected, and Mrs. Hazleton was convinced that Emily did suspect her.

After a brief interview with father and daughter, their fair guest glided quietly up to the room of Lady Hastings, and seated herself by her bedside. She took the sick lady's hand in hers--that white, emaciated hand, once so beautiful and rosy-tipped, and said how delighted she was to see her looking a great deal better.

"Do you think so really?" said Lady Hastings; "I feel dreadfully weak and exhausted, dear Mrs. Hazleton, and sometimes think I shall never recover."

"Oh don't say so," replied Mrs. Hazleton; "your husband's return has evidently done you great good: the chief part of your malady has been mental. Anxiety of mind is often the cause of severe sickness, which passes away as soon it is removed. One great source of uneasiness is now gone, and the only other that remains--I mean this unfortunate engagement of dear Emily to Mr. Marlow--may doubtless, with a little firmness and decision upon your part, be remedied also."

Mrs. Hazleton was very skillful in forcing the subject with which she wished to deal, into a conversation to which it had no reference; and having thus introduced the topic on which she loved to dwell, she went on to handle it with her usual skill, suggesting every thing that could irritate the invalid against Marlow, and render the idea of his marriage with Emily obnoxious in her eyes.

Even when Lady Hastings, moved by some feelings of gratitude and satisfaction by the intelligence of Marlow's efforts to recover her husband's property, communicated the hopes she entertained to her visitor, Mrs. Hazleton contrived to turn the very expectations to Marlow's disadvantage, saying, "If such should indeed be the result, this engagement will be still more unfortunate. With such vast property as dear Emily will then possess, with her beauty, with her accomplishments, with her graces, the hand of a prince would be hardly too much to expect for her; and to see her throw herself away upon a mere country gentleman--a Mr. Marlow--all very well in his way, but a nobody, is indeed sad; and I would certainly prevent it, if I were you, while I had power."

"But how can I prevent it?" asked Lady Hastings; "my husband and Emily are both resolute in such things. I have no power, dear Mrs. Hastings."

"Yon are mistaken, my sweet friend," replied her companion; "the power will indeed soon go from you if these hopes which have been held out do not prove fallacious. You are mistress of this house--of this very fine property. If I understand rightly, neither your husband nor your daughter have at present anything but what they derive from you. This position may soon be altered if your husband be reinstated in the Hastings estates."

"But your would not, Mrs. Hazleton, surely you would not have me use such power ungenerously?" said Lady Hastings.

Mrs. Hazleton saw that she had gone a little too far--or rather perhaps that she had suggested that which was repugnant to the character of her hearer's mind; for in regard to money matters no one was ever more generous or careless of self than Lady Hastings. What was her's was her husband's and her child's--she knew no difference--she made no distinction.

It took Mrs. Hazleton some time to undo what she had done, but she found the means at length. She touched the weak point, the failing of character. A little stratagem, a slight device to win her own way by an indirect method, was quite within the limits of Lady Hastings' principles; and after dwelling some time upon a recapitulation of all the objections against the marriage with Marlow, which could suggest themselves to an ambitious mind, she quietly and in an easy suggestive tone, sketched out a plan, which both to herself and her hearer, seemed certain of success.

Lady Hastings caught at the plan eagerly, and determined to follow it in all the details, which will be seen hereafter.

CHAPTER XXXIX

"I am very ill indeed this morning," said Lady Hastings, addressing her maid about eleven o'clock. "I feel as if I were dying. Call my husband and my daughter to me."

"Lord, my lady," said the maid, "had I not better send for the doctor too? You do not look as if you were dying at all. You look a good deal better, I think, my lady."

"Do I?" said Lady Hastings in a hesitating tone. But she did not want the doctor to be sent for immediately, and repeated her order to call her husband and her daughter.

Emily was with her in an instant, but Sir Philip Hastings was some where absent in the grounds, and nearly half an hour elapsed before he was found. When he entered he gazed in his wife's face with some surprise--more surprise indeed, than alarm; for he knew that she was nervous and hypondriacal, and as the maid had said, she did not look as if she were dying at all. There was no sharpening of the features--no falling in of the temples--none of that pale ashy color, or rather that leaden grayness, which precedes dissolution. He sat down, however, by her bedside, gazing at her with an inquiring look, while Emily stood on the other side of the bed, and the maid at the end; and after speaking a few kind but somewhat rambling words, he was sending for some restoratives, saying "I think, my dear, you alarm yourself without cause."

"I do not indeed, Philip," replied Lady Hastings. "I am sure I shall die, and that before very long--but do not send for any thing. I would rather not take it. It will do me more good a great deal to speak what I have upon my mind--what is weighing me down--what is killing me."

"I am sorry to hear there is any thing," said Sir Philip, whose thoughts, intensely busy with other things, were not yet fully recalled to the scene before him.

"Oh, Philip, how can you say so?" said Lady Hastings, "when you know there is. You need not go," she continued, speaking to the maid who was drawing back as if to quit the room, "I wish to speak to my husband and my daughter before some one who will remember what I say."

Sir Philip however quietly rose, opened the door, and motioned to the girl to quit the room, for such public exhibitions were quite contrary to his notions of domestic economy. "Now, my dear," he said, "what is it you wish to tell me? If there be any thing that you wish done, I will do it if it is in my power."

"It is in your power, Philip," replied Lady Hastings; "you know and Emily knows quite well that her engagement to Mr. Marlow was against my consent, and I must say the greatest shock I ever received in my life. I have never been well since, and every day I see more and more reason to object. It is in the power of either of you, or both, to relieve my mind in this respect--to break off this unhappy engagement, and at least to let me die in peace, with the thought that my daughter has not cast herself away. It is in your power, Philip, to--"

"Stay a moment," said her husband, "it is not in my power."

"Why, are you not her father?" asked Lady Hastings, interrupting him. "Are you not her lawful guardian? Have you not the disposal of her hand?"

"It is not in my power," repeated Sir Philip coldly, "to break my plighted word, to violate my honor, or to live under a load of shame and dishonor."

"Why in such a matter as this," said Lady Hastings, "there is no such disgrace. You can very well say you have thought better of it."

"In which ease I should tell a lie," said Sir Philip dryly.

"It is a thing done every day," argued Lady Hastings.

"I am not a man to do any thing because there are others who do it every day," answered her husband. "Men lie, and cheat, and swindle, and steal, and betray their friends, and relations, and parents, but I can find no reason therein for doing the same. It is not in my power, I repeat. I cannot be a scoundrel, whatever other men may be, and violate my plighted word, or withdraw from my most solemn engagements. Moreover, when Marlow heard of the misfortunes which have befallen us, and learned that Emily would not have one-fourth part of that which she had at one time a right to expect, he showed no inclination to withdraw from his word, even when there was a good excuse, and I will never withdraw from mine, so help me God."

Thus speaking he turned his eyes towards the ground again and fell into a deep reverie. While this conversation had been passing, Emily had sunk upon her knees, trembling in every limb, and hid her face in the coverings of the bed. To her, Lady Hastings now turned. Whether it was that remorse and some degree of shame affected her, when she saw the terrible agitation of her child, I cannot tell, but she paused for a moment as if in hesitation.

She spoke at length, saying "Emily, my child, to you I must appeal, as your father is so obdurate."

Emily made no answer, however, but remained weeping, and Lady Hastings becoming somewhat irritated, went on in a sharper tone. "What! will not my own child listen to the voice of a dying mother?" she asked rather petulantly than sorrowfully, although she tried hard to make her tone gravely reproachful; "will she not pay any attention to her mother's last request?"

"Oh, my mother," answered Emily, raising her head, and speaking more vehemently than was customary with her, "ask me any thing that is just; ask me any thing that is reasonable; but do not ask me to do what is wrong and what is unjust. I have made a promise--do not ask me to break it. There is no circumstance changed which could give even an excuse for such a breach of faith. Marlow has only shown himself more true more faithful, more sincere. Should I be more false, more faithless, more ungenerous than he thought me? Oh no! it is impossible--quite impossible," and she hid her streaming eyes in the bedclothes again, clasping her hands tightly together over her forehead.

Her father, with his arms crossed upon his chest, had kept his eyes fixed upon her while she spoke with a look of doubt and inquiry. Well might he doubt--well might he doubt his own suspicions. There was a truth, a candor, a straightforwardness, in that glowing face which gave the contradiction, plain and clear, to every foul, dishonest charge which had been fabricated against his child. It was impossible in fact that she could have so spoken and so looked, unless she had so felt. The best actress that ever lived could not have performed that part. There would have been something too much or too little. something approaching the exaggerated or the tame. With Emily there was nothing. What she said seemed but the sudden outburst of her heart, pressed for a reply; and as soon as it was spoken she sunk down again in silence, weeping bitterly under the conflict of two strong but equally amiable feelings.

For a moment the sight seemed to rouse Sir Philip Hastings. "She should not, if she would," he said; "voluntarily, and knowing what she did, she consented to the promise I have made, and she neither can nor shall retract. To Marlow, indeed, I may have a few words to say, and he shall once more have the opportunity of acting as he pleases; but Emily is bound as well as myself, and by that bond we must abide."

"What have you to say to Marlow?" asked Lady Hastings in a tone of commonplace curiosity, which did not at all indicate a sense of that terrible situation in which she assumed she was placed.

"That matters not," answered Sir Philip. "It will rest between him and me at his return. How he may act I know not--what he may think I know not; but he shall be a partaker of my thoughts and the master of his own actions. Do not let us pursue this painful subject further. If you feel yourself ill, my love, let us send for further medical help. I do hope and believe that you are not so ill as you imagine; but if you are so there is more need that the physician should be here, and that we should quit topics too painful for discussion, where discussion is altogether useless."

"Well, then, mark me," said Lady Hastings with an air of assumed melancholy dignity, which being quite unnatural to her, bordered somewhat on the burlesque; "mark me, Philip--mark me, Emily! your wife, your mother, makes it her last dying request--her last dying injunction, that you break off this marriage. You may or you may not give me the consolation on this sick bed of knowing that my request will be complied with; but I do not think that either of you will be careless, will be remorseless enough to carry out this engagement after I am gone. I will not threaten, Emily--I will not even attempt to take away from you the wealth for which this young man doubtless seeks you--I will not attempt to deter you by bequeathing you my curse if you do not comply with my injunctions; but I tell you, if you do not make me this promise before I die, you have embittered your mother's last moments, and--"

"Oh, forbear, forbear," cried Emily, starting up. "For God's sake, dear mother, forbear," and clasping her hands wildly over her eyes, she rushed frantically out of the room.

Sir Philip Hastings remained for nearly half an hour longer, and then descended the stairs and passed through the drawing-room. Emily was seated there with her handkerchief upon her eyes, and her whole frame heaving from the agonized sobs which rose from her bosom. Sir Philip paused and gazed at her for a moment or two, but Emily did not say a word, and seemed indeed totally unconscious of his presence. Some movements of compassion, some feeling of sympathy, some doubts of his preconceptions might pass through the bosom of Sir Philip Hastings; but the dark seeds of suspicion had been sown in his bosom--had germinated, grown up, and strengthened--had received confirmation strong and strange, and he murmured to himself as he stood and gazed at her, "Is it anger or sorrow? Is it passion or pain? All this is strange enough. I do not understand it. Her resolution is taken, and taken rightly. Why should she grieve? Why should she be thus moved, when she knows she is doing that which is just, and honest, and faithful?"

He measured a cloud by an ell wand. He gauged her heart, her sensibilities, her mind, by the rigid metre of his own, and he found that the one could not comprehend the other. Turning hastily away after he had finished his contemplation, without proffering one word of consolation or support, he walked away into his library, and ringing a bell, ordered his horse to be saddled directly. While that was being done, he wrote a hasty note to Mr. Short, the surgeon, and when the horse was brought round gave it to a groom to deliver. Then mounting on horseback, he rode away at a quick pace, without having taken any further notice of his daughter.

Emily remained for about half an hour after his departure, exactly in the same position in which he had left her. She noticed nothing that was passing around her; she heard not a horse stop at the door; and when her own maid entered the room and said,--"Doctor Short has come, ma'am, and is with my lady. Sir Philip sent Peter for him; but Peter luckily met him just down beyond the park gates;" Emily hardly seemed to hear her.

A few minutes after, Mr. Short descended quietly from the room of Lady Hastings, and looked into the drawing-room as he passed. Seeing the beautiful girl seated there in that attitude of despondency, he approached her quietly, saying, "Do not, my dear mistress Emily, suffer yourself to be alarmed without cause. I see no reason for the least apprehension. My good lady, your mother is nervous and excited, but there are no very dangerous symptoms about her--certainly none that should cause immediate alarm; and I think upon the whole, that the disease is more mental than corporeal."

Emily had raised her eyes when he had just begun to speak, and she shook her head mournfully at his last words, saying, "I can do nothing to remedy it, Mr. Short--I would at any personal sacrifice, but this involves more--I can do nothing."

"But I have done my best," said Mr. Short with a kindly smile; for he was an old and confidential friend of the whole family, and upon Emily herself had attended from her childhood, during all the little sicknesses of early life. "I asked your excellent mother what had so much excited her, and she told me all that has passed this morning. I think, my dear young lady, I have quieted her a good deal."

"How? how?" exclaimed Emily eagerly. "Oh tell me how, Mr. Short, and I will bless you!"

The good old surgeon seated himself beside her and took her hand in his. "I have only time to speak two words," he said, "but think they will give you comfort. Your mother explained to me that there had been a little discussion this morning when she thought herself dying--though that was all nonsense--and it must have been very painful to you, my dear Mistress Emily. She told me what it was about too, and seemed half sorry already for what she had said. So, as I guessed how matters went--for I know that the dear lady is fond of titles and rank, and all that, and saw she had a great deal mistaken Mr. Marlow's position--I just ventured to tell her that he is the heir of the old Earl of Launceston--that is to say, if the Earl does not marry again, and he is seventy-three, with a wife still living. She had never heard any thing about it, and it seemed to comfort her amazingly. Nevertheless she is in a sad nervous state, and somewhat weak. I do not altogether like that cough she has either; and so, my dear young lady, I will send her over a draught to-night, of which you must give her a tablespoonful every three hours. Give it to her with your own hands; for it is rather strong, and servants are apt to make mistakes. But I think if you go to her now, you will find her in a very different humor from that which she was in this morning. Good bye, good bye. Don't be cast down, Mistress Emily. All will go well yet."

CHAPTER XL

From the house of Sir Philip Hastings Mr. Short rode quickly on to the cottage of Mistress Best, which he had visited once before in the morning. The case of John Ayliffe, however, was becoming more and more urgent every moment, and at each visit the surgeon saw a change in the countenance of the young man which indicated that a greater change still was coming. He had had a choice of evils to deal with; for during the first day after the accident there had been so much fever that he had feared to give any thing to sustain the young man's strength. But long indulgence in stimulating liquors had had its usual effect in weakening the powers of the constitution, and rendering it liable to give way suddenly even where the corporeal powers seemed at their height. Wine had become to John Ayliffe what water is to most men, and he could not bear up without it. Exhaustion had succeeded rapidly to the temporary excitement of fever, and mortification had begun to show itself on the injured limb. Wine had become necessary, and it was administered in frequent and large doses; but as a stimulant it had lost its effect upon the unhappy young man, and when the surgeon returned to the cottage on this occasion, he saw not only that all hope was at an end, but that the end could not be very far distant.

Good Mr. Dixwell was seated by John Ayliffe's side, and looked up to the surgeon with an anxious eye. Mr. Short felt his patient's pulse with a very grave face. It was rapid, but exceedingly feeble--went on for twenty or thirty beats as fast as it could go--then stopped altogether for an instant or two, and then began to beat again as quickly as before.

Mr. Short poured out a tumbler full of port wine, raised John Ayliffe a little, and made him drink it down. After a few minutes he felt his pulse again, and found it somewhat stronger. The sick man looked earnestly in his face as if he wished to ask some question; but he remained silent for several minutes.

At length he said, "Tell me the truth, Short. Am not I dying?"

The surgeon hesitated, but Mr. Dixwell raised his eyes, saying, "Tell him the truth, tell him the truth, my good friend. He is better prepared to bear it than he was yesterday."

"I fear you are sinking, Sir John," said the surgeon.

"I do not feel so much pain in my leg," said the young man.

"That is because mortification has set in," replied Mr. Short.

"Then there is no hope," said John Ayliffe.

The surgeon was silent; and after a moment John Ayliffe said, "God's will be done."

Mr. Dixwell pressed his hand kindly with tears in his eyes; for they were the Christian words he had longed to hear, but hardly hoped for.

There was a long and somewhat sad pause, and then the dying man once more turned his look upon the surgeon, asking, "How long do you think it will be?"

"Three or four hours," replied Mr. Short. "By stimulants, as long as you can take them, it may be protracted a little longer, but not much."

"Every moment is of consequence," said the clergyman. "There is much preparation still needful--much to be acknowledged and repented of--much to be atoned for. What can be done, my good friend to protract the time?"

"Give small quantities of wine very frequently," answered the surgeon, "and perhaps some aqua vitæ--but very little--very little, or you may hurry the catastrophe."

"Well, well," said John Ayliffe, "you can come again, but perhaps by that time I shall be gone. You will find money enough in my pockets, Short, to pay your bill--there is plenty there, and mind you send the rest to my mother."

The surgeon stared, and said to himself, "he is wandering;" but John Ayliffe immediately added, "Don't let that rascal Shanks have it, but send it to my mother;" and saying "Very well, Sir John," he took his leave and departed.

"And now my dear young friend," said Mr. Dixwell, the moment the surgeon was gone, "there is no time to be lost. You have the power of making full atonement for the great offence you have committed to one of your fellow creatures. If you sincerely repent, as I trust you do, Christ has made atonement for your offences towards God. But you must show your penitence by letting your last acts in this life be just and right. Let me go to Sir Philip Hastings."

"I would rather see his daughter, or his wife," said John Ayliffe: "he is so stern, and hard, and gloomy. He will never speak comfort or forgiveness."

"You are mistaken--I can assure you, you are mistaken," answered the clergyman. "I will take upon me to promise that he shall not say one hard word, and grant you full forgiveness."

"Well, well," said the young man, "if it must be he, so be it--but mind to have pen and ink to write it all down--that pen won't write. You know you tried it this morning."

"I will bring one with me," said Mr. Dixwell, rising eager to be gone on his good errand; but John Ayliffe stopped him, saying, "Stay, stay--remember you are not to tell him any thing about it till he is quite away from his own house. I don't choose to have all the people talking of it, and perhaps coming down to stare at me."

Mr. Dixwell was willing to make any terms in order to have what he wished accomplished, and giving Mrs. Best directions to let the patient have some port wine every half hour, he hurried away to the Court.

On inquiring for Sir Philip, the servant said that his master had ridden out.

"Do you know where he is gone, and how long he will be absent?" asked Mr. Dixwell.

"He is gone, I believe, to call at Doctor Juke's, to consult about my lady," replied the man; "and as that is hard upon twenty miles, he can't be back for two or three hours."

"That is most unfortunate," exclaimed the clergyman. "Is your lady up?"

The servant replied in the negative, adding the information that she was very ill.

"Then I must see Mistress Emily," said Mr. Dixwell, walking into the house. "Call her to me as quickly as you can."

The man obeyed, and Emily was with the clergyman in a few moments, while the servant remained in the hall looking out through the open door.

After remaining in conversation with Mr. Dixwell for a few minutes, Emily hurried back to her room, and came down again dressed for walking. She and Mr. Dixwell went out together, and the servant saw them take their way down the road in the direction of Jenny Best's cottage: but when they had gone a couple of hundred yards, the clergyman turned off towards his own house, walking at a very quick pace, while Emily proceeded slowly on her way.

When at a short distance from the cottage, the beautiful girl stopped, and waited till she was rejoined by Mr. Dixwell, who came up very soon, out of breath at the quickness of his pace. "I have ordered the wine down directly," he said, "and I trust we shall be able to keep him up till he has told his story his own way. Now, my dear young lady, follow me;" and walking on he entered the cottage.

Emily was a good deal agitated. Every memory connected with John Ayliffe was painful to her. It seemed as if nothing but misfortune, sorrow, and anxiety, had attended her ever since she first saw him, and all connected themselves more or less with him. The strange sort of mysterious feeling of sympathy which she had experienced when first she beheld him, and which had seemed explained to her when she learned their near relationship, had given place day by day to stronger and stronger personal dislike, and she could not now even come to visit him on his death-bed with the clergyman without feeling a mixture of repugnance and dread which she struggled with not very successfully.

They passed, however, through the outer into the inner room where Mistress Best was sitting with the dying man, reading to him the New Testament. But as soon as Mr. Dixwell, who had led the way, entered, the good woman stopped, and John Ayliffe turned his head faintly towards the door.

"Ah, this is very kind of you," he said when he saw Emily, "I can tell you all better than any one else."

"Sir Philip is absent," said Mr. Dixwell, "and will not be home for several hours."

"Hours!" repeated John Ayliffe. "My time is reduced to minutes!"

Emily approached quietly, and Mrs. Best quitted the room and shut the door. Mr. Dixwell drew the table nearer to the bed, spread some writing paper which he had brought with him upon it, and dipped a pen in the ink, as a hint that no time was to be lost in proceeding.

"Well, well," said John Ayliffe with a sigh, "I won't delay, though it is very hard to have to tell such a story. Mistress Emily, I have done you and your family great wrong and great harm, and I am very, very sorry for it, especially for what I have done against you."

"Then I forgive you from all my heart," cried Emily, who had been inexpressibly shocked at the terrible change which the young man's appearance presented. She had never seen death, nor was aware of the terrible shadow which the dark banner of the great Conqueror often casts before it.

"Thank you, thank you," replied John Ayliffe; "but you must not suppose, Mistress Emily, that all the evil I have done was out of my own head. Others prompted me to a great deal; although I was ready enough to follow their guidance, I must confess. The two principal persons were Shanks the lawyer, and Mrs. Hazleton--Oh, that woman is, I believe, the devil incarnate."

"Hush, hush," said Mr. Dixwell, "I cannot put such words as those down, nor should you speak them. You had better begin in order too, and tell all from the commencement, but calmly and in a Christian spirit, remembering that this is your own confession, and not an accusation of others."

"Well, I will try," said the young man faintly, lifting his hand from the bed-clothes, as if to put it to his head in the act of thought. But he was too weak, and he fell back again, and fixing his eyes on a spot in the wall opposite the foot of the bed, he continued in a sort of dreamy commemorative way as follows: "I loved you--yes, I loved you very much--I feel it now more than ever--I loved you more than you ever knew--more than I myself knew then. (Emily bent her head and hid her eyes with her hands.) It was not," he proceeded to say, "that you were more beautiful than any of the rest-- although that was true too--but there was somehow a look about you, an air when you moved, a manner when you spoke, that made it seem as if you were of a different race from the rest--something higher, brighter, better, and as if your nobler nature shone out like a gleam on all you did--I cannot help thinking that if you could have loved me in return, mine would have been a different fate, a different end, a different and brighter hope even now--"

"You are wandering from the subject, my friend," said Mr. Dixwell. "Time is short."

"I am not altogether wandering," said John Ayliffe, "but feel faint. Give me some more wine." When he had got it, he continued thus: "I found you could not love me--I said in my heart that you would not love me; and my love turned into hate--at least I thought so--and I determined you should rue the day that you had refused me. Long before that, however, Shanks the lawyer had put it into my head that I could take your father's property and title from him, and I resolved some day to try, little knowing all that it would lead me into step by step. I had heard my mother say a hundred times that she had been as good as married to your uncle who was drowned, and that if right had been done I ought to have had the property. So I set to work with Shanks to see what could be done. Sometimes he led, sometimes I led; for he was a coward, and wanted to do all by cunning, and I was bold enough, and thought every thing was to be done by daring. We had both of us got dipped so deep in there was no going back. I tore one leaf out of the parish register myself, to make it seem that your grandfather had caused the record of my mother's marriage to be destroyed--but that was no marriage at all--they never were, married--and that's the truth. I did a great number of other very evil things, and then suddenly Mrs. Hazleton came in to help us; and whenever there was any thing particularly shrewd and keen to be devised, especially if there was a spice of malice in it towards Sir Philip or yourself, Mrs. Hazleton planned it for us--not telling us exactly to do this thing of that, but asking if it could not be done, or if it would be very wrong to do it. But I'll tell you them all in order--all that we did."

He went on to relate a great many particulars with which the reader is already acquainted. He told the whole villanous schemes which had been concocted between himself, the attorney, and Mrs. Hazleton, and which had been in part, or as a whole, executed to the ruin of Sir Philip Hastings' fortune and peace. The good clergyman took down his words with a rapid hand, as he spoke, though it was somewhat difficult; for the voice became more and more faint and low.

"There is no use in trying now," said John Ayliffe in conclusion, "when I am going before God who has seen and known it all. There is no use in trying to conceal any thing. I was as ready to do evil as they were to prompt me, and I did it with a willing heart, though sometimes I was a little frightened at what I was doing, especially in the night when I could not sleep. I am sorry enough for it now--I repent from my whole heart; and now tell me--tell me, can you forgive me?"

"As far as I am concerned, I forgive you entirely," said Emily, with the tears in her eyes, "and I trust that your repentance will be fully accepted. As to my father, I am sure that he will forgive you also, and I think I may take upon myself to say, that he will either come or send to you this night to express his forgiveness."

"No, no, no," said the young man with a great effort. "He must not come--he must not send. I have made the atonement that he (pointing to Mr.

Dixwell) required, and I have but one favor to ask. Pray, pray grant it to me. It is but this. That you will not tell any one of this confession so long as I am still living. He has got it all down. It can't be needed for a few hours, and in a few, a very few, I shall be gone. Mr. Dixwell will tell you when it is all over. Then tell what you like; but I would rather not die with more shame upon my head if I can help it."

The good clergyman was about to reason with him upon the differences between healthful shame, and real shame, and false shame, but Emily gently interposed, saying, "It does not matter, my dear sir; a few hours can make no difference."

Then rising, she once more repeated the words of forgiveness, and added, "I will now go and pray for you, my poor cousin--I will pray that your repentance may be sincere and true--that it may be accepted for Christ's sake, and that God may comfort you and support you even at the very last."

Mr. Dixwell rose too, and telling John Ayliffe that he would return in a few minutes, accompanied Emily back towards her house. They parted, however, at the gates of the garden; and while Emily threaded her way through innumerable gravelled walks, the clergyman went back to the cottage, and once more resumed his place by the side of the dying man.

CHAPTER XLI

Sir Philip Hastings returned to his own house earlier than had been expected, bringing with him the physician he had gone to seek, and whom--contrary to the ordinary course of events--he had found at once. They both went up to Lady Hastings's room, where the physician, according to the usual practice of medical men in consultation, approved of all that his predecessor had done, yet ordered some insignificant changes in the medicines in order to prove that he had not come there for nothing. He took the same view of the case that Mr. Short had taken, declaring that there was no immediate danger; but at the same time he inquired particularly how that lady rested in the night, whether she started in her sleep, was long watchful, and whether she breathed freely during slumber.

The maid's account was not very distinct in regard to several of these points; but she acknowledged that it was her young lady who usually sat up with Lady Hastings till three or four o'clock in the morning.

Sir Philip immediately directed Emily to be summoned, but the maid informed him she had gone out about an hour and a half before, and had not then returned.

When the physician took his leave and departed, Sir Philip summoned the butler to his presence, and inquired, with an eager yet gloomy tone, if he knew where Mistress Emily had gone.

"I really do not, Sir Philip," replied the man. "She went out with Mr. Dixwell, but they parted a little way down the road, and my young lady went on as if she were going to farmer Wallop's or Jenny Best's."

At the latter name Sir Philip started as if a serpent had stung him, and he waved to the man to quit the room. As soon as he was alone he commenced pacing up and down in more agitation than he usually displayed, and once or twice words broke from him which gave some indications of what was passing in his mind.

"Too clear, too clear," lie said, and then after a pause exclaimed, holding up his hands; "so young, and so deceitful! Marlow must be told of this, and then must act as he thinks fit--it were better she were dead--far better! What is the cold, dull corruption of the grave, the mere rotting of the flesh, and the mouldering of the bones, to this corruption of the spirit, this foul dissolution of the whole moral nature?"

He then began to pace up and down more vehemently than before, fixing his eyes upon the ground, and seeming to think profoundly, with a quivering lip and knitted brow. "Hard, hard task for a father," he said--"God of heaven that I should ever dream of such a thing!--yet it might be a duty. What can Marlow be doing during this long unexplained absence? France-- can he have discovered all this and quitted her, seeking, in charity, to make the breach as little painful as possible? Perhaps, after all," he continued, after a few moments' thought, "the man may have been mistaken when he told me that he believed that this young scoundrel was lying ill of a fall at this woman's cottage; yet at the best it was bad enough to quit a sick mother's bedside for long hours, when I too was absent. Can she have done it to show her spleen at this foolish opposition to her marriage?"

There is no character so difficult to deal with--there is none which is such a constant hell to its possessor--as that of a moody man. Sir Philip had been moody, as I have endeavored to show, from his very earliest years; but all the evils of that sort of disposition had increased upon him rapidly during the latter part of his life. Unaware, like all the rest of mankind, of the faults of his own character, he had rather encouraged than struggled against its many great defects. Because he was stern and harsh, he fancied himself just, and forgot that it is not enough for justice to judge rightly of that which is placed clearly and truly before it, and did not remember, or at all events apply the principle, that an accurate search for truth, and an unprejudiced suspension of opinion till truth has been obtained, are necessary steps to justice. Suspicion--always a part and parcel of the character of the moody man--had of late years obtained a strong hold upon him, and unfortunately it had so happened that event after event had occurred to turn his suspicion against his own guiltless child. The very lights and shades of her character, which he could in no degree comprehend, from his own nature being destitute of all such impulsiveness, had not only puzzled him, but laid the foundation of doubts. Then the little incident which I have related in a preceding part of this work, regarding the Italian singing-master--Emily's resolute but unexplained determination to take no more lessons from that man, had set his moody mind to ponder and to doubt still more. The too successful schemes and suggestions of Mrs. Hazleton had given point and vigor to his suspicions, and the betrayal of his private conversation to the government had seemed a climax to the whole, so that he almost believed his fair sweet child a fiend concealed beneath the form of an angel.

It was in vain that he asked himself, What could be her motives? He had an answer ready, that her motives had always been a mystery to him, even in her lightest acts. "There are some people," he thought, "who act without motives--in whom the devil himself seems to have implanted an impulse to do evil without any cause or object, for the mere pleasure of doing wrong."

On the present occasion he had accidentally heard from the farmer, who was the next neighbor of Jenny Best, that he was quite certain Sir John Hastings, as he called him, was lying ill from a fall at that good woman's cottage. His horse had been found at a great distance on a wild common, with the bridle broken, and every appearance of having fallen over in rearing. Blood and other marks of an accident had been discovered on the road. Mr. Short, the surgeon, was seen to pay several visits every day to the old woman's house, and yet maintained the most profound secrecy in regard to his patient. The farmer argued that the surgeon would not be so attentive unless that patient was a person of some importance, and it was clear he was not one of Jenny Best's own family, for every member of it had been well and active after the surgeon's visits had been commenced.

All these considerations, together with the absence of John Ayliffe from his residence, had led the good farmer to a right conclusion, and he had stated the fact broadly to Sir Philip Hastings.

Sir Philip, on his part, had made no particular inquiries, for the very name of John Ayliffe was hateful to him; but when he heard that his daughter had gone forth alone to that very cottage, and had remained there for a considerable time in the same place with the man whom he abhorred, and remembered that the tale which had been boldly put forth of her having visited him in secret, the very blood, as it flowed through his heart, seemed turned into fire, and his brain reeled with anguish and indignation.

Presently the hall door was heard to open, and there was a light step in the passage. Sir Philip darted forth from his room, and met his daughter coming in with a sad and anxious face, and as he thought with traces of tears upon her eyelids.

"Where have you been?" asked her father in a stern low tone.

"I have been to Jenny Best's down the lane, my father," replied Emily, startled by his look and manner, but still speaking the plain truth, as she always did. "Is my mother worse?"

Without a word of reply Sir Philip turned away into his room again and closed the door.

Alarmed by her father's demeanor, Emily hurried up at once to Lady Hastings's room, but found her certainly more cheerful and apparently better.

The assurance given by the physician that there was no immediate danger, nor any very unfavorable symptom, had been in a certain degree a relief to Lady Hastings herself; for, although she had undoubtedly been acting a part when in the morning she had declared herself dying, yet, as very often happens with those who deceive, she had so far partially deceived herself as to believe that she was in reality very ill. She was surprised at Emily's sudden appearance and alarmed look, but her daughter did not think it right to tell her the strange demeanor of Sir Philip, but sitting down as calmly ass he could by her mother's side, talked to her for several minutes on indifferent subjects. It was evident to Emily that, although her father's tone was so harsh, her mother viewed her more kindly than in the morning, and the information which had been given her by the surgeon accounted for the change. The conduct of Sir Philip, however, seemed not to be explained, and Emily could hardly prevent herself from falling into one of those reveries which have often been mentioned before. She struggled against the tendency, however, for some time, till at length she was relieved by the announcement that Mistress Hazleton was below, but when Lady Hastings gave her maid directions to bring her friend up, Emily could refrain no longer from uttering at least one word of warning.

"Give me two minutes more, dear mamma," she said, in a low voice. "I have something very particular to say to you--let Mrs. Hazleton wait but for two minutes."

"Well," said Lady Hastings, languidly; and then turning to the maid she added, "Tell dear Mrs. Hazleton that I will receive her in five minutes, and when I ring my bell, bring her up."

As soon as the maid had retired Emily sank upon her knees by her mother's bedside, and kissed her hand, saying, "I have one great favor to ask, dear mother, and I beseech you to grant it."

"Well, my child," answered Lady Hastings, thinking she was going to petition for a recall of her injunction against the marriage with Marlow, "I have but one object in life, my dear Emily, and that is your happiness. I am willing to make any sacrifice of personal feelings for that object. What is it you desire?"

"It is merely this," replied Emily, "that you would not put any trust or confidence whatever in Mrs. Hazleton. That you would doubt her representations, and confide nothing to her, for a short time at least."

Lady Hastings looked perfectly aghast "What do you mean, Emily?" she said. "What can you mean? Put no trust in Mrs. Hazleton my oldest and dearest friend?"

"She is not your friend," replied Emily, earnestly, "nor my friend, nor my father's friend, but the enemy of every one in this house. I have long had doubts--Marlow changed those doubts into suspicions, and this day I have accidentally received proof positive of her cruel machinations against my father, yourself, and me. This justifies me in speaking as I now do, otherwise I should have remained silent still."

"But explain, explain, my child," said Lady Hastings. "What has she done? What are these proofs you talk of? I cannot comprehend at all unless you explain."

"There would be no time, even if I were not bound by a promise," replied Emily; "but all I ask is that you suspend all trust and confidence in Mrs. Hazleton for one short day--perhaps it may be sooner; but I promise you that at the end of that time, if not before, good Mr. Dixwell shall explain every thing to you, and place in your hands a paper which will render all Mrs. Hazleton's conduct for the last two years perfectly clear and distinct."

"But do tell me something, at least, Emily," urged her mother. "I hate to wait in suspense. You used to be very fond of Mrs. Hazleton and she of you. When did these suspicions of her first begin, and how?"

"Do you not remember a visit I made to her some time ago," replied Emily, "when I remained with her for several days? Then I first learned to doubt her. She then plotted and contrived to induce me to do what would have been the most repugnant to your feelings and my father's, as well as to my own. But moreover she came into my room one night walking in her sleep, and all her bitter hatred showed itself then."

"Good gracious! What did she say? What did she do?" exclaimed Lady Hastings, now thoroughly forgetting herself in the curiosity Emily's words excited.

Her daughter related all that had occurred on the occasion of Mrs. Hazleton's sleeping visit to her room, and repeated her words as nearly as she could recollect them.

"But why, my dearest child, did you not tell us all this before?" asked Lady Hastings.

"Because the words were spoken in sleep," answered Emily, "and excited at the time but a vague doubt. Sleep is full of delusions; and though I thought the dream must be a strange one which could prompt such feelings, yet still it might all be a troublous dream. It was not till afterwards, when I saw cause to believe that Mrs. Hazleton wished to influence me in a way which I thought wrong, that I began to suspect the words that had come unconsciously from the depths of her secret heart. Since then suspicion has increased every day, and now has ripened into certainty. I tell you, dear mother, that good Mr. Dixwell, whom you know and can trust, has the information as well as myself. But we are both bound to be silent as to the particulars for some hours more. I could not let Mrs. Hazleton be with you again, however--remembering, as I do, that seldom has she crossed this threshold or we crossed hers, without some evil befalling us--and not say as much as I have said, to give you the only hint in my power of facts which, if you knew them fully, you could judge of much better than myself. Believe me, dear mother, that as soon as I am permitted--and a very few hours will set me free--I will fly at once to tell you all, and leave you and my father to decide and act as your own good judgment shall direct."

"You had better tell me first, Emily," replied Lady Hastings; "a woman can always best understand the secrets of a woman's heart. I wish you had not made any promise of secrecy; but as you have, so it must be. Has Marlow had any share in this discovery?" she added, with some slight jealousy of his influence over her daughter's mind.

"Not in the least with that which I have made to-day," replied Emily; "but I need not at all conceal from you that he has long suspected Mrs. Hazleton of evil feelings and evil acts towards our whole family; and that he believes that he has discovered almost to a certainty that Mrs. Hazleton aided greatly in all the wrong and injury that has been done my father. The object of his going to France was solely to trace out the whole threads of the intrigue, and he went, not doubting in the least that he should succeed in restoring to my parents all that has been unjustly taken from them. That such a restoration must take place, I now know; but what he has learned or what he has done I cannot tell you, for I am not aware. I am sure, however, that if he brings all he hopes about, it will be his greatest joy to have aided to right you even in a small degree."

"I do believe he is a very excellent and amiable young man," said Lady Hastings thoughtfully.

She seemed as if she were on the point of saying something farther on the subject of Marlow's merits; but then checked herself, and added, "But now indeed, Emily, I think I ought to send for Mrs. Hazleton."

"But you promise me, dear mother," urged Emily eagerly, "that you will put no faith in any thing she tells you, and will not confide in her in any way till you have heard the whole?"

"That I certainly will take care to avoid, my dear," replied Lady Hastings. "After what you have told me, it would be madness to put any confidence in her--especially when a few short hours will reveal all. You are sure, Emily, that it will not be longer!"

"Perfectly certain, my dear mother," answered her daughter. "I would not have promised to refrain from speaking, had I not been certain that the time for such painful concealment must be very short."

"Well, then, my dear child, ring the bell," said Lady Hastings. "I will be very guarded merely on your assurances, for I any sure that you are always candid and sincere whatever your poor father may think."

Emily rung the bell, and retired to her own room, repeating mournfully to herself, "whatever my poor father may think?--Well, well," she added, "the time will soon come when he will be undeceived, and do his child justice. Alas, that it should ever have been otherwise!"

She found relief in tears; and while she wept in solitude Lady Hastings prepared to receive Mrs. Hazleton with cold dignity. She had fully resolved, when Emily left her, to be as silent as possible in regard to every thing that had occurred that day; not to allude, directly or indirectly, to the warning which had been given her, and to leave Mrs. Hazleton to attribute her unwonted reserve to caprice, or any thing else she pleased. But the resolutions of Lady Hastings were very fragile commodities when she fell into the hands of artful people who knew her character, and one was then approaching not easily frustrated in her designs.

CHAPTER XLII

Mrs. Hazleton was an observer of all small particulars. She never seemed to give them any attention indeed, but it is not those who notice them publicly who pay most attention to them in private. Now she had never in her life been detained five minutes when she had come to visit Lady Hastings. Her friend was always only too glad to see her. On the present occasion, she had been kept alone for fully ten-minutes in the drawing-room, and she was not at all pleased with this want of alacrity. Her face was as smooth, as gentle, and as smiling when she entered the sick lady's bed-room, as if she had been full of affection and tender consideration; and before she had reached the bed-side, Lady Hastings felt that it would be a somewhat difficult task to play the cold and reserved part she had imposed upon herself. She resolved, doggedly, however, to act it out; and as Mrs. Hazleton approached, she continued looking at her fair delicate hands, or at the rings--now somewhat too large for the fingers they encircled.

All this was a hint, if not distinct intelligence, to Mrs. Hazleton. She saw that a change of feeling, or at least a change of purpose, had taken place, and that Lady Hastings felt embarrassed by a consciousness which she might or might not choose to communicate. Mrs. Hazleton remained the same, however, and rather enjoyed the hesitation which she perceived than otherwise. She was not without that proud satisfaction which persons of superior mind feel, in witnessing the effects upon weak people of causes which would not give them a moment's trouble. Difficulties and complexities she had been so much accustomed to overcome and to unravel, that she had learned to feel a certain triumphant joy in encountering them. That joy, indeed, would have been changed to despair or rage if she had ever dreamed of being frustrated; but success had made her bold, and she loved to steer her course through agitated waters.

"Well, my dear friend," she said, with the sweet tones of her voice falling from her lips like drops d liquid honey, "You do not seem quite so well to-day. I hope this business which you were to undertake has not agitated you, or perhaps you have not executed your intention; it could be very well put off till you are better."

This was intended to lead to confession; for from a knowledge of Lady Hastings' character, a strong suspicion arose that she had not found courage to carry through the little drama which had been planned between them, and that she was now ashamed to confess her want of resolution.

Lady Hastings remained silent, playing with her rings, and Mrs. Hazleton, a little angry--but very little--gave her one of those delightful little scratches which she was practised in administering, saying, "No one knew any thing about your intentions but myself, so, no one can accuse you of weakness or vacillation."

"I care very little," said Lady Hastings (most untruly) "of what people accuse me. I shall of course form my own resolutions from what I know, and execute them or not, dear Mrs. Hazleton, according to circumstances, which are ever changing. What is inexpedient one day may be quite expedient the next."

Now no one was more fully aware than Mrs. Hazleton that expediency is always the argument of weak minds, and that changing circumstances afford every day fair excuses to men and to multitudes for every kind of weakness under the sun. Her belief was strengthened, that Lady Hastings had not acted as she had promised to act, and she replied with an easy, quiet, half-pitying smile, "Well, it is not of the slightest consequence whether you do it now or a week hence, or not at all. The worst that could come would be Emily's marriage with Marlow, and if you do not care about it, who should? I take it for granted, of course, that you have not acted in the matter so boldly and decidedly as we proposed."

There was an implied superiority in Mrs. Hazleton's words and manner, which Lady Hastings did not like. It roused and elevated her, and she replied somewhat sharply, "You are quite mistaken, my dear friend. I did all that was ever intended; I sent for Emily and my husband, told them that I believed I should not live long, and made it my last request that the engagement with Marlow should be broken off."

"Indeed!" exclaimed Mrs. Hazleton, with even too much eagerness; "What did they say? Did they consent?"

"Far from it," answered Lady Hastings. "My husband said he had made a promise, which he would not violate on any account or consideration whatever, and Emily was much in the same story."

"That shows that your decision was not strongly enough expressed," replied her visitor. "I do not believe that any man or woman could be heartless enough to refuse a wife or mother's last request, if made in so solemn a manner."

"They did refuse, point-blank, however," said Lady Hastings. "But do you know, Mrs. Hazleton," she continued, seeing a provokingly bitter smile on Mrs. Hazleton's face, "do you know, strange to say, I am very glad they did refuse. Upon after consideration, when all anger and irritation was gone, I began to think it was hardly right or fair, or Christian either, to oppose this marriage so strongly, without some better reason than I have to assign. Marlow is a gentleman in all respects, of very good family too, I believe. He is a good and excellent young man. His fortune, too, is not inconsiderable, his prospects good, and his conduct under the deprivations which we have lately suffered, and the loss of at least two-thirds of the fortune he had a right to expect with Emily, has been all that is kind, and amiable, and generous."

Mrs. Hazleton sat by the bedside, fixing her eyes full upon the countenance of the invalid, and betraying not in the least the rage and disappointment that were at her heart. They were not a whit the less bitter, however, or fierce, or malignant; but rather the more so from the effort to smother them. No one for a moment could have imagined that she was angry, even in the least degree; and yet no disappointed demon ever felt greater fury at being frustrated by the weakness or vacillation of a tool.

After staying for a moment to take breath, Lady Hastings proceeded, saying, "All these considerations, dear Mrs. Hazleton, have made me resolve to make amends for what I have said--to withdraw the opposition I have hitherto shown--and consent to the marriage."

Mrs. Hazleton retired for a moment into herself. For a minute or two she was as silent as death--her cheek grew a little paler--her eyes lost their lustre, and became dead and cold--they seemed looking at nothing, seeing nothing--there was no speculation in them. The only thing that indicated life and emotion was a slight quivering of the beautifully-chiselled lip. There was a word echoing in the dark chambers of her heart in replying to Lady Hastings. It was "Never!" but it was not spoken; and after a short and thoughtful pause she recovered herself fully, and set about her work again.

"My dear friend," she said, in a sweet tone, "you have doubtless good reasons for what you do. Far be it from me to say one word against your doing what you think fit; only I should like to know what has made such a change in your views, because I think perhaps you may be deceived."

"Oh, no, I am not deceived," replied Lady Hastings, "but really I cannot enter into explanations. I have heard a great deal lately about many things--especially this morning; but I--I--in fact, I promised not to tell you."

Lady Hastings thought that in making this distinct declaration she was performing a very magnanimous feat; but her little speech, short as it was, contained three separate clauses or propositions, with each of which Mrs. Hazleton proposed to deal separately. First, she asserted that she was not deceived, and to this her companion replied, with a slight incredulous smile, "Are you quite sure, my friend? Here you are lying on a bed of sickness, with no power of obtaining accurate information; while those who are combined to win you to their wishes have every opportunity of conveying hints to you, both directly and indirectly, which may not be altogether false, but yet bear with them a false impression."

"Oh, but there can be no possible doubt," said Lady Hastings, "that Marlow is the heir of the Earl of Launceston."

Mrs. Hazleton's brow contracted, and a quick flush passed over her cheek. She had never before given attention to the fact--she had never thought of it at all--but the moment it was mentioned, her knowledge of the families of the nobility, and Mr. Marlow's connections, showed her that the assertion was probably true. "It may be so," she said, "but I am very doubtful. However, I will inquire, and let you know the truth, to-morrow. And now, my dear friend, let us turn to something else. You say you have heard a great deal to-day, and that you have promised not to tell _me_--me--for you marked that word particularly. Now here I have a right to demand some explanation; for your very words show that some person or persons endeavor to prejudice your mind against me. What you have heard must be some false charge. Otherwise the one who has been your friend for years, who has been faithful, constant, attentive, kind, to the utmost limit of her poor abilities, would not be selected for exclusion from your confidence. They seek, in fact, by some false rumor, or ridiculous tale, which you have not the means of investigating yourself, to deprive you of advice and support. I charge no one in particular; but some one has done this--if they had nothing to fear from frankness, they would not inculcate a want of candor towards one who loves you, as they well know."

"Why the fact is Emily said," replied Lady Hastings, "that could only be for a short time, and----"

"Emily!" cried Mrs. Hazleton with a laugh, "Emily indeed! Oh, then the matter is easily understood--but pray what did Emily say? Dear Emily, she is a charming girl--rather wayward--rather wilful--not always quite so candid to her friends as I could wish; but these are all thoughts which will pass away with more knowledge of the world. She will learn to discriminate between true friends and false ones--to trust and confide entirely and without hesitation in those who really love her, and not to repose her confidence in the dark and mysterious.--Now I will undertake to say that Emily has thrown out hints and inuendoes, without giving you very clear and explicit information. She has asked you to wait patiently for a time. It is always the dear child's way; but I did not think she would practice it upon her own mother."

Now most people would have imagined, as Lady Hastings did imagine, that Mrs. Hazleton's words proceeded from spite--mere spite; but such was not the case: it was all art. She sought to pique Lady Hastings, knowing very well that when once heated or angry, she lost all caution; and her great object at that moment was to ascertain what Emily knew, and what Emily had said. She was successful to a certain degree. She did pique Lady Hastings, who replied at once, and somewhat sharply, though with the ordinary forms of courtesy. "I do not think you altogether do Emily justice, dear Mrs. Hazleton, although you have in some degree divined the course she has pursued. She did not exactly throw out inuendoes; but she made bold and distinct charges, and though she did not proceed to the proofs, because there was no time to do so, and also because there were particular reasons for not doing so, yet she promised within a very few hours to establish every assertion that she made beyond the possibility of doubt.

"I thought so," said Mrs. Hazleton, in a somewhat abstracted tone, casting her eyes round the room and taking up, apparently unconcerned, the vial of medicine which stood by Lady Hastings' bedside. "Pray, my dear friend, when the revelation is made--if it ever be made--inform me of the particulars."

"If it ever be made," exclaimed Lady Hastings. "No revelation needs to be made, Mrs. Hazleton--nothing is wanting but the proofs. Emily was explicit enough as to the facts. She said that you had aided and assisted in depriving my husband of his property, that in that and many other particulars you had acted any thing but a friendly part, that you were moved by a spirit of hatred against us all, and that very seldom had there been any communications between our house and yours without some evil following it--which is true enough."

She spoke with a good deal of vehemence, and raised herself somewhat on her elbow, as if to utter her words more freely. In the mean while Mrs. Hazleton sat silent and calm--as far as the exterior went at least--with her eyes fixed upon a particular spot in the quilt from which they never moved till Lady Hastings had done.

"Grave charges," she said at length, "very grave charges to bring against one whom she has known from her infancy, and for whom she has professed some regard--but no less false than grave, my dear friend. Now either one of two things has happened: the first, which I mention merely as a possibility, but without at all believing that such is the case--the first is, I say, that Emily, judging your opposition to her proposed unequal marriage to be abetted by myself, has devised these charges out of her own head, in order to withdraw your confidence from me and gain her own objects: the second is--and this is much more likely--that she has been informed by some one, either maliciously or mistakenly, of some suspicions and doubts such as are always more or less current in a country place, and has perhaps embellished them a little in their transmission to you.--The latter is certainly the most probable.--I suppose she did not tell you from whom she received the information."

"Not exactly," answered Lady Hastings, "but one thing I know, which is, that Mr. Dixwell the rector has all the same information, and if I understood her rightly, has got it down in writing."

Mrs. Hazleton's cheek grew a shade paler; but she answered at once "I am glad to hear that; for now we come to something definite. All these charges must be substantiated, dear friend--that is, if they can be substantiated--" she added with a smile.

"You can easily understand that, attached to you by the bonds of a long friendship, I cannot suffer my name to be traduced, or my conduct impeached, even by your own daughter, without insisting upon a full explanation, and clear, satisfactory proofs, or a recantation of the charges. Emily must establish what she has said, if she can.--I am in no haste about it; it may be to-morrow, or the next day, or the day after--whenever it suits you and her in short; but it must be done. Conscious that I am innocent of such great offences, I can wait patiently; and I do not think, my dear friend, that although I see you have been a little startled by these strange tales, you will give any credence to them in your heart till they are proved. Dear Emily is evidently very much in love with Mr. Marlow, and is anxious to remove all opposition to her marriage with him. But I think she must take some other means; for these will certainly break down beneath her."

She spoke so calmly, and in so quiet and gentle a tone--her whole look and manner was so tranquilly confident--that lady Hastings could hardly believe that she was in any degree guilty.

"Well, I cannot tell," she said, "how this may turn out, but I do not think her marriage with Mr. Marlow can have any thing to do with it. I have fully and entirely resolved to cease all opposition to her union; on which I see my daughter's happiness is staked, and I shall certainly immediately signify my consent both to Emily and to my husband."

"Wait a little--wait a little" said Mrs. Hazleton with a significant nod of the head. "I have no mysteries, my dear friend. I have nothing to conceal or to hold back. You are going, however, to act upon information which is very doubtful. I believe that you have been deceived, whoever has told you that Mr. Marlow is the heir to the Earl of Launceston, and it is but an act of friendship on my part to procure you more certain intelligence. You shall have it I promise you, before four and twenty hours are over, and all I ask is that you will not commit yourself by giving your consent till that intelligence has been obtained. You cannot say that you consent if Mr. Marlow proves to be the heir of that nobleman, but will not consent if such be not the case.--That would never do, and therefore your consent would be irrevocable. But on the other hand there can be no great harm in waiting four and twenty hours at the utmost. I have plenty of books of heraldry and genealogy, which will soon let me into the facts, and you shall know them plainly and straightforwardly at once. You can then decide and state your decision firmly and calmly, with just reason and upon good grounds."

Lady Hastings was silent. She saw that Mrs. Hazleton had detected the motives of her sudden change of views, and she did not much like being detected. She had fully made up her mind, too, that Marlow was to become Earl and her daughter Countess of Launceston, and the very thought of such not being the result was a sort of half disappointment to her. Now Lady Hastings did not like being disappointed at all, and moreover she had made up her mind to have a scene of reconciliation, and tenderness, and gratitude with her husband and her daughter, from which--being of a truly affectionate disposition--she thought she should derive great pleasure.

Thus she hesitated for a moment as to what she should answer, and Mrs. Hazleton, determined not to let the effect of what she had said subside before she had bound her more firmly, added, after waiting a short time for a reply, "you will promise me, will you not, that you will not distinctly recall your injunction, and give your consent to the marriage till you have seen me again; provided I do not keep you in suspense more than four and twenty hours? It is but reasonable too, and just, and you would, I am sure, repent bitterly if you were to find afterwards that your consent to this very unequal marriage had been obtained by deceit, and that you bad been made a mere fool of--Really at the very first sight, even if I had not good reason to believe that this story of the heirship is either a mistake or a misrepresentation, it seems so like a stage trick--the cunning plot of some knavish servant or convenient friend in a drama--that I should be very doubtful. Will you not promise me then?"

"Well, there can be no great harm in waiting that length of time," said Lady Hastings. "I do not mind promising that; but of course you will let me know within four and twenty hours."

"I will," replied Mrs. Hazleton firmly; "earlier if it be possible; but the fact is, I have some business to settle to-morrow of great importance. My lawyer, Mr. Shanks--whom I believe to be a great rogue--persuaded me to lend some money upon security which he pronounced himself to be good. I knew not what it was for; as we women of course can be no judges of such things; but I have just discovered that it was to pay off some debts of this young man who calls himself Sir John Hastings. Now I don't know whether the papers have been signed, or any thing about it; and I hear that the young man himself is absent, no one knows where. It makes me very uneasy; and I have sent for Shanks to come to me to-morrow morning. It may therefore be the middle of the day before I can get here; but I will not delay a moment, you may be perfectly sure."

She had risen as she spoke, and after pressing the hand of Lady Hastings tenderly in her own, she glided calmly out of the room with her usual graceful movement, and entering her carriage with a face as serene as a summer sky, ordered the coachman to drive home in a voice that wavered not in its lightest tone.

CHAPTER XLIII

Mrs. Hazelton entered the carriage, I have said, at the end of the last chapter, without the slightest appearance of agitation or excitement. Although now and then a flush, and now and then a paleness, had spread over her face during the conversation with Lady Hastings, though her eye had emitted an occasional flash, and at other times had seemed fixed and meaningless, such indications of internal warfare were all banished when she left the room, the fair smooth cheek had its natural color, the eye was as tranquil as that of indifferent old age.

The coachman cracked his long whip, before four magnificent large horses heaved the ponderous vehicle from its resting place, and Mrs. Hazleton sank back in the carriage and gave herself up to thought--but not to thought only. Then all the smothered agitation; then all the strong contending passions broke forth in fierce and fiery warfare. It is impossible to disentangle them and lay them out, as on a map, before the reader's mind. It is impossible to say which at first predominated, rage, or fear, or disappointment, or the thirst of vengeance. One passion it is true--the one which might be called the master passion of her nature--soon soared towering above the rest, like one of those mighty spirits which rise to the dizzy and dangerous pinnacle of power in the midst of the turbulence and tempest which accompany great social earthquakes. But at first all was confusion.

"Never," she repeated to herself--"never!--it shall never be. If I slay her with my own hand it shall never be--foiled--frustrated in every thing; and by this mere empty, moody child, who has been my stumbling block, my enemy, my obstruction, in all my paths. No, no, it shall never be!"

A new strain of thought seemed to strike her; her head leaned forward; her eyes closed, and her lips quivered.

There are many kinds of conscience, and every one has some sort, such as it is. What I mean is, that there is almost in every heart a voice of warning and reproof which counsels us to regret certain actions, and which speaks in different tones to different men. To the worldly--those who are habitually of the earth earthly--it holds out the menace of earthly shame and misfortune and sorrow. It recapitulates the mistakes we have committed, points to the evil consequences of evil deeds, shows how the insincerities and falsehoods of our former course have proved fruitless, and how the cunning devices, and skilful contrivances, and artful stratagems, have ended in mortification and reproach and contempt; while still the gloomy prospects of detection and exposure and public contumely and personal punishment, are held up before our eyes as the grim portrait of the future.

I need not pause here to show how conscience affects those who, however guilty, have a higher sense--those who have a cloudy belief in a future state--who acknowledge in their own hearts a God of justice--who look to judgment, and feel that there must be an immortality of weal or woe. Mrs. Hazleton was of the former class. The grave was a barrier to her sight, beyond which there was no seeing. She had been brought up for this world, lived in this world, thought, devised, schemed, plotted for this world. She never thought of another world at all. She went to church regularly every Sunday, read the prayers with every appearance of devotion, even listened to the sermon if the preacher preached well, and went home more practically atheist than many who have professed themselves so.

What were her thoughts, then, now? They were all earthly still. Even conscience spoke to her in earthly language, as if there were no other means of reaching her heart but that. Its very menaces were all earthly. She reviewed her conduct for the last two or three years, and bitterly reproached herself for several faults she discovered therein--faults of contrivance, of design, of execution. She had made mistakes; and for a time she gave herself up to bitter repentance for that great crime.

"Caught in my own trap," she said; "frustrated by a girl--a child!--ay! and with exposure, perhaps punishment, before me. How she triumphs, doubtless, in that little malignant heart. How she will triumph when she brings forward her proofs, and overwhelms me with them--if she has them. Oh, yes, she has them! She is mighty careful never to say any thing of which she is not certain. I have remarked that in her from a child. She has them beyond doubt, and now she is sitting anticipating the pleasure of crushing me--enjoying the retrospect of my frustrated endeavors--thinking how she and Marlow will laugh together over a whole list of attempts that have failed, and purposes that I have not been able to execute. Yes, yes, they will laugh loud and gaily, and at the very altar, perhaps, will think with triumph that they are filling for me the last drop of scorn and disappointment. Never,

never, never! It shall never be. That is the only way, methinks;" and she fell into dark and silent thought again.

The fit lasted some time, and then she spoke again, muttering the words between her teeth as she had previously done. "They will never marry with a mother's curse upon their union! Oh, no, no, I know her too well. She will not do that. That weak poppet may die before she recalls her opposition--must die--and then they will live on loving and wretched. But it must be made as bitter as possible. It must not stop there."

Again she paused and thought, and then said to herself, "That drug which the Italian monk sold me would do well enough if I did but fully know its effects. There are things which leave terrible signs behind them--besides it is old, and may have lost its virtue. I must run no risk of that--and it must be speedy as well as sure. I have but four and twenty hours--the time is very short;" and relapsing into silence again, she continued in deep and silent meditation till the carriage stopped at her own gates.

Mrs. Hazleton sat in the library that night for two or three hours, and studied diligently a large folio volume which she had taken down herself. She read, and she seemed puzzled. A servant entered to ask some unimportant question, and she waved him away impatiently. Then leaning her head upon her hand she thought profoundly. She calculated in her own mind what Emily knew--how much--how intimately, and how she had learned it. Such a thing as remorse she knew not; but she had some fear, though very little--a sort of shrinking from the commission of acts more daring and terrible than any she had yet performed. There was something appalling--there is always something appalling--in the commission of a great new crime, and the turning back, as it were, of the mind of Mrs. Hazleton from the search for means to accomplish a deed determined, in order to calculate the necessity of that deed, proceeded from this sort of awe at the next highest step of evil to those which she had already committed.

"She must know all," said Mrs. Hazleton to herself, after having considered the matter for some moments deeply. "And she must have learned it accurately. I know her caution well. From whom can she have learned it?"

"From that young villain Ayliffe," was the prompt reply. "I was too harsh with him, and in his fit of rage he has gone away at once to tell this girl--or perhaps that old fool Dixwell. Most likely he has furnished her with evidence too, before he fled the country. Without that I could have set Marlow's discoveries at naught. Yet I doubt his having gone to Dixwell; he always despised him. Mean as he was himself; he looked upon him as a meaner. He would not go to him to whine and cant over him. He would go to the girl herself. Her he always loved, even in the midst of his violence and his rage. He would go to her or write to her beyond all doubt. She must be silenced. But I must deal with another first. Come what will, this marriage shall not take place. Besides, she is the most dangerous of the two. The girl might be frightened or awed into secrecy, and it will take longer time to reach her, but nothing will keep that weak woman's tongue from babbling, and in four and twenty hours her consent will be given to this marriage. If I can but contrive it rightly, that at least may be stopped, and a part of my revenge obtained at all events. It must be so--it must be so."

She turned to the leaves of the book again, but nothing in the contents seemed to give her satisfaction. "That will be too long," she said, after having read about a third of a page. "Three or four days to operate! Who could wait three or four days when the object is security, tranquility, or revenge? Besides the case admits of no delay. Before three of four days all will be over."

She read again, and was discontented with what she read. "That will leave traces," she said. "It must be the Italian's dose, I believe, after all. Those monks are very skilful men, and perhaps it may not have lost its efficiency. It is easily tried," she exclaimed suddenly, and ascending quietly to her own dressing-room, she sought out from the drawer of an old cabinet a small packet of white powder, which she concealed in the palm of her hand. Then descending to the library again, she sat for a few minutes in dull, heavy thought, and then rang a hand-bell which stood upon her table.

"Bring me a small quantity of meat cut fine for the dog," she said, as soon as her servant appeared. "He seems ill; what has been the matter with him?"

"Nothing, madam," said the man, looking under the table where lay a beautiful small spaniel sound asleep. "He has been quite well all day."

"He has had something like a fit," said Mrs. Hazleton.

"Dear me, perhaps he is going mad," replied the man. "Had I not better kill him?"

"Kill him!" exclaimed Mrs. Hazleton; "on no account whatever. Bring me a small plate of meat."

The man did as he was ordered, and on his return found the dog sitting at his mistress's feet, looking up in her face.

"Ah, Dorset," she said, speaking to the animal in a kindly tone, "you are better now, are you?"

The man seemed inclined to linger to see whether the dog would eat: but Mrs. Hazleton took the plate from him, and threw the poor beast a small piece, which he devoured eagerly.

"There that will do," said Mrs. Hazleton. "You may leave the room."

When she was alone again, she paused for a moment or two, then deliberately unfolded the packet, and put a very small quantity of the powder it contained upon a piece of the meat. This morsel she threw to the poor animal, who swallowed it at once, and then she set down the plate upon the ground, which he cleared in a moment. After that Mrs. Hazleton turned to her reading again, and looked round once at the end of about two minutes. The dog had resumed his sleeping attitude, and she read on. Hardly a minute more had passed ere the poor brute started up, ran round once or twice, as if seized with violent convulsions, staggered for an instant to and fro, and fell over on its side. Mrs. Hazleton rang the hell violently, and two servants ran in at once. "He is dying," she cried; "he is dying."

"Keep out of his way, madam," exclaimed one of the men, evidently in great fear himself, "there is no knowing what he may do."

The next instant the poor dog started once more upon his feet, uttered a loud and terrific yell, and fell dead upon the floor.

"Poor thing," said Mrs. Hazleton. "Poor Dorset! He is dead; take him away."

The two men seemed unwilling to touch him, but when quite satisfied that there was no more life left in him, they carried him away, and Mrs. Hazleton remained alone.

"Speedy enough," said the lady, replacing the large volume on the shelf. "We need no distillations and compoundings. This is as efficacious as ever. Now let me see. I must try and remember the size of the bottle, and the color of the stuff that was in it." She thought of these matters for some minutes, and then retired to rest.

Did she sleep well or ill that night? God knows. But if she slept well, the friends of hell must sometimes have repose.

The next morning very early, Mrs. Hazleton walked out. As the reader knows, she lived at no great distance from the little town, even by the high-road, and that was shortened considerably by a path through the park. There was a poor man in the place, an apothecary, who had came down there in the hope of carrying away some of the practice of good Mr. Short. He had not been very successful, and his stock of medicines was not very great: but he had all that Mrs. Hazleton wanted. Her demands indeed were simple enough--merely a little logwood, a little saffron, and a little madder. Having obtained these she asked to see some vials, and selected one containing somewhat less than half a pint.

The good man packed all these up with zealous care, saying that he would send them up to the house in a few minutes. Mrs. Hazleton, however, said she would carry them herself; but the very idea of the great lady carrying home a parcel, even through her own park, shocked the little apothecary extremely, and he pressed hard to be permitted to send his own boy, till Mrs. Hazleton replied in a rather peremptory tone, "I always say what I mean, sir. Be so good as to give me the parcel."

When she reached her own house, she ordered her carriage to be at the door at half past twelve in order to convey her to the dwelling of Sir Philip Hastings. Upon a very nice calculation the drive, commenced at that hour, would bring her to the place of her destination shortly after that precise period of the day when Lady Hastings was accustomed to take an hour's sleep. But Mrs. Hazleton had laid out her plan, and did not thus act by accident.

Almost every lady in those days acted the part of a Lady Bountiful in her neighborhood, and gave, not alone assistance in food and money to the cottagers and poor people about her, but medicine and sometimes medical advice. Both the latter were very simple indeed; but the preparation of these simple medicines entailed the necessity of what was called a still-room in each great house. In fact to be a Lady Bountiful, and to have a still-room, were two of the conventionalities of the day, from which no lady, having more than a very moderate fortune, could then hope to escape. Mrs. Hazleton was in the still-room, then, when her dear friend, who had already on one occasion given the death blow to her schemes upon Mr. Marlow's heart, drove up to the door and asked to see her.

The servant replied that his mistress was busy in the still-room, but that he would go and call her in a moment.

"Oh, dear, no," replied the lady, entering the house with an elastic step; "I will go and join her there, and surprise her in her charitable works. I know the way quite well--you needn't come--you needn't come;" and on she went to the still-room, which she entered without ceremony.

Mrs. Hazleton was, at that moment, in the act of pouring a purpleish sort of fluid, out of a glass dish with a lip to it, into an apothecary's vial. She turned round sharply at the sound of the opening door, thinking that it was produced by a servant intruding upon her uncalled. When she saw her friend, however, whose indiscreet advice she had neither forgotten nor forgiven, her face for a moment turned burning red, and then as pale as death; and she had nearly let the glass fall from her hand.

What was said on either part matters very little. Mrs. Hazleton was too wise to speak as sharply as she felt, and led the way from the still-room as fast as possible; but her dear friend had in one momentary glance seen every thing--the glass bowl, the vial, the fluid, and--more particularly than all--Mrs. Hazleton's sudden changes of complexion on her entrance.

CHAPTER XLIV

Sir Philip Hastings sat at breakfast with his daughter the morning of the same day on which Mrs. Hazleton in the still-room was subjected to her dear friend's unpleasant intrusion. He was calmer than he had been since his return; but it was a gloomy, thoughtful sort of calmness--that sort of superficial tranquility which is sometimes displayed under the influence of overpowering feelings, as the sea, so sailors tell us, is sometimes actually beaten down by the force of the winds that sweep over it. His brow was contracted with a deep frown, but it was by no means varied. It was stern, fixed, immoveable. To his daughter he spoke not a word, except when she bade him good morning, and asked after his health; and then he only replied "Well."

When breakfast was nearly over, a servant brought in some letters, and handed two to his master and one to Emily. Sir Philip's were soon read; but Emily's was longer, and she was still perusing it, with apparently much emotion, when the servant returned to the room. Sir Philip, during the half hour they had been previously together, had abstained from turning his eyes towards her. He had looked at the table cloth, or straight at the wall; but now he was gazing at her so intently, with a strange, eager, haggard expression of countenance that he did not even notice the entrance of the servant till the man spoke to him.

"Please your worship" said the servant "Master Atkinson of the Hill farm, near Hartwell, wishes to speak to you on some justice business."

Sir Philip started, and murmured between his teeth. "Justice--ay, justice!--who did you say?"

The man repeated what he had said before, and his master replied, "shew him in."

He then remained for a moment or two with his head leaning on his hand, and seemingly making an effort to recall his thoughts from some distant point; and when Mr. Atkinson entered, he spoke to him tranquilly enough.

"Pray be seated, Mr. Atkinson," he said, "what is it you want? I have meddled little with magisterial affairs lately."

"I want a warrant, sir," replied Mr. Atkinson. "And against a near neighbor and relation of yours; so I am sure you are not a man to refuse me justice."

"Not if it were my nearest and my dearest," replied Sir Philip, in a deep and hollow tone. "Who is the person?"

"A young man calling himself Sir John Hastings," said Mr. Atkinson. "We are afraid of his getting out of the country. He knows he has been found out, and he is hiding somewhere not very far off; but I and a constable will find him."

Emily had lain down her letter by her side, and was listening attentively. It was clear she was greatly moved by what she heard. Her face turned white and red. Her lip quivered as if she would fain have spoken; but she hesitated and remained silent for a moment. She thought of the unhappy young man lying on his death bed; for she had as yet received no intimation of his death from Mr. Dixwell, and of his seeing himself seized upon by the officers of justice, his last thoughts disturbed, all his anxious strivings after penitence, all his communings with his own heart, all his efforts to prepare for meeting with death, and God, and judgment, scattered by worldly shame and earthly anguish--she felt for him--she would fain have petitioned for him; but she was misunderstood, and, what was worse, she knew it--she felt it--she could not speak--she dare not say any thing, though her heart seemed as if it would break, and her only consolation was that all would be explained, that her motives, her conduct, would all be clear and comprehended in a a very few short hours. She knew, however, that she could not bear much more without weeping; for the letter which she had received from Marlow, telling her that he had arrived in London, and would set off to see her, as soon as some needful business, in the capital had been transacted, had agitated her much, and even pleasureable emotions will often shake the unnervous so as to weaken rather than strengthen us when called upon to contend with others of a different kind.

She rose then and left the room with a sad look and wavering step, and Sir Philip gazed at her as she passed with a look impossible to describe, saying to himself, "So--is it so?"

The next instant, however, he turned to the farmer, who was a man of a superior class to the ordinary yeomen of that day, saying, "What is your charge, sir?"

"Oh, plenty of charges, sir," replied the man; "fraud, conspiracy, perjury, forgery, in regard to all which I am ready to give information on my oath."

Sir Philip leaned his head upon his hand, and thought bitterly for two or three minutes. Then raising his eyes full to Atkinson's face, he said, "Were this young man my own child, were he my son, or were he my brother, were he a very dear friend, I should not have the slightest hesitation, Mr. Atkinson. I would take the information, and grant you a warrant at once-- nay; I will do so still, if you insist upon it; for it shall never be said that any consideration made me refuse justice. But I would have you remember that Sir John Hastings is my enemy; that he has, justly or unjustly, deprived me of fortune and station, and throughout the only transactions we have had together, has shown a spirit of malignity against me which might well make men believe that I must entertain similar feelings towards him. To sign a warrant against him, therefore, would be very painful to me, although I believe him to be capable of the crimes with which you charge him, and know you to be too honest a man to make such an accusation without a reasonable confidence in its truth. But I would have you consider whether it may not bring suspicion upon all your proceedings, if your very first step therein is to obtain a warrant against this man from his known and open enemy."

"But what am I to do, Sir Philip?" asked the farmer. "I am afraid he will escape. I know that he is hiding in this very neighborhood, in this very parish, within half a mile of this house."

A groan burst from the heart of Sir Philip Hastings. He had spoken his remonstrance clearly, slowly, and deliberately, forcibly bending his thoughts altogether to the subject before him; but he had been deeply and terribly moved all the time, and this direct allusion to the hiding place of John Ayliffe, to the very house which his daughter had visited on the previous day, roused all the terrible feelings, the jealous anger, the indignation, the horror, the contempt which had been stirred up in him, by what he thought her indecent, if not criminal act. It was too much for his self-command, and that groan burst forth in the struggle against himself.

He recovered himself speedily, however, and he replied, "Apply to Mr. Dixwell: he is a magistrate, and lives hardly a stone's throw from this house. You will lose but little time, save me from great pain, and both you and me from unjust imputations."

"Oh, I am not afraid of any imputations," said Mr. Atkinson. "I have personally no interest in the matter. You have, Sir, a great interest in it and if you would just hear what the case is, you would see that no one should look more sharply than you to the matter, in order that no time may be lost."

"I would rather not hear the case at all," replied Sir Philip. "If I have a personal interest in it, as you say, it would ill befit me to meddle. Go to Mr. Dixwell, my good friend. Explain the whole to him, and although perhaps he is not the brightest man that ever lived, yet he is a good man and an honest man, who will do justice in this matter."

"Very well, sir, very well," replied the farmer, a little mortified; for to say the truth, he had anticipated some little accession of importance from lending a helping hand to restore Sir Philip Hastings to the rights of which he had been unjustly deprived, and taking his leave he went away, thinking the worthy baronet the most impracticable man he had ever met with in his life. "I always knew that he was crotchety," he said to himself, "and carried his notions of right and wrong to a desperate great length; but I did not know that he went so far as this. I don't believe that if he saw a man running away with his own apples, he would stop him without a warrant from another justice. Yet he can be severe enough when he is not concerned himself, as we all know. He'd hang every poacher in the land for that matter, saying, as I have heard him many a time, that it is much worse to steal any thing that is unprotected, than if it is protected."

With these thoughts he rode straight away to the house of Mr. Dixwell, but to his mortification he found that the worthy clergyman was out. "Can you tell me where he is?" he asked of the servant, "I want him on business of the greatest importance."

The woman hesitated for a moment, but the expression of perplexity and anxiety on the good farmer's face overcame her scruples, and she replied, "I did not exactly hear him say where he was going, but I saw him take the foot-path down to Jenny Best's."

Atkinson turned his horse's head at once, and rode along the road till he reached the cottage. There he fastened his horse to a tree, and went in. The outer room was vacant; but through the partition he heard a voice speaking in a slow, measured tone, as if in prayer; and after waiting and hesitating for a moment or two, he struck upon the table with his knuckles to call attention to his presence.

The moment after, the door opened slowly and quietly, and Jenny Best herself first put out her head, and then came into the room with a curtsy, closing the door behind her.

"Good day, Jenny," said the farmer; "is Mr. Dixwell here?"

"Yes, Master Atkinson," replied the good dame; "he is in there, praying with a sick person."

"Why how is that?" asked Mr. Atkinson. "Best is not ill, I hope, nor your son."

"No, sir," answered the old woman; "it is a young man who broke his leg close by our door the other day;" and seeing him about to ask further questions, which she might have had difficulty in parrying, she added, "I will call the parson to you, sir."

Thus saying, she retreated again into the inner room, and in a few moments Mr. Dixwell himself appeared.

"God day, Atkinson," he said; "you have been absent on a journey, I hear."

"Yes, your Reverence," replied the farmer, "and it is in consequence of that journey that I come to you now. I want a warrant from you, Mr. Dixwell; and that as quick as possible."

"Why, I cannot give you a warrant here," said the clergyman, hesitating. "I have no clerk with me, nor any forms of warrants, and I cannot very well go home just now. It can, do no harm waiting an hour or two, I suppose."

"It may do a great deal of harm," replied the farmer, "for as great a rogue and as bad a fellow as ever lived may escape from justice if it is not granted immediately."

"Can't you go to Mr. Hastings?" said the clergyman. "He would give you one directly, if the case justifies it."

"He sent me to your Reverence," replied the farmer. "In one word, the case is this, Mr. Dixwell. I have to charge a man, whom, I suppose, I must call a gentleman, upon oath, with fraud, perjury, and forgery. Shanks, one of the conspirators we have got already. But this man--this fellow who calls himself Sir John Hastings, I mean, is hiding away here--in this very cottage, sir, I am told--and may make his escape at any minute. Now that I am here, and a magistrate with me, I tell you fairly, sir, I will not quit the place till I have him in custody."

He spoke in a very sharp and decided tone; for to say the truth he had a vague suspicion that Mr. Dixwell, whose good-nature was well known, knew very well where John Ayliffe was, and might be trying to convert him, with the full intention of afterwards aiding him to escape. The clergyman answered at once, however, "he is here, Master Atkinson, but he is very ill, and will soon be in sterner custody than yours."

There was a good deal of the bull-dog spirit of the English yeoman in the good farmer's character, and he replied tartly, "I don't care for that. He shall be in my custody first."

Mr. Dixwell looked pained and offended. His brow contracted a good deal, and laying his hand upon the farmer's wrist, he led him towards the door of the inner room, saying, "You are hard and incredulous, sir. But come with me, and you shall see his state with your own eyes."

The farmer suffered himself to be led along, and Mr. Dixwell opened the door, and entered the room with a quiet and reverent step. The sunshine was streaming through the little window upon the floor, and by its cheerful light, contrasting strangely with the gray darkness of the face which lay upon the bed of death. There was not a sound, but the footfalls of the two persons who entered; for the old woman had seated herself by the bedside, and was gazing silently at the face of the sick man.

At first, Mr. Atkinson thought that he was dead; and life indeed lingered on with but the very faintest spark. He seemed utterly unconscious; for the eyes even did not move at the sound of the opening door, and the farmer was a good deal shocked at the hardness of his judgment. He was not one, however, to give up his purpose easily, and when Mr. Dixwell said, "you can now see and judge for yourself--is he likely to escape, do you think?" Atkinson answered in a low but determined tone, "No, but I do not think I ought to leave him as long as there is any life in him."

"You can do as you please," said Mr. Dixwell, in a tone of much displeasure. "Only be silent. There is a seat;" and leaving him, he took his place again by the dying man's side.

Though shocked, and feeling perhaps a little ashamed, Mr. Atkinson. with that dogged sort of resolution which I have before spoken of; resisted his own feelings, and would not give up the field. He thought he was doing his duty, and that is generally quite sufficient for an Englishman. Nothing could move him, so long as breath was in the body of the unhappy young man. He remained seated there, perfectly still and silent, as hour after hour slipped away, with his head bent down, and his arms crossed upon his chest.

The approach of death was very slow with John Ayliffe: he lingered long after all the powers of the body seemed extinct. Hand or foot he could not move--his sunken eyes remained half closed--the hue of death was upon his face, but yet the chest heaved, the breath came and went, sometimes rapidly, sometimes very slowly; and for along time Mr. Dixwell could not tell whether he was conscious at all or not. At the end of two hours, however, life seemed to make an effort against the great enemy, though it was a very feeble one, and intellect had no share in it. He began to mutter a few words from time to time, but they were wild and incoherent, and the faint sounds referred to dogs and horses, to wine and money. He seemed to think himself talking to his servants, gave orders, and asked questions, and told them to light a fire, he was so cold. This went on till the shades of evening began to fall, and then Mr. Short, the surgeon, came in and felt his pulse.

"It is very strange," said the surgeon, "that this has lasted so long. But it must be over in a few minutes now. I can hardly feel a pulsation."

Mr. Dixwell did not reply, and the surgeon remained gazing on the dying man's face till it was necessary to ask for a light. Jenny Best brought in a solitary candle, and whether it was the effect of the sudden though feeble glare, I cannot tell, John Ayliffe opened his eyes, and said, more distinctly than before, "I am going--I am going--this is death--yes, this is death! Pray for me, Mr. Dixwell--pray for me--I do repent--yes, I have hope."

The jaw quivered a little as he uttered the last words, but at the same moment John Best, the good woman's husband, entered the room with a hurried step, drew Mr. Short, the surgeon, aside, and whispered something in his ear.

"Good Heaven!" exclaimed the surgeon. "Impossible, Best! Has the man got a horse? mine's at the farm."

"Yes, sir, yes!" replied the man, eagerly. "He has 'got a horse; but you had better make haste."

Mr. Short dashed out of the room; but before he left it, John Ayliffe was a corpse.

CHAPTER XLV

Mrs. Hazleton found the inconvenience of having a dear friend. It was in vain that she tried to get rid of her visitor. The visitor would not be got rid of. She was deaf to hints; she paid no attention to any kind of inuendoes; and she looked so knowing, so full of important secrets, so quietly mischievous, that Mrs. Hazleton was cowed by that most unnerving of all things, the consciousness of meditated crime. She could not help thinking that the fair widow saw into her thoughts and purposes--she could not help doubting the impenetrability of the veil behind which hypocrisy hides the hideout features of unruly passion--she could not help thinking that the keen-sighted and astute must perceive some of the movements at least of the rude movers of the painted puppets of the face--the smile, the gay looks, the sparkling eyes, the calm placid brow, the dignified serenity, which act their part in the glittering scene of the world, too often worked by the most harsh, foul, and brutal of all the motives of the human heart. But she was irritated too, as well as fearful; and there was a sort of combat went on between impatience and apprehension. Had she given way to inclination she would have ordered one of her servants to take the intruder by the shoulders and put her out of doors; but for more than an hour after the time she had fixed for setting out, vague fears--however groundless and absurd--were sufficiently powerful to restrain her temper. She was not of a character, however, to be long cowed by any thing. She had great confidence in herself--in her own resources--in her own conduct and good fortune likewise. That confidence might have been a little shaken indeed by events which had lately occurred; but anger soon rallied it, and brought it back to her aid. She asked herself if she were a fool to dread that woman-- what it was she had discovered--what it was that she could testify. She had merely seen her doing what almost every lady did a hundred times in the year in those day--preparing some simples in the still-room; and gradually as she found that gentle hints proved unsuccessful, she resumed her natural dignity of demeanor. That again gave way to a chilling silence, and then to a somewhat irritable imperiousness, and rising from her chair, she begged her visitor to excuse her, alleging that she had business of importance to transact which would occupy her during the whole day.

Not one of all the variation of conduct--not one sign, however slight, of impatience, doubt, or anger--escaped the keen eye that was fixed upon her. Mrs. Hazleton, under the influence of conscience, did not exactly betray the dark secrets of her own heart, but she raised into importance, an act in itself the most trifling, which would have passed without any notice had she not been anxious to conceal it.

As soon as her visitor, taking a hint that could not be mistaken, had quitted the room and the house, with an air of pique and ill-humor, Mrs. Hazleton returned to the still-room and recommenced her operations there; but she found her hand shaking and her whole frame agitated.

"Am I a fool," she asked herself, "to be thus moved by an empty gossip like that? I must conquer this, or I shall be unfit for my task."

She sat down at a table, leaned her head upon her hand, gazed forth out of the little window, forced her mind away from the present, thought of birds and flowers, and pictures and statues, and of the two sunshiny worlds of art and nature--of every thing in short but the dark, dark cares of her own passions. It was a trick she had learned to play with herself--one of those pieces of internal policy by which she had contrived so often and so long, to rule and master with despotic sway the frequent rebellions of the body against the tyranny of the mind.

She had not sat there two minutes, however, ere there was a tap at the door, and she started with a quick and jarring thrill, as if that knock had been a summons of fate. The next instant she looked quickly around, however, and was satisfied that whoever entered could find no cause for suspicion. She was there seated quietly at the table. The vial was out of sight, the fatal powder hidden in the palm of her hand, and she said aloud, "Come in."

The butler entered, bowing profoundly and saying, "The carriage is at the door, madam, and Wilson has just come back from the house of Mr. Shanks, but he could not find him."

The man hesitated a little as if he wished to add something more, and Mrs. Hazleton replied in a somewhat sharp tone, "I told you when I sent it away just now that I would tell you when I was ready. I shall not be so for half an hour; but let it wait, and do not admit any one. Mr. Shanks must be found, and informed that I want to see him early to-morrow, as I shall go to London on the following day."

"I am sorry to say, madam," replied the butler, "that if the talk of the town is true, he will not be able to come. They say he has been apprehended on a charge of perjury and forgery in regard to that business of Sir Philip Hastings, and has been sent off to the county jail."

Mrs. Hazleton looked certainly a little aghast, and merely saying "Indeed!" she waved her hand for the man to withdraw.

She then sat silent and motionless for at least five minutes. What passed within her I cannot tell; but when she rose, though pale as marble, she was firm, calm, and self-possessed as ever. She turned the key in the lock; she drew a curtain which covered the lower half of the window, farther across, so that no eye from without, except the eye of God, could see what she was doing there within. She then drew forth the vial from its nook, opened out the small packet of powder, and poured part of it into a glass. She seemed as if she were going to pour the whole, but she paused in doing so, and folded up the rest again, saying, "That must be fully enough; I will keep the rest; it may be serviceable, and I can get no more."

She gazed down upon the ground near her feet with a look of cold, stern, but awful resolution, as if there had been an open grave before her; and then she placed the packet in her glove, poured a little distilled water into the glass, shook it, and held the mixture up to the light. The powder had in great part dissolved, but not entirely, and she added a small quantity more of the distilled water, and poured the whole into the vial, which was already about one-third full of a dark colored liquid.

"Now I will go," she said, concealing the bottle. But when she reached the door, and had her hand upon the lock, she paused and remained in very deep thought for an instant, with her brow slightly contracted and her lip quivering. Heaven knows what she thought of then,--whether it was doubt, or fear, or pity, or remorse--but she said in a low tone, "Down, fool! it shall be done," and she passed out of the room.

She paused suddenly in the little passage which led to the still-room, by a pair of double doors, into the principal part of the house, perceiving with some degree of consternation that she had been unconsciously carrying the vial with its dark colored contents in her hand, exposed to the view of all observers. Her eye ran round the passage with a quick and eager glance; but there was no one in sight, and she felt reassured. Even at that moment she could smile at her own heedlessness, and she did smile as she placed the bottle in her pocket, saying to herself, "How foolish! I must not suffer such fits of absence to come upon me, or I shall spoil all."

She then walked quietly to her dressing-room, arranged her dress for the little journey before her, and descended again to the hall, where the servants were waiting for her corning. After she had entered the carriage, however, she again fell into a fit of deep thought, closed her eyes, and remained as if half asleep for nearly an hour. Perhaps it would be too much to scrutinize the state or changes of her feelings during that long, painful lapse of thought. That there was a struggle--a terrible struggle--can hardly be doubted--that opportunity was given her for repentance, for desistance, between the purpose and the deed, we know; and there can be little doubt that the small, still voice--which is ever the voice of God--spoke to her from the spirit-depth within, and warned her to forbear. But she was of an unconquerable nature; nothing could turn her; nothing could overpower her, when she had once resolved on any act. There was no persuasion had effect; no remonstrance was powerful. Reason, conscience, habit itself, were but dust in the balance in the face of one of her determinations.

She roused herself suddenly from her fit of moody abstraction, when the carriage was still more than a mile from the house of Sir Philip Hastings. She looked at the watch which hung by her side, and gazed at the sky; and then she said to herself, "That woman's impertinent intrusion was intolerable. However; I shall get there an hour before the twenty-four hours have passed, and doubtless she will have kept her word and refrained from speaking till she has seen me; but I am afraid I shall find her woke up from her midday doze, and that may make the matter somewhat difficult. Difficult! why I have seen jugglers do tricks a thousand times to which this is a mere trifle. My sleight of hand will not fail me, I think;" and then she set her mind to work to plan out every step of her proceedings.

All was clearly and definitely arranged by the time she arrived at the door of Sir Philip Hastings' house. Her face was cleared of every cloud, her whole demeanor under perfect control. She was the Mrs. Hazleton, the calm, dignified, graceful Mrs. Hazleton, which the world knew; and when she descended from the carriage with a slow but easy step, and spoke to the coachman about one of the springs which had creaked and made a noise on the way, not one of Sir Philip Hastings' servants could have believed that her mind was occupied with any thing more grave than the idle frivolous thoughts of an every-day society.

CHAPTER XLVI

Mrs. Hazleton fancied herself in high good luck; for just as she was passing through the door into the hall, Lady Hastings' maid crossed and made her a curtsey. Mrs. Hazleton beckoned her up, saying in a quiet, easy, every-day tone, "I suppose your lady is awake by this time?"

"No, madam," replied the maid, "she is asleep still. She did not take her nap as early as usual to-day; for Mistress Emily was with her, and my lady would not go to sleep till she went out to take a walk."

Mrs. Hazleton was somewhat alarmed at this intelligence; for she had not much confidence in her good friend's discretion. "How is Miss Emily?" she said in a tender tone. "She seemed very sad and low when last I saw her."

"She is just the same, Madam," replied the maid. "She did not seem very cheerful when she went out, and has been crying a good deal to-day."

Mrs. Hazleton was better satisfied, and paused for an instant to think; but the maid interrupted her cogitations by saying--"I think I may wake my lady now, if you please to come up, Madam."

"Oh, dear, no," replied Mrs. Hazleton. "Do not wake her. I will go in quietly and sit with her till she wakes naturally. It is a pity to deprive her of one moment's calm sleep. You needn't come, you needn't come. I will ring for you when your mistress wakes;" and she quietly ascended the stairs, though the maid offered some civil remonstrances to her undertaking the task of watching by her sleeping mistress.

The most careful affection could not have prompted greater precautions in opening the door of the sick lady's chamber, than those which were taken by Mrs. Hazleton. It was a good solid door, however, well seasoned, and well hung, and moved upon its hinges without noise. She closed it with the same care, and then with a soft tread glided up to the side of the bed.

Lady Hastings was sleeping profoundly and quietly; and as she lay in an attitude of easy grace, a shadow of her youthful beauty seemed to have returned, and all the traces of after cares and anxiety were banished for the time. On the table, near the bed-head, stood the vial of medicine, with the glass and spoon; and Mrs. Hazleton eyed it for a moment or two without touching it. She saw that she had hit the color exactly; but the quantity in that vial, and the one she had with her, was somewhat different. She felt puzzled and doubtful. She asked herself--"Would the difference be discovered when the time came for giving her the medicine?" and a certain degree of trepidation seized her. But she was bold, and said to herself--"They will never see it. They suspect nothing. They will never see it." She took the vial from her pocket, and held it for an instant or two in her hand. Again a doubt and hesitation took possession of her. She gazed at the sleeper with a haggard eye. The face was so calm, so sweet, so gentle in expression, that the pleasant look perhaps did move her a little with remorse. The voice within said again, and again, "Forbear!" She tried to deafen herself against it, or to fill the ear of conscience with delusive sounds. "She is dying," she said--"She will die--she cannot recover. It is but taking away a few short hours, in order to stop that fatal marriage, which shall never be. I am becoming a fool--a weak irresolute fool."

Just as she thus thought, Lady Hastings moved uneasily, as if to wake from her slumber. That moment was decisive. With a hurried hand, and quick as light, Mrs. Hazleton changed the two vials, and concealed the one which she had taken away.

Then it was, probably for the first time, that all the awful consequences of the deed, for time and for eternity, flashed upon her. The scales fell from her eyes: no longer passion, or mortified vanity, or irritated pride, or disappointed love, distorted the objects or concealed their forms. She stood there consciously a murderer. She trembled in every limb; and, unable to support herself, sunk down in the chair that stood near. Had Lady Hastings slept on, Mrs. Hazleton would have been saved; for her impulse was immediately to reverse the very act she had done--all would have been saved--all to whom that act brought wretchedness. But the movement of the chair--the sound of the vial touching the marble table--the rustle of the thick silk--dispelled what remained of slumber, and Lady Hastings opened her eyes drowsily, and looked round. At the very moment she would have given worlds to recall it. The deed became irrevocable. The barrier of Fate fell: it was amongst the things done; it was written in the book of God as a great crime committed. Nothing remained but to insure, that the end she aimed at would be obtained; that the evil consequences, in this world at least, should be averted from herself. There was a terrible struggle to recover her self-command--a wrestling of the spirit--against the turbulent and fierce emotions which shook the body. She was still much agitated when Lady Hastings recognized her and began to speak; but her determination was taken to obtain the utmost that she could from the act she had committed--to have the full price of her crime. She was no Judas Iscariot, to be content with the thirty pieces of silver for the innocent blood, and then hang herself in despair. Oh no! She had sold her own soul, and she would have its price.

But yet, as I have said, the struggle was terrible, and lasted longer than usual with her.

"Dear me, my kind friend, is that you?" said Lady Hastings. "Have you been here long? I did not hear you come in."

Her words, and her tone, were gentle and affectionate. All the coldness and the sharpness of the preceding day seemed to have passed away, and to have been forgotten; but words and tone were equally jarring to the feelings of Mrs. Hazleton. The sharpest language, the most angry manner, would have been a relief to her. They would have afforded her some sort of strength--some sort of support.

It is painful enough to hear sweet music when we are very sad. I have known it rise almost to agony; but the tones of friendship and regard, of gentleness and tender kindness, to the ear of hatred and malice, must be more terrible still.

"I have been here but a moment," said Mrs. Hazleton, gloomily--almost peevishly. "I suppose it was my coming in woke you; but I am sure I made as little noise as possible."

"Why, what is the matter?" said Lady Hastings. "You look quite pale and agitated, and you speak quite crossly."

"Your sudden waking startled me," said Mrs. Hazleton; "and, besides, you looked so ill, my dear friend. I almost thought you were dead till you began to move."

There was malice in the sentence, simple as it seemed, and it had its effect. Nervous, hypochondriac, Lady Hastings was frightened at the mere sound, and her heart beat strangely at the very thought of being supposed dead. It seemed to her to augur that she was very ill; that she was much worse than her friends allowed her to believe; that they anticipated her speedy dissolution, and she remained silent and sad for several minutes, giving Mrs. Hazleton time to recover herself completely. She was a little piqued too at the abruptness of Mrs. Hazleton's manner. Neither the speech, nor the mode, nor the speaker, pleased her; and she replied at length--"Nevertheless, I feel a good deal better to-day. I have slept well for, I dare say, a couple of hours; and my dear child Emily has been with me all the morning. I must say she bears opposition and contradiction very sweetly."

She knew that would not please Mrs. Hazleton, and she laid some emphasis on the words by way of retaliation. It was petty, but it was quite in her character. "Now I think of it," she added, "you promised to tell me what you discovered in regard to Marlow's relationship to Lord Launceston. I find--but never mind. Tell me what you have found out."

Mrs. Hazleton hesitated. The first impulse was to tell a lie--to assert that Marlow was not the old earl's heir; but there was something in Lady Hastings' manner which made her suspect that she had received more certain information, and she made up her mind to speak the truth.

"It is very true," she said; "Mr. Marlow is the old lord's nearest male relation, and heir to his title. I suspect," she added with a silly sounding laugh, "you have found this out yourself, my dear friend, and have made your peace with Emily, by withdrawing your opposition to her marriage."

Her heart was very bitter at that moment; for she really did suspect all that she said. The idea presented itself to her mind (producing a feeling of fierce disappointment), of all her efforts being rendered fruitless, her dark schemes frustrated, her cunning contrivances without effect, at the very moment when the crime, by which she proposed to insure success, was so far consummated as to be beyond recall. She was relieved on that score in a moment.

"Oh dear no," cried Lady Hastings. "I promised you, my dear friend, that I would say nothing till I saw you, and I have said nothing either to my husband or Emily. But I will of course now tell her all immediately, and I do confess it will give me greater satisfaction than any act of my whole life, to withdraw the opposition to her marriage which has made her so miserable, and to bid her be happy with the man of her own choice--an excellent good young man he is too. He has been laboring, I find, for the last fortnight or three weeks, night and day, in our service, and has detected the horrible conspiracy by which my husband was deprived of his rights and property. I shall tell Emily, with great joy, as soon as ever she comes back, that were it for nothing but this zeal in our cause, I would receive him joyfully as my son-in-law."

"You had better wait till to-morrow morning," said Mrs. Hazleton, in a cold but significant tone.

"Oh dear no," said Lady Hastings, somewhat petulantly, "I have waited quite long enough--perhaps too long. You surely would not have me protract my child's anxiety and sorrow unnecessarily. No, I will tell her the moment she returns. She read me part of a letter from Marlow to-day, which shows me that he has lost no time in seeking to serve us and make us happy, and I will lose no time in making my child and him happy also."

"As you please," replied Mrs. Hazleton; "I only thought that in this changeable world, there are so many unexpected things occurring between one day and another, it might be well for you to pause and consider a little--in order, I mean, that after-thought may not show you reason to withdraw your consent, as you now withdraw your objection."

"My consent once given, shall never be withdrawn," replied Lady Hastings, in a determined tone.

Mrs. Hazleton looked at the vial by the bedside, and then at her watch. "You had better avoid all agitation," she said, "and at all events before you speak with Emily, take a dose of the medicine, which Short tells me he has given you to soothe and calm your spirits--shall I give you one now?"

"No, I thank you," replied Lady Hastings, briefly; "not at present."

"Is it not the time?" said Mrs. Hazleton, looking at her watch again; "the good man told me you were to take it very regularly."

"But he told me," replied Lady Hastings, "that nobody was to give it to me but Emily, and she will be back at the right time, I am sure. What o'clock is it?"

"Past five," replied Mrs. Hazleton, advancing the hour a little.

"Then it wants three quarters of an hour to the time," said Lady Hastings, "and Emily has only gone to take a walk. We are expecting Marlow to-night, so she will not go far I am sure."

Mrs. Hazleton fell into profound thought. In proposing to give Lady Hastings the portion herself, she had deviated a little from her original plan. She had intended all along, that the mortal draught should be administered by the hand of Emily, and she had only been tempted to depart from that purpose by the fear of Lady Hastings withdrawing her opposition to her daughter's marriage with Marlow before the deed was fully accomplished.

There was no help for it, however. She was obliged to take her chance of the result; and while she mused at that moment, vague notions--what shall I call them?--not exactly schemes or purposes, but rather dreams of turning suspicion upon Emily herself, of making men believe--suspect, even if they could not prove--that the daughter knowingly deprived the mother of life, crossed her imagination. She meditated rather longer than was quite decorous, and then suddenly recollecting herself she said, "By the way, has Emily yet condescended to particularize her astounding charges against your poor friend? I am really anxious to hear them, and although I confess that the matter has afforded me some amusement, it has brought painful feelings and doubts with it too: I have sometimes fancied, my dear friend, that there is a slight aberration in your poor Emily's mind, and I can account for her conduct in this instance by no other mode. You know her grandfather, Sir John, had moments when he was hardly sane. I have heard your own good father declare upon one occasion, that Sir John was as mad as a lunatic. Tell me then, has Emily brought forward any proofs, or alluded to these accusations since I saw you? You said she would explain all in a few hours."

"She has not as yet explained all," replied Lady Hastings, "but I cannot deny that she has alluded to the charges, and repeated them all distinctly. She said that the delay had been rather longer than she expected; but that as soon as Mr. Dixwell came, every thing should be told."

"The suspense is unpleasant," said Mrs. Hazleton, somewhat sarcastically; "I trust the young lady does not play with the feelings of her lover as she does with those of her friends, otherwise I should pity Marlow."

Lady Hastings was a good deal nettled. "I do not think he much deserves your pity," she replied; "and besides, I think he is quite satisfied with Emily's conduct, as I am also. I am quite confident she has good reason for what she says, my dear Madam--not that I mean to assert that the charges are true, by any means--she may be mistaken, you know--she may be misinformed-- but that she brings them in good faith, and fully believes that she can prove them distinctly, I do not for a moment doubt. If she is wrong, nobody will be more grieved, or more ready to make atonement than herself; but whether she is right or wrong, remains to be proved."

"All that I have to request then is," said Mrs. Hazleton, "that you will be kind enough to let me know, immediately you are yourself informed, what are the specific charges, and upon what grounds they rest. That they must be false, I know; and therefore I shall give myself no uneasiness about them. All I regret is, that you should be troubled about what must be frivolous and absurd. Nevertheless, I must beg you to let me hear immediately."

"Sir Philip will do that," replied Lady Hastings, coldly. "If Emily is right in her views, the matter will require the intervention of a man. It will be too serious for a woman to deal with."

"Oh, very well," said Mrs. Hazleton, with an air of offended dignity. "Good morning, my dear Lady;" and she quitted the room.

She paused upon the broad staircase for two or three minutes, leaning upon the balustrade in deep thought; but when she descended to the hall, she asked a servant who stood there if Mistress Emily had returned. The man replied in the negative, and she then inquired for Sir Philip, asking to see him.

The servant said he was in his library, and proceeded to announce her. She followed him so closely as to enter the room almost at the same moment, and beheld Sir Philip Hastings, with his head leaning on his hand, sitting at the table and gazing earnestly down upon it. There was a book before him, but it was closed.

"I beg pardon for intruding, my dear sir," said Mrs. Hazleton, "but I wished to ask if you know where Emily is. I want to speak with her."

"I know nothing about her," said Sir Philip, abruptly; and then muttered to himself, "would I knew more."

"I thought I saw her in the fields as I came," said Mrs. Hazleton, "gathering flowers and herbs--she is fond of botany, I believe."

"I know not," said Sir Philip, recovering himself a little. "Pray be seated, Madam--I have not attended much to her studies lately."

"Thank you, I must go," said Mrs. Hazleton. "Perhaps I shall meet her as I drive along. Do not let me interrupt you, do not let me interrupt you;" and she quietly quitted the room.

"Gathering herbs!" said Sir Philip Hastings, "what new whim is this?"

CHAPTER XLVII

Emily Hastings was not three hundred yards from the house when Mrs. Hazleton drove away from the house door. She had never been more than three hundred yards from it during that day. She had gathered no herbs, she had wandered through no fields; but, at her mother's earnest request, she had gone out to breathe the fresh air for half an hour, and had ascended through the gardens to a little terrace on the hill, where she had continued to walk up and down under the shade of some tall trees; had seen Mrs. Hazleton arrive, and saw her depart. The scene which the terrace commanded was very beautiful in itself, and the house below, the well-cultivated gardens, a fountain here and there, neat hedge-rows, and trim, well-ordered fields, gave the whole an air of home comfort, and peaceful affluence, such as few countries but England can display.

I have shown, or should have shown, that Emily was somewhat of an impressible character, and the brightness and the pleasant character of the scene had its usual effect in cheering. Certainly, to any one who had stood near her, looking over even that fair prospect, she herself would have been the loveliest object in it. Every year had brought out some new beauty in her face, and without diminishing one charm of extreme youth, had expanded her fair form into womanly richness. The contour of every limb was perfect: the whole in symmetry complete; and her movements, as she walked to and fro, upon the terrace, were all full of that easy, floating grace, which requires a combination of youth and health, and fine proportion, and a pure, high mind. If there was a defect it was that she was somewhat pale that day; for she had not slept at all during the preceding night from agitated feelings, and busy thoughts that would not rest. But the slight degree of languor, which watching and anxiety had given, was not without its own peculiar charm, and the liquid brightness of her eyes seemed but the more dazzling for the drooping of the eyelid, with its long sweeping fringe.

There was a mixture, too, strange as it may seem to say so, of sadness and cheerfulness, in the expression of her face that day--perhaps I should say an alternation of the two expressions; but the change from the one to the other was too rapid for distinctness; and the well of feelings from which the expressions flowed, was of very mingled waters. The scene of death and suffering which she had lately witnessed at the cottage, her father's wild and gloomy manner, her mother's sickness, the displeasure of one parent, however unjust, and the opposition of another, to her dearest wishes, however unreasonable, naturally produced anxiety and sadness. But then again, on the other hand, Marlow's letter had cheered and comforted her much; the prospect of seeing him so speedily, rejoiced her more than she had even anticipated, and the certainty that a few short hours would remove for ever all doubts as to her conduct, her thoughts and her feelings, from the mind of both her parents, and especially from that of her father, gave her strength and happy confidence.

Poor Emily! How lovely she looked as she walked along there with the ever varying expressions fluttering over her face, and her rich nut-brown hair, free and uncovered, floating in curls on the sportive breath of the breeze.

When first she came out the general tone of her feelings was sad; but the bright hopes seemed to in vigor in the open air, and her mind fixed more and more gladly on the theme of Marlow's letter. As it did so she extracted fresh motives of comfort from it. He had given her many details in regard to his late proceedings. He had openly and plainly spoken of the conduct of Mrs. Hazleton, and told her he could prove the facts which he asserted. He had not even hinted at an injunction to secrecy, and although her first impulse had been to wait for his arrival and let him explain the whole himself, yet, as it was now getting late in the day, and he had not come- -as the obligation to secrecy, laid upon her by John Ayliffe, might not be removed till the following morning, and her mother was evidently anxious and uneasy for want of all explanations--Emily thought she might be fully justified in reading more of Marlow's letter to Lady Hastings than she had hitherto done, and showing her that she had asserted nothing without reasonable cause. The sight of Mrs. Hazleton's carriage arriving confirmed her in this intention. She knew that fair lady to possess very great influence over her mother's mind. She believed that influence to have been always exerted balefully, and she judged it better, much better, to cut it short at once, rather than suffer it to endure even for another day.

When she saw the carriage drive away, then, she returned rapidly to the house, went to her room to get Marlow's letter, and then proceeded to her mother's chamber.

"Mrs. Hazleton has been here, my love," said Lady Hastings, as soon as Emily approached, "and really, she has been very strange and disagreeable. She seems, not to have the slightest consideration for me; but even in my weak state, says every thing that can agitate and annoy me."

"I trust, my dear mother, that you will see her no more," said Emily. "The full proofs of what I told you concerning her. I cannot yet give; but Marlow lays me under no injunction to secrecy, and I have brought his letter to read you the part in which he speaks of her. That will show you quite enough to convince you that Mrs. Hazleton should never be permitted within these doors again."

"Oh read it, pray read it, my dear," said Lady Hastings. "I am all anxiety to know the facts; for really one does not know how to behave to this woman, and I feel in a very awkward position towards her."

Emily sat down by the bedside and read, word for word, all that Marlow had written in reference to Mrs. Hazleton, which was interspersed, here and there, with many kindly and respectful expressions towards Lady Hastings and her husband, which he knew well would be gratifying to her whom he addressed. His statements were all clear and precise, and from them Lady Hastings learned he had obtained proof, from various different sources, that her seeming friend had knowingly and willingly supplied John Ayliffe with the means of carrying on his fraudulent suit against Sir Philip Hastings: that she had been his counsel and cooperator in all his proceedings, and had suggested many of the most criminal steps he had taken. The last passage which Emily read was remarkable: "To see into the dark abyss of that woman's heart, my dearest Emily," he said, "is more than I can pretend to do; but it is perfectly clear that she has been moved in all her proceedings for some years, by bitter personal hatred towards Sir Philip, Lady Hastings, and yourself. Mere self-interest--to which she is by no means insensible on ordinary occasions--has been sacrificed to the gratification of malice, and she has even gone so far as to place herself in a situation of considerable peril for the purpose of ruining your excellent father, and making your mother and yourself unhappy. What offence has been committed by any of your family to merit such persevering and ruthless hatred, I cannot tell. I only know that it must have been unintentional; but that it has not been the less bitterly revenged. Perhaps the disclosures which must be made as soon as I return, may give us some insight into the cause; but at present I can only tell you the result."

"My dear Emily," said Lady Hastings, "your father should know this immediately. He has been very sad and gloomy since his return. I really cannot tell what is the matter with him; but something weighs upon his spirits, evidently; but this news will give him relief, or, at all events, will divert his thoughts. It was very natural, my dear girl, that you should first tell your mother, but I really think that we must now take him into our councils."

"I will go and ask him to come here, at once," said Emily. "I think my dear father has not understood me rightly lately, and has chilled me by cold looks and words when I would fain have spoken to him, and poured my whole thoughts into his bosom. Oh, I shall be glad to do any thing to regain his confidence; and although I know it must be regained in a very, very short space of time, yet I would gladly do any thing to prevent its being withheld from me even a moment longer."

She took a step towards the door as she spoke; but Lady Hastings; unhappily, called her back. "Stay, my Emily," she said. "Come hither, my dear child; I have something to say that will cheer you and comfort you, and give you strength to meet any little crosses of your father's with patience and resignation. He has been sorely tried, and is much troubled. But I was going to say, dear Emily," and she threw her arms round her daughter's neck as she leaned over her, "that I have been thinking much of all that was said the other day, in regard to your marriage with Marlow. I see that your heart is set upon it, and that you can only be happy in a union with him. I know him to be a good and excellent young man; and after all that he has done to serve us, I must not interpose your wishes any longer; although, perhaps, I might have chosen differently for you had the choice rested with me. I give you, therefore, my full and free consent, Emily, and trust you will be as happy as you deserve, my dear girl. I think you might very well have made a higher alliance, but----"

"But none that would have made me half so happy," replied Emily, embracing her mother. "Oh, dear mother, if you could know the load you take from my heart, you would be amply repaid for any sacrifice of opinion you make to your child's happiness. I cannot conceive any situation more painful to be placed in than a conflict between two duties. My positive promise to Marlow, my obedience to you, are now reconciled, and I thank you a thousand thousand times for having thus relieved me from so terrible a struggle."

The tears rose in her eyes as she spoke, and Lady Hastings made her sit down by her bedside, saying--"Nay, my dear child, do not suffer yourself to be so much agitated. I did not know till the other day," she said, feeling some self-reproach at having been brought to play the part she had acted lately, "I did not know till the other day that you were really so much in love, my Emily. But I have known what such feelings are, and can sympathize with you. Indeed I should have yielded long ago if it had not been for the persuasions of that horrid Mrs. Hazleton. She always stood in the way of every thing I wanted to do, and would not even let me know the truth about your real feelings--pretending all the time to be my friend too!"

"She has been a friend to none of us, I fear," replied Emily, "and to me especially an enemy; although I cannot at all tell what I ever did to merit such pertinacious hatred as she seems to feel towards me."

"Do you know, my child," said Lady Hastings, with a meaning smile, "I have been sometimes inclined to think that she wished to marry Marlow herself?"

Emily started and looked aghast, and then that delicate feeling, that sensitiveness for the dignity of woman's nature, which none, I suspect, but woman's heart can clearly comprehend, caused her cheek to glow like a rose with shame at the very thought of a woman loving unloved, and seeking unsought. She felt, however, at once, that there might be--that there probably was--much truth in what her mother said, that she had touched the true point, and had discovered one at least of the causes of Mrs. Hazleton's strange conduct. Nevertheless, she answered, "Oh, dear mother, I hope it is not so. Sure I am that Marlow would never trifle with any woman's love, and I cannot think that Mrs. Hazleton would so degrade herself as even to dream of a man who never dreamt of her; besides, she is old enough to be his mother."

"Not quite, my child, not quite," replied Lady Hastings. "She is, I believe, younger than I am; and though old enough to be your mother, Emily, I could not have been Marlow's, unless I had married at ten years old. Besides, she is very beautiful, and she knows it, and may have thought that such beauty as hers, and her great wealth, might well make up for a small difference of years."

"Perhaps you are right," replied Emily, thoughtfully, as many a circumstance flashed upon her memory, which had seemed, to her dark and mysterious in times past; but to which the cause suggested by her mother seemed now to afford a key. "But if it was me, only, she hated," added Emily, "why should she so persecute my father and yourself?"

"Perhaps," replied Lady Hastings, speaking with a clear-sighted wisdom which she seldom evinced, "perhaps because she knew that the most terrible blows are those which are aimed at us through those we love. Besides, one cannot tell what offence your father may have given. He is very plain spoken, and not accustomed to deal very tenderly. Now Mrs. Hazleton is not well pleased to hear plain truths, nor to bear with patience any sharpness or abruptness of manner. Moreover, my child, I have heard that it was old Sir John Hastings' wish, when we were all young and free, that your father should marry Mrs. Hazleton. But he preferred another, perhaps less worthy of him in every respect."

"Oh, no, no." cried Emily, with eager affection. "More worthy of him a thousand times in all ways. More good--more kind--more beautiful."

"Nay, nay, flatterer," said Lady Hastings, with a smile. "I was well enough to look at once, Emily, and more to his taste. That is enough. My glass tells me clearly that I cannot compete with Mrs. Hazleton now. But it is growing dark, my dear, I must have lights."

"I will ring for them, and then go and seek my father," replied Emily.

She rang, and the maid appeared from the anteroom, just as Lady Hastings was saying that it was time to take her medicine. Emily took up the vial and the spoon, poured out the quantity prescribed, with a steady hand, very unlike that with which Mrs. Hazleton had held the same bottle an hour before, and having put the dose into a wine-glass, handed it to her mother.

"Bring lights," said Lady Hastings, addressing her maid; and the moment after, she raised the glass to her lips, and drank the contents.

"It tastes very odd, Emily," she said, "I think it must be spoiled by the heat of the room."

"Indeed," said Emily. "That is very strange. The last vial kept quite well. But Mr. Short will be here to-night, and we will make him send some more."

She paused for a moment or two, and then added, "Now, shall I go for my father?"

"No," said Lady Hastings, somewhat faintly; "wait till the girl comes back with the lights."

She was silent for a few moments, and then raised herself suddenly on her arm, saying in a tone of great alarm, "Emily, Emily! I feel very ill.--Good God, I feel very ill!"

Emily sprang to her side and threw her arm round her; but the next instant Lady Hastings uttered a fearful scream, like the cry of a sea-bird, and her head fell back upon her daughter's arm.

Emily rang the bell violently: ran to the door and shrieked loudly for aid; for she saw too well that her mother was dying.

The maid, several of the other servants, and Sir Philip Hastings himself, rushed into the room. Lights were brought: Mr. Short was sent for; but ere the servant had well passed the gates, Lady Hastings, after a few convulsive sobs, had yielded up her spirit.

CHAPTER XLVIII

When the surgeon entered the room of Lady Hastings there was a profound silence. Sir Philip Hastings was standing by his wife's bedside, motionless as a statue; gazing with a knitted brow and fixed stony eye upon the features of her whom he had so well and constantly loved. Emily lay fainting upon the floor, with her head supported by one of the maids, while another tried to recall her to life. Two more servants were the room, but they, like all the rest, remained silent in presence of the awful scene before them. The windows were not yet closed, and the faint, struggling, gray twilight, came in, and mingled sombrely with the pale light of the wax candles, giving even a more deathlike hue to the face of the corpse, and throwing strange crossing lights and shades upon features which remained convulsed even after the agony of death was past.

"Good God! Sir Philip, what is this I hear?" exclaimed Mr. Short before he caught the whole particulars of the scene.

Sir Philip Hastings made no answer. He did not even seem to hear; and the surgeon advanced to the bedside, and gazed for an instant on the face of Lady Hastings. He took her hand in his. It was still warm; but when he put his fingers on her wrist, no pulse vibrated beneath his touch. The heart, too, was quite still: not a flutter indicated a lingering spark of vitality. The breath was gone; and though the surgeon sought on the dressing-table for a small mirror, and applied it to the lips, it remained undimmed. He shook his head sadly; but yet he made some efforts. He took a vial of essence from his pocket, and applied it to the nostrils; he opened a vein, and a few drops of blood issued from it, but stopped immediately; and several other experiments he tried, that not a lingering doubt might remain of death having taken possession completely.

At length he ceased, saying, "It is in vain. How did this happen? It is very strange. There was not an indication of such an event yesterday. She was decidedly better."

"And so she was this morning, sir," said Lady, Hastings' maid; "she slept quite well too, sir, before Mrs. Hazleton came."

Sir Philip Hastings remained profoundly silent; but Mr. Short gave a sudden start at the name of Mrs. Hazleton, and asked the maid when that lady had left her mistress.

"Not half an hour before her death, sir," replied the maid; "and even for a little time after she was gone, my lady seemed quite well and cheerful with Mistress Emily."

"Were you with her when she was seized so suddenly?" asked the surgeon.

"No, sir," said the maid. "No one was with her but Mistress Emily. My lady had sent me away for lights; but just when I was coming up the stairs, I heard my young lady ringing the bell violently, and screaming for help, and in two minutes after I came in my lady was dead."

"I must hear the first symptoms," said Mr. Short, "and this dear young lady needs attending to. If I know her right, this shock will well nigh kill her."

He moved towards Emily as he spoke, but in passing across, his eye lighted upon the vial which was standing upon the table at the bedside, with the spoon and wine-glass which had been used in administering the medicine. Something in the appearance of the bottle seemed to strike him suddenly, and he raised it sharply and held it to the candle. "Good God!" exclaimed Mr. Short; "Good God!" and his face turned as pale as death, and a fit of trembling seized upon him.

It was several moments before he uttered another word. He put his hand to his brow, and seemed to think deeply and anxiously. Then he examined the bottle again, took out the cork, held it to his nostrils, tasted a single drop poured upon the end of his finger, and shook his head sadly and solemnly. Every eye but those of the maid, who was supporting Emily's head, was now turned upon him. There was something in his manner so unusual, so strange, that even the attention of Sir Philip Hastings was attracted by it; and he looked gloomily at the surgeon for a moment, as if in a dreamy wonder at his proceedings.

At length, Mr. Short spoke again. "Can any body tell me," he said, "when Lady Hastings took a dose of this stuff?"

No one remarked the irreverent term which he applied to the contents of the vial; for every one who listened to him would probably have given it the same name, had it been a mithridate; but the maid of the deceased lady replied at once, "Only a few minutes before she died, sir. I saw her take it myself."

"Who gave it to her?" demanded the surgeon, sternly.

"My young lady, sir," answered the maid, "just before I went for the lights, and I am sure she did not give her a drop too much of it; for she measured it out carefully in the spoon before she put it into the glass."

Mr. Short remained silent again, and Sir Philip Hastings spoke for the first time with a great effort.

"What is the matter, sir?" he asked, gloomily; "you seem confounded, thunder-struck. What has befallen to draw your eyes from that?" and he pointed to the bed of his dead wife.

"I am bound to say, Sir Philip," replied Mr. Short, "that it is my belief that the dose given to Lady Hastings from that bottle, has been the cause of her death. In a word, I believe it to be poison."

Sir Philip Hastings gazed in his face with a wild look of horror. His teeth chattered in his head, his whole frame shook visibly to the eyes of those around, but he uttered not a word, and it was the maid who answered, exclaiming in a shrill voice, "Oh, how horrible! How could you send my lady such stuff?"

"I never sent it to her, woman!" said Mr. Short, sternly; "if you had eyes you would see that it is not of the same color, nor has it the same taste of that which I sent. It is different in every respect; and if no other proof were wanting that which I sent Lady Hastings was harmless, it would be sufficient to say, that the last vial I brought was delivered to you yourself yesterday quite full, that Lady Hastings ought to have taken four or five doses of that medicine between that time and this, and----"

"Oh, yes!" exclaimed the maid, interrupting him, "she took it quite regularly. I saw Mistress Emily give her three doses myself."

"Well, did those hurt her?" asked Mr. Short, sharply.

"I can't say they did," replied the woman, "indeed she always seemed better a little while after taking them."

"Well that shows that this is not the same," said Mr. Short; "besides, this bottle has never come out of my surgery. I always choose mine perfectly clear and white, that I may be enabled to see if the medicine is at all troubled or not. This has a green tinge, and must have come from some common druggist's, and the stuff that it contains must be strictly analyzed."

As he spoke, Sir Philip Hastings strode up to him, grasped his hand, and wrung it hard, saying in a hollow husky tone, and pointing to the bottle, "What is it you mean? What is it all about? What is that?"

"Poison! Sir Philip," replied Mr. Short, moved by the feelings of the moment beyond all his ordinary prudence; "poison! and I very much fear that it has been administered to your poor lady intentionally."

"Gathering herbs!--gathering herbs!" screamed Sir Philip Hastings, like a madman; and tearing the hair out of his head, he rushed away from the room, and locked himself into his library.

No one could tell to what his words alluded, nor did they trouble themselves much to discover; for every one at once concluded that the shock of his wife's sudden death, and the discovery of its terrible cause, had driven him insane.

"Oh, do run after my master, sir," cried the maid; "he has gone into the library, I heard him bang the door."

"Has he got any arms there?" asked Mr. Short, "there used to be pistols at the Hall."

"No, sir, no," exclaimed one of the housemaids, "they are not there. They are in his dressing-room out yonder."

"Well, then, I will leave him alone for the present," said the surgeon; "here is one who demands more immediate care. Poor young lady! If she should discover, in her present state of grief, how her mother has died, and that her hand has been employed to produce such a catastrophe, it will destroy either her life or her intellect."

"But who could have done it, sir?" exclaimed Lady Hastings' maid.

"Never you mind that for the present," said Mr. Short; "I have my suspicions; but they are no more than suspicions at present. You stay with me here, and let the other woman carry your poor young lady to her room. I will be with her presently, and will give her what will do her good. One of you, as soon as possible, send me up a man-servant--a groom would be best."

His orders were obeyed promptly; for he spoke with a tone of decision and command which the terrible circumstances of the moment enabled him to assume; although in ordinary circumstances he was a man of mild and gentle character.

As soon as poor Emily was borne away to her own chamber, Mr. Short turned to the maid again, inquiring, "How long had Mistress Hazleton gone when your mistress was seized with these fatal convulsions?"

"About half an hour, sir," said the maid. "It couldn't have been longer. Mrs. Hazleton came when my lady was asleep, and went in alone, saying she would not disturb her."

"Ha!" cried the surgeon; "was she with her for any time alone?"

"All the time that she staid, sir," replied the maid; "for I did not like to go in, and Mistress Emily was walking on the terrace up the hill."

"I suppose then you cannot tell how long Mrs. Hazleton remained alone with your lady before she woke?"

"Yes, I can pretty nearly, sir," answered the maid, "for though Mrs. Hazleton told me not to come in with her, and said she would ring when my lady waked, I came after her into the anteroom, and sat there all the time. For about five minutes, or it might be ten, all was quiet enough; but at the end of that time I heard my lady and Mrs. Hazleton begin to speak."

"You heard no other sounds previously?" asked the surgeon.

"Nothing but the rustle of Mrs. Hazleton's gown, as she moved about once or twice," said the maid, "and of that I can't be rightly sure."

"You did not by chance look through the key-hole?" asked Mr. Short.

"No, that I didn't," said the maid, tossing her head, "I never did such a thing in my life."

"Well, well. Get me a sheet of paper," replied the surgeon, "and a pen and ink--oh, they are here are they?" But before he could sit down to write, a groom crept in through the half-open door, and received orders from the surgeon to saddle a horse instantly and return. Mr. Short then sat down and wrote as follows:

"Ma. ATKINSON:--As you are high constable of Hartwell, I write as a justice of the peace for the county of ----, to authorize and require you to follow immediately the carriage of The Honorable Mistress Hazleton, to apprehend that lady and to keep her in your safe custody, taking care that her person be immediately searched by some proper person, and that any vials, bottles, powders, or other objects whatsoever bearing the appearance of drugs or medicines, or of having contained them, be carefully preserved, and marked for identification. I have not time or menus to fill up a regular warrant; but I will justify you in, and be responsible for, whatever you may do to insure that Mrs. Hazleton has no means or opportunity allowed her of concealing or making away with any thing she has carried away from this house, where Lady Hastings has just deceased from the effects of poison. You had better take the fresh horse of the bearer, and lose not an instant in overtaking the carriage."

He then signed his name just as the groom returned; but ere he gave the man the paper he added in a postscript:

"You had better search the carriage minutely, and make any preliminary investigation that you may think fit before I arrive. The hints given above will be sufficient for your guidance."

"Take this paper immediately to Jenny Best's cottage," said Mr. Short to the groom. "Ask if Mr. Atkinson is there. Should he be so, give it to him, and let him take your horse if he requires it. Should you not find him there, seek for him either at the house of Mr. Dixwell, or at the farm close by. Should he be at neither of those places, follow him on to his house near Hartwell at full speed. Do you understand?"

"Oh, quite well, sir," said the groom, who was a shrewd, keen fellow; and he left the room without more words.

When he got down to the hall door, however, he thought he might as well know more of his errand, and read the paper which he had received with the butler and the foot man. A brief consultation followed between them, and not a little horror and anger was excited by the information they had gained from the paper, for Lady Hastings had been well loved by her servants, and Mrs. Hazleton was but little loved by any of her inferiors in station.

"Go you on, John, as fast as possible," said the footman, "I'll get, a horse and come after you as fast as possible with Harry; for this grand dame has three servants with her, and mayn't choose to be taken easily."

"Ay, come along, come along," said the groom; "we'll run her down, I'll warrant," and hurrying away he got to his horse's back.

In the mean time Mr. Short had proceeded to the room of poor Emily Hastings, whom he found recovering from her fainting fit, and sobbing in the bitterness of grief.

"Oh, Mr. Short," she said, "this is very terrible. There surely was something wrong about that medicine, for my poor mother was taken ill the moment she had swallowed it. She had had the same quantity three times to-day before; but she said that it tasted strange and unpleasant. It could not surely have been spoiled by keeping so short a time, and that could not have killed her even if it had been so. Pray do examine it."

"I will, I will, my dear," replied Mr. Short kindly, "but I don't think the medicine I sent could spoil, and if it did it could have no evil effect. Now quiet yourself, my dear Mistress Emily; I am going to give you a draught which will soothe your nerves, and fit you better to bear all these terrible things."

He then had recourse to the little store of medicines he usually carried in his pocket, and administered first a stimulant and then a somewhat powerful narcotic. For about ten minutes he remained seated by Emily's bedside with her own maid standing at the foot, and during that time the poor girl spoke once or twice, asking anxiously after her father, and expressing a great desire to go to him. Gradually, however, her eyelid's began to droop, her sentences remained unfinished, and, in the end, she fell into a deep and profound sleep.

"She will not wake for six or eight hours," said Mr. Short, addressing the maid. "But when she does wake it would be better you should be with her, my good girl. If you like, therefore, you can go and take some rest in the meanwhile; but order yourself to be called at the end of five hours."

"If you are quite sure that she will remain asleep, sir," said the maid, "I will lie down, for I am sure sorrow wearies one more than work."

"She won't wake," said Mr. Short, "for six hours at least. I will now go and see Sir Philip," and descending the stairs he knocked at the door of the library, thinking that probably he should find it locked. The stern voice of Sir Philip Hastings, however, said "Come in," in a wonderfully calm tone; and when the surgeon entered he found Sir Philip seated at the library table, and apparently reading a Greek book, the contents of which Mr. Short could not at all divine.

CHAPTER XLIX

I must now follow the groom on his road, first to the cottage of good Jenny Best, where he learned that Mr. Atkinson had gone away some five minutes before, and then to the house of the neighboring farm, where he found the person he sought still seated on his horse, but talking to the tenant at the door.

"Here, Mr. Atkinson," cried the groom as he came up; "here's a note for you from Mr. Short the surgeon--a sort of warrant, I believe; for he's a justice of the peace, you know, as well as a surgeon. Read it quick, Mr. Atkinson, read it quick; for it won't keep hot long; and if that woman isn't caught I think I'll hang myself."

"Bring us a light, farmer," said Mr. Atkinson, "quickly. What is all this about, John?"

"Why, Madam Hazleton has poisoned my lady, and she's as dead as a door nail," said the groom, "that's all; and bad enough too. Zounds, I thought she'd do some mischief; she was always so hard upon her horses."

"Good heaven!" exclaimed Mr. Atkinson, "you do not mean to say that she has certainly poisoned Lady Hastings?"

"Why, Mr. Short believes it, and every one believes it," answered the groom.

Mr. Atkinson might have endeavored to reduce the number comprised in the term "every body" to its just proportions; but before he could do so, the farmer returned with a light shaded from the wind by his hat; and the good high constable of Hartwell, bending over his saddle, read hurriedly Mr. Short's brief note.

"What's the matter? what's the matter?" cried the farmer; and great was his surprise and consternation to hear that Lady Hastings was dead, and that strong suspicion existed of her having been poisoned by Mrs. Hazleton. There is a stern, dogged love of justice, however, in the English peasant, which rises into energy and excitement; and the farmer was instantly heard calling for his horse.

"Zounds, I'll ride with you, Atkinson," he said. "This great dame has got so many servants, she may think fit to set the law at defiance; but she must be taught that high people cannot poison other people any more than low ones. But you go on; you go on. I'll catch you up, perhaps. If not, I'll come in time, don't you be afraid."

"I'm going along too," said the groom, "and two others are coming; so if her tall men show fight, I think we'll leather their jackets."

Away they went as fast as they could go, and to say truth, Mr. Atkinson was not at all sorry to have some assistance; for without ever committing any one act which could be characterized as criminal, unjust, or wrong, within the knowledge of her neighbors, Mrs. Hazleton had somehow impressed the minds of all who surrounded her with the conviction, that hers was a most daring and remorseless nature. The general world received their impression of her character--and often a false one, be it good or evil--by her greater and more important actions: the little circle that surrounds us forms a slower but more certain judgment from minute but often repeated traits.

On rode Mr. Atkinson and the groom, as fast as their horses could carry them. Wherever there was turf by the road-side they galloped; and at the rate of progression made by carriages in that day, they made sure they must be gaining very rapidly upon the object of their pursuit. When first they set out it was very dark; but at the end of twenty minutes, in which period they had ridden somewhat more than four miles, the edge of the moon began to appear above the horizon, and her light showed them well nigh another mile on the road before them. Still no carriage was in sight, and the groom exclaimed, "Dang it, Mr. Atkinson, we must spur on, or she will get home before we catch her."

It is impossible to run after any thing without feeling some of the eagerness of the foxhound, and, it is not to be denied that Mr. Atkinson shared in some degree in the impetuous spirit of the chase with the groom. He said nothing about it, indeed; but he made his spurs mark his horse's sides, and on they went up the opposite slope at a quicker pace than ever. From the top was a very considerable descent into the bottom of the valley; in which Hartwell is situated; but the moon had not yet risen high enough to illuminate more than half the scene, and darkness, doubly dark, seemed to have gathered over the low grounds beneath the eyes of the two horsemen.

Mr. Atkinson thought he perceived some large object below, moving on towards Hartwell; but he could not be sure of it till he had descended some way down the hill, when the carriage of Mrs. Hazleton, mounting a little rise into the moonlight, became plainly visible to the eye. The groom took off his cap and waved it, saying, "Tally ho!" but neither he nor his companion paused in their rapid course, but went thundering down at the risk of their necks, and of their horses' knees. The carriage moved slowly; the pursuers went very fast: and at the end of about four minutes they had reached and passed the two mounted men-servants, who, as customary in those days, rode behind the vehicle. Robberies on the highway were by no means uncommon; so that it was the custom for the attendants upon a carriage to travel armed, and Mrs. Hazleton's two men instantly laid their hands upon the holsters of their pistols, when those too rapid riders passed them at such a furious pace. Mr. Atkinson, however, was not a man to be easily frightened from any thing he undertook, and wheeling his horse sharply when in a little advance of the coachman, he exclaimed, "In the King's name I command you to stop. I am James Atkinson, high constable of Hartwell. You know me, sir; and I command you in the King's name to stop!"

"Why, Master Atkinson, what is all this about?" cried the coachman. "There is nobody but Mrs. Hazleton here. Don't you know the carriage?"

"Quite well," replied Mr. Atkinson; "but you hear what I say, and will disobey at your peril. John, ride round to the other side, while I speak to the lady here." -

Now Mrs. Hazleton had heard the whole of this conversation, and had there been sufficient light, Mr. Atkinson, whose eye was turned towards where she sat, would have seen her turn deadly pale. It might naturally be supposed that in any ordinary circumstances she would have directed her first attention to the side from which the sounds proceeded; but so far from that being the case, she instantly put her hand in her pocket, and was almost in the act of throwing something into the road, when John the groom presented himself at the window, and she stopped suddenly.

"What is it, Mr. Atkinson?" she exclaimed, turning to the other window, and speaking in a tone of high indignation. "Why do you presume to stop my carriage on the King's highway?"

"Because I am ordered, Madam, by lawful authority, so to do." replied Mr. Atkinson. "I am sorry, Madam, to tell you that you must consider yourself as a prisoner."

Mrs. Hazleton would fain have asked upon what charge; but she did not dare, and for a moment strength and courage failed her. It was but for a moment, however, and in the next she exclaimed in a loud and more imperious tone than ever, "This is a pretence for robbery or insult. Drive on, coachman. Mathew--Rogerson--clear the way!"

She reckoned wrongly, however, if she counted upon any great zeal in her servants. The two men hesitated; for the King's name was a tower of strength which they did not at all like to assail. Their mistress repeated her order in an angry tone, and one of them, with habitual deference to her commands, went so far as to cock the pistol which he now held in his hand; but at that moment the adverse party received an accession of strength which rendered all assistance hopeless. The other two servants of Sir Philip Hastings came down the hill at full speed, and a gentleman, followed by a servant, rode up from the side of Hartwell, and addressed Mr. Atkinson by his name.

"Ah, Mr. Marlow!" said Mr. Atkinson. "You come at a very melancholy moment, sir, and to witness a very unpleasant scene; but, nevertheless; I must require your assistance, sir, as this lady seems inclined to resist the law."

"What is the matter?" asked Marlow. "I hope there is no mistake here. If I see rightly this is Mrs. Hazleton's carriage. What is she charged with?"

"Murder, sir," replied. Mr. Atkinson, who had been a little irritated by the lady's resistance, and spoke more plainly than he might otherwise have done. "The murder of Lady Hastings by poison."

It was spoken. She heard the words clearly and distinctly. She had been detected. Some small oversight--some accidental circumstance--some precaution forgotten--some accidental word, or gesture, had betrayed the dark secret, revealed the terrible crime. It was all known to men, as well as to God, and Mrs. Hazleton sunk back in the carriage overpowered by the agony of detection.

"Oh, ho; here come the other men," said Mr. Atkinson, as the two servants of Sir Philip Hastings rode up. "Now, coachman, drive on till I tell you to stop. You, John, keep close to the other window, and watch it well. I will take care of this one. The others come behind. Mr. Marlow, you had perhaps better ride with us for half a mile or so; for I must stop at the house of Widow Warmington, as I have orders to make a strict search."

"Oh, take me to my own house--take me to my own house," said Mrs. Hazleton, in a faint tone.

"I dare not venture to do that, Madam," said Mr. Atkinson; "for we are nearly three miles distant, and accidents might happen by the way which would defeat the ends of justice. I must have a full search made at the very first place where I can procure lights. That will be at Mrs. Warmington's; but she is a friend of your own, Madam, and you will be received there with all kindness."

Mrs. Hazleton did not reply; and the carriage drove on, Mr. Atkinson keeping a keen watch upon one window, and the groom riding close to the other.

A few minutes brought them to the house of the shrewd widow, and the bell was rung sharply by one of the servants. A woman servant appeared in answer to the summons, and without asking whether her mistress was at home, or not, Atkinson took the candle from her hand, saying, "Lend me the light for a moment. I wish to light Mrs. Hazleton into the house. Now, Madam, will you please to descend.--John, dismount, and come round here; assist Mrs. Hazleton to alight, and come with us on her other side."

Mrs. Hazleton saw that she could not double or turn there. She withdrew her hand from her pocket where she had hitherto held it, resumed her forgotten air of dignity, and though, to say the truth, she would rather have met her "dearest foe in heaven," than have entered that house so escorted, she walked with a firm step and dauntless eye, with the high constable on one side, and groom on the other.

"They shall not see me quail," she said to herself. "They shall not see me quail. I know the worst, and I can meet it--I have had my revenge."

In the mean time, the maid had run in haste to tell her mistress the marvels of the scene she had just witnessed, and Mrs. Warmington had gathered enough, without divining the whole, to rejoice her with anticipated triumph. The arrest of Shanks the attorney on a charge of conspiracy and forgery, had set going the hundred tongues of Rumor, few of which had spared the name of Mrs. Hazleton; and Mrs. Warmington, at the worst, suspected that her dear friend was implicated in the guilt of the attorney. That, however, was sufficient to give the widow considerable satisfaction, for she had not forgotten either some coldness and neglect with which Mrs. Hazleton had treated her for some time, or her impatient and insolent conduct that morning; and though upon the strength of her plumpness, and easy manners, people looked upon Mrs. Warmington as a very good natured person, yet fat people can be very vindictive sometimes.

"Good gracious me, my dear, what is the matter?" exclaimed Mrs. Warmington, as the prisoner was brought in, while Mr. Atkinson, in a speaking to those behind, exclaimed, "Let no one touch or approach the carriage till I return."

Mrs. Hazleton made no answer to her dear friend's questions, and the high constable, taking a little step forward, said, "I beg pardon, Mrs. Warmington, for intruding into your house; but I have been ordered to apprehend this lady, and to have her person and her carriage strictly searched, without giving the opportunity for the concealment or destruction of any thing. It seems to me that Mrs. Hazleton has something bulky in that left hand pocket. As I do not like to put my hand rudely upon a lady, may I ask you, Madam, to let me see what that pocket contains?"

Without the slightest hesitation, but with a good deal of curiosity, Mrs. Warmington advanced at once and took hold of the rich silk brocade of the prisoner's gown.

"Out, woman!" cried Mrs. Hazleton, with the fire flashing from her eyes; and she struck her.

But Mrs. Warmington did not quit her hold or her purpose. "Good gracious, what a termagant!" she exclaimed, and at once thrust her right hand into the pocket, and drew forth the vial which had been sent by the surgeon to Lady Hastings.

"Dear me!" exclaimed Mrs. Warmington. "Why, this is the very bottle I saw you mixing stuff in this morning, when you seemed so angry and vexed at my coming into the still-room.--No, it isn't the same either; but it was one very like this, only darker in the the color."

"Ha!" said Mr. Atkinson. "Madam, will you have the goodness to put a mark upon that bottle by which you can know it again?--Scratch it with a diamond or something."

"Oh, poor I have no diamonds," said Mrs. Warmington. "My dear, will you lend me that ring?"

Mrs. Hazleton gave her a withering glance, but made no reply; and Marlow pointed to two peculiar spots in the glass of the bottle, saying, "By those marks it will be known, so that it cannot be mistaken." His words were addressed to Mr. Atkinson; for he felt disgusted and sickened by the heartless and insulting tone of Mrs. Warmington towards her former friend.

At the sound of his voice--for she had not yet looked at him--Mrs. Hazleton started and looked round. It is not possible to tell the feelings which affected her heart at that moment, or to picture with the pen the varied expressions, all terrible, which swept over her beautiful countenance like a storm. She remembered how she had loved him. Perhaps at that moment she knew for the first time how much she had loved him. She felt too, how strongly love and hate had been mingled together by the fiery alchemy of disappointment, as veins of incongruous metals have been mixed by the great convulsions of the early earth. She felt too, at that moment, that it was this love and this hate which had been the cause of her deepest crimes, and all their consequences--the awful situation in which she there stood, the lingering tortures of imprisonment, the agonies of trial, and the bitter consummation of the scaffold.

"Oh, Marlow, Marlow," she cried--in a tone for the first time sorrowful--"to see you mingling in these acts!"

"I have nothing to do with the present business, Mrs. Hazleton," replied Marlow, "but I am bound to say that in consequence of information I have procured, it would have been my duty to have caused your apprehension upon other charges, had not this, of which I know nothing, been preferred against you. All is discovered, madam all is known. With a slight clue, at first, I have pursued the intricate labyrinth of your conduct for the last two years to its conclusion, and every thing has been made plain as day.

"You, Marlow, you?" cried Mrs. Hazleton, fixing her eyes steadfastly upon him, and then adding, as he bowed his head in token of assent, "but all is not known, even to you. You shall know all, however, before I die; and perhaps to know all may wring your heart, hard though it be. But what am I talking of?" she continued, her face becoming suddenly suffused with crimson, and her fine features convulsed with rage. "All is discovered, is it? And you have done it it? What matters it to me, then, whose heart is wrung--or what becomes of you, or me, or any one? A drop more or less is nothing in the overflowing well. Why should I struggle longer? Why should I hide any thing? Why should I fly from this charge to meet another? I did it--I poisoned her--I put the drug by her bedside. It is all true--I did it all--I have had my revenge as far as it could be obtained, and now do with me what you like. But remember, Marlow, remember, if Emily Hastings marries you, she does it with a mother's curse upon her head--a curse that will fall upon her heart like a mildew, and wither it for ever--a curse that will dry up the source of all fond affections, blacken the brightest hours, and embitter the purest joys--a dying mother's curse! She knows it--she has heard it--it can never be recalled. I have put that beyond fate. Ha ha! It is upon you both; and if you venture to unite your unhappy destinies, may that curse cling to you and blast you for ever."

She spoke with all the vehemence of intense passion, breaking, for the first time in life, through strong habitual self-control; and when she had done, she cast herself into a chair, and covered her eyes with her hands.

She wept not; but her whole frame heaved and shivered, with the terrible emotion that tore her heart.

In the mean time, Marlow and Mrs. Warmington and the high constable spoke upon it, consulting what was to be done with her. The prison system of England was at that time as bad as it could be, and those who condemned and abhorred her the most, were anxious to spare her as long as possible the horrors of the jail. At length, after many difficulties, and a good deal of hesitation, Mr. Atkinson agreed, at the suggestion of Mrs. Warmington, to leave her in the house where she then was, under the charge of a constable to be sent for from Hartwell. There was a high upper room from which there was no possibility of escape, with an antechamber in which the constable could watch, and there he was determined to confine her till she could be brought before the magistrate on the following day.

"I must have her thoroughly searched in the first place," said Mr. Atkinson; "for she may have some more of the poison about her, and in her present state, after all she has confessed, she is just as likely to swallow it as not. However, Mr. Marlow, you had better, I think, ride on as fast as possible to see Sir Philip Hastings, and tell him what has occurred here. If I judge rightly, your presence will be very needful there."

"It will indeed," said Marlow, a sudden vague apprehension of he knew not what, seizing upon him; "God grant I have not tarried too long already;" and quitting the room, he sprang upon his horse's back again.

CHAPTER L

Sir Philip Hastings, I have said, was reading a Greek book when Mr. Short entered the library. His face was grave, and very stern; but all traces of the terrible agitation with which he had quited the side of his wife's death-bed, were now gone from his face. He hardly looked up when the surgeon entered. He seemed not only reading, but absorbed by what he read. Mr. Short thought the paroxysm of grief was passed, and that the mind of Sir Philip Hastings, settling down into a calm melancholy, was seeking its habitual relief in books. He knew, as every medical man must know, the various whimsical resources to which the heart of man flies, as if for refuge, in moments of great affliction. The trifles with which some will occupy themselves--the intense abstraction for which others will labor--the imaginations, the visions, the fancies to which others again will apply, not for consolation, not for comfort; but for escape from the one dark predominant idea. He said a few words to Sir Philip then, of a kindly but somewhat commonplace character, and the baronet looked up, gazing at him across the candles which stood upon the library table. Had Mr. Short's attention been particularly called to Sir Philip's countenance, he would have perceived at once, that the pupils of the eyes were strangely and unnaturally contracted, and that from time to time a certain nervous twitching of the muscles curled the lip, and indented the cheek. But he did not remark these facts: he merely saw that Sir Philip was reading: that he had recovered his calmness; and he judged that that which might be strange in other men, might not be strange in him. In regard to what he believed the great cause of Sir Philip's grief, his wife's death, he thought it better to say nothing; but he naturally concluded that a father would be anxious to hear of a daughter's health under such circumstances, and therefore he told him that Emily was better and more composed.

Sir Philip made a slight, but impatient motion of the hand, but Mr. Short went on to say, "As she was so severely and terribly affected, Sir Philip, I have given Mistress Emily a composing draught, which has already had the intended effect of throwing her into profound slumber. It will insure her, I think, at least six, if not seven hours of calm repose, and I trust she will rise better able to bear her grief than she would be now, were she conscious of it."

Sir Philip mattered something between his teeth which the surgeon did not hear, and Mr. Short proceeded, saying, "Will you permit me to suggest, Sir Philip, that it would be better for you too, my dear sir, to take something which would counteract the depressing effect of sorrow."

"I thank you, sir, I thank you," replied Sir Philip, laying his hand upon the book; "I have no need. The mind under suffering seeks medicines for the mind. The body is not affected. It is well--too well. Here is my doctor;" and he raised his hand and let it fall upon the book again.

"Well then, I will leave you for to-night, Sir Philip," said the surgeon; "to-morrow I must intrude upon you on business of great importance. I will now take my leave."

Sir Philip rose ceremoniously from his chair and bowed his head; gazing upon the surgeon as he left the room and shut the door, with a keen, cunning, watchful look from under his overhanging eyebrows.

"Ha!" he said, when the surgeon had left the room, "he thought to catch me--to find out what I intended to do--slumber!--calm, tranquil repose--so near a murdered mother! God of heaven!" and he bent down his head till his forehead touched the pages of the book, and remained with his face thus concealed for several minutes.

It is to be remarked that not one person, with a single exception, to whom the circumstances of Lady Hastings' death were known, even dreamed of suspecting Emily. They all knew her, comprehended her character, loved her, had faith in her, except her own unhappy father. But with him, if the death of his unhappy wife were terrible, his suspicions of his daughter were a thousand fold more so. To his distorted vision a multitude of circumstances brought proof all powerful. "She has tried to destroy her father," he thought, "and she has not scrupled to destroy her mother. In the one case there seemed no object. In the other there was the great object of revenge, with others perhaps more mean, but not less potent. Try her cause what way I will, the same result appears. The mother opposes the daughter's marriage to the man she loves--threatens to frustrate the dearest wish of her heart,--and nothing but death will satisfy her. This is, the end then of all these reveries--these alternate fits of gloom and levity. The ill balanced mind has lost its equipoise, and all has given way to passion. But what must I do---oh God! what must I do?"

His thoughts are here given, not exactly as they presented themselves; for they were more vague, confused, and disjointed; but such was the sum and substance of them. He raised his head from the book and looked up, and after thinking for a moment or two he said, "This Josephus--this Jew--gives numerous instances, if I remember right, of justice done by fathers upon their children--ay, and by the express command of God. The priest of the Most High was punished for yielding to human weakness in the case of his sons. The warrior Jephtha spared not his best beloved. What does the Roman teach? Not to show pity to those the nearest to us by blood, the closest in affection, where justice demands unwavering execution. It mast be so. There is but the choice left, to give her over to hands of strangers, to add public shame, and public punishment to that which justice demands, or to do that myself which they must inevitably do. She must die--such a monster must not remain upon the earth. She has plotted against her father's life--she has colleagued with his fraudulent enemies--she has betrayed the heart that fondly trusted her--she has visited secretly the haunts of a low, vulgar ruffian--she has aided and abetted those who have plundered her own parents--she has ended by the murder of the mother who so fondly loved her. I--I am bound, by every duty to society, to deliver it from one, who for my curse, and its bane, I brought into the world. She must be put to death; and no hand but mine must do it."

He gazed gloomily down upon the table for several minutes, and then paced the room rapidly with agony in every line of his face. He wrung his hands hard together. He lifted up his eyes towards heaven, and often, often, he cried out, "Oh God! Oh God! Is there no hope?--no doubt?--no opening for pause or hesitation?"

"None, none, none," he said at length, and sank down into his chair again.

His eye wandered round the room, as if seeking some object he could not see, and then he murmured, "So beautiful--so young--so engaging--just eighteen summers; and yet such a load of crime!"

He bent his head again, and a few drops of agony fell from his eyes upon the table. Then clasping his forehead tight with his hand, he remained for several minutes thoughtful and silent. He seemed to grow calmer; but it was a deceitful seeming; and there was a wild, unnatural light in his eyes which, notwithstanding all the apparent shrewdness of his reasoning--the seeming connection and clearness of his argument, would have shown to those expert in such matters, that there was something not right within the brain.

At length he said to himself in a whisper, as if he was afraid that some one should hear him, "She sleeps--the man said she sleeps--now is the time--I must not hesitate--I must not falter--now is the time!" and he rose and approached the door.

Once, he stopped for a moment--once, doubt and irresolution took possession of him. But then he cast them off; and moved on again.

With a slow step, but firm and noiseless tread, he crossed the hall and mounted the stairs. No one saw him: the servants were scattered: there was no one to oppose his progress, or to say, "Forbear!"

He reached his daughter's room, opened the door quietly, went in, and closed it. Then he gazed eagerly around. The curtains were withdrawn: his fair, sweet child lay sleeping calmly as an infant. He could see all around. Father and child were there. There was no one else.

Still he gazed around, seeking perhaps for something with which to do the fatal deed! His eye rested on a packet of papers upon the table. It contained those which Marlow had left with poor gentle Emily to justify her to her father in case of need.

Oh, would he but take them up! Would he but read the words within!

He turns away--he steals toward the bed! Drop the curtain! I can write no more. Emily is gone!

CHAPTER LI

When Mr. Short, the surgeon, left the presence of Sir Philip Hastings, he found the butler seated in an arm-chair in the hall, cogitating sadly over all the lamentable events of the day. He was an old servant of the family, and full of that personal interest in every member of it which now, alas, in these times of improvement and utilitarianism (or as it should be called, selfishness reduced to rule), when it seems to be the great object of every one to bring men down to the level of a mere machine, is no longer, or very rarely, met with. He rose as soon as the surgeon appeared, and inquired eagerly after his poor master. "I am afraid he is touched here, sir," he said, laying his finger on his forehead. "He has not been at all right ever since he came back from London, and I am sure, when he came down to-night, calling out in such a way about gathering herbs, I thought he had gone clean crazy."

"He has become quite calm and composed now," replied Mr. Short; "though of course he is very sad: but as I can do no good by staying with him, I must go down to the farm for my horse, and ride away where my presence is immediately wanted."

"They have brought your horse up from the farm, sir," said the butler. "It is in the stable-yard."

Thither Mr. Short immediately proceeded, mounted, and rode away. When he had gone about five miles, or perhaps a little more, he perceived that two horsemen were approaching him rapidly, and he looked sharp towards them, thinking they might be Mr. Atkinson and the groom. As they came near, the outlines of the figures showed him that such was not the case; but the foremost of the two pulled up suddenly as he was passing, and Marlow's voice exclaimed, "Is that Mr. Short?"

"Yes, sir, yes, Mr. Marlow," replied the surgeon. "I am very glad indeed you have come; for there has been terrible work this day at the house of poor Sir Philip Hastings. Lady Hastings is no more, and--"

"I have heard the whole sad history," replied Marlow, "and am riding as fast as possible to see what can be done for Sir Philip, and my poor Emily.

I only stopped to tell you that Mrs. Hazleton has been taken, the vial of medicine found upon her, and that she has boldly confessed the fact of having poisoned poor Lady Hastings. You will find her and Atkinson, the high constable, at the house of Mrs. Warmington.--Good night, Mr. Short; good night;" and Marlow spurred on again.

The delay had been very short, but it was fatal.

When Marlow reached the front entrance of the court, he threw his rein to the groom and without the ceremony of ringing, entered the house. There was a lamp burning in the hall, which was vacant; but Marlow heard a step upon the great staircase, and looked up. A dark shadowy figure was coming staggering down, and as it entered the sphere of the light in the hall, Marlow recognized the form, rather than the features, of Sir Philip Hastings. His face was ashy pale: not a trace of color was discernible in any part: the very lips were white; and the gray hair stood ragged and wild upon his head. His haggard and sunken eye fell upon Marlow; but he was passing onward to the library, as if he did not know him, tottering and reeling like a drunken man, when Marlow, very much shocked, stopped him, exclaiming, "Good God, Sir Philip, do you not know me?"

The unhappy man started, turned round, and grasped him tightly by the wrist, saying, in a hoarse whisper, and looking over his shoulder towards the staircase, "Do not go there, do not go there--come hither--you do not know what has happened."

"I do, indeed, Sir Philip," replied Marlow, in a soothing tone, "I have heard--"

"No, no, no, no!" said Sir Philip Hastings. "No one knows but I--there was no one there--I did it all myself.--Come hither, I say!" and he drew Marlow on towards the library.

"He has lost his senses," thought Marlow. "I must try and soothe him before I see my Poor Emily. I will try and turn his mind to other things;" and, suffering himself to be led forward, he entered the library with Sir Philip Hastings, who instantly cast himself into a chair, and pressed his hands before his eyes.

Marlow stood and gazed at him for a moment in silent compassion, and then he said, "Take comfort, Sir Philip. Take comfort. I bring you a great store of news; and what I have to tell will require great bodily and mental exertions from you, to deal with all the painful circumstances in which you are placed. I have followed out every thread of the shameful conspiracy against you--not a turning of the whole rascally scheme is undiscovered."

"She had her share in that too," said Sir Philip, looking up in his face, with a wild, uncertain sort of questioning look.

"I know it," replied Marlow, thinking he spoke of Mrs. Hazleton, "She was the prime mover in it all."

Sir Philip wrung his hands tight, one within the other, murmuring "Oh, God; oh, God!"

"But," continued Marlow, "she will soon expiate her crimes; for she has been taken, and proofs of her guilt found upon her, so strong and convincing, that she did not think fit even to conceal the fact, but confessed her crime at once."

Sir Philip started, and grasped both the arms of the chair in which he sat, tight in his thin white hands, gazing at Marlow with a look of bewildered horror that cannot be described. Marlow went on, however, saying, "I had previously told her, indeed, that I had discovered all her dark and treacherous schemes--how she had labored to make this whole family miserable--how she had attempted to blacken the character of my dear Emily--imitated her handwriting--induced you to misunderstand her whole conduct, and thrown dark hints and suspicions in your way. She knew that she could not escape this charge, even if she could conceal her guilt of to-day, and she confessed the whole."

"Who--who--who?" cried Sir Philip Hastings, almost in a scream. "Of whom are you talking, man?"

"Of Mrs. Hazleton," replied Marlow. "Were you not speaking of her?"

Sir Philip Hastings stretched forth his hands, as if to push him farther from him; but his only reply was a deep groan, and, after a moment's pause, Marlow proceeded, "I, thought you were speaking of her--of her whose task it has been, ever since poor Emily's ill-starred visit to her house, to calumniate and wrong that dear innocent girl--to make you think her guilty of bitter indiscretions, if not great crimes--who, more than any one, aided to wrong you, and who now openly avows that she placed the poison in your poor wife's room in order to destroy her."

"And I have killed her!--and I have killed her!" cried Sir Philip Hastings, rising up erect and tall--"and I have killed her!"

"Good God, whom?" exclaimed Marlow, with his heart beating as if it would burst through his side. "Whom do you mean, sir?"

Sir Philip remained silent for a moment, pressing his hands tight upon his temples, and then, answered in a slow, solemn voice, "Your Emily--my Emily--my own sweet--" but he did not finish the sentence; for ere the last words could be uttered, he fell forward on the floor like a dead man.

For an instant, stupified and horror-struck, Marlow remained motionless, hardly comprehending, hardly believing what he had heard. The next instant, however, he rushed out of the library, and found the butler with the late Lady Hastings' maid, passing through the back of the house towards the front staircase.

"Which is Emily's room?" he cried,--"Which is Emily's room?"

"She is asleep, sir," said the maid.

"Which is her room?" cried Marlow, vehemently. "He is mad--he is mad--your master is mad--he says he has killed her. Which is her room?" and he darted up the staircase.

"The third on the right, sir," cried the butler, following with the maid, as fast as possible; and Marlow darted towards the door.

A fit of trembling, however, seized him as he laid his hand upon the lock. "He must have exaggerated," he said to himself. "He has been unkind--harsh--he calls that killing her--I will open it gently," and he and the two servants entered it nearly together.

All was quiet. All was still. The light was burning on the table. There was a large heavy pillow cast down by the side of the bed, and the bed coverings were in some disorder.

No need of such a stealthy pace, Marlow! You may tread firm and boldly. Even your beloved step will not wake her. The body sleeps till the day of judgment. The spirit has gone where the wicked cease from troubling, and the weary are at rest.

The beautiful face was calm and tranquil; though beneath each of the closed eyes was a deep bluish mark, and the lips had lost their redness. The fair delicate hands grasped the bed-clothes tightly, and the whole position of the figure showed that death had not taken place without a convulsive struggle. Marlow tried, with trembling hands, to unclasp the fingers from the bed-clothes, and though he could not do it, he fancied he felt warmth in the palms of the hands. A momentary gleam of hope came upon him. More assistance was called: every effort that could be suggested was made; but it was all in vain. Consciousness--breath--life--could never be restored. There was not a dry eye amongst all those around, when the young lover, giving up the hopeless task, cast himself on his knees by the bedside, and pressed his face upon the dead hand of her whom he had loved so well.

Just at that moment the voice of Sir Philip Hastings was heard below singing a stanza of some light song. It was the most horrible sound that ever was heard!

Two of the servants ran down in haste, and the sight of the living was as terrible as that of the dead. Philip Hastings had recovered from his fit without assistance, had raised himself, and was now walking about the room with the same sort of zigzag, tottering step with which he bad met Marlow on his return. A stream of blood from a wound which he had inflicted on his forehead when he fell, was still pouring down his face, rendering its deathlike paleness only the more ghastly. His mouth was slightly drawn aside, giving a strange sinister expression to his countenance; but from his eyes, once so full of thought and intellect, every trace of reason had vanished. He held his hands before him, and the fingers of the one beat time upon the back of the other to the air that he was singing, and which he continued to sing even after the entrance of the servants. He uttered not a word to them on their appearance: he took not the slightest notice of them till the butler, seeing his condition, took him by the arm, and asked if he had not better go to bed.

Then, Sir Philip attempted to answer, but his words when spoken were indistinct as well as confused, and it became evident that he had a stroke of palsy. The servants knew hardly what to do. Marlow they did not dare to disturb in his deep grief: the surgeon was by this time far away: their mistress, and her fair unhappy daughter were dead: their master had become an idiot. It was the greatest possible relief to them when they beheld Mr. Dixwell the clergyman enter the library. Some boy employed about the stables or the kitchen, had carried down a vague tale of the horrors to the Rectory; and the good clergyman, though exhausted with all the fatigues and anxiety of the day, had hurried down at once to see what could be done for the survivors of that doomed family. He comprehended the situation of Sir Philip Hastings in a moment; but he put many questions to the butler as to what preceded the terrible event, the effects of which he beheld. The old servant answered little. To most of the questions he merely shook his heal sadly; but that mute reply was sufficient; and Mr. Dixwell, taking Sir Philip by the hand, said, "You had better retire to rest, sir--you are not well."

Sir Philip Hastings gave an unmeaning smile, but followed the clergyman mildly, and having seen him to a bedroom, and left him in the hands of his servants, Mr. Dixwell turned his step towards the chamber of poor Emily.

Marlow had risen from his knees; but was still standing by the bedside with his arms folded on his chest. His face was stern and sorrowful; but perfectly calm.

Mr. Dixwell approached quietly, and in a melancholy tone, addressed to him some words of consolation--commonplace enough indeed, but well intended.

Marlow laid his hand upon the clergyman's arm, and pointed to Emily's beautiful but ghastly face. He only added, "In vain!--Do what is needful--Do what is right--I am incapable;" and leaving the room, he descended to the library, where he closed the door, and remained in silence and solitude till day broke on the following morning.

CHAPTER LII

Mrs. Warmington became a person of some importance with the people of Hartwell. All thoughts were turned towards her house. Everybody wished they could get in and see and hear more; for the news had spread rapidly and wide, colored and distorted; but yet falling far short of the whole terrible truth. When Mr. Short himself arrived in town, he found three other magistrates had already assembled, and that Mr. Atkinson and Sir Philip Hastings' groom, John, were already giving them some desultory and informal information as to the apprehension of Mrs. Hazleton and its causes. The first consideration after his appearance amongst them, was what was to be done with the prisoner; for one of the justices--a gentleman of old family in the county, who had not much liked the appointment of the surgeon to the bench, and had generally found motives for differing in opinion with him ever since--objected to leaving Mrs. Hazleton, even for the night, in any other place than the common jail. The more merciful opinion of the majority, however, prevailed. Atkinson gave every assurance that the constable whom he had placed in charge of the lady was perfectly to be depended upon, and that the room in which she was locked up, was too high to admit the possibility of escape. Thus it was determined that Mrs. Hazleton should be left where she was for the night, and brought before the magistrates for examination at an early hour on the following morning.

Even after this decision was come to, however, the conversation or consultation, if it may be so called, was prolonged for some time in a gossiping, idle sort of way. Gentlemen sat upon the edge of the table with their hats on, or leaned against the mantelpiece, beating their boots with their riding-whips, and some marvelled, and some inquired, and some expounded the law with the dignity and confidence, if not with the sagacity and learning of a Judge. They were still engaged in this discussion when the news of Emily's death was brought to Hartwell, and produced a painful and terrible sensation in the breasts of the lightest and most careless of those present. The man who conveyed the intelligence brought also a summons to Mr. Short to return immediately to Sir Philip Hastings, and only waiting to get a fresh horse, the surgeon set out upon his return with a very sad and sorrowful heart. He would not disturb Mr. Marlow; though he was informed that he was in the library; but he remained with Sir Philip Hastings himself during the greater part of the night, and only set out for his own house to take a little repose before the meeting of the magistrates, some quarter of an hour before the first dawn of day.

Full of painful thoughts he rode on at a quick pace, till the yellow and russet hues of the morning began to appear in the east. He then slackened his pace a little, and naturally, as he approached the house of Mrs. Warmington, he raised his eye towards the windows of the room in which he knew that the beautiful demon, who had produced so much misery to others and herself, had been imprisoned.

Mr. Short was riding on but suddenly a sound met his ear, and as his eyes ran down the building from the windows above, to a small plot of grass which the lady of the house called the lawn, he drew up his horse, and rode sharply up to the gate.

But it is time now to turn to Mrs. Hazleton. Lodged in the upper chamber which had been decided upon as the one fittest for their purpose, by Mr. Atkinson and the rest, with the constable from Hartwell domiciled in the anteroom, and the door between locked, Mrs. Hazleton gave herself up to despair; for her state of mind well deserved that name, although her feelings were very different from those which are commonly designated by that name. Surely to feel that every earthly hope has passed away--to see that further struggle for any object of desire is vain--to know that the struggles which have already taken place have been fruitless--to feel that their objects have been base, unworthy, criminal--to perceive no gleam of light on either side of the tomb--to have the present a wilderness, the future an abyss, the past and its memories a hell--surely this is despair! It matters not with what firmness, or what fierceness it may be borne: it matters not what fiery passions, what sturdy resolutions, what weak regrets, what agonizing fears, mingle with the state. This is despair! and such was the feeling of Mrs. Hazleton. She saw vast opportunities, a splendid position in society, wealth, beauty, wit, mind, accomplishments, all thrown away, and for the gratification of base passions exchanged for disgrace, and crime, and a horrible death. It was a bad bargain; but she felt she had played her whole for revenge and had lost; and she abode the issue resolutely.

All these advantages which I have enumerated, and many more, Mrs. Hazleton had possessed; but she wanted two things which are absolutely necessary to human happiness and human virtue--heart and principle. The one she never could have obtained; for by nature she was heartless.

eloquent words. He hears not the door open; he sees not that tall, venerable, but somewhat stiff and gaunt figure, enter and approach him. He reads on, till the old man's Geneva cloak brushes his arm, and his hand is upon his shoulder. Then he starts up--looks around--but says nothing. A faint smile, pleasant yet grave, crosses his finely cut lip; but that is the only welcome, as he raises his eyes to the face that bends over him. Can that boy in years be already aged in heart?

It is clear that the old man--the old clergyman, for so he evidently is-- has no very tender nature. Every line of his face forbids the supposition. The expression itself is grave, not to say stern. There is powerful thought about it, but small gentleness. He seems one of those who have been tried and hardened in some one of the many fiery furnaces which the world provides for the test of men of strong minds and strong hearts. There has been much persecution in the land; there have been changes, from the rigid and severe to the light and frivolous--from the light and frivolous to the bitter and cruel. There have been tyrants of all shapes and all characters within the last forty years, and fools, and knaves, and madmen, to cry them on in every course of evil. In all these chances and changes, what fixed and rigid mind could escape the fangs of persecution and wrong? He had known both; but they had changed him little. His was originally an unbending spirit: it grew more tough and stubborn by the habit of resistance; but its original bent was still the same.

Fortune--heaven's will--or his own inclination, had denied him wife or child; and near relation he had none. A friend he had: that boy's father, who had sheltered him in evil times, protected him as far as possible against the rage of enemies, and bestowed upon him the small living which afforded him support. He did his duty therein conscientiously, but with a firm unyielding spirit, adhering to the Calvinistic tenets which he had early received, in spite of the universal falling off of companions and neighbors. He would not have yielded an iota to have saved his head.

With all his hardness, he had one object of affection, to which all that was gentle in his nature was bent. That object wits the boy by whom he now stood, and for whom he had a great--an almost parental regard. Perhaps it was that he thought the lad not very well treated; and, as such had been his own case, there was sympathy in the matter. But besides, he had been intrusted with his education from a very early period, had taken a pleasure in the task, had found his scholar apt, willing, and affectionate, with a sufficient touch of his own character in the boy to make the sympathy strong, and yet sufficient diversity to interest and to excite.

The old man was tenderer toward him than toward any other being upon earth; and he sometimes feared that his early injunctions to study and perseverance were somewhat too strictly followed--even to the detriment of health. He often looked with some anxiety at the increasing paleness of the cheek, at the too vivid gleam of the eye, at the eager nervous quivering of the lip, and said within himself, "This is overdone."

He did not like to check, after he had encouraged--to draw the rein where he had been using the spur. There is something of vanity in us all, and the sternest is not without that share which makes man shrink from the imputation of error, even when made by his own heart. He did not choose to think that the lad had needed no urging forward and yet he would fain have had him relax a little more, and strove at times to make him do so. But the impulse had been given: it had carried the youth over the difficulties and obstacles in the way to knowledge, and now he went on to acquire it, with an eagerness, a thirst, that had something fearful in it. A bent, too, had been given to his mind--nay, to his character, partly by the stern uncompromising character of him to whom his education had been solely intrusted, partly by his own peculiar situation, and partly by the subjects on which his reading had chiefly turned.

The stern old Roman of the early republic; the deeds of heroic virtue--as virtue was understood by the Romans; the sacrifice of all tender affections, all the sensibilities of our nature to the rigid thought of what is right; the remorseless disregard of feelings implanted by God, when opposed to the notion of duties of man's creation, excited his wonder and his admiration, and would have hardened and perverted his heart, had not that heart been naturally full of kindlier affections. As it was, there often existed a struggle--a sort of hypothetical struggle--in his bosom, between the mind and the heart. He asked himself sometimes, if he could sacrifice any of those he knew and loved--his father, his mother, his brother, to the good of his country, to some grave duty; and he felt pained and roused to resistance of his own affections when he perceived what a pang it would cost him.

Yet his home was not a very happy one; the kindlier things of domestic life had not gathered green around him. His father was varying and uneven in temper, especially toward his second son; sometimes stern and gloomy, sometimes irascible almost to a degree of insanity. Generous, brave, and upright, he was; but every one said, that a wound he had received on the head in the wars, had marvelously increased the infirmities of his temper.

The mother, indeed, was full of tenderness and gentleness; and doubtless it was through her veins that the milk of human kindness had found its way into that strange boy's heart. But yet she loved her eldest son best, and unfortunately showed it.

The brother was a wild, rash, reckless young man, some three years older; fond of the other, yet often pleased to irritate--or at least to try, for he seldom succeeded. He was the favorite, however, somewhat spoiled, much indulged; and whatever was done, was done for him. He was the person most considered in the house; his were the parties of pleasure: his the advantages. Even now the family was absent, in order to let him see the capital of his native land, to open his mind to the general world, to show him life on a more extended scale than could be done in the country; and his younger brother was left at home, to pursue his studies in dull solitude.

Yet he did not complain; there was not even a murmur at his heart. He thought it all quite right. His destiny was before him. He was to form his fortune for himself, by his own abilities, his own learning, his own exertions. It was needful he should study, and his greatest ambition for the time was to enter with distinction at the University; his brightest thoughts of pleasure, the comparative freedom and independence of a collegiate life.

Not that he did not find it dull; that gloomy old house, inhabited by none but himself and few servants. Sometimes it seemed to oppress him with a sense of terrible loneliness; sometimes it drove him to think of the strange difference of human destinies, and why it should be that--because it had pleased Heaven one man should be born a little sooner or a little later than another, or in some other place--such a wide interval should be placed between the different degrees of happiness and fortune.

He felt, however, that such speculations were not good; they led him beyond his depth; he involved himself in subtilties more common in those days than in ours; he lost his way; and with passionate eagerness flew to his books, to drive the mists and shadows from his mind. Such had been the case even now: and there he sat, unconscious that a complete and total change was coming over his destiny.

Oh, the dark workshop of Fate! what strange things go on therein, affecting human misery and joy, repairing or breaking shackles for the mind, the means of carrying us forward in a glorious cause, the relentless weights which hurry us down to destruction! While you sit there and read--while I sit here and write, who can say what strange alterations, what combinations in the must discrepant things may be going on around--without our will, without our knowledge--to alter the whole course of our future existence? Doubtless, could man make his own fate, he would mar it;

and the impossibility of doing so is good. The freedom of his own actions is sufficient, nay, somewhat too much; and it is well for the world, aye, and for himself--that there is an overruling Providence which so shapes circumstances around him, that he cannot go beyond his limit, flutter as he will.

There is something in that old man's face more than is common with him--a deeper gravity even than ordinary, yet mingled with a tenderness that is rare. There is something like hesitation, too--ay, hesitation even in him who during a stormy life has seldom known what it is to doubt or to deliberate: a man of strict and ready preparation, whose fixed, clear, definite mind was always prompt and competent to act.

"Come, Philip, my son," he said, laying his hand, as I have stated, on the lad's shoulder, "enough of study for to-day. You read too hard. You run before my precepts. The body must have thought as well as the mind; and if you let the whole summer day pass without exercise, you will soon find that under the weight of corporeal sickness the intellect will flag and the spirit droop. I am going for a walk. Come with me; and we will converse of high things by the way."

"Study is my task and my duty, sir." replied the boy; "my father tells me so, you have told me so often, and as for health I fear not. I seem refreshed when I get up from reading, especially such books as this. It is only when I have been out long, riding or walking, that I feel tired."

"A proof that you should ride and walk the more," replied the old man. "Come, put on your hat and cloak. You shall read no more to-day. There are other thoughts before you; you know, Philip," he continued, "that by reading we get but materials, which we must use to build up an edifice in our own minds. If all our thoughts are derived from others gone before us, we are but robbers of the dead, and live upon labors not our own."

"Elder sons," replied the boy, with a laugh, "who take an inheritance for which they toiled not."

"Something worse than that," replied the clergyman, "for we gather what we do not employ rightly--what we have every right to possess, but upon the sole condition of using well. Each man possessed of intellect is bound to make his own mind, not to have it made for him; to adapt it to the times and circumstances in which he lives, squaring it by just rules, and employing the best materials he can find."

"Well, sir, I am ready," replied the youth, after a moment of deep thought; and he and his old preceptor issued forth together down the long staircase, with the slant sunshine pouring through the windows upon the unequal steps, and illuminating the motes in the thick atmosphere we breathe, like fancy brightening the idle floating things which surround us in this world of vanity.

They walked across the park toward the stile. The youth was silent, for the old man's last words seemed to have awakened a train of thought altogether new.

His companion was silent also; for there was something working within him which embarrassed and distressed him. He had something to tell that young man, and he knew not how to tell it. For the first time in his life he perceived, from the difficulty he experienced in deciding upon his course, how little he really knew of his pupil's character. He had dealt much with his mind, and that he comprehended well--its depth, its clearness, its powers; but his heart and disposition he had not scanned so accurately. He had a surmise, indeed, that there were feelings strong and intense within; but he thought that the mind ruled them with habitual sway that nothing could shake. Yet he paused and pondered; and once he stopped, as if about to speak, but went on again and said nothing.

At length, as they approached the park wall, he laid his finger on his temple, muttering to himself, "Yes, the quicker the better. 'Tis well to mingle two passions. Surprise will share with grief--if much grief there be." Then turning to the young man, he said, "Philip, I think you loved your brother Arthur?"

He spoke loudly, and in plain distinct tones; but the lad did not seem to remark the past tense he used. "Certainly, sir," he said, "I love him dearly. What of that?"

"Then you will be very happy to hear," replied the old man, "that he had been singularly fortunate--I mean that he has been removed from earth and all its allurements--the vanities, the sins, the follies of the world in which he seemed destined to move, before he could be corrupted by its evils, or his spirit receive a taint from its vices."

The young man turned and gazed on him with inquiring eyes, as if still he did not comprehend what he meant.

"He was drowned," said the clergyman, "on Saturday last, while sailing with a party of pleasure on the Thames;" and Philip fell at his feet as senseless as if he had shot him.

CHAPTER II

I must not dwell long upon the youthful scenes of the lad I have just introduced to the reader; but as it is absolutely needful that his peculiar character should be clearly understood, I must suffer it to display itself a little farther before I step from his boyhood to his maturity.

We left Philip Hastings senseless upon the ground, at the feet of his old preceptor, struck down by the sudden intelligence he had received, without warning or preparation.

The old man was immeasurably shocked at what he had done, and he reproached himself bitterly; but he had been a man of action all his life, who never suffered thought, whether pleasant or painful, to impede him. He could think while he acted, and as he was a strong man too, he had no great difficulty in taking the slight, pale youth up in his arms, and carrying him over the park stile, which was close at hand, as the reader may remember. He had made up his mind at once to bear his young charge to a small cottage belonging to a laborer on the other side of the road which ran under the park wall; but on reaching it, he found that the whole family were out walking in the fields, and both doors and windows were closed.

This was a great disappointment to him, although there was a very handsome house, in modern taste, not two hundred yards off. But there were circumstances which made him unwilling to bear the son of Sir John Hastings to the dwelling of his next neighbor. Next neighbors are not always friends; and even the clergyman of the parish may have his likings and dislikings.

Colonel Marshal and Sir John Hastings were political opponents. The latter was of the Calvinistic branch of the Church of England--not absolutely a non-juror, but suspected even of having, a tendency that way. He was sturdy and stiff in his political opinions, too, and had but small consideration for the conscientious views and sincere opinions of others. To say the truth, he was but little inclined to believe that any one who differed from him had conscientious views or sincere opinions at all; and certainly the demeanor, if not the conduct, of the worthy Colonel did not betoken any fixed notion or strong principles. He was a man of the Court--gay, lively, even witty, making a jest of most things, however grave and worthy of reverence. He played high, generally won, was shrewd, complaisant, and particular in his deference to kings and prime ministers. Moreover, he was of the very highest of the High Church party--so high, indeed, that those who belonged to the Low Church party, fancied he must soon topple over into Catholicism.

In truth, I believe, had the heart of the Colonel been very strictly examined, it would have been found very empty of anything like real religion. But then the king was a Roman Catholic, and it was pleasant to be as near him as possible.

It may be asked, why then did not the Colonel go the same length as his Majesty? The answer is very simple. Colonel Marshal was a shrewd observer of the signs of the times. At the card table, after the three first cards were played, he could tell where every other card in the pack was placed. Now in politics he was nearly as discerning; and he perceived that, although King James had a great number of honors in his hand, he did not hold the trumps, and would eventually lose the game. Had it been otherwise, there is no saying what sort of religion he might have adopted. There is no reason to think that Transubstantiation would have stood in the way at all; and as for the Council of Trent, he would have swallowed it like a roll for his breakfast.

For this man, then, Sir John Hastings had both a thorough hatred and a profound contempt, and he extended the same sensations to every member of the family. In the estimation of the worthy old clergyman the Colonel did not stand much higher; but he was more liberal toward the Colonel's family. Lady Annabelle Marshal, his wife, was, when in the country, a very regular attendant at his church. She had been exceedingly beautiful, was still handsome, and she had, moreover, a sweet, saint-like, placid expression, not untouched by melancholy, which was very winning, even in an old man's eyes. She was known, too, to have made a very good wife to a not very good husband; and, to say the truth, Dr. Paulding both pitied and esteemed her. He went but little to the house, indeed, for Colonel Marshal was odious to him; and the Colonel returned the compliment by never going to the church.

Such were the reasons which rendered the thought of carrying young Philip Hastings up to The Court--as Colonel Marshal's house was called--anything but agreeable to the good clergyman. But then, what could he do? He looked in the boy's face. It was like that of a corpse. Not a sign of returning animation showed itself. He had heard of persons dying under such sudden affections of the mind; and so still, so death-like, was the form and countenance before him, as he laid the lad down for a moment on the bench at the cottage door, that his heart misgave him, and a trembling feeling of dread came over his old frame. He hesitated no longer, but after a moment's pause to gain breath, caught young Hastings up in his arms again, and hurried away with him toward Colonel Marshal's house.

I have said that is was a modern mansion; that is to imply, that it was modern in that day. Heaven only knows what has become of it now; but Louis Quatorze, though he had no hand in the building of it, had many of its sins to answer for--and the rest belonged to Mansard. It was the strangest possible contrast to the old-fashioned country seat of Sir John Hastings, who had his joke at it, and at the owner too--for he, too, could jest in a bitter way--and he used to say that he wondered his neighbor had not added his own name to the building, to distinguish it from all other courts; and then it would have been Court Marshal. Many were the windows of the house; many the ornaments; pilasters running up between the casements, with sunken panels, covered over with quaint wreaths of flowers, as if each had an embroidered waistcoat on; and a large flight of steps running down from the great doorway, decorated with Cupids and cornucopias running over with this most indigestible kind of stone-fruit.

The path from the gates up to the house was well graveled, and ran in and out amongst sundry parterres, and basins of water, with the Tritons, &c., of the age, all spouting away as hard as a large reservoir on the top of the neighboring slope could make them. But for serviceable purposes these basins were vain, as the water was never suffered to rise nearly to the brim; and good Dr. Paulding gazed on them without hope, as he passed on toward the broad flight of steps.

There, however, he found something of a more comfortable aspect. The path he had been obliged to take had one convenience to the dwellers in the mansion. Every window in that side of the house commanded a view of it, and the Doctor and his burden were seen by one pair of eyes at least.

Running down the steps without any of the frightful appendages of the day upon her head, but her own bright beautiful hair curling wild like the tendrils of a vine, came a lovely girl of fourteen or fifteen, just past the ugly age, and blushing in the spring of womanhood. There was eagerness and some alarm in her face: for the air and haste of the worthy clergyman,

The other might have been bestowed upon her by her parents. But they had failed to do so; for their own proper principles had been too scanty for them to bestow any on their daughter. Yet, strange to say, the lack of heart somewhat mitigated the intensity of the lady's sufferings now. She felt not her situation as bitterly as other persons with a greater portion of sensibility would inevitably have done. She had so trained herself to resist all small emotions, that they had in reality become obliterated. Fiery passions she could feel; for the earthquake rends the granite which the chisel will not touch, and these affected her now as much as ever.

At that very moment, as she sat there, with her head resting on her hand, what is the meaning of that stern, knitted brow, that fixed, steadfast gaze forward, that tight compression of the lips and teeth At that moment Nero's wish was in the bosom of Mrs. Hazleton. Could she have slaughtered half the human race to blot out all evidence of her crimes, and to escape the grinning shame which she knew awaited her, she would have done it without remorse. Other feelings, too, were present. A sense of anger at herself for having suffered herself to be in the slightest degree moved or agitated by any thing that had occurred; a determined effort, too, was there--I will not call it a struggle--to regain entire command of herself--to be as calm, as graceful, as self-possessed, as dignified as when in high prosperity with unsullied fame. It might be, in a certain sense, playing a part, and doubtless the celebrated Madame Tiquet did the same; but she was playing a part for her own eyes, as well as those of others. She resolved to be firm, and she was firm. "Death," she said, "is before me: for that I am prepared. It cannot agitate a nerve, or make a limb shake. All other evils are trifles compared with this. Why then should I suffer them to affect me in the least? No, no, they shall not see me quail!"

After she had thus thought for some two hours, gaining more and more self-command every moment, as she turned and re-turned all the points of her situation in her own mind, and viewed them in every different aspect, she rose to retire to rest, lay down, and tried to sleep. At first importunate thought troubled her. The same kind of ideas went on--the same reasonings upon them--and slumber for more than one hour would not visit her eyelids. But she was a very resolute woman, and at length she determined that she would not think: she would banish thought altogether; she would not let the mind rest for one moment upon any subject whatsoever; and she succeeded. The absence of thought is sleep; and she slept; but resolution ended where sleep begun, and the images she had banished waking, returned to the mind in slumber. Her rest was troubled. Growing fancies seemed to come thick upon her mind; though the eyes remained closed, the features were agitated; the lips moved. Sometimes she laughed; sometimes she moaned piteously; sometimes tears found their way through her closed eyelids; and sobs struggled in her bosom.

At length, between three and four o'clock in the morning, Mrs. Hazleton rose up in bed. She opened her eyes, too; but there was a dull glassy look about them--a fixed leaden stare, not natural to her waking hours. Slowly she got out of bed, approached the table, took up a candle which she had left burning there, and which was now nearly down to the socket, and walked straight to the door, saying aloud, "Very dark--very dark--every thing is dark."

She tried the door, but found it locked; and the constable slept on. She then returned to the table, seated herself, and for some five or ten minutes continued to twist her long hair round her fingers. She then rose again, and went straight to the window, threw it up, and seemed to look out. "Chilly--chilly," she said. "I most walk to warm myself."

The sill of the window was somewhat high, but that was no obstacle; for there was a chair near, and Mrs. Hazleton placed it for herself with as much care as if she had been wide awake. When this was done she stepped lightly upon it, and put her knee upon the window-sill, raised herself suddenly upright, and struck her head sharply against the upper part of the window. It is probable that the blow woke her, but at all events it destroyed her balance, and she fell forward at once out of the window.

There was a loud shriek, and then a deep groan. But the constable slept on, and no one knew the fate that had befallen her 'till Mr. Short, the surgeon, passing the house, was attracted to the spot where she had fallen, by a moan, and the sight of a white object lying beneath the window.

A loud ringing of the bell, and knocking at the door, soon roused the inhabitants of the house, and the mangled form of Mrs. Hazleton was carried in and stretched upon a bed. She was not dead; and although almost every bone was broken, except the skull, and the terrible injuries she had received precluded all possibility of recovery, she regained her senses before three o'clock of the same day, and continued to linger for somewhat more than a fortnight in agonies both of mind and body, too terrible to be described. With the rapid, though gradual weakening of the corporeal frame, the powers of the mind became enfeebled--the vigorous resolution failed--the self-command abandoned her. Half an hour's death she could have borne with stoical firmness, but a fortnight's was too much. The thoughts she could shut out in vigorous health, forced themselves upon her as she lay there like a crushed worm, and the tortures of hell got hold upon her, long before the spirit departed. Yet a sparkle of the old spirit showed itself even to her last hour. That she was conscious of an eternity, that she was convinced of after judgment, of the reward of good, and of the punishment of evil, that she believed in a God, a hell, a heaven, there can be no doubt--indeed her words more than once implied it--and the anguish of mind under which she seemed to writhe proved it. But yet, she refused all religious consolation; expressed no penitence: no sorrow for what she had done, and scoffed at the surgeon when he hinted that repentance might avail her even then. It seemed that, as with the earthly future, she had made up her mind at once, when first detected, to meet her fate boldly; so with the judgment of the immortal future, she was resolute to encounter it unbending. When urged, nearly at her last hour, to show some repentance, she replied, in the weak and faltering voice of death, but in as determined a tone as ever, "It is all trash. An hour's repentance could do no good even if I could repent. But I do not. Nobody does repent. They regret their failure, are terrified by their punishment; but they and I would do exactly the same again if we hoped for success and impunity. Talk to me no more of it. I do not wish to think of hell till it has hold upon me, if that should ever be."

She said no more from that moment forward, and in about an hour after, her spirit went to meet the fate she had so boldly dared.

But few persons remain to be noticed in this concluding chapter, and with regard to their after history, the imagination of the reader might perhaps be left to deal, without further information. A few words, however, may be said, merely to give a clue to their after fate.

The prosecution of Mr. Shanks, the attorney, was carried on but languidly, and it is certain that he was not convicted of the higher offence of forgery. On some charge, however, it would seem he was sentenced to two years' imprisonment, and the last that is heard of him, shows him blacking shoes at the inn in Carrington, then a very old man, in the reign of George the First.

Sir Philip Hastings never recovered his senses, not did he seem to have any recollection of the horrible events with which his earthly history may be said to have closed; but his life was not far extended. For about six months he continued in the same lamentable state in which we have last depicted him, sometimes singing, sometimes laughing, and sometimes absorbed in deep melancholy. At the end of that period, another paralytic stroke left him in a state of complete fatuity, from which, in two years, he was relieved by death.

If the reader will look into the annals of the reign of Queen Anne, he will find frequent mention in the campaigns of Marlborough and Eugene, of a Major, a Colonel, and a General Marlow. They were all the same person; and they will find that officer often reported as severely wounded. I cannot trace his history much farther; but the genealogies of those times show, that in 1712, one Earl of Launceston died at the age of eighty-seven, and was succeeded by the eighth Earl, who only survived three years, and the title with him became extinct, as it is particularly marked that he died unmarried. As this last of the race is distinguished by the title of Lieutenant-General, the Earl of Launceston, there can be no doubt that this was the lover and promised husband of poor Emily Hastings.

It is a sad tale, and rarely perhaps has any such tragedy darkened the page of domestic history in England. A whole family were swept away, and most of those connected with them, in a very short space of time; but it is not the number of deaths within that period that gives its gloominess to the page--for every domestic history is little but a record of deaths--but the circumstances. Youth, beauty, virtue, gentleness, kindness, honor, integrity, punctilious rectitude: reason, energy, wisdom, sometimes, nay often, have no effect as a screen from misfortune, sorrow, and death. Were this world all, what a frightful chaos would human life be. But the very sorrows and adversities of the good, prove that there is a life beyond, where all will be made even.